"Louie!" she cries even be[...] see if I am still there. "L[...] dropping her totebag to the floor and extending her arms wide.

Before I can shift my weight to my pins and escape, she is on me like a tomato-red tornado. "Oh, Louie," she sighs. "You should see your shoes."

I should indeed see my shoes; that would be some news worth getting on the Internet. What, pray tell, are they? Two-tone wingtips? High-heeled sneakers? Perhaps they are fuzzy-wuzzy slippers.

The emotional stress caused by the sudden return of the gentleman known as Max has tipped poor Miss Temple over the edge. Naturally, her delusion would be in the area of fancy footwear, since she was a teensy bit nuts on the subject even when she was sane.

"Oh Louie, they are *sooo* gorgeous. Entirely covered in teeny, tiny Austrian crystals, and white like diamonds, except when the rainbow reflections are dancing off them. And, then, on the back of the heel, on each shoe, a darling figure of a black cat."

I do not like what I am thinking one itsy bit. *Darling? Teeny, tiny?* I have not heard Miss Temple resort to such nauseating descriptives in the entire time we have shared more than a roof. What has come over her?

"They're called 'Halloween Jinx' and I can win a pair free! All I have to do is find a shoe like these hidden somewhere in semi-plain sight in Las Vegas. And, then…Mama's gonna get a brand-new pair of shoes, Louie, oh, yes!"

Then she leans closer to whisper a tender something in my ear. What she murmurs is the hush-hush retail price of the prize shoes. I pause in mid-purr.

That is no small patch of cabbage that she is talking about.

By Carole Nelson Douglas from Tom Doherty Associates

MYSTERY

MIDNIGHT LOUIE MYSTERIES:
Catnap
Pussyfoot
Cat on a Blue Monday
Cat in a Crimson Haze
Cat in a Diamond Dazzle
Cat with an Emerald Eye
Cat in a Flamingo Fedora
Cat in a Golden Garland
Cat on a Hyacinth Hunt
Cat in an Indigo Mood
Cat in a Jeweled Jumpsuit
Cat in a Kiwi Con
Midnight Louie's Pet Detectives (anthology)

IRENE ADLER ADVENTURES:
Good Night, Mr. Holmes
Good Morning, Irene
Irene at Large
Irene's Last Waltz

Marilyn: Shades of Blonde (anthology)

HISTORICAL ROMANCE
Amberleigh*
Lady Rogue*
Fair Wind, Fiery Star

SCIENCE FICTION
Probe*
Counterprobe*

FANTASY
TALISWOMAN:
Cup of Clay
Seed upon the Wind

SWORD AND CIRCLET:
Keepers of Edanvant
Heir of Rengarth
Seven of Swords

*also mystery

CAROLE NELSON DOUGLAS

CAT IN A DIAMOND DAZZLE

A MIDNIGHT LOUIE MYSTERY

FORGE®

A TOM DOHERTY ASSOCIATES BOOK
NEW YORK

This is a work of fiction. All the characters and events portrayed in this book are either products of the author's imagination or are used fictitiously.

CAT IN A DIAMOND DAZZLE

Copyright © 1996 by Carole Nelson Douglas

All rights reserved, including the right to reproduce this book, or portions thereof, in any form.

Cover art by Joe DeVito

A Forge Book
Published by Tom Doherty Associates, LLC
175 Fifth Avenue
New York, NY 10010

www.tor.com

Forge® is a registered trademark of Tom Doherty Associates, LLC.

ISBN: 0-812-55506-6
Library of Congress Catalog Card Number: 95-53239

First edition: May 1996
First mass market edition: February 1997

Printed in the United States of America

0 9 8 7 6 5 4 3

For the real and original Midnight Louie;
nine lives were not enough

Contents

Prologue: Mine Eyes Dazzle . . .   13

Chapter 1: Return of the Native   15

Chapter 2: Still the Same Old Story . . .   22

Chapter 3: A Fight for Love and Glory . . .   31

Chapter 4: Yvette to Be Alone   46

Chapter 5: A Really Big Shoe-down   49

Chapter 6: Little Cat Feet   57

Chapter 7: Boys Town   61

Chapter 8: Deep Waters   82

Chapter 9: Spray for Rain   91

Chapter 10: Pirates Ahoy!   98

Chapter 11: Blue Dahlia Bogey Boogie   112

Chapter 12: Hearse and Rehearsal   120

Chapter 13: Murder on the Hoof   134

Chapter 14: Every Little Breeze . . .   148

Chapter 15: Hocus Focus   156

Interlude: Ah, Sweet Mystery of Hystery   175

Chapter 16: Bugged Out   179

Chapter 17: . . . Seems to Whisper Louise   190

Chapter 18: Every Large Breezy . . .   197

Chapter 19: Ship of Jewels   206

Chapter 20: Long John Louie   220

Chapter 21: Opening Knights   223

Interlude: Hysterical Again   241

8 • Contents

Chapter 22: Morning, Moon and Molina   244

Chapter 23: Catfood vs. Dogmeat   259

Chapter 24: Jake of All Trades   267

Chapter 25: True Confessions   277

Chapter 26: Another Opening, Another Shoe   284

Chapter 27: Witch Switch   295

Chapter 28: Romantic Rendezvous   301

Chapter 29: Four Queens Get the Boot   311

Interlude: It's Hystery!   322

Chapter 30: Undressed Rehearsal   325

Chapter 31: Murderous Suspicions   340

Chapter 32: Interview with the Execution.   352

Chapter 33: A Clue to Chew On   357

Chapter 34: Last Act   364

Chapter 35: Love in Vein   378

Chapter 36: Swept Away   384

Chapter 37: Confess   398

Chapter 38: Checkmate   405

Tailpiece: Midnight Louie Celebrates   410

       Carole Nelson Douglas Talks Shoes and Show Biz   413

"No mask like open truth to cover lies,
As to go naked is the best disguise."

—Congreve, *The Double Dealer* (1694)

Cat in a
Diamond Dazzle

Mine Eyes Dazzle . . .

Well, knock me over with a wolverine and suck me up with a second-hand Hoover.

I could not be more surprised had Mr. Elvis Presley himself materialized in Miss Temple Barr's living room, although I doubt that even the King would have the gall to wear a Hawaiian shirt of such particularly lurid design.

This last item of apparel is so electrifyingly florid that I am forced to squint my eyes semi-shut. A pity. That delays my analysis of the individual who has committed the taste-defying act of wearing such a garment.

Miss Temple Barr, however, is not one to be distracted by an aura of rotting flora when there is an intruder in the house.

And there is no doubt that the gentleman who has been kind enough to fetch her sunglasses from the patio is an intruder, although he is apparently known to her. He is vaguely familiar to me as well, though it pains me to admit acquaintance with one so deficient in wardrobe coordination skills.

In fact, as mine eyes adjust to the pineapple/passion fruit dazzle, I manage to study this trespasser from head to toe. This is a time-consuming job, given the dude's impressive height, but luckily I am lying down, so it is not a physical strain.

Here are the facts: the intruder is a thirty-something Caucasian male, six-feet-something in height, whipsnake-narrow in width, with a head of thick black hair that is almost as shiny and well-tended as mine.

I must say I approve of the hair, if little else.

But I am not an ace detective for naught, and am as able to draw an inference as an inside straight. Despite the lurid gasoline-spill tinted sunglasses that shade this dude's eyes, I would bet that they are as green as string beans. Maybe greener, since most of the string beans of my acquaintance have been overcooked to an unappetizing avocado color.

This is not a dagger I see before me but something almost as dangerous to the status quo: the missing Mr. Mystifying Max. As you may well imagine, the two main characters in this sudden encounter are too busy eyeing each other to spare a glance for little me.

As you may also imagine, I do not intend to take the unauthorized re-entry of a former resident of the premises lying down, even if he is considerably bigger than I.

But you do not have to imagine: Midnight Louie is on the scene to describe the encounter in living color, with Vistavision, sound effects and even Smellorama.

Right now my keen sniffer is absorbing the scents of ozone-crackling tension along with a delicate undercurrent of pheromone. If anyone could bottle this stuff, we all would have something to write home about. Meanwhile, the world at large can only rely upon the sage instincts and keen observational skills of its humble on-the-scene reporter, yours truly.

Stay tuned.

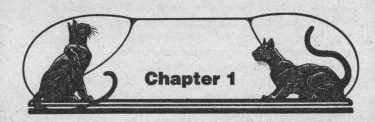

Return of the Native

Max Kinsella looked like a surreal figure lost in a garishly vacant Dali landscape. Temple couldn't believe her eyes.

Nor could her mind assemble several clear but alien impressions into a recognizable image . . . neon-storm, carnival-midway Hawaiian shirt. Oil-slick rainbow sunshades . . . dark, virtual-reality lenses locking the wearer into an intimated vast but hidden world. Height like the Eiffel Tower: familiar but looming larger than memory.

She was viewing not Max Kinsella, but Max Headroom, some berserk computer-image accident and traveling freak show. Kaleidoscopic Technicolor Hologram Man. Unreal, man. Unreal.

The seashore roared in Temple's ears. She sensed her own space, time and particular place in such sharp but distant clarity that it too had become a dislocated Dali landscape, seen but not felt. Not truly comprehended.

Well-corseted Victorian ladies, she guessed, would have swooned by now. The only buttressing piece of clothing holding

Temple together at the moment was the soft sash of her martial arts gi, and it was no excuse for suffering an attack of the vapors.

She became aware of her bare feet planted on the fuzzy comfort of her fake goat-hair rug. At the same instant, she became even more alert to her hatred of ever being seen at such a childish disadvantage.

And then, despite the ludicrous shock of Max's reappearance, and his appearance, reality shattered her Technicolor daze like a fist smashing a stained-glass window.

She heard the eternal, prosaic hum of the air conditioner, and began to recognize again the bland familiarity of her domestic terrain. She even began to recall Max being as normal a part of this interior decor as she was. She began to believe he was there, as she still was. That this time it was really, really Max. That he was . . . alive.

A thrum of relief overrode numb disbelief.

Then another emotion came roaring out from the icebox of time-frozen emotions in which she had stored Max with the wistful care of someone preserving a prom-night corsage.

A muscular emotion, part fire and part tempered steel, it had a hot, coal-fire heart and a one-track mind. Its long-dampered engine began racing, chug-chugging with impatience, building up a head of steam in countertime to the shock-slowed beat of her heart.

The memory engine was gathering speed and sweeping her into its impetuous train. She saw the past—their past—glide by in stately panorama.

Meeting at the Guthrie Theatre. That night's magic show— prestidigitation in the heart of darkness—the stage a velvet-black hole lit by the spotlights' cyclic fireworks. Walking beside the lamplight-dappled water in Loring Park in a lukewarm summer night. Leaving Minneapolis. Landing in Las Vegas so lost in each other they were like shell-shocked aliens on terra infirma.

Electra, the Circle Ritz, the Goliath and more magic shows in the dark, more days in the light, more nights in black satin and falling stars afloat on water. . . . Azure days, quicksilver nights.

Temple was now a mere passenger aboard the locomotive of her own emotions, drawn along by one particular, as-yet unnameable sensation. She leaned out the train window and tilted her head to read the passing sign: the town of Joy in the state of Disbelief. Utter, driving, unstoppable joy.

The train steamed forward, sure of itself, carving a path through space and time, back to the future, escaping the past and tearing into the present. Everything else slipped away like air. The engine was climbing the steepest grade of incredulity, penetrating the darkest tunnel of doubt, ready to huff and puff across the widest chasm of uncertainty, ready to overleap any chasm, whether a bridge stretched beneath it or not. . . .

"Max—" Temple heard her voice whisper. *You're alive,* her mind shouted.

Max didn't seem to hear either his spoken name or her nameless emotions. Maybe the pistons of her joy were pounding too loudly. Then he spoke, too.

"Who's the blond?"

Temple frowned at words as indecipherable as vernacular Martian. Nonsense syllables. Why would Max speak gobbledegook at such a moment?

"You're alive," she whispered, still lagging behind real time.

Who's the blond? What blond? Some woman he wanted to saw in half, some blonde magician's assistant? Christie Brinkley? Huh?

Then the present reasserted itself in flash cards of detail. Temple saw herself passing through the past twenty-four hours as if watching a secret videotape of her every movement. Then she understood.

The parquet floor of her apartment shuddered and became so solid it hurt. Sunlight lancing through the open French door that framed Max's bizarre silhouette made her eyes water.

Her train of joy derailed with a sickening crash, a jack-knifing, twisting tangle of each car in its long train. Passengers named Trust and Hope and Love were cast out upon the surreal countryside like so many dice gone awry.

Yet everything collapsed in slow motion, like all disasters both physical and psychic. She had one split second to mourn the ruined scene, to count the dead and to inspect the walking wounded, particularly herself. Then her strange travelog of emotion ended with her at home.

She studied Max's Technicolor facade, knowing the man behind it, inside it, and not knowing him at all. With one cold question, he had cast himself again into the farthest, protective deep freeze of her emotions. Fresh damage smashed Temple's train wreck of joy into smaller pieces. His words, so distant, so judging, struck her heart to the hilt, a long, Arthurian sword thrust so deep it might never be drawn out. If only she *were* stone . . .

A new emotion surfaced through an ocean of hurt, and it struck back.

"Are your eyes really green?" she said, just as flatly.

So there they stood, after all this time, asking idiot questions that could only be answered with anger and self-justification.

Max stood unmoving, as he in turn struggled to decode her remark. Then he took off his sunglasses, folded and hung them from the dreadful shirt's breast pocket.

His eyes were still green, Temple saw, but were they *really*? He wasn't saying, was he? Just showing. Magicians were very good at dodging the issues, any issue. They would show, but not tell.

"You've been *watching* me," she said. Accused.

"Had to. For your sake as well as mine."

Her theatrical ear listened for the trace of a brogue, and the sword in her heart (stupid but inescapable cliche) twisted. Trust was in terminal condition and growing weaker every second. Hope was declared dead. Love was in a coma and would probably linger there for life, such as it was.

Still, "your sake" implied something.

"Max—!" She shoved her fingers into her hair.

He put a shushing finger to his lips, his (maybe green) eyes warning silence.

She glanced quickly around the room. Was it bugged?

Max, reading her concern, shook his head. "No one's listening to us but us, and that's two too many."

He moved further into the room, in a smooth big-cat glide meant to soothe. Max had the seamless, gravity-defying, sight-deceiving motion of a master mime. He stopped four feet away, behind the sofa.

"He's new."

Who? Temple was still moving in four-four time in a sixteenth-note world. She followed Max's feline-green glance to the sofa seat.

Oh. Louie.

"A stray cat I found at the Convention Center."

Max extended a cautious arm, the dark hairs on it gleaming as satin as Louie's well-licked coat. His fingers stroked Louie's head.

The cat growled, deep and long.

Max didn't jerk his hand away, as most people would. "He likes it here."

"Why shouldn't he? He gets food and affection, and comes and goes as he pleases."

An awkward silence prevailed, as certain personal parallels were drawn by both parties.

Max stepped cautiously around the sofa, nodding at Temple. "That's something new."

"My gi?" Goodness, she sounded casual, Temple thought. She lifted a tail of the flour-sack-pale sash. "I'm learning self-defense." Studying the yet-alien garb, she added, "Matt's my teacher."

How easily Max had moved from direct route to circuitous, just like a cat mincing around a foreign object. Here she was answering his very first question, whether she wanted to or not. *Who's the blond?* "Matt Devine. New neighbor."

"Self-defense is an admirable art." Max was noncommittal. He smiled then, that Max smile that could charm china birds off jade-bejeweled trees. "But I don't think that outfit does you justice."

Temple's shoulders dropped as her eyes winced shut. "In other words, I look like Dopey the dwarf."

In that unguarded instant, Max took his opening. Temple heard nothing, no movement. Yet she felt his hands under her elbows, then he was lifting her up, as before, until her face was level with his. Temple forced herself not to wince again.

He lifted her higher this time, so she was looking down on him, as if they were in bed. She stared into his hypnotically green eyes—

warm, amused, probing—and their traitorous color stopped her cold again.

"You look adorable," he said. "You always underestimate yourself, Temple." His light tone changed. "Don't underestimate me."

The betraying, inevitable tears hung like isinglass curtains before her vision, frozen from falling.

"Max . . . *why*?"

"I can't say."

"Then why do you expect *me* to spill my guts?"

He lowered her to the floor so swiftly she felt she'd been on a carnival ride. "I have a lot of unreasonable expectations." He looked around. Temple was shocked to see that his hair had grown so long it was gathered into a pony tail. "Like expecting things to stay the same. But they don't, do they?"

"Some things do." Like *her* hairstyle. "Look, why don't we start over, sit down and talk?"

"Aren't you expected somewhere?" He eyed the gi.

"This." She tightened the sash as if wringing her hands instead of cotton ties. "I'll run down and say that something came up."

Max grinned. "Considering my method of arrival, that's not only apt, but precisely truthful."

"You climbed up the outside? Like Louie? Why?"

"The cat climbs up the outside, too?" Max glanced at the animal, not necessarily pleased to note a similarity. "I imagine we slink around for the same reasons."

"Hunting?" Temple asked.

"Or hiding." Max reached for the sunglasses again. "But don't call off your lesson. I'll come down and watch."

"Max, no! I'd feel . . . dumb. And if you are hiding—"

"Not too seriously at the moment, or I wouldn't be here."

Temple shook her head. "At least explain the Easter-egg shirt."

"Authentic fifties-vintage Goodwill."

"I know *what* it is, I want to know *why* you're wearing it."

"Why? Can't you tell? Naked isn't the best disguise, Temple. In Las Vegas, loud is."

She couldn't help laughing, which was better than crying. Trying to convince Max *not* to go where he was not wanted was always hopeless. She shrugged, picked up her keys and her sunglasses and left the apartment.

Max followed, on silent cat feet.

Her last glimpse of Midnight Louie showed that he remained sprawled like a sultan on her sofa, but his eyes were narrowed, both possessive . . . and suspicious.

Chapter 2

Still the Same Old Story . . .

Temple felt like she was being escorted to her execution. Here she was, wearing some jailhouse set of baggy pajamas, in custody of a guard of sorts, leaving the shady security of the Circle Ritz for the brutal sunlight of the execution yard.

All she had to do was whip off the sash of her gi and tie it over her eyes. She wished she could, because then she wouldn't see Matt Devine's pale figure waiting under the soaring palm tree.

The military beat of some lines by Kipling even ran through her head, slightly amended: *"Matt is Matt and Max is Max, and never the twain shall meet."*

Didn't she just wish! Didn't she just wish a sudden exit to China would open up before her feet? Didn't she just wish the Wizard of Oz would swoop down in a balloon gondola to whisk her away, only she wasn't wearing the proper shoes for leaving Oz and how could she go home to Kansas when this—however bizarre— was it?

The dolorous convict shuffle of her slip-on jute sandals over concrete made her glance down. A fate worse than death: facing the music in tacky footwear. Mata Hari would have hung her well-hatted head in shame if she had lived to see this.

Matt had been warming up with Oriental shadow boxing on the blue vinyl practice mats under the palm tree. He straightened at Temple's approach, looking beyond her with an expression of polite puzzlement.

Damn Max, here he was playing the professional magician again, the man holding all the cards, while other people tried to guess what number and suit was on them.

"Ready?" By now Matt sounded puzzled as well as looked it.

Before she could answer, Max stepped in, literally, moving between them. "Don't mind me. I'm just a spectator."

Matt's expression still interrogated Temple.

Might as well get it over with, she thought. Ready, aim, fire.

"This is . . . Max Kinsella."

Max stood there grinning, his arms folded over his chest, but not concealing nearly enough of the obscene shirt.

Temple finished her unwelcome duties. "Matt Devine is the new neighbor in eleven." Not *our* new neighbor.

Temple had to give Catholic seminary discipline an A-plus. Matt didn't turn a gilded hair.

"You left before I moved in," he said calmly to Max, extending a hand.

Max uncoiled enough to shake it. "You're Temple's martial arts guru, I hear." He glanced her way. "She never had much interest in breaking her fingernails before."

"That was before," Matt answered, perfectly cordial and perfectly calm, "she was assaulted by some nasty thugs."

Temple winced, but not at the memory of the attack.

That was nothing compared to the spot she was in now: caught between two men who didn't know one another, each suspecting he had good reason to distrust/resent/hate (take your pick) the guts of the other.

"Listen," Temple said, trying to be the good hostess and keep the guests from dismembering one another. "That was a happy accident. Every liberated female should learn how to defend herself. Woman doth not live by Mace alone."

Max flashed her a knowing glance, but was not deterred.

"So you're a martial arts instructor?" he asked Matt.

"I'm a martial arts student," Matt corrected with his usual modesty.

Max did the Mr. Spock thing with his left eyebrow, and Temple ached to try her latest knee jab on him.

From the corner of her eye, she saw that Midnight Louie had bestirred himself and found his own mysterious way down. He sat in the shade of the palm tree, where he disciplined one apparently dirty paw. Things must be at a sad pass when even Midnight Louie was worried enough to play chaperone.

The silence prolonged past the comfort barrier as the two men regarded each other. Ooh, Temple hated being in the middle of unspoken man stuff! Why couldn't they just behave in a civil, amenable manner, instead of getting stiff and suspicious, with all the usual ugly undertones of possession and trespassing?

The tension in the air was still as electric as Max's shirt. Each man had taken upon himself the role of protecting Temple against the other. Didn't they get it? She didn't need protection against anything but the two of *them!*

"So when did Temple get mugged?" Max asked Matt.

Was she not supposed to be here, or something? Temple wondered. "A few weeks ago," she answered.

"It wasn't just a mugging." Anger tightened Matt's voice into a vocal cudgel. "It was a beating, a bad one. The creeps were looking for you."

Max forgot the other man and turned toward Temple with an expression Temple had never seen on Max's face: horrified.

"Temple? Are you all right?" From the urgency of his tone, her attack might have occurred just yesterday. She nodded quickly, but his questions continued. "Who were they? When—?"

"We kind of thought," Matt put in, "you might know who they were, since they sure knew who you were."

Max ignored him, thank God. He stepped closer to Temple,

suddenly casting her in his shade. His hand lifted her face, as if searching for visible wounds.

"I'm sorry," he said, sounding it. "I didn't expect that. That's why I left, to—"

The intimacy level was like old times, just her and Max, and no one else in the whole, wide, wacky world. Matt wouldn't understand the power of such a pull. He must be thinking. . . .

"Yoohoo!" Electra Lark's fruity tones came caroling toward them from the Circle Ritz. "Max Kinsella, is that you in the King-Kong-in-Honolulu disguise? Come on, let me look at you, you devilish stranger, you."

Electra did what Temple could not do, what only a woman over sixty could do. She ran up and enveloped Max in a muumuu hug that competed with his shirt, then broke away to give him a piercing inspection.

Temple let the breath she had been holding ease out slowly, so no one would notice.

Matt, however, had. She watched his fists unclench.

Electra had rushed outside so fast she was panting. She was also patting at her pixie-length hair, dyed today a wholesome persimmon color.

"I'd know you anywhere, you rascal," she told Max. "What a fab surprise. I'm sure you want to inspect the Hesketh Vampire, to make sure that I'm not abusing it. Say, that is one slick motorcycle. Come on back to the shed, and I'll show you how I've got it bedded down."

Max laughed at her excitement, but eyed Temple over Electra's spikey waves of magenta hair. "We haven't had much chance—"

"Go ahead," Temple said. "We'll talk later. I want to run up and change anyway."

"No lesson today?" Max asked sardonically.

"Not in martial arts," she answered flatly enough that it stung.

"Max!" Electra urged. "Shake a leg. It's been so long and I know you have a million questions."

He allowed himself to be led off, recognizing Electra's unspoken promise to fill him in on what had happened since he left. Now was Temple's chance to bring Matt up to date. Divide and conquer. She turned to him.

"Let's go in."

Matt was no readier than Max to move. His head had followed Electra's fading chatter as she and Max vanished around the cedar fence. Now he turned back to Temple.

"Aren't you afraid he might disappear again?"

She shrugged. "No such luck for any of us, I fear. Okay. It's my turn to say, 'Shake a leg,' before both of mine collapse."

He fell into step with her as they edged into the unfiltered sunlight by the pool.

"Did Electra do that on purpose?" Matt asked. "Distract him, I mean?"

"I sure hope so. You guys were getting difficult. I wish you hadn't told Max about my . . . attack."

"I only told the truth."

"And you only wanted to make him feel guilty."

"That's what I've been trained to do," Matt said wryly. "Not really. I've been trained to make myself feel guilty, so it's nice to have a chance to foist the emotion off on someone else, someone who deserves it."

"Maybe."

Matt held the door open for Temple. She scraped through on the obnoxiously loud sandals. Inside, the dim back hall's familiar tranquility was as soothing as a massage. Temple sighed.

"When did he show up?" Matt asked.

"Just now. On my patio." She laughed at Matt's politely appalled expression. "He's a magician. He thrives on sudden entrances."

"And exits."

"Ouch." She sighed again. "I guess we have a lot to talk about."

"I guess you do."

They were silent in the elevator, Matt noticing without comment when Temple pressed the button for the fourth floor only. His floor, not hers.

The deserted late-afternoon halls glowed with the everpresent electric sconces necessary to a circular building, where daylight only enters the perimeter living quarters.

"How do you feel about this sudden resurrection?" Matt asked as they followed the curved passage to the cul-de-sac ending at his front door.

Temple had to consider. "Happy that Max's alive. Furious that he seems to think he can pop in and out of my life without fuss or folderol. Confused. Worried. Molina wants to interrogate him about a murder case."

"Really." Matt leaned against the wall beside his door, his face shadowed by the building's equivalent of an overhead porch light.

"I didn't tell you." But I have to now, she thought. "Molina dug up some . . . disturbing omissions in Max's past; disturbing because I didn't know anything about them."

"Does that change how you feel about him?"

"No . . . only whether I was smart to rely on feeling." She leaned against the opposite wall, hands behind her back. "It does cast a pall on the past."

"He implied a few moments ago that he left because he expected trouble."

"Yes. Why? Molina would say I should suspect him of being a thief or an international terrorist. One thing's for sure: something made him leave, and I hope it wasn't me."

"He wouldn't be back if it was. But isn't that the real question?"

"What?"

"*Why* is he back? Why now?"

"Yeah, why now? And why didn't I think to ask?"

"Maybe you were a little off-balance."

"Maybe I was balancing on one foot, on one spike heel on a beach ball. Lord, when he walked through that French door in that unbelievable getup—"

"He doesn't usually dress like that?"

"No! Max is a conservative dresser, really. Slacks and sweaters in low-key colors that won't distract from his personal act. I've often suggested he could be a little more . . . imaginative."

"It worked."

Temple began to smile, then sobered quickly. "No, I only wish he had gone off the deep end simply as a fashion statement. But he said it himself this afternoon: loud is the best disguise."

"Sounds like he's back on the scene prematurely. Can you figure out why?"

"No. He said it was dangerous for him to hang around."

"For him, or you?"

"For both of us, I guess. That makes Molina's suspicions pretty feasible, doesn't it?"

Matt nodded soberly. He hadn't even cracked a smile when she'd laughed at Max's new look. In the artificial light his expression was almost morose.

"Matt, you've been asking me how I feel, but what about you?"

"What do you mean?" He leaned away from the wall, as if putting up his guard.

"Only that you must have assumed what I finally did: that Max was history. Now he's demonstrably a current event. Doesn't that make you wonder about . . . us?"

"Us." He repeated the word flatly. "It didn't seem necessary to think about an 'us' until he showed up again. Temple, I've got to respect your previous commitment. You and Max may not have been married, but you were a couple, presumably sincere about your mutual involvement. Since Max is back now, I wish you both the best of luck. I think you ought to work at patching things up. Whatever the reason for his absence, he obviously hasn't forgotten you."

"Very . . . true. Very wise advice, Contact Man. So that's it? Some bland platitudes and patient good counsel? That's how you *feel* about it? That's all?"

"Hey, don't get upset—"

"Why shouldn't I get upset? Every man I know seems to take his coming and going in my life as no big deal. Is there some sort of maturity bug going around? You sure didn't act like Mr. Cool downstairs."

"I'm just trying to do the best thing—"

"The best thing is to be honest, and that includes with yourself as well as me. I sure don't know where I stand with Max, and I would go really bananas if I can't know where I stand with you."

He suddenly leaned back against the wall, letting even his head seek its unwavering support. "Guilty. Again. No, I'm not thrilled that he's back. I don't think he deserves you. If he hadn't run off, you wouldn't have had to play a punching bag for some apes who are still at large. He didn't see you after that; I did."

"Matt, maybe you're not just mad at Max."

"Who else?" he asked, frowning.

"How about your father—your real father who left your mother and left her open to your abusive stepfather?"

"I don't care about him!" He seemed surprised by his own admission.

"Maybe you do," she said. "And maybe you care about me."

"You." He pushed himself away from the wall. The light was behind him and she could hardly see his face, but she could feel the anger he had barely controlled with Max. "Of course I care about you, Temple," he said in a lower voice. "You're my guardian angel in this strange, new, secular world I've entered. When I saw him, knew who he was, what claims he had on you . . . I saw all those ugly emotions I've always loathed rushing forward like an invisible army. It's what I've always been afraid of—fury and rage, fear, anxiety and abandonment. I felt like I'd been left bleeding and naked in the middle of the Las Vegas Strip."

"Matt—" She moved to him, and he caught her arms like a man in desperate need of human contact, but still determined to hold her at arm's length.

"Temple, I realized then how much you've pulled me into the real world I've got to enter if I'm to leave the past behind. I realized then, when it was too late, how I really feel about you."

"Yes?"

They were facing each other, the light washing their faces on one side only, so bright it was blinding, and casting the other side in shadow.

It was one of those rare moments of intense personal truth. Both their voices had sunk to a whisper.

"Temple—" Matt sounded truly bereft, "I think I . . . I think I need you."

Well. Not quite the revelation she had expected, but heartfelt nonetheless. What had she done? Led him just far enough ahead so that he would fall without her support? She had been more successful at reaching him than she thought, she realized, and such breakthroughs always have a price. What she owed Max, and what she owed Matt, couldn't, would never, fall neatly into separate compartments. And she would probably never be content with a compromise.

While these conflicting thoughts jostled in her mind, Matt abruptly drew her close and kissed her square and hard on the mouth. He had come a long, long way, thanks to her, and now the guilt was on her head.

How did she feel right now? That she had everything she had ever wanted, and it was all wrong. Max back, and she not sure she wanted him that way. Matt committing commitment, and she regretting that she had brought him to a brink she might no longer be willing or able to cross.

"I'm sorry," he was saying, "that wasn't fair. I did that badly—"

"No! No." Temple threw her hands up in the air, then threw her arms around his shoulders. She embraced him the way Electra had welcomed Max back, sort of.

"No matter what happens," she whispered fiercely in his ear, "we will always be friends."

The fadeout from *Casablanca* it was not.

Chapter 3

A Fight for Love and Glory . . .

Winking neon from the sign outside cast pink and blue stripes into the large, darkened room. Pink for girls, blue for boys. The garish pastel light lashed many pale, motionless faces, but each time it struck Temple's cheek she blinked.

Still, the rhythmic wink of obscenely cheery neon had a hypnotic effect she found peaceful. She edged down the seat so the lucent tattoo beat across her knee instead of her face, slightly dislodging a bench partner in the process.

"Sorry," she whispered in automatic apology, though doing so was ridiculous. A Las Vegas wedding chapel, particularly one as eccentric as the Lovers' Knot, was not really a church.

Yet the silence remained profound, the atmosphere oddly serene. Pulsing neon flashed like heat lightning on the lattice archway at the room's front. Silk flowers intertwined the slats.

Temple appreciated the comfortable, well-stuffed bulk of the woman on her left. Her face under a broad-brimmed straw hat was unreservedly lumpy as well as quiet. A rhinestone beauty mark on the woman's cheekbone gleamed like a frozen tear.

Sitting among the congregation, staring at the blinking bars of light like a slot-machine junkie, made Temple feel like Goldilocks. She had found a "just right" place to be.

The side door creaked, then admitted an expanding bar of ordinary incandescent light. Temple jumped like an experimental gerbil, then huddled against the commodious woman beside her, almost dislodging the hat.

Sorry, she didn't quite whisper aloud. She seldom found it necessary to make herself smaller than usual.

Whoever had opened the door wasn't about to stop with a quick glance around. Footsteps ground over a floor gritty from dozens of rice-strewings.

Temple watched the shadow explore the room's fringes, feeling as stupid as a kid playing the game of "statue" and forced to hold stock still, or maybe feeling more like "It" in a game of hide and seek that she was much too old for. The longer she kept her presence quiet, the more idiotic she would look if she were discovered.

Still she said nothing, and moved no more than her neighbors.

The shadow paused by the dark hummock of the organ.

Temple bit her lip. Surely Matt hadn't come down again, perhaps seeking the same ersatz solace that she did?

The shadow, sure-footed, reached the room's ceremonial center, just an empty space meant for two, or three at most. It stopped dead center in the arch, head sweeping left and right like a spotlight.

"What on earth—?" Electra Lark's voice interrogated herself. "I never finished the Erica Kane figure that's supposed to go there. And poor old Sophie's hat has slipped."

She came scurrying down the center aisle, not about to be fooled by a living body among all these mannequins of her own making.

"It's me." Temple sat forward. The bracketing soft-sculpture people collapsed into each other behind her.

"Temple! Oh, my great-aunt Gilda's garters! You nearly scared the frost out of my hair. I thought it might be a burglar, or some sort of sex fiend."

"Just your local PR person," Temple confirmed in a foolish found-out voice.

Electra lifted the woman dubbed Sophie into the pew ahead, then took her place on the seat, settling some papers on her lap.

"I was looking for you, I admit, but I'd given up and decided to see if everything was ship-shape here. What are you doing in the chapel?"

"I thought it would be quiet."

"So it *was*," Electra said, chuckling. "No wedding's scheduled for a week. Now, listen. I told Max he could house-sit the Kellers's condo while they're in Nova Scotia."

"Oh, Electra! That isn't fair. My condo is half his."

"He hasn't exactly been paying his half of the maintenance and mortgage lately, has he? Besides, Louie might not make him real welcome."

"Louie is not the issue."

"I know, dear. Obviously, you two need a little time—"

Temple snorted in despair at Electra's understatement.

"Anyway, the upshot is that Max wants nothing to do with the Circle Ritz. Says it's too public for him. So you're off the hook."

"Am I?"

"For the moment. You and Max will still have to sit down and talk things over."

"And over and over . . . how do I get in such messes? I'd rather be confronting a murderer right now."

"I hope not, because that would make me a rather nasty customer, not to mention dangerous to be with alone in the dark."

"It's not quite dark."

"No, it isn't, dear, and you can't see that yet."

Electra sighed and settled against the hard seat, a human replica of the soft-sculpture figure she had dislodged.

"How did Matt take the resurrection of the Mystifying Max?" she asked.

"Like a plaster saint. So calm and so concerned about me. I could have kicked him."

"How did Max take Matt?"

"Like indigestion. Max and Louie don't get along either. I could kick them both. But since I abhor senseless violence, I think I'll relocate to Point Barrow, Alaska, instead."

"No, you won't." Electra rattled her papers. "That's why I was looking for you. That's why the chapel is closed for a week. I need a roommate for a conference I'm attending and you need to get away from all this. Best part is it starts tomorrow."

"Conference? I've had it up to here with stage-managing those events, and I can't leave town with my Crystal Phoenix renovation commitments."

"That's the beauty part. The conference is right here in town, at the Phoenix. What more could you ask for a convenient get-away? You and I can bunk at your home-away-from-home for six stress-free days and let the males in your life—Max, Louie, and Matt—rethink their absurdly territorial positions."

"Well, there's hope for Louie, but I doubt that Matt or Max will be bellying up to the bar together anytime soon. What kind of conference is this, anyway? For Justices of the Peace?"

"Hardly. A dull lot, you know. Quit sulking in the pews and come on into the light, dear."

Temple slid along the varnished wooden bench to follow Electra to the wall-hugging organ, where she fanned out her papers, then snapped on the music lamp atop the console.

"*Voila!*"

Temple blinked at the sudden bright light, trying to read a glossy brochure and flyer. But no text, however clever and copious, could compete with the lush four-color image of a hotly embracing, half-dressed couple.

"What kind of conference is this?" she asked suspiciously.

"G.R.O.W.L.—Great Readers Of Wonderful Literature. Just think, they're holding this year's deal right here in Vegas! At the Crystal Phoenix. Six days of glamour at a classy hotel, Crystal days and Crystal nights. Balls, banquets, cocktail receptions and lots of daytime panels on the how and why of the romance novel. All the big-time authors will attend, and the hunkiest cover models. They have a costume show, a cover model pageant, even a 'star search' writing contest for readers who want to write."

"Electra! You don't read this stuff?"

Electra inserted her muumuu between Temple and her precious papers. "It isn't 'stuff,' and I do. In fact, I plan to enter the writing contest. Why are you so sure it's junk?"

"I didn't say that. It's just that the grocery store rack romance covers are so lurid. Talk about selling raw meat."

"Not all of the covers are like that. And what's wrong with a little sensuality, anyway?"

"Nothing, but it shouldn't be packaged so embarrassingly like sausage, and that's what those muscle-bound, semi-nude, male cover models look like."

"Aha! So you've looked."

"Who could miss them?"

"But you've never read a romance novel?"

"Not since . . . oh, *Wuthering Heights*."

"I can't believe that." Electra glared at her over the concentrated gleam of the music lamp until Temple felt like she was being grilled by a cop. Romance patrol on your tail.

"Okay," Temple said, thinking hard and trying to be honest. "I read some Georgette Heyer Regency romances in high school. You know, romantic farce among the upper classes, skirting the indiscreet but very proper after all, as discreet as Jane Austen. *Those* male cover models all looked like Bob Cratchet in Beau Brummell clothes."

"Heyer is a classic author," Electra said reverently, "but a bit prim by today's standards. Even the Regency romance has caught up with the times. Face it, the period is historically more correct with a peek behind the bedcurtains. The Regency rake had a high old time."

"I don't know why I'm standing here debating books I haven't read with you when my life is last week's powdered milk without water at the moment."

"You see! You haven't kept up with the romance field. You need to get acquainted with modern times between the covers. You

might learn something that would help your current situation."
Electra finished with a significant waggle of her silvery eyebrows
that made her resemble a demonic fairy godmother beckoning an
innocent to a night at the erotomaniac's ball.

Temple laughed, which was an improvement on her previous
mood. "Honestly. You think I could learn something from a paperback romance novel? Please. Life is earnest, life is real. Life is
nothing like a date with Fabio on a really good hair day—his, not
yours. That kind of self-deceptive escapism has zilch to do with
my . . . domestic dilemma."

"A *Domestic Dilemma*," Electra parroted, assuming a strange,
simpering demeanor Temple had never seen before. "A Regency
romance by Henrietta Hayfield under the, ah, old Garnet imprint." She bit a lip. "Published in the late seventies, I think. The
heroine is a runaway heiress who disguises herself as a chimney
sweep and marries an earl with an allergy to soot. Stunning romantic tension, but no sensual fireworks in either the hearth or
the bedroom. Did I mention that the conference is going to have
a trivia contest, too?" she finished modestly.

"How appropriate!" Temple said, steaming. "I know you mean
well, Electra, but the last thing I need now is visions of Scarlet Pim-
pernels or scarlet women dancing in my girlish imagination. I need
my feet on the ground, not my head in the clouds. I'm going to my
. . . rooms."

Electra thrust the bundle of papers at Temple. "At least look
over the conference materials, dear. I've never known you to have
a closed mind. It might be fun."

"Fun is not in my game plan at the moment."

Temple stomped out of the wedding chapel on her noisome sandals, enjoying shattering the silence that she had sought, and so
soon lost.

Still, the encounter with Electra had eased her emotional shell
shock. A lethargy of despair lifted with her as she jolted upward
in the creaking elevator.

She pulled the door key from her jumpsuit pocket and entered
the condominium, flipping on the kitchen switch. Fluorescent
light burned the black-and-white decor kitchen into etched sharp-

ness. It oozed just far enough into the living room beyond to reveal the sofa and its two occupants.

One end was again in the possession of Midnight Louie, his eyes glowing green in the semi-dark; at the other end sat Max Kinsella. His eyes did not glow green.

Temple wasn't surprised to find him there this time, but she did feel the lover's knot in her gut kink again. Max, seeing her, reached up a long arm to turn on the reading lamp over the sofa, bathing himself and his Hawaiian shirt in an incandescent spill of buttery light.

Temple set the materials Electra had given her on the edge of the kitchen counter and went to face the music.

"This time," Max said, "I was perfectly house-trained. I used my key." He leaned forward, the object in hand. When Temple didn't take the key, he set it down on the coffee table.

With both ends of the sofa occupied, Temple didn't relish putting herself in the middle. So she sat on the coffee table facing the sofa, something only a lightweight like herself could do without tipping it over.

Maybe it was the downpour of light from above, but Max looked worried, or, rather, he looked like he was trying not to look worried.

"I don't understand," she said for openers.

He shrugged. "My breaking and entering via the balcony seemed to upset you. I can be civil and use a door like anyone else. You can keep that." He nodded at the key on the glass-topped table.

Temple felt like another fictional little-girl-lost, only this time it was Alice confronting tables bearing alien objects that could abruptly change her perceptions of herself and the world around her. Did her reaction to current events make her a mature Big Girl, or an emotionally shrunken Little Girl? Go ask Alice.

"It's your key," she finally said.

"You can give it back when you really believe that."

"Electra said you won't stay at the Circle Ritz."

"Can't," Max corrected. "This was meant to be a flying visit to let you know I was alive."

"Thanks, I guess."

He was silent. At the sofa's other end, Louie maintained his noncommittal stare. Then he suddenly hiked a hind leg over one shoulder and began grooming his business end, all the while keeping a glaring eye on Max.

Temple had never before seen a cat give anyone the finger, and laughed. Max deserved a feline finger, at least.

"He doesn't like me," Max noted.

"Oh, I doubt Louie is reacting in terms of like or dislike. He's just not sure you won't commit an indiscretion on his sofa."

"He must know my history." Max directed a significant, and searing, look at Temple.

That look could have made a nun blush, but Temple was drained of frivolous blood. She looked at the floor.

"Temple, what's happened with us?" he wanted to know.

"Max! What *us*? You were gone, without word or warning, for over five months. Lieutenant Molina even implied that you might be dead, although Lieutenant Molina mostly implied that you were an escaped murderer whose whereabouts she wanted to know."

"Electra clued me in on your recent crime-solving exploits, but she didn't mention this Molina bozo. He had no right planting nonsense in your mind—"

"Is your Interpol record nonsense?"

"My Interpol record—?"

"Play innocent, but your hidden baby blues won't fool me, and they *are* baby blues. I saw it right there on the Interpol card in black and white: six-foot-two, eyes of blue. Sure, you could grow an extra inch or two, but your eyes wouldn't change color. Would *you* trust somebody who even lied about their eye color?"

Max's frown was still worrying at the Interpol news. "What the devil could that damned interfering lieutenant have dug up?"

"How about IRA involvement? That bring back any forgotten chapters and verses? You know, following the black velvet band for the good of dear auld Ireland and all that. I didn't even know that you were Irish-born."

"I wasn't."

"Then what were you doing in Ireland at the tender age of seventeen, being suspected of IRA activities?"

"I was a tourist! That whole business was a mix-up. This Molina didn't have anything more recent than that old Interpol bulletin, did he?"

"No . . ." Temple found Max's assumption that Molina was male as irritating as a hovering gnat, yet it was not worth swatting down when much bigger issues were swarming en masse. "That still doesn't explain why your local disappearing act became semipermanent. Or why you never said good-bye. Or called. Nor does it explain away the body in the ceiling of the Goliath casino. Or the *other* body in the ceiling of the Crystal Phoenix casino just a couple of days ago . . . or why you wear those damn green contact lenses that I've never seen you putting in or taking out. That took premeditation, Max, and plenty of it! What did you take me for, a loyal and gullible audience of one?"

"Temple." He leaned forward to put his hands on her arms. "We've got lots to talk about. We can't possibly catch up on five months all at once."

"Not just months, Max, years! After you left, when Lieutenant Molina came around asking questions, I realized that I knew hardly anything about your past."

"That works both ways," he pointed out. "We did get carried away with ourselves."

"Me? You're saying I have a past worth exploring? Hah!"

"The past five months certainly sound eventful." He was smiling.

"Why is Lieutenant Molina so anxious to find you? And what about those men who—?"

Max's hands slid down her forearms until they enclosed her fingers. His touch was as warm as always. If "cold hands, warm heart" was a truism, did "warm hands, cold heart" apply?

"Temple, that assault on you never should have happened. That's why I left, why I never contacted you, no matter how much I wanted to. My disappearing act was supposed to draw them away from you."

"Then you know who they are; you know why they want you."

"No." He considered. "I suspected that someone like them might be after me, that's true enough. I can even guess why, but I can't tell you. If you know anything, you're in danger."

"I'm in danger ignorant, too. I might as well know why."

Max shook his head, releasing her hands. "I can't say. It's not only my decision—and certainly not my inclination—to keep you in the dark, believe that. And I can't stay here right now to sort all this out."

"All what? Me? The condominium? The hotel casino murders? Who Jack the Ripper really was? Don't tell me you're confessing to all or any of the above?"

His features both softened and sharpened. All of his attention focused on her. "Exasperation is the last resort of the uncertain, Temple."

While she contemplated that, he reached out and drew her onto the sofa, into the lean-back corner with him, so she was tucked between the crook of his arm and his shoulder like a jig-saw puzzle piece slipping into its well-worn dovetail.

Tension evaporated.

"You're all that I care about," he said simply, "but unfortunately not all that I have to be concerned about."

Max sighed, which wasn't like the Max she knew, but then she had apparently never known the real Max (maybe the complete Max would be a better way to put it).

"I suppose I was naive," he said, almost to himself, and that didn't sound like the old Max either. "I had no business getting involved with you."

"Now's a great time to figure that out."

"With anyone, really. But you changed my mind—fast."

"I thought you changed me, and my life."

His arms tightened around her and he rested his head on top of hers. Their position gave Temple that same seductive, cozy feeling you get bundled up with someone you love on a toboggan, poised atop an exhilarating hill, on the brink of a thrilling but familiar ride. Toboggan rides, she reminded herself, hadn't done much for Mattie Silver and Ethan Frome.

"We may have made a fast merge on the highway of love, but

it wasn't a whim," he said wryly. "And it wasn't undertaken lightly, by either of us. Remember how we exchanged our 'papers,' how we rigorously practiced safe sex for six months? We did everything right."

"I remember rigorous, and it certainly didn't feel like practice, or that safe, even if it was," she said, remembering also the sweet anticipation of sex in the slow lane. "We were so cute and quaint, kind of like in the Dark Ages, when engaged couples waited until they were married. It actually was a lot more exciting that way."

"We were responsible," he said. "We took care that we didn't hurt each other. Temple, I've been faithful. I haven't thrown that away."

"I've been celibate, too." A bittersweet thought clothed in ambivalence shrouded the naked truth. Did her attraction to Matt in his absence add up to infidelity? Why did honesty so often unravel at the edges?

His embrace tightened. "Then there's nothing to stop us starting where we left off."

"Not exactly. There's *nobody* to stop us . . . except us. I tried not to listen to other people's doubts, but you were gone, and, after a while, I didn't have glib answers anymore."

"Maybe you shouldn't discuss me in absentia."

"Aha, so that's where you were all this time: off on a foreign junket in Absentia."

After a shocked moment, Max laughed, the free-wheeling spree of delight that always made her smile. She was smiling now.

He pulled her on top of him. "God, I've missed that."

"What?" Still smiling, and backsliding into that half-audible, almost-coy lover's Q&A session.

"My paprika girl." His big hand tousled her hair. "Always surprising, and full of spunk."

"Thank you," Temple said, as expected.

"I hate spunk," he answered with feeling, on cue.

And they laughed again.

Because they were back, in Max's Loring Park resident hotel, a quaint rambling old place painted ersatz-Victorian yellow, filled with actors and other artsy itinerants. They were on the lumpy liv-

ing room sofa, while the small television set droned reruns of
Mary Tyler Moore's old seventies sitcom, and she was playing
Mary and he was Mr. Grant for an acerbic moment, and they were
beginning to get very well acquainted indeed.

Temple couldn't say whether Max kissed her, or she kissed him,
and that had been the way it had always been, too. And she
couldn't say when it started or when it stopped, but they were still
doing it when Midnight Louie rose and walked pointedly over
their lower legs, all twenty-some pounds of him stalking indignantly off now that things had gotten mushy.

The cat's withdrawal brought her to her senses, or away from
them. She pushed herself up and away, but slowly.

"What is it? What's really come between us?" Max asked.

"Time. Truth. It can't be the same, Max. It just can't. I'm not
the same."

"Is it Devine? He's damn good-looking, and damnably nice. I
can see—"

"No, you can't see. Not a thing." She put a hand on his shoulder, assuring, consoling. "Matt's not the threat you think."

"Why not? Is he married?"

"No, but he's not free."

"Then he's divorcing. . . ."

"Not in the way you think."

"What way?"

"I can't say."

But she wanted to, wanted to explain why their association
could look so romantic and be so platonic thus far, despite some
fairly adolescent tangos in the dark. But she couldn't expose Matt
like that. Max watched her with that patented judicious, astute
Max look. They were so different, and so much the same.

"Divided loyalties." The ruefulness in Max's voice reflected his
own acquaintance with such struggles of the conscience. "You
can't betray a confidence. Your silence means you're committed
elsewhere to some degree, Temple."

"So does yours."

They regarded each other sadly. Telling the truth, yet saying
nothing.

Temple moved back to her side of the sofa; actually Louie's, but even he had walked out on this painful impasse. From the kitchen she heard the astounding sound of Free-to-be-Feline pellets being crunched. Either nothing else was set out to eat, or he was making an unprecedented statement.

"It's not Matt," she said finally, not expecting Max to believe her. "It's the mystery. We all have a right to our own mysteries, but yours are too deep. I have to wonder now if I've been misled. Taken. Used."

Three little words, and she could see him conceal an internal wince at each one. He lashed out in turn, but not at her.

"Then it's that damnable police lieutenant Molina, planting poisonous seeds, but doing what? Arresting me? No, not even if I walked up and held my wrists out for the cuffs. Because I'm not . . . guilty of anything arrestable. You're going to let some pathologically suspicious detective come between us?"

"Frank is coming between us—"

"Frank? That's his name?"

Temple smiled at his latest erroneous conclusion. "Frank Ness, maybe a relative of Elliot, do you think? Molina's just a messenger, Max. An unwelcome one, but a bit player, believe me. You've got to accept responsibility. You said earlier that maybe you shouldn't have 'let' us happen, that you had no right."

"But I had an inclination, a need."

"What I need to know, what I have a right to know, is what you can't tell me about yourself, bad or good or indifferent. That's the sad thing, if you'd just trust me—"

"There's no trust in what began in Ireland all those innocent years ago, Temple, only serial suspicion. It's not that I don't trust you, or myself, it's the whole mean and uncouth world out there. I suppose I should be grateful you have someone around to look after you," he added in a bitter mumble, as if accusing himself of dereliction of duty.

"Yeah," Temple said assertively. "Me."

"Temple, I have always respected your independence."

"Good, because I've had to develop a bit more of it lately."

"Good."

"Fine. Then everybody's happy. Max, if you really knew what kind of danger I've faced and survived lately, you'd stop acting like a knight errant and offer me a job as a bodyguard."

"If I knew, I'd probably ship you back to your family in Minneapolis."

Temple shook her head. "Too late. Can't go back, and I'm glad. I thank you for that. Can't go back to being a professional innocent, either."

"Too bad. Absence is overrated; it doesn't make the heart grow fonder."

Resignation had settled on his expressive form like an invisible cloak. He was a mime at heart; despite his phenomenal emotional and facial control, his body language always gave him away, at least to her. Temple felt her uncertainty and resolve melting into compassion, anguish, the vague grip of chronic misery.

"Max, you idiot, this wouldn't be so bloody bewildering if I didn't want to just jump right back to where we were! Maybe with some time, some talk—"

"I haven't got time! And talk is academic." He sat forward on the couch, staring at the bare glass top of her coffee table as if studying his faint reflection. "Temple, your suspicions are absolutely right, in a way. That ancient Interpol card marked the beginning of the whole mess. It began with a death. There have been more, and will be more. So maybe that means that I don't deserve a life. But you . . . I won't risk you, even if that means I must risk losing you."

"Will you stay in Las Vegas?"

His fingers entwined tightly, making his two hands into one bare-knuckled, white-capped mountain range, like some Oriental form of isometric exercise symboling intense inner conflict. "I can't say."

"Will you come up and see me sometime?" A suggestion of Mae West in the delivery barely disguised her underlying seriousness.

He glanced up from contemplating some dark well in his past

and future, truly startled. Temple just smiled. One didn't often shock the Mystifying Max.

She managed to keep the smile light and bright. "I didn't say it was hopeless, Max. Just use the door now and again. And knock first."

Chapter 4

Yvette to Be Alone

Humans are a curious species. I mean that in both senses of the word: they are odd in their own practices, and nosy about the habits of others.

So they are always writing books about my kind purporting to explain our comings and goings and endearing little domestic quirks. They are especially obsessed by our bathroom routines for some reason, although we have bent over backwards to use their indoor facilities and I have not observed them making any reciprocal effort to adapt our outdoor etiquette in these matters.

When they are not speculating about our potty practices, they are puzzling over our enduring attraction to paper goods. Be it newsprint, tax forms or the pages of an open book, we can always be found on it (or, on occasion, under it). Why?

The answer is apparently too obvious to arrive at. Where do they suppose we get our legendary savoir faire, our wise demeanor and sage expressions? We are absorbing the contents of the printed matter in our own cryptic, inimitable way. I do not propose that we actually read line by line, but proximity is enough. Perhaps you have heard certain veterinarians seriously advising humans to shred newspapers as substitute litter box material for felines who have had that sometimes necessary procedure that I call a "claw draw."

How idiotic! What do they take us for? Such humans will tell you that their discriminating domestic partners usually refuse to use these substitute box fillers. And why? Not because of the caustic perfume of printer's ink, but because all of those tumbled and shredded bits of words and phrases confuse our sense of order. Although we often may be inclined to demonstrate our opinion of much of human literature with a well-deserved scratch and deposit, we do not wish to deface potential reading matter.

However, I am not here to discuss human behavior, however disgusting.

I merely cite these facts of feline behavior to explain how it is that when Miss Temple Barr returns from seeing Mr. Max Kinsella to the door, she finds me rising and stretching atop the brochures and flyers on the kitchen countertop.

"Oh, Louie, shoo!" she greets me in her usual melodious tones of affection. "Have you wrinkled all of Electra's information?"

Wrinkled it? I have conquered it. As I rise I know several key facts: one is the imminent arrival of hundreds of romance-lovers. This is no news. Las Vegas is full of romance-lovers, else it would not have so many wedding chapels.

What has set my synapses singing is the news that the female hostess of the main event at this amorous gathering is none other than Miss Savannah Ashleigh, the so-called film star. And where Miss Savannah Ashleigh goeth, her little lamb is sure to goeth also. I refer to none other than the Divine Yvette, *mon amour* of fur, the pinnacle of Persian pussyhood, the shaded silver sultana of Rodeo Drive.

"Louie! Don't drool on the convention brochure." Miss Temple is now berating me. "Surely, you are not one of these cover model maniacs?"

Please. Naked muscle does not do a thing for me. The usually percipacious Miss Barr has evidently missed the key image: a

small head shot of Miss Savannah Ashleigh, her waves of platinum hair bleached to match the natural silver of my beloved's soft
locks.

"Ooooh," says Miss Temple, her piquant little features wrinkling. "Savannah Ashleigh is hosting the cover model pageant.
That has-been could not get work as Heather Locklear's stand-
in. Am I glad I am not handling PR for this do—temperamental
cover hunks would be bad enough. Savannah Ashleigh would be
too much. Louie—! Give that back!"

Even as my little doll battles me for possession of the convention brochure, I keep my claws in and my lip zipped. She suddenly freezes in mid-fight and opens those baby blue-grays as
wide as all outdoors.

"Why, Louie, that Ashleigh woman has a cat you're sweet on
. . . what is its name? Iva . . . Ivory . . . Minuet . . . Minaret?"

The Divine Yvette is not an "It," but I will not deign to tell Miss
Temple so. I do not speak to humans, on principal, because some
of them are so unspeakable to my kind.

Miss Temple does not expect an answer from me anyway.
"Even cats get the long-gone, lonesome blues, I guess," she goes
on. "I am sure that Savannah Ashleigh drags the poor thing everywhere she goes. So, feel free, Louie, to mosey on over to the
Phoenix to visit Electra and me during the G.R.O.W.L. convention. You can even say hello to your lost inamorata."

In amor what? Poor Miss Temple. Her mind is more than somewhat muddled from her recent encounter with the Mystifying Max.
No doubt she has already forgotten that there is good reason I
would not be eager to race over to the Crystal Phoenix to mix
whiskers with the Divine Yvette.

I cannot touch tootsie to premises without risking an encounter
with my own unwelcome offspring, the exceedingly un-divine Midnight Louise. No matter that the Divine Yvette waits and wonders
in her lonely canvas carrier.

A romance conference may be convening at the Crystal
Phoenix, but love is not in the cards for two lonely persons from
the opposite side of the tracks. The Divine Yvette is forever Pretty
Paws, and I am plain dirt.

Chapter 5

A Really Big
Shoe-down

"It's no use, Louie," Temple announced at 10:30 P.M., slapping back the covers so quickly that the cat was forced to edge aside.

Midnight Louie, rearranged in the Sphinx/Leo position so prominent in Las Vegas nowadays, regarded her sitting form with polite yet bored amazement. Cats were as good as concealing their thoughts as . . . well, the Sphinx.

"I just can't sleep," she went on aloud despite Louie's obvious disinterest, "and I won't spend any more time tossing and twitching over men whose names begin with the letter M. There is more to life than angst in the first degree. I'm outta here."

She picked up the red shoe phone and sparred a round of numbers into it, by heart. It wasn't answered until the fourth ring, but Temple felt no guilt whatsoever. She'd had it with guilt.

"Did I wake you? Sorry. I won't take more than a minute. Electra, get me out of here! It's a go on your GROWLers. Whisk me away to Wishful Thinking Land. Reality . . . mucks. Eight tomorrow morning? No problem."

She set the phone down on its high red heel and disconnecting black sole, then regarded Midnight Louie in her turn. "There's only one place a girl can go when everything has gone wrong in her life, and I'm on my way."

Temple jumped up, tore off her Garfield T-shirt, no doubt to Louie's supreme relief, and sprinted over to her fifties dresser with the foot-deep drawers.

Pantyhose hurled left and right until she found a pair that lacked runs, snags and holes in the toes. Her flurry of action had lured Louie from the bed to the floor, where he was playing footsie with the rejected pantyhose.

"Eat 'em if you want to," Temple advised him in atypical abandon. "Why keep defective hose around that I'll never wear?" That line might also apply to certain human beings whose first names began with the letter M, but, like Scarlett, Temple wasn't going to think about that until tomorrow.

She donned a linen culotte and top in such a cheery shade of butter-substitute yellow that it would make teeth grit for miles around, snarled a brush through her bed-tousled curls and left the bedroom.

In five minutes flat she had her red patent leather tote bag on the passenger seat and was weaving the aqua Geo Storm in and out of the Las Vegas Strip's twenty-four-hour traffic jam.

Caesars Palace was lit up like a wedding cake, all illuminated white columns. The image did nothing for Temple's mood, but she parked the Storm in the lot and hoofed her way into the churning crowds. The dark casino with its thousand pinpoints of low intensity light was a blurred, sound-barrier-breaking, warp-speed passage to her.

Seconds later she broke into the tasteful beige ambiance of the hotel's marble-lined Forum shopping area. Here she finally paused, although it was a detour on her ultimate route. Despite the hour and the hot action in the casino, crowds still jostled through the tangled byways of shopfronts. Temple hitched the tote bag straps higher on her shoulder. *Don't mess with me, purse-snatchers!*

She was coming up fast on the pale Cararra-marble backside of Michelangelo's David, a replica that loomed eighteen virtually nude feet into the mall's airy classical vault. The surrounding rotunda was painted bawdy-house red with oodles of white plasterwork, creating an intimate bedroom ambiance for David's marbled muscles. *Another slick imposter,* Temple thought darkly. A costly imitation of the real thing. *Just like certain relationships!*

She cast David's insouciantly bare, ultra-masculine form a glance. His name decidedly did not begin with an M. Soon she would be seeing similar territoriality in the flesh at Electra's G.R.O.W.L. conference. Growl! So what!

Like Caesar, she stood at a personal Rubicon: between two vastly different paths. Hah! Did her subconscious think it was referring to matters metaphysical? No. This choice was far more crucial than a mere fork in the rocky road of her lovelife.

Should she go east, or should she go west? East lay the more familiar turf of the Appian Way, a well-heeled shopper's paradise of vamp and sole, most of them not manmade, but the real thing.

West lay the Place-She-Dare-Not-Contemplate and remain sane, the Place-She-Had-Been-Ignoring, the guaranteed site of temptation beyond budget. Temple had never laid eyes on the exact location, though she had known of its existence for months. To plunge into such a dangerous region in her state of emotional chaos was folly, but there are times when only exquisite excess will soothe the savage soul. Sole.

Even now she thought she could hear the siren song of high heels tapping, could see the sad, stirring vision of rows of unoccupied shoes lined up like doggies in a window, hoping for a possessor. . . . Pick me. Pick *me!* *Pick* me!

She turned right, west, and marched to her doom and to her delight. Odd how often those opposite concepts went together!

First, she decided on a frontal attack, which was the long way around, but a brisk walk does wonders to soothe the savage heart. She retraced her way through the casino and out the sweeping front entrance flanked by more reproductions of classic statues. Given the mating habits of the Roman gods they represented, reproductions were oddly apt. Temple followed the curving walk from pool to pool of dramatic lighting, pausing only under the huge rotating Planet Hollywood sign at the midway point.

By the time she reached the Strip, she was braced for the background clatter of cars and foot traffic, and bathed in millions of kilowatts of a neon symphony. Caesars's warm white incandescence glowed on her left; the Mirage's sophisticated coppery cliffside shone amid tropical splendor. The Mirage volcano emitted a cigarette cough as it prepared to whoop and roar with artificial fireworks, the Strip's only chain smoker.

But Temple was pointed between these titans of the Las Vegas Strip, toward her own temple, a rotunda bristling with gilded horses flaunting their twenty-four-carat hooves. A hop on the moving sidewalk and she was wafted, alongside a stream of tourists, up a gentle incline toward The Forum Shops at Caesars Palace. (Omit the apostrophe in Caesars, she mentally reminded herself, like a good PR girl who knows all the local quirks, and even some national ones: the Dr in Dr Pepper never has a period, nor does the S in Harry S Truman, nor does Caesars Palace sport an apostrophe.)

Like Jean Paul Sartre's Hell, the novice found No Exit from The Forum Shops except through Caesars' casino. Las Vegas architecture was as canny as a maze. Despite all the bells and whistles, the object was to maroon visitors right where the management wanted them: dead center in a casino.

No such illusions would do for Temple tonight. This was a serious pilgrimage. So she brushed by aimless tourists with single-minded skill. Many people had slowed to gawk at the eternally blue trompe l'oeil sky, where wispy clouds shimmered in a shifting bath of sunset haze. She dodged around the massive marble obstacle of the first indoor fountain. A ring of people was awaiting the hourly animation of Bacchus, Plutus, Apollo and Venus, but Temple rushed through, unimpressed by the dome's laser-lashed storming sky, or the emerald constellations of stars that twinkled through.

She streaked past Planet Hollywood like a copper-topped comet, did not pause to watch its indoor world-shaped sign turn above the neon-framed cave of the trendy restaurant. She detoured around the gigantic sculpted fountain in the ersatz street's center, not even glancing at the honored Italian names under the surrounding Greek pediments surmounted by statuary: Versace, Gucci, Escada, Armani. Once again it was Romans over the Greeks, and everybody else, by a designer logo.

She knew most of the stores here, but kept an eye out for the newest one. By now the black yawning maw of Caesars, glinting with the gold teeth of casino lighting, loomed beyond the Forum Shops's eternal twilight glow like a monster mouth.

Where was it? Had she overshot her goal? No! Her feet were tiring. Even the businesslike clicks of her high heels on the marble floor had lost the perky, reassuring sound of her own intent existence.

She squinted at the shop signs above the doors, deliberately underplayed to showcase the brilliantly lit shop windows below. Temple's heart began beating faster as she recognized part of a name. Surely that first word . . . Seteu? Yes! She had never seen it before, but she would have known it anywhere. Her feet moved faster.

She crossed lanes in the stream of shoppers like the Storm darting through traffic, her chin lifted so she could see above the madding (and Texas-tall) crowd to the object of her outing.

Was that woman in the high-tech rubber jumpsuit going to dash in the door before her? Not on her life!

Temple's feet barely touched ground as she scuttled through the moving mob, slipping through the open door a step before the Rubber Jumpsuit.

Ah. Ahhhh.

Here all was not only classical, but class. The understated gleam of travertine walls, warm backlighting that showcased (shoecased?) glass shelves artfully lined with goods. She was aware of miniature dressmaking forms attired in gold brocade, of purses and the odd accessory scattered artfully hither and yon. But they were not the Main Event.

Temple contemplated the static, yet somehow anticipatory peace of a shoe store. All those smooth, unsullied soles waiting to glide over the plush carpet like magical skates. All those unscuffed toes and heels primed to pose before the floor-level mirrors. All those clever bows and straps and decorative heels. All that evening glitz and glitter waiting to accompany all the little girls from Kansas and the cinder-choked hearth to battle and to balls.

Unlike skirts and dresses and belts, shoes do not allow their owners to outgrow them. Carefully kept, they do not wear out, like socks and hose and human knees and friendships. Age cannot wither, nor custom stale their infinite variety of color, cut and style.

Temple moved slowly, softly in the large room, a connoisseur in an art gallery. No longer would she have to haunt Saks and Neiman Marcus sales at the Strip's Fashion Show Mall for unsold size fives. Oz had come to her. The Wizard had landed, gently, on the Yellow Brick Road and she needed more than ruby red slippers for the journey. Suddenly last summer, this stand-alone shop of shoes designed by Stuart Weitzman had miraculously appeared in her own back yard. SW shoes by the yard awaited her. She sighed. It was meant to be. All she had to do now was afford them.

Temple edged along the store's perimeter, dazzled by the glimpse of one exquisite shoe after another. Even the vanilla-colored casual shoes had their own subtle glamour, although, when it came to shoes, Temple liked them high, narrow and handsome. Temple found herself catching a ghostly reflection of herself, and stumbled back in amazement.

A Plexiglas-box-topped pedestal had served as her imperfect mirror. Beyond the translucent outline beckoned even greater wonders: a wall of dancing shoes with solid rhinestone-covered heels, each glittering like a size-five rainbow, some diamond-bright, others gleaming with sapphires and rubies and emeralds.

"Those are Pavé Collection models custom-designed by Mr. Weitzman," a gentle voice noted beside her.

"I know." Temple could not take her eyes off the treasure trove of shoes. "I've heard of them. They're fabulous."

"They can be designed to match a particular gown or any theme of the customer's choosing."

Temple nodded in a dream. "How much—?"

The saleswoman told her, in an even gentler voice with not a hint of condescension.

Temple nodded. She wasn't surprised. She also was not about

to ever become the owner of a pair of Pavé Collection shoes. At least she would have visiting privileges.

"Thank you." Temple tried to sound as if she needed time to decide which several styles she wished to purchase.

The saleswoman drifted away diplomatically, leaving Temple to contemplate the cruelties of budget. Temple remained transfixed. To her this was Stonehenge, Avalon, Nirvana. The cares of the day, as Stephen Foster or someone equally antique would put it, faded away. Some women found such surcease of sorrow in chocolate. Temple always found it in an exquisite pair of high heels. At least her addiction was not fattening (especially not to the wallet).

Which one of the black satin pumps would she pick? The one covered in winking red ladybugs, with matching bag? The Deco-inspired one of a woman (on the heel) walking a Scottie (on the toe) with a long glittering leash (along the instep)? The golden glitz of a sun/moon/stars motif?

Visions of Austrian crystals dancing in her head, Temple finally focussed on the contents of the Plexiglas plinth standing like a prow, a figurehead before the wall of Pavé Collection shoes. Behind the clear Plexiglas floated a pair of diamond-white shoes, Cinderella shoes paved in crystal. A card explained the Pavé Collection philosophy: up to 14,000 hand-set Austrian crystals encrusting each and every pair.

Temple edged around the pedestal, careful not to touch it, to jar the precious cargo inside. And then . . . and then . . .

Holy cats!

She was nose-to-nose with Midnight Louie. Well, a black, Austrian-crystal cat, anyway, with great personal presence, climbed the back of each glittering heel, a single emerald stone winking at his eye.

Solely cats!

A second card was propped on a delicate easel on the pedestal's other side. *Halloween's coming,* it announced in elegant script. *Find a pair of these "Jinx" black-cat, hidden somewhere in Las Vegas, by October 31 and claim a pair in your size as the prize.*

Yes! Temple clasped her hands. The answer to a lovesick

maiden's prayer. Not men whose first names began with M, but shoes whose name began with "Midnight" as in Louie. What more could a modern-day Cinderella wish for? Stuff the vacillating prince; get it on with the cool shoes!

Obviously, she was destined to find and win these shoes. Obviously, this was a heaven-sent distraction from her current personal conundrum. Obviously, Las Vegas's prime crime-solving amateur could beat out every other candidate in the Streak for the Shoes.

Temple marched up to a person that she assumed was the saleswoman who had addressed her earlier; she had been too dazzled to notice much but the shoes.

"Do I need an entry blank?"

The woman's face, which was about her age, looked politely inquiring. Surely she too had only one thing on her mind? How could she work here and not?

"For the Midnight Louie shoes . . . I mean, the Halloween Jinx shoes."

"Oh. Just spot them by October thirty-first, then drop by and fill out a card with your name and address."

"Piece of chocolate cheesecake," Temple said, as satisfied as if she had eaten the whole, metaphorical thing.

She left the store, hardly noticing the crowd, and wended her way back through the crowded casino, not even glancing into the Appian Way at David with his sling and no G-string as she passed.

For some reason, she felt ravenous.

Chapter 6

Little Cat Feet

It has been a busy day, and I am in no mood for late-night distur-
bances in routine.

In my own living room, I have had to defend my turf against the
invasion of the seven-foot-tall man.

On my own personal sofa, I have had to share my cushions with
a stranger, while gazing upon a shirt the color of lizard leavings.

In the privacy of my bedchamber, I have been forced to endure
more tossing and turning from Miss Temple Barr than a crepe
suzette could expect to encounter in an omelet pan.

When the lady of the house returns, I am not prepared for the
general air of celebration. Those of my kind do not celebrate, except internally.

This does not stop Miss Temple Barr from thrusting me into the
midst of her excitement.

"Louie!" she cries even before she has entered our bedroom
to see if I am still there.

"Louie!" She stands in the doorway, dropping her totebag to the floor and extending her arms wide.

She is obviously prepared for a swoop. If there is anything I loathe more than a swoop, I would be hard-pressed to name it.

Before I can shift my weight to my pins and escape, she is on me like a tomato-red tornado. You would think that she would have learned by now that it is impossible to hug a dude of my persuasion, not to mention dimensions. But she does so anyway, resting her rusty curls on my velvet-tailored shoulders. I just hope that she does not shed.

"Oh, Louie," she sighs. "You should see your shoes."

I should indeed see my shoes; that would be some news worth getting on the Internet. What, pray tell, are they? Two-tone wingtips? High-heeled sneakers, now that they make such a thing? Perhaps they are fuzzy-wuzzy slippers. As if I would trade my hardy, super-sensitive foot-leather for such clumsy accoutrements!

The emotional stress caused by the sudden return of the gentleman known as Max has tipped poor Miss Temple over the edge. Naturally, her delusion would be in the area of fancy footwear, since she was a teensy bit nuts on the subject even when she was sane.

But she need not try to involve a plain-and-simple shoeless schmoe from Idaho in her mental breakdown. Pretty soon she will be buying me little red sweaters and rubber galoshes for my tootsy-wootsies. No thank you! I have always been a free soul, and spurn clothes of any kind, including collars and ties.

My aloof reaction to her less-than-joyous news has not penetrated the euphoric fog that Miss Temple Barr's illness has wrapped around her.

She insists on confiding more mania to my twitching ears.

"Oh, Louie, they are *sooo* gorgeous. Entirely covered in teeny, tiny Austrian crystals, and white like diamonds, except when the rainbow reflections are dancing off them. And, then, on the back of the heel, on each shoe, a darling figure of a black cat, reaching up, who knows for what? Maybe for Free-to-be-Feline, do you think?

I think, all right, and I do not like what I am thinking one itsy bit. *Darling? Teeny, tiny?* I have not heard Miss Temple resort to such nauseating descriptives in the entire time we have shared more than a roof. What has come over her?

"They're called 'Halloween Jinx' and I can win a pair free!"

Win a pair free. Normally, Miss Temple eschews redundancy. I am truly concerned for her well-being, not to mention my own.

"All I have to do is find a shoe like these hidden somewhere in semi-plain sight in Las Vegas. And, then . . . Mama's gonna get a brand-new pair of shoes, Louie, oh, yes!

Mama? Spare me! I remember my maternal parent well, and she in no way resembled Miss Temple Barr by any stretch of my imagination or Miss Temple's.

"Hey, don't squirm away!" she pleads, crawling along on her knees beside the bed to keep me pinned to the coverlet. You would think I was a dude named Max, or Matt. "You're my lucky charm, Louie. Those shoes don't know it yet, but they have your name on them, and they are going to end up on my feet. It was meant to be."

I do not want my name bandied about on any pair of shoes, no matter how luxurious. However, I flop over on my side and allow her to massage my back and shoulders. When they get these little fits upon them, there is no containing them. At least they can apply that manic energy for my betterment. Mmmmm, not bad. Miss Temple is an A-one masseuse when she puts her mind to it, and those long, red nails . . . well, I am mollified after the previous hysterics.

"Oh, Louie," she says again. I am beginning to think that I am Irish. "Oh, Louie. Why is life always so complicated?"

I can tell by her tone that we are no longer discussing prize shoes, but deep matters of philosophy.

She sighs again. I do not know why humans are given such puny means of expressing themselves. If they could release their tensions, fears and pleasures with a long, deep purring session, they would not need psychiatrists and such.

But they are deficient in this area as well, and I am forced to do Miss Temple's purring for her.

She leans her head on my broad stomach, ear down, all the better to hear my masculine roaring and rumbling. I was not born to be a pillow, but there are times when I serve as such.

"I am not going to think about anything for the next five days, except finding those shoes. Do not tell anyone that I am going with Electra to a romance convention, though. That could ruin my reputation. Here I am, with two men in my life, and no life, except getting away from it all at a romance-novel convention full of cover hunks!"

Hey, *I* am a coverlet hunk.

She must have grasped the picture, because she leans closer to whisper a tender something in my ear. What she murmurs is the hush-hush retail price of the prize shoes.

I pause in mid-purr. That is no small patch of cabbage that she is talking about. Of course, any shoes bearing my always-elegant image would be worth a pretty penny.

I conclude that Miss Temple should lose the lukewarm dudes and go after the cool cat shoes.

Chapter 7

Boys Town

"What are you going to wear to the ball, dear?"

The words were sweetly intoned, yet Electra Lark looked like a fairy godmother who'd been kidnapped by MTV and forced to work in music videos.

Temple eyed Electra's puce/chartreuse muumuu and post-punk snare-do. "Nothing pumpkin-colored, though it may be appropriate to the season. It clashes with my hair. What ball?"

"The Midsummer Night's Dream Dance. Every G.R.O.W.L. convention has a big costume ball one evening. I thought you'd want to avoid looking out of place."

"Costumes! Can't I just wear my usual rags, Godmother? With, of course, a stunning pair of crystal shoes. In fact, I might have exactly the pair in a couple of weeks."

"Two weeks is too late. And, sure, some people wear ordinary evening clothes." Electra sniffed, as if black tie were too, too tawdry. "I guess you could, too."

Temple threw up her hands, then the hairbrush she was pack-ing. It landed among her lingerie on the bed.

"And what, Godmother dear, does one wear to a Midsummer Night's Dream ball in mid-October?"

"I'm going as Puck's grandmother," Electra said, "floaty silver lamé and gray chiffon, with genuine woodland camouflage in iri-descent glue-on glitter. And trifocals."

"You don't wear trifocals yet."

"No, but Puck's grandmother would be awfully old by now. Haven't you got something kicky, dear?"

"You've seen my shoe collection."

"Oh, my yes." Electra turned to the gaping closet doors. "Awe-some. But I've never seen a long gown in your closet, come to think of it."

"Come to think of it, I haven't got one. The hems always have to be taken up for me, so I don't bother. Plus long skirts obscure the important stuff, like my shoes."

"And your svelte little ankles and dimpled knees. Very wise. But nothing formal and floor-sweeping. A pity." Electra looked vaguely disappointed, as if she might burst into a tearful "bibbity bobbity boo-hoo."

"Oh, for heaven sakes, Electra! I do have a Lucretia Borgia getup I bought at a Guthrie Theatre costume sale years ago, think-ing it might be useful for a Renaissance Fair sometime. It came with these knee-length, beribboned tresses of red hair that matched mine, so I couldn't resist. Real human hair, too."

"Rapunzel. Perfect! Now, you'll need a welcome wagon outfit, something vaguely Western would work nicely; a dressy man-eating ensemble for the cover hunk pageant; and an awards banquet outfit—that beaded number you wore to the Gridiron is fine for that, and you won't be trotting up to the microphone for any awards . . . you're not planning to enter the romance-writing contest, are you?"

"Why should I write romantic fiction when I can't get any trac-tion in the romantic *faction* part of my life at the moment? Be-sides, didn't the entrants have to submit their work weeks ago?"

"No, that's the fun of this contest! We all get the rules in our convention packets, so we have four days to whip up three chapters and an outline. The winner will be announced at the awards banquet Sunday night after all the real writers' awards are given."

"You're actually going to enter this contest?"

"Absolutely. I've read enough romances to have the drill down pat. Say, could you bring along that cute little laptop of yours?"

"Oho, so that's why I need to escape my emotional Waterloo at the Circle Ritz for a few days! You need my megabytes."

"It's still a nice getaway. Now, where's that costume?"

"Oh, I don't know, somewhere in the lower depths of my closet in a big polyethelene dry-cleaner bag."

Temple sighed, grunted and then dove into a space where none but dust bunnies had gone since she had moved into the Circle Ritz almost a year earlier.

"Yeowww!" she complained, jumping back. "Something stuck me."

"You don't suppose it could be a scorpion?" Electra, the ever-consciencious landlady, shoved several of Temple's best outfits aside for a clearer view.

But the culprit did not possess a stinger in its tail, although a tail was standard-issue for its kind.

Midnight Louie lay curled up on a floor-trailing plastic bag. He greeted his unmasking with a lion-size yawn, and an additional, contented flex of his claws.

"So that's where he goes when I can't find him anywhere," Temple said.

"He's just having a Midsummer Night's nap in a peaceful place. Cats like that sort of retreat."

"How do you know?" Temple asked. "I thought you were allergic to cats?"

"That doesn't mean I don't know their habits. In fact, that may be why I'm so allergic to them. Don't worry about the costume. If Louie's wrinkled it, I can take it upstairs and use my industrial steamer on it."

"Industrial steamer! I'm impressed."

"No, but your gown will be," Electra said. "I intend to get you packed and over to the Phoenix within six hours."

"What about Louie?" Temple wondered as Electra dove into the closet to yank the heaped plastic out from under him.

"He can go as Puss in Boots, but he'll have to get his own wardrobe mistress."

Within five hours Temple, Electra and more garment bags than two unescorted ladies should carry were camped out in the Crystal Phoenix's bustling lobby behind a long, broad line of similar souls. Midnight Louie had been left lounging on the clothing-strewn wreck that was Temple's bedspread at the moment.

"Shouldn't we have told someone we were coming here?" Temple wondered queasily.

"Why?" Electra sounded indignant. "That is the advantage of being single; no one is owed an explanation. If they want to know so bad, they'll find out, believe me. Besides, who did you plan to notify? The maintenance man, or gentlemen boarders named Max and Matt?"

"I didn't have anyone specifically in mind," Temple began in a wishy-washy manner she much despised.

"Besides, they'd just laugh at us."

"Why?" Temple didn't ask who "they" were.

"Obviously, you haven't been a romance reader, or you'd know. To the nonromance-reading public, we're silly, love-starved women with so little going on in our lives we have to read these laughable tales of sex and seduction."

Temple hoped she didn't look as appalled as she felt. "I was thinking of this as just another convention. It didn't occur to me I'd be taken for a romance junkie merely by being here."

"What's wrong with that?" Electra demanded.

Before Temple could explain that she belonged to enough disadvantaged categories—women, short women, unlucky red-headed women, deserted women, assaulted women—without getting dragooned into yet another one of which she was utterly innocent . . . someone bumped into her from behind.

The offense was repeated, with feeling.

"Hey!" Temple spun around, ready to lambaste.

The offender's identity struck her dumb.

"Well, well," he said, practically purring. "Had no idea you were this hard up, T.B. I can point you to a dozen places in Las Vegas where you can put a little romance in your life, besides this hen party." He glanced at the long line of women waiting to register for their rooms. "What a bunch of losers."

"So that's what you're doing here, Buchanan."

"Hey! As you often say so eloquently. Sleaze is my beat." He leaned closer than was necessary or particularly healthy, batting his thick black eyelashes up and down the better to look Temple up and down. "You don't want to ogle these beefcake cover models, T.B. Half of 'em are queer and the other half are iffy. If I'd have known you were at loose ends and had a yen for romance, we might have got something going. No wonder you're so snappish to me. You just need a good—"

"Jerk!" Electra growled like a watchdog at Temple's side. "Who is this little man, Temple?"

"Not the Duchess of Windsor's darling, I'll tell you that. Meet Crawford Buchanan, author of the Broadside column for the *Las Vegas Scoop*."

"Oh, yes, I've seen it," Electra allowed. "Usually with used cat litter on it."

"I'm not covering this for the *Scoop*." Buchanan disdainfully adjusted the hang of his ivory linen jacket. "I'm the local liaison for *Hot Heads*, the national TV news mag, you know. I'll be providing a blow-by-blow account on all five days of the GROWLers' time to howl. If you're nice to me"—he leaned almost close enough to polish Temple's teeth with his own—"I'll make sure you get an on-camera interview. I'll even identify you as a local flack. Be good for business."

"I'm here *on* business," she announced airily, stepping back and right onto Electra's toe. "For the Phoenix." She hoped that was vague enough. "The only air time I need is room to breathe about six miles from you!"

"Women." Crawford smiled smarmily at Electra, as if—being silver-haired—she wasn't quite one anymore. "You can always tell they like you when they're testy."

"Sorry," Temple said, leaping off of Electra's toe the moment Crawford Buchanan had removed himself.

"Why?" Electra looked puzzled.

Mortified, Temple turned to see who her spike heel had nailed to the floor, and more important, who was so stoic as to mumble no word of protest.

Oh my. There he was. David in the flesh, only seven feet high instead of eighteen. Temple looked up, and up. Max was tall, but effacingly narrow. This guy was built more like an inverted sky-scraper. Unlike one of those needle-nosed buildings, he widened as he went up to Schwarzenegger proportions. Unlike David and Arnold, he draped his upper development in a modest curtain of bicep-brushing hair—pseudo sun-streaked, honestly straight and artfully untamed.

Temple had the oddest sensation of being within stomping distance of a massive palomino horse. All right. Palomino stallion. Okay, revise that. Palomino stud.

"I'm sorry," she said, "for stepping on you."

"You step on Fabrizio?" His tanned face crinkled (adorably, Temple assumed) with amusement. "No. Fabrizio must avoid stepping on lovely lady." With that he grinned (tenderly) and picked her up (manfully) in one fell swoop.

Some women in line turned to stare, then coo. Some blushed. Fabrizio crushed Temple to his manly chest, bared thanks to an unlaced not-so-manly poet's shirt. His skin was tanned, supernaturally hairless and his pectorals swelled to such unbelieveable dimensions that Temple marveled that he was allowed out in public without a Wonderbra.

Electronic flashes exploded along the registration line, but a hotter, more dazzling light went nova on the sidelines. Temple knew that blinding brilliance from days of old, though at that time she had been the tormenter hiding behind it.

"Looks like America's favorite male cover model, Fabrizio, has found a maiden fair already." Crawford Buchanan's oozing baritone rose from beyond the nebula of wattage. "How does it feel, miss, to be where every woman in America wants to be? How does it feel to be in the great Fabrizio's arms?"

The great Fabrizio was nuzzling her neck and swinging his gilded locks into her nose, which itched.

"Like . . . like, my friend Flicka," Temple said brightly. To the Great Fabrizio, she was less creative. "I have a terrible fear of heights," she murmured fretfully. "I may be sick to my stomach any second. Put me down."

She emphasized her wishes by doing what she would try with an errant horse who had rudely cantered off with her. She kicked him in the washboard belly with one long, sharp spur of high heel.

"Oof." Fabrizio swung her to the floor faster than a square-dancing partner. But he was still grinning. Apparently huge size muffled the sense of feeling. So much for the sensitive nineties kind of guy.

Women had deserted their places in line to cluster around the monument in their midst, squeezing Temple out of the picture, thank God. All of them carried black canvas bags emblazoned with the hot-pink letters of G.R.O.W.L., which made them seem quite fierce.

"Quick!" Electra's foot nudged their piled luggage forward over the smooth marble floor. "We can slip ahead in the line."

"Don't you want to stay here and ogle Fabrizio?" Temple wondered in a hoarse whisper.

Electra cast an interested look over her shoulder and past her swinging earrings. "Too much competition right now. He certainly liked you."

"I was easy to pick on and pick up. Look, there goes another one."

A slender woman with long, braided hair, wearing a country-print smock, was giggling in the grasp of Fabrizio. More electronic flashes popped as more women deserted the line to ooh and ahhh.

"Bet he won't pick up *that* one." Electra jerked her head to a heavyset woman in a olive-green jogging suit painted from wrist to ankle with violets. "You're right. That big galoot doesn't tax his torso unnecessarily."

"It's probably insured by Lloyd's of London against sudden hair growth, yellow waxy buildup and drool," Temple said wickedly. "I already regret being here," she added as they stepped up to the registration desk.

"Maybe, but imagine what the boys back at the Circle Ritz will think if they happen to catch *Hot Heads* tonight."

"Never happen," Temple predicted with confidence. "Matt will be on the job at ConTact by ten-thirty P.M., and who knows where Max will be? Not before his nearest television set, I'll wager."

Temple felt odd about checking into the Crystal Phoenix. In their eighth-floor room, she and Electra took turns hanging up their duds. Electra had whipped articles out of Temple's closet without waiting for their owner's advice and consent. And, in truth, Temple didn't much care what she wore.

She threw herself tummy-down on the window-side double bed and began leafing through the usual tourist attraction guide. "I almost never see these things. Maybe it'll give me a clue to the whereabouts of the shoes."

"You're not going to gallivant all over Las Vegas and miss half the convention, I hope," Electra said, laying out an impressive arsenal of hair products on the long dressing table surface between bathroom and bedroom. Temple had enthused about the Midnight Louie shoes all the way over in the car.

"Maybe. This really isn't my thing. I only came along to use your extra ticket."

"Then maybe you could hop down and pick up our registration materials while I finish unpacking."

Temple glimpsed Electra wrestling a cloud of chiffon and glitter into the narrow closet. It seemed to be dueling the brocaded train of her lavender velvet Renaissance gown for privilege of place.

"Okay." She pulled the wallet on a string from her tote bag, made sure she had the room entry card, then headed down to the ballroom floor.

Electra was humming happily off-key as she left.

This "getaway," Temple mused in the familiar elevator on the way down, was more for Electra's sake than hers. Presiding at weddings night and day must become quite a grind. No wonder

Electra was a dedicated romance reader, given her profession. Seeing all those dewy couples must create an artificially sweetened view of life, love and lust.

More women melded in the ballroom lobby, swamping the registration table. Luckily, the designation A–L was less lightly patronized than M–Z. Temple slipped into line and shuffled forward dutifully. At first she tried to decide if crowd control could be improved by any rearrangement of the premises. She had, after all, a big stake in the Phoenix's operations now that she was its official updating consultant. Then she found herself concentrating on fragments of conversation.

"I love those big, bad boys."

"Too juvenile. I'll take the strong, silent type."

"Alpha males are where it's at, ladies."

"But not on the covers. Beefcake is boring."

"Oh, look! There's Sharon Rose. Hold my place in line."

At a side table, authors were displaying promotional materials for their books. Temple didn't recognize any of the women, though her line-mates certainly did.

"Shannon Little," a nearby voice whispered reverently. "The Lightning Lord Saga."

Temple realized that Shannon Little must be the spectacularly large woman attired totally in purple, down to the ostrich-plume pen she carried like a wimpy scepter. She was fanning out a sheaf of four-color posters when another woman made a beeline for her.

"Where are my promo materials?" the newcomer asked. "I put them out half an hour ago."

"Oh, I adjusted the layout," Shannon Little said with vague, airy waves of her pudgy fingers and fluffy pen. "Everyone expects to see my books here in front, next to my dear friend Misty Meadows."

Even Temple recognized that name. Misty Meadows was such a perennial bestselling author that she had starred in a memorable TV ad. The ad, which supposedly showed her relaxing at home, featured a site that resembled Kensington Palace and gardens.

"You just swept my stuff away?" The other author was younger, smaller and more polite than Little, but equally unidentifiable to Temple.

"Surely you don't mind?" Shannon Little sounded ever so slightly put upon. "Misty and I always display together."

"Misty's stuff was already out when I came and used the available space for mine. If I can find another free spot, I'll move, but—"

"Never mind!" Shannon Little swept her flyers into a ragged pile. "I'll go someplace else if I must."

A slight woman with hip-length brown hair glided serenely past the tense scene.

"Misty Meadows," murmured a woman ahead of Temple in line.

Temple eyed the famous bestseller: middle-aged, middle-sized, well-dressed and totally oblivious to her "dear friend" Shannon Little.

The territory-defending author pulled her materials from the jumbled pile at the table's rear and began laying them out—again. Shannon Little sailed away like a Spanish galley, ponderous and stiff, her flyers clutched against her generous purple bosom, which had nothing in common with her selfish spirit.

Temple heard a wave of chuckles agitate the women around her.

"La Little got caught making too much of herself again," the woman behind her muttered.

"You must be a veteran of these things," Temple said, turning with a smile. She was startled to find herself eye to eye with the woman. Usually she had to look up. So she looked down. Yup, the woman was wearing high heels, too. Hallelujah, another shrimp on stilts in the world! Let's hear it for "littles" that live up to their names.

The woman grinned at her. "What a bitch. We're not all like that."

"You're an author?" Temple couldn't help being impressed. Authors made things up, which was much more taxing than spitting out the facts over and over in ever-inventive forms.

" 'Fraid so." The woman cast a wry look after the fading purple sails of the Bad Ship Shannon Little.

Now this was her idea of a romance author, Temple thought,

eyeing the outspoken woman. She was in her well-preserved fifties, petite and chic in a careless sort of way, with her oversize designer glasses and cheerful silk scarf. She also had a face willing to wrinkle and a sense of humor unafraid to call a spade a spade and a witch a bitch. Now the woman had returned her attention to the line and was assessing Temple in turn.

Parallel frown lines made sudden quote marks above the bridge of her glasses. She peered sharply at Temple's face, then looked at her hair. For the first time, the woman sounded uncertain.

"Tem-ple?" She drew back as if denying her own suspicions. "You can't be . . . Little Temple."

"I am not little!" Temple's knee-jerk denial had even more kick, since she'd just seen a woman named Little misbehave. She did not want to be associated with that creature in any way.

The woman behind her in line laughed until her glasses gleamed from the shockwaves. "You *are* Temple, all right. Said the same thing twenty years ago. Don't you remember me?"

"No. Should I?"

"Maybe not. I'm your aunt, but I haven't been around since you were . . . well, little. Sorry."

"Aunt? I don't have any missing aunts. Except . . . Aunt Ursula!" she shrieked.

"Shhh!" Her aunt cast nervous glances around. "I don't go by *that* name anymore."

"You went to New York to become an actress," Temple said, not so much recalling as accusing. "Mother said you would starve."

"Well, I didn't, did I? But I didn't miss that prophecy by much. You got my Christmas cards, didn't you?"

"When I lived at home, but I haven't lived at home for nine years."

Ursula shrugged. "Good for you. Let's get our paperwork, and then I'll buy you a drink. We've got a lot to talk about."

Temple hesitated. Given her current emotional quandary, she really didn't want to delve into ancient family matters at the same time, and anything involving her parents' generation had to be old news.

Still, it gave her something besides Crawford Buchanan, the

Great Fabrizio and Shannon Little to think about while shuffling forward six inches at a time.

When she reached the long table, the harried woman behind it had her sign a computer listing for Electra Lark and Guest, then handed her two heavy canvas bags fat with folders, flyers, give-aways and free books.

She stepped out of line as best she could to wait for her aunt—imagine that, her long-lost Aunt Ursula who was now going under another name, apparently. Temple watched the woman conduct her business, searching for comparisons with her mother and her Minnesota aunts. None came. The ex-Ursula greeted, signed, sympathized and bore away the ear-marked bag in such a charming, efficient manner that Temple writhed in envy and lusted for reaching a certain age, when no one would mistake her for a girl.

"Now." Her aunt used a long, elegant middle finger to thrust the bridge of her glasses more firmly on her aquiline nose. Maybe that autocratic nose gave her the air of authority. "I'm dying for a martini. Come on."

Or maybe it was her deep, textured voice. Temple's had a slight rasp that some considered endearing, but Auntie Whoever's voice held a true froggy dew reminiscent of Tallulah Bankhead or Tammy Grimes.

Bemused, Temple followed the authoritative tap of her aunt's conservative but expensive heels—Bally, she would guess. But then why wouldn't her aunt be authoritative in every respect? She had said she was an author, hadn't she? But a *romance* author? Why hadn't Mom said anything about that?

Soon they were ensconced at a tiny round marble-topped table beside the Phoenix's meandering indoor stream, overhung by thriving tropical plants and crowded at foot-level by the sagging weight of their convention bags. A waitress buzzed by with the usual round brown tray. Her aunt ordered a Gibson, cocked her eyebrows and waited while Temple dithered.

"A Bloody Mary, I guess."

The waitress swooped away on her rounds.

"Who's your friend?" her aunt asked, looking down.

Temple fully expected to follow her gaze and find Midnight

Louie blinking up at her, so well-trained was she to his uncatlike comings and goings. All she saw was three black canvas bags full of words, woo and woe, not wool.

"Oh. The other bag's for my landlady, Electra. She's the romance buff. I just came along for the ride."

"Yes, I saw you mounted on the human roller coaster. Awesome, isn't he?"

"Fabrizio? More like paw-some."

Her aunt's contralto laugh would have been a whoop if it weren't so basso. "Breezy, they call him for short. Say, do you mind if I smoke? I'll keep the fumes aimed in a neutral direction."

"I do, but I guess relatives have an escape clause."

"Terrible habit." Her aunt lit a Virginia Slim with a match from a yup Sardi's box. "I try to quit once a month. But at least I don't bite babies."

Temple blinked as her aunt finished her lighting-up ritual by smiling expectantly, then went back to something that intrigued her. "Tell me what you meant about not using 'Ursula' anymore."

"Well, it's a godawful name."

"I know."

"That's right! Sis stuck that on you as a middle name, didn't she? Probably thought making me your godmother would be a good influence on me. It wasn't."

"You're my godmother! I'd forgotten that. You've been gone for such a long time, and have been strangely out of touch."

"Strangely out of touch." Her aunt gazed up at the twinkling fairy lights entwining the greenery. "An off-Broadway director said that about me once, in less innocuous tones."

She leaned away from the tiny table as the waitress bent to set their drinks down, then produced a fan of bills that earned an especially deep departing dip from the server.

"Ah, Temple dear," her flowing delivery went on, not missing a beat, "my life's long story is not worth even a short retelling. In fact, one picture is worth a thousand words."

She reached into the bag at her feet, then slapped something to the marble tabletop.

After Temple finished recoiling, she pulled the object, a fat paperback book, to her side of the table. The smooth raised surface of its title lettering felt like gigantic Braille beneath her fingertips. "Sulah Savage . . . *Night of a Thousand Stars*," she read aloud. "You? You're Sulah Savage?"

Aunt Ursula sipped and inhaled in happy sequence. "You've heard of her!"

"Not until now."

"Oh. She's doing quite well. I considered using 'Sue,' but it didn't have the proper ring. Much too Buddy Holly. Certainly 'Ursula Carlson' wasn't going to sell books, or anything else. Why on earth did they name me that?"

"Why on earth did they pass it on to me?" Temple leaned across the table. "There's this odious man in town—"

"Only one? That's not the Las Vegas I expected."

"The only one I know. He's always calling me by my initials, like I was a disease."

"Ah. T.B."

"Right. I live in absolute dread that he'll learn my middle name."

"T.U.B. Not the image a forward-looking young woman wants to cultivate in this age of low-fat everything, including, one presumes, initials. What is your line of work, anyway?"

"I used to be a local TV reporter."

"Thespian blood, I knew it!"

"Then I became PR director for the Guthrie Theatre."

"Good old Guth! Sir Tyrone would be so proud. And see how the Thespian blood continues to seep out?"

"Please, less gory imagery. Now I do freelance PR around town. In fact, I just landed this hotel, which is doing a total makeover."

"Whatever brought an artless Minnesota babe-in-the-North-Woods to Vegas?"

Temple winced. "A traveling magician named Max."

"A magician. Another theatrical link. Temple, you were obviously born to trod the boards."

"What about you? Didn't you leave home at some absurdly young age to act in New York?"

"Yes. One tends to do that sort of thing at absurdly young ages."

"And?"

"I did act in New York, and did a lot of other things in New York. Couldn't model, too short. So I sold perfume at Saks, and worked for an answering service and dog-walked, acting every now and again. And then, one day almost twenty years ago, I discovered Sulah."

"You've been publishing novels for twenty years and the family never knew?"

"The family never wanted to know. You know them. Rooted in Midwestern conservatism. I could never stand a life of Thou Shalt Nots. Thou shalt not move more than a mile from thy birth home. Thou shalt not ever leave the first job or husband thou hast. Thou shalt not express thyself. Thou shalt not smoke."

She made a face and stubbed out her cigarette in the tiny crystal phoenix-shaped ashtray provided. The Phoenix's smoking accoutrements seemed elegant even in this age of enforced social responsibility.

"Aunt . . . what do I call you?"

"Kit. Just Kit. Please. I never had any children and I'm not about to start now. Thank God you're well past the age of consent—aren't you?" When Temple nodded, she went on. "My middle name's Katherine, and I always liked Christopher Marlowe's plays. People have been calling me Kit for thirty years."

"But your cards home—"

"—were signed Ursula. I know. Thou shalt not change thy given name, either. Why did Sister Sarah ever give you the progressive first name of Temple, anyway? I remember Mom and Dad were speechless about it."

"Maybe it was her one tiny rebellion. I was her last chance, after all."

"And look at your brothers and sister: Cindy, John, Bob and Larry. You must have been her menopause baby."

"No, I'm sure not." Temple answered with a tinge of horror. Surely her mother had not been *that* old when she was born, had she? Then she realized that her mother must be almost seventy.

"Neutral names are all the rage now," Kit said contemplatively. "Who can tell whether a stockbroker named Tyler or Morgan is a boy or a girl? Maybe that's good. Maybe it'll be easier for women to get the jobs they want. Look at the young woman named Shannon who was accidentally accepted at The Citadel, a bastion of male exclusivity, otherwise known as a bastardy. They're still kicking up over it."

"Hmm," said Temple, who hadn't found her ambiguous name any particular advantage in the struggle for survival. The name Shannon had also reminded her of the morning's incident. "Are all romance writers as awful as that Little woman?"

"Shannon Large, you mean? No, but the media love to accent the ridiculous in this genre. Unfortunately, we used to have several candidates for that crown in the early days, and a few such dinosaurs survive. Romance Queens of the genus Tyrannosaurus Regina. But most romance writers are as everyday as Hamburger Helper: hard-working women—and a few brave men—who labor in obscurity to earn five figures, all of them with no more personal pizzazz or prima donna temperament than a sponge mop. I, of course, am not one of them."

Kit flicked an errant tobacco flake off her tongue with such panache that Temple regarded the gesture as a hallmark of breeding rather than evidence of the filthy habit that it was.

"Are you thinking of writing romances?" her aunt asked.

"No! But Electra might be."

"Well, tell your friend to talk to me if she wants any advice from the published."

"Did your previous remark mean that you earn more than five figures?"

"Not at first."

"But now?"

Kit nodded and sipped her Gibson as demurely as a cat lapping up tapwater. "It's not been easy. Most romance writers have been cruelly exploited for years—don't laugh, I'm not dramatizing, although I admit that I do have tendencies."

"But why romances?"

"Because they are Theatre, my dear! Action, Adventure, Passion. Nobody mounts Marlowe and Webster anymore. Poor old Shakespeare is always being updated until we have punk-rock Romeos and Juliets, Julius Caesar is a Mafia don and *The Tempest* is done as a *Star Trek* episode, with Caliban a Klingon. Historical romances offer me sweep, swash and buckle, tragic separations and ecstatic reunions, villains grand enough to gnaw the scenery with their pointed fangs and forked tongues, language that flows as it was wont in previous centuries, and only clicks and stutters like a banal telegram in more modern works. It has imagination! Optimism! Happy endings—after much travail and torment, of course. It is just like Real Life, if you think about it."

Around them, patrons burst into polite applause. Kit inclined her mahogany-red head and lit another cigarette. She would make a magnificent Madwoman of Chaillot, Temple thought, instantly revising her thought. Kit was a bit young for the part, yet Giraudoux's play was one of those lovely exercises in language so seldom performed anymore. No wonder her aunt wrote instead of acted.

"Miss Barr?"

The voice was masculine, ever sweet and low, and came from above. Had Gabriel descended? Temple glanced up to find a dramatically dark, long-haired man in a shirt that laced up the front looking down at her.

Obviously a heartbreaker, but how the chromium picolinate did he know her? Kit's raised eyebrows across the table were asking the same question after reaching a similar conclusion.

The soft-spoken deference in his voice and stance oozed unconscious, but nonetheless effective charm. She knew him from somewhere . . .

"Cheyenne," he reminded her with a shy (or possibly sensual) smile.

Oh, yes. Cheyenne. One of the male strippers in the Rhinestone G-strip competition. He of the intriguingly ambiguous (or was that ambidexterous?) sexual preference and ethnic origin.

"Are you competing here?" she asked in confusion.

He nodded. "A lot more rewarding than the last contest you saw me in. Fabio has made millions in endorsements, and this wannabe Fabrizio hopes to cash in on the same market. I figure it's time for a different type."

Temple hated to tell him that brunettes always came in second to blonds of either sex. Redheads were even worse off, despite
the current rage for red on Hollywood actress' heads.

Kit tipped her head and showed lazy cat-slit eyes. "Fabio was
the first; he'll make the most."

Cheyenne smiled his ever-appreciative smile. "Still plenty left
for the rest of us. I've just come back from some European modeling gigs—London, Oslo, Amsterdam, Berlin, Rome. In fact—"

His hot fudge gaze slid like brunette lava over Temple's features, one by one. But this time another, less intimate message
seemed to be behind it. Something as icy as anxiety.

"Maybe we could get together this evening for a few minutes,
Miss Barr. I have a big deal brewing. It won't be announced for a
couple of days, but . . . " he laughed disarmingly. "I might need a
publicist, or at least some friendly advice. I could buy you a drink."

Temple weighed the flattery of a tête-a-tête with one of Love's
Leading Lotharios against her lust for the Midnight Louie shoes.
Feet won, hands down.

"Thanks, but I've got a previous engagement tonight. Anytime
later on during the convention, though."

Did honest disappointment fleet across that lean, sculpted face?
Temple's pulses throbbed with a frisson of regret.

"Later will have to do, then. Thanks." Cheyenne's wry smile
broadened to public dimensions as his gaze flitted between them.
"Both of you ladies are welcome to drop in on our pageant rehearsal in the Peacock Theater tomorrow morning. My act has a
surprise built in that'll knock everybody dead. Eight o'clock."

"That early?" Kit complained.

"The guys want to be mingling with the conventioneers by
ten A.M. That builds audience applause for the actual competition
and *that* influences our distinguished panel of judges. Can I count
on your claps, ladies?"

"Absolutely," Kit boomed in her foggiest voice, "a standing
ovation."

With a farewell crinkle of his sloe eyes, Cheyenne retreated
through the engulfing greenery as lithely as a snake one might find
in Eden.

"I think he's sweet on you," Kit said.

"No . . . I'm ages older. I mean, most of these guys are only twenty-two or something."

"Men reach their sexual peak at eighteen."

"You could have fooled me. They hardly seem old enough to enter into a mature relationship until the mid-twenties."

"Who's talking maturity?"

"I guess I'm behind the times," Temple admitted. "What do you think of these male cover-model contests?"

Kit coughed and gulped the last of her Gibson, then clapped a fanned hand to her throat. "Really? Outside of ogling opportunity? Grounds for murder. Outrageous exploitation—and not of the boys onstage. We women write the books, read the books, yet these coverboys get all the publicity and big-dollar endorsements. When was the last time you saw a mere romance author on a TV talk show or a television commercial? Yet there is Fabio, the Studmuffin of Scent, spritzing away like Schwarzenegger posing as a madly overgrown chef with his "I Can't Believe It's Not Butter" spray that wouldn't melt in his fine Italian mouth. Then there's his overblown book contract, that some unsung woman is penning for low dough and no glory. Maybe women should have equal ogling opportunity with men, but the fact is that we're amateurs at it, and we get damn little out of it. Even when the tables are turned, we come out on the short end of the stick economically. That said"— Kit leaned closer, a drift of smoky breath wafting toward Temple; she lowered her voice to true Tallulah range—"I'd take that one home for Christmas any day of the year, wouldn't you?"

"Ummm, pass. His health pedigree strikes me as risky. Besides, I distrust these guys on principle. There's something smarmy about a man who makes his living off women. I believe they used to call them gigolos in your day."

"Oooh. Nasty little snapper, aren't you, niece?"

"I suppose," Temple added, "you are dying to go to that model contest rehearsal at the crack of dawn tomorrow."

"*Mais oui, cherie.*"

"Mom would be shocked to know that you turned out to be a dirty middle-aged woman."

"Your mother would be shocked if I had turned out a saint, so why give her the satisfaction? This boy-toy thing is such a fabulous sideshow, anyway. What's the harm in sneaking a preview peek? Perhaps it will inspire you to enter the Love's Leading Amateur contest."

Temple nodded sourly. "Sometimes I do indeed feel the champion of the world in that arena."

"I can't stay out too late," Electra warned when Temple returned to their room and suggested an afternoon outing to the new MGM Grand. "My two-day writing seminar starts bright and early at ten A.M. tomorrow."

"You'll be up even earlier if you join Aunt Kit and me in the cover-model pageant run-through. Cheyenne especially invited me."

"Ooh, Cheyenne. I remember that sexy young man from the strippers' contest. He'd be terrific on Indian romance covers."

"Kit said that romance writers resent male cover models getting all the attention, instead of the authors and books."

"Maybe the publishers have overdone the hunk appeal, but as a reader, I'm not so much offended as bemused."

"Cover hunks. The expression suggests narcissistic, oily characters living off women."

"Equal opportunity, dear. Picture-perfect girls have been doing that for years with men. At least someone is bothering to court our good opinion. When you reach my age and width, that counts for a lot. Now, about this outing today with your long-lost aunt—"

"It'll be fun for Kit and us to check out the MGM Grand Wizard of Oz display and the theme park out back. And don't worry, Kit isn't like an aunt at all; you'll love her. I haven't seen her in years. I'm amazed she recognized me. Best of all, she's an author who can give you tips for your contest entry."

"I don't recall reading anything by a Kit—"

"Not her pen name. That's Sulah Savage."

"No!"

"Yes."

"Not the author of *Quicksilver Moon?*"

"Don't ask me."

"Sulah Savage is one of my favorite authors! I'd go through the buffet line at the Bucket O' Blood to spend some time with her. Why didn't you say so in the first place?"

"I didn't know how notorious she was."

"Well, shake a shoe, hon. I can't speak for you, but I'm ready. We're off to see the Wizard."

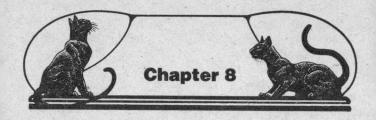

Chapter 8

Deep Waters

Lap-swimming was the most relentlessly routine discipline in the physical fitness lexicon.

And yet, Matt often thought while beating his way back and forth through the choppy chlorinated water, the combination of robotic motion and buoyant mental freedom produced a body/mind synergy with virtual reality overtones.

A swimmer became his own iron lung; breathing became a measured necessity rather than a forgotten art. While every muscle fought to keep the body afloat on its liquid treadmill, the mind made unauthorized excursions to the lower depths. Sometimes, while swimming in some pristine, heavenly blue pool, Matt's imagination plummeted to a childhood level of primal fear. He would recall an ancient episode from a Flash Gordon film serial. The-evil-emperor-Ming from the planet Mongo, the guy with the Snow-White stepmother upstanding collar, had Flash tossed into a huge water tank . . . with a giant octopus.

Matt's glancing glimpses of sun-dappled water shadows below

would suddenly sprout lurking tentacles where there were only pool-grooming hoses or the shadow of a palm blade. Or he would conjure the slice of a shark fin, thanks to more recent Spielbergian memories.

Today Matt saw or sensed no monsters of the deep, except the thrashing confusion in his own psyche. Every stroke accentuated the I-am-a-camera viewpoint. The airy, dry world above the Circle Ritz pool became a series of rapid intercuts: sky, palm tree, building edge, ruffle of agitated surface water, deeper water sliced by his body like a gelatinous aquamarine by a gemologist's diamond-edged blade.

Back and forth, his every motion was both ultimate effort and easy birdlike glide through an alien element. Sun. Sky. Spray. Kicking, carving. Thinking without thinking about it. Meeting monsters of the id and ego in the vasty depths. Glimpsing Leviathan in a teacup, Neptune in the iris of a chlorinated eye.

Matt touched warm concrete, pushed away, turned, then churned back the length of the modest pool in eight easy strokes of utter effort.

Sky. Sun. Shadow.

Plough the water into forever-vanishing furrows.

Sun. Sky. Shadow.

Shadow?

Matt reversed himself like a motor, instantly upright, treading water, his face and breath caught between warring elements. His eyelashes strained a liquid veil from his waterlogged vision.

The new silhouette of a bush beside the pool turned into a squatting man, knees jackknifed, elbows akimbo. Primitive man adapted such postures easily; overcivilized man didn't have the joints or the humility for it.

Matt squinted into the corona of sunlight surrounding the figure. The black-by-contrast center resolved into lurid focus: Max Kinsella's protective coloring, a Hawaiian shirt.

Matt's squint became a frown. He felt like a grunt surprised by a Viet Cong during R&R.

"Something I can do for you?" he asked, implying that was the last thing he was inclined to do.

"Talk."

Matt grabbed the pool's thick curved lip, sank, gained buoyancy and pushed himself out of the water. He dripped like sunken treasure for a few silent moments.

Kinsella never moved, despite the puddle of water inching toward his tennis-shoed feet. No wonder Matt hadn't heard his approach.

Matt sat dripping on the pool's edge, unhappy and not too worried about showing it. He hated having to leave the protective overcoat of the water, the self-immersion in amniotic fluid, the cover for his almost-nakedness.

That's what he relished about the Circle Ritz. Almost none of its tenants used the pristine but out-of-date pool. No witnesses to his moment of leaving the water, a time when flashes of vulnerability would wring him like cramps. In high school he had avoided gym, using whatever subterfuge he could; he had avoided eyes and questions. Now, he no longer had body bruises to hide, but the habit had transferred to a shame of his body. No matter how much he understood that none of the old pain showed, or how much he was beginning to believe that his body might be a source of pleasure and admiration, he still hated revealing himself. Perhaps his pride feared pity, but no one could see the long-invisible wounds. Perhaps his fear dreaded pride.

Kinsella unbent with a dancer's fluidity. Matt couldn't hear a knee creak, but hastened to rise with him, as if to keep them on the same level, despite the considerable height difference. His usual self-consciousness in situations like this had another, nastier overtone. With Temple it took the form of sexual shyness. Now, Matt felt insufficient in another way, in strength and size. He was eight years old again, and helpless against a man's height and anger. At almost six feet, he had pretty much shaken that inner shrinking sensation, but Kinsella was unusually tall.

"You're quite an athlete," Kinsella commented as he turned a gaudy back on Matt to walk to the table and chairs Electra kept by the pool.

"Not really. I swim some." Matt grimaced at his automatic self-deprecation, grabbed his towel from the foot of an ancient lounge chair and followed. "I don't consider the martial arts work athletics."

"Discipline, then."

Matt shrugged, not bothering to mention his favorite term, meditation.

"I don't see that we have much to talk about," he said. Then he sat, dripping and dabbing at the rivulets sprinting down his face, wishing he could don his clothes.

Kinsella's dubious look seemed practiced. A magician was an actor as much as anything.

"We have something in common," Kinsella said. "Not," he added speedily as Matt maintained a cool so effective he could feel his face freezing, "Temple."

"I wasn't thinking of Temple," Matt answered just as quickly.

"Shame on you," Kinsella suggested smoothly. "She's worth thinking about. Even when she's on retreat."

"Is she on retreat, or *in* retreat?"

"Probably both. Not that I blame her. Look. You don't know me . . . or, rather, you don't know anything about me that isn't misleading. But we have more than Temple in common."

"Such as?"

Matt suspected that he was watching a master of deception at work—on him. Kinsella must thrive on putting other people off balance and keeping them that way. Why had Temple taken off, leaving them—him—alone to confront each other? Matt suspected that she and Electra had skedaddled together, and knew he shouldn't begrudge her a temporary escape. But the last thing on earth he wanted to discuss with Max Kinsella was Temple, especially with their most recent and most intimate evening still lingering on his mind like an uncertain sin.

"So what is our common bond?" Matt inquired, assuming his most nonjudgmental confessional tone but bracing for more surprises.

"Dead men," Kinsella reported with gusto and a flash of cat-green eyes.

"Dead men in general?" Matt asked, still wearing his parish priest mask, though Kinsella had no reason to know of its existence. "Or special dead men?"

"How many dead men do you know?" Kinsella shot back.

"A few. And I guess all dead men are special."

"Hmm. You've heard about mine, I suppose."

"I don't think so."

"Temple didn't tell you about the man that was found dead in a custom cubby-hole in the ceiling above the Goliath gambling tables? Found dead the very night I vanished, never to be seen again . . . until now?"

"You may find your own disappearance astounding, but some of us don't."

"I bore you. Pity. I'm out of practice, I see."

"What *did* you do while you were missing in action?"

"None of your business." With a charismatically mischievous grin.

"Neither are my dead men."

"There's where you may be wrong, boyo. I think our late unlamenteds' deaths may be connected."

"How do you even know about the one that was related to me?"

"Would the name Molina mean anything to you?"

"*She's* talking to you?"

"She?" Kinsella sounded startled.

"She," Matt confirmed. "She wants to interrogate you in the worst way; you haven't obliged her?"

"Not yet, but if she *is* a viable conduit of information, I'm back now. Shall we say that proximity is everything."

"In that case, I can see why you're a suspect in the Goliath death."

"Not that kind of proximity," Kinsella said. "Dead men." He tilted back until the white plastic chair balanced at a gravity-defying angle. "Think about it. Mine at the Goliath five months ago; yours at the Crystal Phoenix last week."

"Mine? Yours? Death doesn't recognize the possessive."

Kinsella let the chair's front legs snap to the concrete. "Figures of speech are relative. Your dead man is more yours than mine is mine. Yours was a relative."

"How did you—?"

"Temple dropped an allusion, I picked it up and followed it to the morgue."

"Not technically a relative."

"A lot of people we have to live with aren't technically relatives."

"A . . . stepfather."

"Close enough to count. Stepparents can be sore points."

"He wasn't a parent to anything but his own indulgences."

Kinsella's quicksilver features hardened with some emotion. Perhaps it was chagrin. "Sorry. I didn't know the connection was that close."

"It wasn't. I hadn't seen him in years."

Kinsella nodded, no doubt calculating the unspoken facts and weighing whether to bring them up or not.

"You never will see him again, as it turned out," he mused a bit morosely.

"But I did. After his death. Maybe."

Kinsella perked up like an Irish setter at the mention of quail. "Why 'maybe'?"

"I hadn't seen the man in seventeen years. In fact, I couldn't really identify him. Time had been hard at work, and death finished the job. He seemed a . . . stranger. Death had changed him, his face. Standing there in the morgue, in that ludicrously Spartan viewing room, I couldn't be sure who it was."

Kinsella mulled that, his long fingers flexing on the shaded plastic table, as if miming a magic trick.

"To be or not to be . . . Cliff Effinger. At least yours has a name and face."

"You didn't know the dead man at the Goliath?"

Kinsella shook his head.

"You still could have killed him."

A pause, then a nod.

"Did you?"

"No." With a slow, sad, sweet smile that acknowledged what such denials were worth on the open market. "Did you kill your stepfather?"

"Unfortunately, no. I don't think so. And no one else is asking, anyway."

Kinsella didn't pursue Matt's odd uncertainty. "What about this Lieutenant Molina?"

"She doesn't give up. She'll still be looking for you."

"Maybe."

"What does that mean?"

"Why did she ask you to identify the body?"

"Because I finally confessed my . . . relationship to Effinger."

"So?"

"She had a dead man in the morgue and she needed someone to confirm his identity."

"No, she didn't."

"What do you mean?"

"This stepfather of yours did the usual bad stepfather things, didn't he?"

Matt felt his muscles stiffen even as he maintained his relaxed posture. Had Temple told Max—?

Kinsella went on as if unaware of Matt's hesitation. "At least he did if he was Cliff Effinger. I asked around. Effinger left his happy hometown for Vegas, drank, gambled, got arrested for all sorts of lowlife offenses that don't add up to much jail time, but do comprise a long, documented trail. Look, Devine. Cliff Effinger left his fingerprints all over this town. Why did this Ms. Molina need you to schlepp on down to the morgue and stare at the copper pennies on his eyes?"

Kinsella's eyes—disconcertingly Midnight-Louie green—focused on Matt like quizzical laser beams. Confused, Matt clutched at any nearby floating assumptions.

"I'm sure Lieutenant Molina had a reason—"

"So am I," Kinsella put in, with feeling. He leaned forward on the little chair, propping his forearms on his thighs. "Think about it. There was no reason to put you through that charade."

"Sometimes," Matt answered slowly, "women like that want you to confront yourself."

"She's that mean?"

"Not mean. Just in a position of authority with a benign sense of mission." He remembered Sister Seraphina prodding him into performing an annointing of the sick on Miss Tyler. The elderly nun had wanted him to face the fact that his former priesthood was always with him. Maybe Molina had wanted him to face his stepfather's death and his own hatred of the man. But she was a police detective, not a therapist. Besides, she couldn't have known about Effinger's family abuse, unless Temple had told her, and Temple was hardly on speaking terms with either Molina or Kinsella these days.

Speak of the devil. He looked up again to find Kinsella studying him. Except for the eyes, Max Kinsella was not a mesmerizingly handsome man. His face was angular and intelligent, his features so mobile that one glimpsed many men behind the frequently exchanged masks. Matt had encountered such chimerical personalities before; every one had concealed a secret and insecure core. Every one could have charmed the snake off the Tree of All Knowledge in Eden.

"You're right," Matt admitted, wondering why he hated that fact so much, hated it almost as much as being virtually naked before a man in a Hawaiian shirt. "Having me identify a man with a police record doesn't make sense. I was so . . . confused at the time, that never dawned on me."

"Trust the police to confuse you. So you hadn't seen your stepfather in years?"

Matt nodded.

"And did it do you any good?"

"Did what?"

"Seeing him dead?"

"No."

"Hmmm. You weren't surprised by his manner of death, though?"

"He left home when I was sixteen."

"Voluntarily?"

Matt shrugged. He wasn't going to perform a post mortem on his family life for the benefit of the Mystifying Max.

"Maybe you don't care what he was up to all those years since then. I do, though."

"Why?"

The man stared at him as Midnight Louie was wont to do: an expression impassive, yet superior, and even vaguely prodding. An unspoken "Well?"

Matt saw the light, and didn't like it. "You're not sure Cliff Effinger *is* dead, are you?"

"Look at *me*. The rumors of my demise were false."

Matt forgot Kinsella for once, plunging again into the cool, shifting ocean of the past. "I'd like to know for sure, for my mother's sake," he admitted despite himself.

"For your mother's sake." Repeated sardonically. "Well, then." Kinsella clapped flat palms to the tabletop. The gesture should have hurt. He grinned. "I'd say that we have more than one common interest. Let's forget our unflattering assumptions about each other and look into our pair of dead men."

"You're a loner. Why the buddy act?"

"I'm also supposed to be missing. I try to keep my personal appearances to a bare minimum."

Matt winced at the expression.

"Besides," Kinsella said, "it's better for Temple if most of the folk out there still think so. I could use a front man."

Matt laughed. "Another magic act, with me as the distraction. What do I get out of this?"

"You may find out who killed your stepfather, and why. Or . . . you may find out that he still needs killing."

"And why would I care?"

"Because, trust me, you do," Kinsella said, rising. "You can't help it."

Chapter 9

Spray for Rain

Although I dare not enter the Crystal Phoenix until I can check out the whereabouts and mood of my ungrateful offspring, Midnight Louise, I can lurk outside. This I do, for two good reasons. I am determined to rekindle the relationship between me and Miss Savannah Ashleigh's purebred pride and joy, the Divine Yvette. I am also not averse to keeping an eye on my other little doll, for it has not been lost upon me that she is somewhat at loose ends, what with one thing and another. Frankly, I fear for her sanity.

So there I am, keeping unobtrusive watch for any comings and goings of an intriguing nature. That is how I come to see a certain party of three exiting the Crystal Phoenix Hotel and Casino. For those unfamiliar with my usual turf, the Phoenix is a modest establishment more noted for class than crass. Once I pick up the trio's trail, I recognize two of the subjects at once: Miss Temple Barr and Miss Electra Lark, for the simple reason that neither of them are unknown to me.

The third is a puzzler, though in some ways a riper version of Miss Temple. Anyway, they link arms and amble down the Strip, laughing and talking like old friends. This is suspicious in itself, for I have never laid eyes on the new doll, who looks old enough to be Miss Temple's mother or Miss Electra's sister. Could she be both? Anything is possible in the Naked City. (Some call the Big Crabapple of New York the Naked City, but Las Vegas is better qualified for that nickname, whether you count half-naked chorus girls or stripped-bare gamblers who leave this town in little more than suspenders and a barrel.)

Midnight Louie does not require the presence of an unexplained person to realize that something is up. Miss Temple and Miss Electra have skipped out on the Circle Ritz far too abruptly to evade my whisker-trigger suspicions. I hope that this outing will enlighten me. I have little trouble tailing them along the Strip, which is crowded with foot traffic. I am always well beneath notice among foot traffic. Certain advantages pertain to being the little guy.

The ladies' path heads south. I watch the Luxor's obelisk steadily swell at the Strip's southern end. It spikes the brilliant blue autumn sky like a giant's upside down thumbtack. Meanwhile, I keep a profile lower than a craps player on a losing streak, darting from one island of landscaping to the other, as if chasing butterflies. Such subterfuge hardly seems necessary. Most folks afoot in Las Vegas are gawking up at towering hotels and signs. That is why a slack-jawed jaywalker perishes every three days in this town, that and maybe all the free drinks at the casinos and not enough brain cells to bet on something other than traffic flow. These jaywalkers are a mystery anyway. I cannot see any advantage in it. You will not catch Midnight Louie walking a jay across the Strip during rush hour—not even a trained cockatoo.

Anyway, there I am crouching in the petunias before I hop into the next nest of marigolds or what have you. And so on. In a matter of blocks (and blocks along the Las Vegas Strip are on the gargantuan side, on both sides!) it becomes apparent where the ladies three are heading: only one hotel stands head and maned shoulders above the others this side of the Strip: the MGM Grand. This sweeping structure of green glass is reminiscent not so much of the Emerald City in Oz as it is of a tidal wave halted in mid-crash. The MGM Grand's 5005 rooms make it the world's largest hotel. It takes its calculated leisure in an architectural sprawl that covers twice the acreage of the other Strip behemoths. Naturally, it is completely fitting that the door dude to this mirrored Babylon on the Mojave should be a fellow with feline tendencies.

Sure enough, Leo the lion's ocher stucco head soon dominates the horizon. These so-called Big Cats! They think they own everything they survey, simply because they are taller than the next guy. On the subject of true stature, I am shoulder to shoulder with Miss Temple Barr, figuratively speaking, of course.

Figuratively speaking, though, this Leo is one impressive dude. Large but angular, with world-class green eyes the size of billboards. My subjects skirt Leo's muscular paws without a glance up at his lordly yet amiable face, so eager are they to pursue their mysterious mission. Then Miss Electra Lark stops dead. Tourists part like the Red Sea around her as she turns, looks back and points with a lack of politeness that only a tourist could get away with.

I do not pause to think, but spring for camouflage—right into the pansies and decorative cabbages sprouting at the base of Leo's immaculate pedicure. I have heard of cabbages and kings, and Leo is a self-proclaimed King of the beasts, but pansies? Really, Leo, what do we have here—L-a-a-ammm-bert, the Sheepish Lion?

I am not surprised by the presence of this effete flora, but I am about to be shocked nearly out of my leather soles.

Meanwhile, Miss Electra continues to wave her arm about like an undisciplined tail. Miss Temple and the stranger stop to gawk at what I discern to be the blue and red peaks of the Camelot Hotel and Casino's fools'-capped mock-Medieval towers, kitty-corner (sorry, Leo) from our location.

The Camelot is old chapeau, pardon the expression. I have seen its pointy-hatted wizard glowering down from the Camelot drawbridge onto the Strip for several years now. I like to fancy that this maybe-Merlin has cast a spell on old Leo, dooming the big guy to eternal gate-keeping function at the opposite hostelry. Imagine sitting there day after day, able to do nothing more than light up the night with your big green eyes. This is definitely the downside of working as the house cat at a hotel.

While I crouch and contemplate the sad state of feline pride in these latter days, hordes of human feet hoof into the MGM Grand's maw of brass-and-glass doors. A subtle hissing noise, like a chorus of cicadae, cranks up all around me. Although we are far from the open desert, this sound has a terrible, impending nature, like a thousand rattlesnakes about to strike.

And then I am struck!

A dozen sites on my body sting as I am pelted relentlessly. I leap out of the pansies, crying, "I am dying, Egypt, dying." (Oops. That line is more appropriate to the Sphinx in front of the Luxor down the Strip.) Anyway, I stagger from the flora like Jimmy Cagney hit by a machine gun. Those pansies were poisonous. And the hail of bullets continues. Except that they are wet.

The awful truth triumphs. Leo, the MGM lion, has a spraying problem, and it's pretty pervasive. The pansies beam dewily through a fresh veil of waterdrops.

I shake myself off, hoping to share my bounty with the passing mob. Then I nip through the row of doors with the huge brass doorpulls formed from an intertwined "O" and "Z" behind a Nikon of Japanese tourists clicking away like beetles.

Once inside, I stop, dismayed . . . even outraged. I am inside, not outside, but the sky is frowning and boiling with clouds as if ready to rain on my parade again in earnest. Lightning flashes among the clouds' cumulus blue underbellies. Thunder growls like my stomach on another Free-to-be-Feline morning. I blink my baby greens. How can this be? I admit that I have never bothered to check out the inside of the MGM Grand Hotel, but I did expect it to at least be indoors.

In fact, the unexpected presence of water outside and the scene of impending downpour inside have an unforeseen effect on me. I suddenly remember how long it has been since I performed any actions of a deliquifying nature. Luckily, dead ahead I spot a gentle grassy knoll suffering from a measles of red poppies, so I sprint for relief.

Even more fortunately, a man's voice booms from the gondola of a balloon tethered nearby. (This is not one of your dinky helium objects so prevalent at birthday parties, but the Mother of All Balloons, big enough to serve as transportation.) Every human eye is craned upward to the gesturing figure and the scowling sky beyond, green with oncoming storm. Of course it is really a ceiling, though it is high enough to pass for a sky. In contrast, the so-called grass is barely tall enough to shelter a midget mouse, say Mickey or Minnie (though they are not MGM properties). Furthermore, the blades have a distasteful plastic feel, and as for scent—if you favor privies perfumed with polyethelene, you are in the perfect spot for happy-ever-aftering, but not in Cam-el-ot. So much for the musical interlude. I do not like Muzak in my biffy and I am not very invisible in this ersatz poppy field. While here, though, I sniff the notorious blooms for signs of harvest. Great place to hide an illegal patch of real poppies. No such luck in this case.

A wood that affords more privacy and some real dirt looms beyond the poppy fields' ever-blooming condition. I dash into its welcoming shadows and camouflaging color, earth-brown. In a wink, I have hidden behind an aluminum garbage can someone has thoughtfully plopped down between two trees. From my vantage point I survey the poppy fields. Against the bilious sky, the crusty old dude in the balloon gondola harangues the attentive crowd while laser-green lightning boogies across the boiling clouds above. Beyond the gathering storm glows a serene, celestial expanse of gilt stars in a Midnight-blue sky, the exact color of my coat's glossy highlights when it is groomed to black satin. I recognize that odd artifice known as wallpaper when I see it, even when it is on the ceiling. Yet I remain thoroughly confused. Ap-

parently the MGM Grand lobby has chosen to combine the worst
of indoor and outdoor worlds.

Then I nearly leap into the next county when the silver garbage
can beside me starts creaking into motion and begins sounding
off. I dodge behind a tree . . . made from another foul-smelling
unnatural substance. The crowd edges my way, oohing and
Ozing.

Only then do I spot the solution to my confusion: a motionless
quartet—five if you count the shrimpy canine—stands frozen amid
the plastic poppies. They are not collecting for the Veterans of
Foreign Wars, believe me, but posing. Even from the rear they are
recognizable: that miserable Cowardly Lion who has given
cathood a bad name; the twin of my nearby orating garbage can,
the Tin Woodman; young Dorothy Gale from Kansas in her
checked jumper and red-sequined pumps (Miss Temple would
shudder at wearing pale blue anklets with such spiffy shoes); and
the Scarecrow who fell down on the job.

Of course that wretched, flea-bitten, cute-as-a-cupcake black
mite Toto is there, too. I am in full agreement with the Wicked
Witch, who appears to have won their last confrontation after all:
stuff him and put him in a theme-hotel vignette.

At least I sniff genuine dirt beneath my feet and am able to
scratch up a few thimbles full so I can attend to my emergency
needs. Public buildings are always short on rest rooms, although
casinos are usually generous in this department. The last thing
the management wants is eager gamblers distracted from the
siren call of snake eyes and a natural by any calls of nature.

Relieved in all departments, I tippy-toe through the ersatz
woods and out into the chiming, glittering casino beyond, where
I can dart unseen among the shadows of slot machines and black-
jack tables.

And dart I do, until I can catch up with the proper trio of shoes:
Miss Temple's pink metallic sneakers, Miss Electra's earth sandals and Madame X's air-cushion white tennis shoes with purple
and lime-green accents. As I slink under the long, rainbow archway into the casino proper, I feel a bit like that little windup pooch

Toto, who spent most of *The Wizard of Oz* fox-trotting behind the principal players.

This is not Kansas anymore. I am not even sure that it is Las Vegas.

Chapter 10

Pirates Ahoy!

"Where are we headed?"

Electra wistfully eyed empty tables spreading into the casino from a dazzling variety of restaurants.

"Look at the fabulous boutique!" Kit gazed left toward display windows crammed with wearable glitz that bounced an acquisitive glint from her eyeglass lenses.

"We are here on business, ladies," Temple reminded them. Her brisk trot did not slow to match their dawdling, window-shopping pace. The enterprise she had in mind was shoe biz.

"Where do we conduct this so-called business?" Electra huffed to catch up with her. "We've been walking for ages. I had no idea the MGM Grand was so misnamed. It should be the MGM Gargantuan."

"Theme park out back." Temple wasted no words as she hustled past gaudy neon game arcades toward the pale horizontal slit of glass doors leading to the great outdoors. "It's just about to open."

Electra groaned. "That means a lot more walking."

"Good for us," Temple sang back, hopping on a down escalator.

Soon their weary feet were beating the merciless cement that was carved into pseudo-flagstones. Sunshine as warm as drawn butter poured down on the crowd massing behind chain barriers while a troupe of spritely teenage entertainers bid them a tuneful welcome, with acrobatics and dancing. After they posed and froze for the expected applause, two clowns parted the chains. The camera-hung mob surged like misplaced souls in a *Twilight Zone* episode into an empty townscape of picturesque storefronts housing shops, eateries and amusement rides.

"Reminds me of H. P. Lovecraft's Innsmouth," Kit mused with ominous emphasis. "All quaint and picturesque on the outside, yet who knows what inbred spawn lurks behind the Williamsburg colors and the blank blackness beyond the polished window-glass?"

"Actresses!" Temple complained to the world at large, none of whom stopped rushing past to listen. "Everything is a stage set for you. This is Disneyland on the desert. What could be more wholesome?"

"Exactly why I suspect the worst," Kit said.

"Oh!" Electra was transported, foot discomfort forgotten. "Look! A wedding chapel. Got to dash in and check it out."

Kit and Temple edged into the tiny foyer while Electra dove through a doorway toward the nuptial mysteries beyond. They loitered nervously beside a window framed by peach organdy curtains not seen in such poufy array since Mr. Blandings Built His Dream House.

Wedding paraphernalia—miniature caketop couples, silk flower bouquets and boutonnieres, white satin garters—decorated several shelves of a built-in display cabinet.

Kit lifted the tiny tag trailing from a massive bouquet, then dropped it like a hot petunia. "Pricey! And that's just for Insty–Prince Charming–type weddings. Imagine what a full church ceremony must cost!"

"You ever do it?"

"What?" Kit looked alarmed and eyed the crowded foyer.

"Get married."

"No. I didn't mean *not* to, but it didn't happen."

"Hmm."

"What's the matter, kid? Feeling like an Old Maid? At your age?"

"Well, you were my age once, and unmarried. Maybe Old Maidism runs in families."

"It's called being single nowadays, and it's not so bad, especially in New York City, which is crammed with places to go and people to go there with."

"So is Las Vegas." Temple flattened against the display case as an influx of gawkers brushed against them. "I wish Electra would hurry. I don't want to miss the next show."

"Aha! So we're here to let them entertain us. That should be interesting."

"Not up to Broadway standards, I'm sure."

Kit made a masque-of-tragedy face as she studied Temple. "We're sure down at the kissy corners today." Her features reversed into a grin, and Temple found the corners of her mouth perking up despite herself. "Man trouble, huh?" Kit diagnosed.

"Men."

"*Men.* I'm impressed. Plurals always impress the shallow at heart, such as people who own two Mercedes. You're more of a vamp than you look."

"Not really. We're talking serial heartbreakers here." Temple felt obligated to explain her situation. "Max—he's . . . he *was* a magician—and I lived together for more than a year, then he vanished just as Matt showed up at the Circle Ritz. And we got along, more or less, but now Max is back—so I'm caught in the middle of two relationships that don't amount to much. Because how can I trust Max again after he pulled his vanishing act? And Matt, being a hotline counselor, is much too polite to trespass on what he now sees as Max's territory . . . so, as far as I'm concerned, they're both welcome to join the French Foreign Legion and I'll just shack up with Louie forever."

Temple's contemplative focus on a petite wax wedding couple lifted to see her aunt's eyes as round as blueberries and tiny, gawking convex people reflected in her oversize lenses. Temple turned to face an audience. Her scattershot recital had stopped spellbound tourists in their tracks.

"What is this Louie-guy's occupation?" asked a woman in a Padres cap and tortoise T-shirt.

"Er, house sitter."

"Stick with the hotline guy," she advised, "steadier job."

"The magician." Her husband, a tall, beak-nosed man with sunburned forearms was no less definite. "He'll always surprise you."

Temple blushed as lobster-red as the man's arms and turned back to the bridal display.

"You hadn't mentioned any Louie before." Kit produced an auntly frown. "House sitters can be a shiftless lot."

"So is Louie," Temple whispered. "He's a cat!"

"Oh. Good choice. Do you think he'd wear a pink carnation for the wedding?"

Temple giggled with Kit's accompaniment. They were still lost in laughter when Electra stormed out of the inner sanctum.

"Standard stuff, and way too country for my taste. Enough dried flowers to give Dorothy's Scarecrow hay fever. Folks are getting married, not emigrating to the *Waltons* set for a honeymoon. Why are you two snickering at the tools of the trade? Cynics! You don't think I make my dough from officiating, do you? No, its the 'options' and 'accessories' and 'video albums.' " She turned on Temple. "All right, Little Miss Marcher, where do we really have to go?"

"It's 'Little Miss *Marker*,' " Kit corrected, turning Temple away from the display and hustling her down the few wooden steps to the ersatz street. "I thought you'd be old enough to know that," she chided Electra.

"I am! And I'm even old enough to remember it wrong sometimes. Where are we going?"

Temple consulted the glossy folded map of the attraction.

"Down this street and to the left. I want the 'dueling pirates' show."

Kit shook her head. "Whyever for?"

"What do pirates have?" Temple asked in turn.

"Swords," Kit replied.

"Sashes," Electra suggested.

"Tattoos." Kit's eyes danced behind her lenses as she envisioned an ever-more-lurid scene.

"That's sailors," Electra objected. "Pirates just have solo earrings and bare chests."

"Yo, ho, ho and a bottle of tanning lotion. I can dig that," Kit answered.

Temple interrupted before the senior citizens in the party turned truly bawdy. "Chests. Dig. What do those two words suggest to you?"

"Lots of fun?" Kit's expression lifted hopefully.

"Treasure," came Temple's wet-blanket response. "We are not attending the cover-hunk pageant yet, ladies. We are out and about on serious business. We have priceless shoes to find. Where could they be hidden in plain sight?"

"Ah." Electra nodded sagely. "A chest of pirate treasure. But wouldn't one of those be buried to the hinges in sand, dear?"

"Not if it's a prop in a theme-park attraction. Come on."

"Are you certain that this 'dueling pirate' show uses a treasure chest?" Kit followed Temple even while she objected to the expedition's direction.

"No, but I have a hunch it might."

Electra nudged Kit's ribs. "Temple's hunches are A-one, especially in the murder department."

"Ooh, do you think we'll have a murder while I'm here?" Kit waxed instantly rhapsodic. "I was in 'Inspector Hound' once, but I've only seen stage corpses. Do you suppose a dueling pirate might do away with a fellow buccaneer?"

"Over hidden shoes?" Temple was indignant. "Hardly. Listen, I've had enough of murder as well as of men."

"*Of Murder and Men.*" Kit paused to envision a marquee. "That has a ring. You should write a play."

"I want to *see* a play right now."

Temple circled behind the pair to herd them toward a souvenir shop, wherein she purchased three tickets to the pirates, then spurred them into the line outside the attraction. The pointed masts of a sailing ship bristled above the entry roofline.

Kit, a true actress, plunged into character. "Brace the mizzenmast, me lads, and we'll make home port by dawn," she urged in a disconcerting basso.

"Do they brace mizzenmasts?" Electra wondered.

"Well, they ought to."

Temple, meanwhile, shuffled forward in line, feeling a moth eating a hole of excitement in her stomach. Was she right? Were the glamorous black-cat shoes tucked amongst swags of pirate pearls and Spanish silver? Would she hit the jackpot on her first jaunt? For once she was out to solve an innocent mystery, and a personally rewarding one. No dead pirates, she promised herself.

Once inside, she quickly eyed the setup. A pool masqueraded as a lagoon, with a pirate ship anchored at the rear. The audience sat opposite the ship in a steeply raked amphitheater, open-aired except for a sun-shading roof.

"The higher we go the better we'll see," Kit suggested *sotto voce*, as if passing on the secrets of the ancients.

"Too high, and I won't get a good look at any treasure chest," Temple said.

"Which may or may not be here," Electra pointed out.

After much vacillating, aisle-blocking and whispered consultation, the party settled on seats four rows up. By then, quite a crowd had entered. They were forced to shuffle into the row, off center to the empty pier area facing the water.

"Don't you think the actors would make off with the shoes if they found them?" Kit asked.

"No, they'd probably be in on the scheme." Temple pursed her lips and knotted her eyebrows to match. "Or they don't know. I doubt the shoes will be obvious, but they should be . . . reachable."

"For who?" Electra jeered. "The Seven Dwarves? Or the Giant in the beanstalk?"

"Wrong play," Temple said just as a swashbuckling figure shot from the top of the seats to the waterfront below on a rope and a reel instead of a wing and a prayer.

Enter stage left a band of pirate scum, fair maiden in hand.

Actually the fair maiden rode in a chiffon-curtained sedan chair, with the pirate scum toting the poles thereof. When she left her shelter, the chiffon collapsed to reveal the real object the poles supported.

"Yes!" Temple barely restrained herself from leaping out of her seat.

The pirates set down their treasure chest, its suggestively agape lid spilling ropes of pearls and glitter into the bright sunshine.

The action below resolved into a comic opera musical interlude for the pirate scum, who were led by a villainous but impressively muscular first mate, bare of shirt, chest hair and tattoos. Had he heard about the Incredible Hunk contest at the Crystal Phoenix?

Our hero was the pirate captain who had shot from the sky in wide-sleeved shirt, sash and head bandana. In the course of rescuing the maiden, defending his ship and treasure chest and quelling a mutiny, the entire cast ran, skirmished, swung on ropes and cavorted from the platform before the audience to a tower to the ship and another tower. Tension ran high as the audience waited to see who would plummet into the lagoon and get wet first.

While all eyes ogled the athletic action at home and aboard, Temple stepped over the seatback before her and slid down into the next row.

Twin gasps from the rear indicated that Kit and Electra had noticed Temple's unconventional change of seats. Luckily, the lusty action below kept the rest of the audience unaware.

Temple settled into the vacant seat like a slowly sinking ship, then sat immobile until the pirate crew cavorted from pier to the ship's deck and masts.

She again rose, stepped down into an empty seat in the lower row and sat. Only two rows below reposed the treasure chest, set aside and forgotten at what amounted to stage right.

Meanwhile, the cast was engaging in frantic swordplay at stage left. Luckily, Temple was on the fringe of the seated audience. She had only to make her way down two more rows, and the treasure chest would be hers, all hers. At least for the few seconds a look required.

At closer view, the chest was unpromising, even disappointingly tawdry. The gilt paint streaking its exterior was thin and hastily applied. Like some eternally gape-jawed village idiot, it sat lolling its tongue of cheap pearl ropes at the audience. None of the contents thus revealed were worth more than fifteen cents. Temple glimpsed the foot of a gilded goblet. A string of plastic red beads. Swaths of red, green and gold glitter mired in glossy slicks of yellowing glue.

Stage props, like the actors themselves, were designed to appeal most from a flattering distance.

Would Temple entrust a delicate, expensive pair of Austrian crystal-studded shoes to such a lowly container? No, but the least likely the looks, the better the hiding place.

Shrieks from her right made Temple jump like a thief in a spotlight. She glanced to the playing area. Some pirate crew horseplay had splashed the front-row occupants with a whiplash of water.

Under cover of squeals and claps, Temple darted down two rows and sank down right before the pirate treasure.

She clasped her hands like a princess bride, hardly believing she was now front-row center, staring at the object of her outing. The temptingly ajar lid looked permanently glued into place. She would have to get on her knees and peer into its shadowed mouth, perhaps even pry it open more, if possible. A good thing she wasn't wearing pantyhose, she thought, as she knee-walked into position and twisted to peer inside the lid. Something pale and glittering as a shark's tooth tickled her eye. She craned her head closer to the chest, hearing distant shouts and laughter.

Was it a crystal-encrusted toe? Or a . . . a fork tine? And stainless steel at that? What kind of pirate treasure were these yahoos passing off here—?

A strong hand clasped her elbow and jerked her upright.

Temple gasped and turned. The frowning first mate was leering at her, his trusty rubber dagger clenched in his impeccably white, even teeth.

"Aha!" he said so broadly that Temple thought he could walk the plank on his villainous tone alone. "Another meddling but comely lass. Booty for below."

Another pirate came swinging down like Tarzan to alight beside them. "We'll take her aboard," her captor decreed, pulling Temple nearer in his sweaty embrace to stage-whisper, "Just hang on and put your feet on the knot. You'll be fine."

Even as he spoke he grabbed a passing cable and stepped up on the heavy knot, holding Temple with only one arm.

Before she could blink, they were sailing over the lagoon like blind mice clinging to the pendulum of a grandfather clock. Temple's feet flailed for the advertised knot, but she was too short to reach it, so she clung to the sailor and the rope, watching the blurred world shoot past like running water colors. Somewhere in that sea of smudged faces were Electra and Kit.

The first mate landed with a jolt on an upper deck, letting the rope swing back across the water.

"That's what you get for lusting after pirate treasure," he announced to Temple and the world at large, thanks to the wonders of portable mikes and modern sound systems.

"Oh, please, sir," she pled prettily, "I must return to my aged and ill grandmother and great-aunt." The microphones hidden about the scene bounced her voice from waterline to rooftop.

Something else bounced: the poop deck as the pirate captain swung jauntily to deck, where he engaged the first mate in a bit of choreographed swordplay. What was not choreographed was Temple's presence. She had no refuge but cowering against the mast while the pretend pirates traded steel and corny lines.

The audience, safe in their seats across what looked like a hundred feet of cold water (it was October and the nights grew chill), laughed at her plight.

At last the first mate dropped his sword to the deck and performed three backward flips to elude the captain's vengeful blade.

"Worry not," the victor announced, grinning beneath his red bandana, "I will return you safe and sound to yon shore."

With that he seized Temple in one arm and the convenient rope in another.

"Oh, no," she protested, "I'd rather swim."

"That can be arranged!" The first mate was charging them, dagger at the ready, as the captain shoved off with a booted foot.

Once again Temple was airborn with a strange man (very strange), swinging at a tummy-twisting speed over the water wide to the pier.

They landed with only an instant to debark before the rope swung back. The captain escorted her to an empty seat with a bow . . . which a mutinous crewman took advantage of, hitting the red bandana with a belaying pin.

While the captain kissed concrete, the first mate swung over to recapture the real fair maiden, who hopped aboard the rope like a pro, protesting all the while.

Temple slumped in her seat, her head spinning from the motion, the noise, the uncertainty. She sat still for the rest of the show, and applauded when the last "Avast, ye cowardly dogs!" had been shouted and the last crewman had taken a watery dive.

So she remained while Kit and Electra edged toward her as the audience filed out of the amphitheater.

"Are you all right?"

Either Kit or Electra had asked that question, and Temple didn't care which.

"Right as rum," she declared, standing and swaying slightly, as if still aboard a rope. "Except I think I'm seasick."

"You looked so cute swinging back and forth," Electra said. "Much cuter than that other girl."

" 'That other girl' is a gymnast," Temple pointed out. "I'm not. If I looked cute, I must seek more opportunities for sheer terror, then, and have my picture taken." Her usually gritty voice had been scared into a growl. "I should sue those swashbuckling goons."

She stiffened as one of the offenders bounded over: the first mate, his sword tabled and his grin more friendly than fiendish this time.

"Say, you did okay. I figured you would. We're supposed to interact with the audience, and you made a great target, sneaking a peak into our treasure chest. I hope you didn't mind the ride. It's pretty safe."

"Pretty?"

"And so are you," he said with a bow.

Smarmy talk would get him nowhere. Temple didn't respond.

"Why were you so interested in the chest, anyway?" he asked.

"Well." Temple paused. Her last attempt to explain a complicated situation had gathered a gaping crowd at the wedding chapel. Somehow she didn't think rhinestone cat shoes would fly here, even if she had. "I'm a high school drama teacher," she said, lying through her pirate-white teeth. "We're putting on *The Merchant of Venice.* I wanted some ideas for doing the three suitors' chests for the play."

"Cool." The first mate nodded, his long blond hair going along for the ride. He smiled dutifully at Kit and Electra, then bounded to wherever pirate scum go to wait for the next show.

"No shoes, huh?" Electra joined Kit in staring at the abandoned treasure chest.

"Nothing but some plastic pearls and a tin fork." Temple brightened. "Maybe I don't think big enough."

"This is a pretty big chest," Kit pointed out.

"Not the chest! The site. Where we need to try next is the Treasure Island Hotel. That place must be crawling with treasure chests."

"Not us," Electra said. "Our aged grandmotherly hearts can't take watching you swing from a poop deck."

"Also our aging great-auntly hearts," Kit added.

"Come on, I had to say something to earn audience sympathy!"

"Too bad you didn't get ours," Electra said.

"We need to get back to our duties at the convention." Kit looked speculatively at Electra. "Maybe we can find our own manly dope-on-a-rope who has a scissors phobia and a serious case of myopia."

She and Kit turned to join the people shuffling out of the amphitheater. One was not shuffling. One had stopped by the entrance, hat in hand, to grin at the oncoming trio.

"Eightball! What are you doing here?" Temple asked.

"No need to ask what you're up to, is there? Thinking of joining the Big Top?" He gestured with his dapper straw fedora to the ship's mast-tops. "Circus Circus might have an opening. I know the security head there."

"I intend to keep my feet on the ground from now on," Temple said with grim determination.

"And I intend to make sure that she does," Electra added.

Eightball offered her a nod and a tight smile. Then he clamped the hat on his balding head and asked Electra, "That Hesketh Vampire still running smooth as polished steel?"

"Absolutely, when I've got time to take her out for a howl."

"Noticed you were away from the Ritz," he said.

"Did you?" Electra sounded unaccountably pleased. "How did that happen?"

Eightball's toe stubbed the damp concrete, which had been baptized by the buccaneers' shenanigans. "Went to say hello to Matt. He mentioned that you and Miss Barr had headed for the hills. Didn't know where."

"Didn't he? I guess we should be pleased that he noticed we were gone." Electra winked at Temple. "Well, I'm going to school at the Crystal Phoenix, and Temple is there to make sure that I crack the books."

"School at the Phoenix?" Eightball dislodged the hat to scratch his head. "This lady the schoolmarm?" He nodded at Kit, who had been patiently waiting for an introduction.

"Kit Carlson." She extended her hand for a businesslike shake. "Mr. . . . Eightball."

"Heck, Eightball's my handle. Last name is O'Rourke."

"Eightball is a private detective," Temple put in helpfully.

Kit arched her eyebrows. "Really? Maybe you could drop by our romance convention. A lot of romance writers are moving into mystery and intrigue. You'd be a great visiting expert."

"No way, ladies. I don't have nothing to do with those books."

Mention of romance had Eightball backing away as if he had seen a snake. With a parting nod and an edgy adjustment of his hat, Eightball O'Rourke joined the crowds ambling through the theme park.

"You see what I mean," Kit said with a sigh.

Temple nodded. "Even the word 'romance' is poison to some men."

"They're just afraid to admit their romantic feelings," Electra added. "It's not macho."

"Except for *The Bridges of Madison County*," Temple said. "Maybe Clint Eastwood playing the lead made romantic love manly again."

"Don't mention that dirty rotten book!" Kit's face flushed with feeling. "One man writes a hasty, three-hanky romance glorifying adultery. Give it a nonromance title and it's suddenly respectable. Booksellers who sneer at paperback romance fiction can't push it at their clients fast enough. It becomes a major bestseller. Hundreds of women have written romances celebrating monogamy and female empowerment, but *they're* chopped liver, even the megasellers, when it comes to respect. Besides, everyone thinks that silly Francesca was so noble to stay with her husband and kids after her fling with the traveling photographer . . . but what happened after the f-stop was over and Mr. Snapshot packed up his light meters and moved on? She lived a lie with her own family for the rest of her life, presumably."

"Easy, easy." Electra patted Kit's shoulder. "The reviewers didn't much care for Waller either. Speaking for myself, I can hardly wait to get back to the hotel and start my contest romance. But, say," she added, guiding Kit into the slipstream of tourists, "maybe I should consider using a *male* pseudonym now—"

Temple trailed them, momentarily immune to such issues as men and romance and money-making schemes. She was pondering where she should search for the Midnight Louie shoes next.

One woman's passion is another woman's feet.

Chapter 11

Blue Dahlia Bogey Boogie

Lieutenant Molina wouldn't have housed a homicide suspect in it, but Carmen loved her tacky dressing room at the Blue Dahlia.

It was only a large storage closet that the management had dedicated to her use. She had furnished it with a battered '30s Goodwill dressing table, the film-noir kind with a big round mirror centered between two low pillars of drawers. The maintenance man had scrounged a couple strips of makeup lights to act as sconces on either side.

A matching bench was too low for her height, and the lighting looked better than it lit, but the forties nightclub dressing-room ambiance tickled her fantasy. When she got out the Carmen paraphernalia, she felt like a big girl playing a little girl playing dress up.

The act of singing under a spotlight, however tiny the stage, the ritual of assuming another persona and then losing herself in the lyrical landscapes of the great old songs, these were all creation and recreation to her. She never changed clothes and left right after a performance. Instead, she sat and drank the whiskey and soda Rudy always had waiting on the blue-mirrored glass atop the dressing table. She hummed some Gershwin, thought of nothing and everything, and replayed the music in her mind. She was lucky to have this romantic escape from the realities of her profession.

She studied herself in the mirror. Lieutenant Molina didn't look in mirrors, but Carmen could, being a creature of smoke and illusion. Matt Devine's comment that her Carmen persona provided a playground for a policewoman's sensual side floated to the forefront of her thoughts.

Her mirror image rolled her eyes. How weird for an ex-priest to express such an intimate insight! Even now she felt slightly embarrassed, whether by the remark's source or its truth, she wasn't sure. But Devine had used the dry, dispassionate tones of a trained counselor, and his perception was probably true.

Some women who went into police work, especially on the patrol level, reveled in the ultra-feminine: long nails, bleached hair, hard-edged makeup. That only reinforced any innate chauvinism and made the men's wives uneasy. Women hankering after careers rather than personal attention kept a rigorously neutral profile. Sure, they were called tough bitches and lezzies for it, but in time the lack of nonsense won out and won over.

So successful had C. R. Molina been at this form of defensive coloration that her showy alter ego had become something of a risk. If word of Carmen got out now, she would not like it.

She touched the signature blue dahlia, pulling a loose bobby pin from her hair and dropping it into a top drawer. The drawers, cramped and cheaply made, tended to slide awry. She bent her attention on making the drawer shut and only accomplished it with a bang.

When she looked up, she was no longer alone in the room, or the broom closet, rather.

The closed door framed a man's figure, as if he were painted on it. A professional description leaped into her mind: six-three or -four, 180 pounds, black slacks, black turtleneck sweater, black hair. Eyes indeterminate. Of course she hadn't heard or seen him come in; Michael Aloysius Xavier Kinsella was a magician, wasn't he? At least sometimes.

If his unconventional entrance was supposed to surprise or alarm her, he wasn't counting on the steadiest nerves in the LVMPD. Who did he think she was, anyway, and why was he here?

"Thanks for knocking." She lowered her eyes to the dressing table as if searching for something among the sparse accoutrements and didn't have to worry about watching him at all.

She looked up again when he pushed himself away from the door with a gymnast's ultra-controlled ease. "The situation didn't seem to call for formalities."

"What situation? Are you a fan?"

His smile was slight, and slightly mischievous. "Only since tonight."

"A new customer. Still, you could knock. We're not that hard up."

"Not if I wanted to enter unseen."

"Don't tell me. A deranged fan. I've always wanted one."

"I've always wanted an explanation."

"Of what?"

"Yourself."

"I don't see why."

"You should, Lieutenant."

"As you should know that I want an explanation of my own. But not here. I believe the expression is 'downtown.' "

"I believe you have to take what you can get."

She didn't answer, never having settled for that, but well aware that he had chosen this time and place to suit his purpose.

She spun around on the bench to face him in something other than the deceptive, reflective glass-made-mirror by a dark, poisonous cloud of silver nitrate.

"So what brought you back, Kinsella, after all this time?" she asked in her usual flat, professional tones, empty even of curiosity.

"Apparently you have nothing better to do than harrass Temple."

She felt humor flare when she least wanted it, but had no time to veil the impulse. "I would say that the case is just the opposite."

"You don't appear very harrassable."

"Let's say that Miss Barr has a talent for getting underfoot at the scene of a crime. Since she has never been very forthcoming about your past, present and future whereabouts, I make a point of asking whenever the occasion presents itself."

"Apparently an occasion presented itself to produce my class photo from Interpol."

She leaned back against the dressing table, resting her head in ı ˉ hand, and smiled. "You know, it really is rather intriguing to be the ˜•ı˜˜gatee for a change. Is this what you did for the IRA?"

His head shook in wry disgust. "That old bureaucratic snafu means nothing, except to Temple."

"They say love is blind, but I guess it's not color-blind." She stood slowly, and tilted her head again. "Let's see, are they green, or blue?"

"Nobody's business," Kinsella said tightly. "I had no idea the police were so interested in professional illusions. That Interpol alert was a farce when it was issued seventeen years ago, and it's unconscionable ancient history now. Why brandish it in front of Temple?"

"Good psychology." She sat again, preferring to appear more casually in control. "Her idiotic loyalty to you made her a hostile witness. I needed to wake her up to the fact that I had good reason to be interested in you and your whereabouts."

"So you had to unmask me as some sort of imposter."

She shrugged. "Aren't you? I'm not one of your admiring audience, Kinsella. I'm not a gullible little girl from the Heartland. Don't expect me to buy for a moment the notion that you abandoned a lucrative performing career on an inexplicable whim. And where is all that money you made performing, anyway? Miss Barr often struggles to pay her mortgage and monthly maintenance on her own income. Why sign her up as a co-owner if you had planned to skip out so soon?"

"Does your job allow you to sling suspicions at any passing stranger?"

"Do you think you can vanish just as a dead body is discovered on your turf and not stir up interest?"

"The Goliath is a big place, Lieutenant. That's why it's called the Goliath. The employees alone number in the thousands, not to mention guests and gamblers. Why should I have anything at all to do with that dead body of yours?"

"Because all of a sudden, you weren't there."

"My contract with the hotel had ended; there was no reason for me to stay."

"Except for Temple Barr and the Circle Ritz." She folded her arms. "I always suspected you'd come back."

"Good for you. Why shouldn't I? And what do I find when I do? Your baseless suspicions have put Temple in an ugly spotlight. Where's your sense of responsibility? Temple has nothing to do with anything you might suspect. Having the police interested in her might attract the wrong elements."

"Besides yourself, I suppose you mean?"

"You know what I mean. Pick on someone your own size, Lieutenant."

She stiffened at the implication. "I would if he would stay visible."

"Look." Kinsella spread his hands in a disingenuous gesture. "I presume there are no warrants out for me."

"Not . . . yet. But I do want to talk to you, and officially. What's wrong with that? What are you afraid of?"

"Not you," he said quickly. Too quickly. "Listen. I'll make you a deal."

"You'll offer a deal. I doubt I'll take it."

"Get me copies of the mug shots and rap sheets on the men who roughed up Temple, and I'll come in quietly for a talk, but not publicly. No downtown."

" 'Get you'? Get real! Why should I trade you police information for a few moments of your precious time, on your terms? Besides, Miss Barr only made tentative identifications. I can't unleash a rogue citizen on unsuspecting crooks."

"Since when are the police so solicitous of petty career criminals?"

"You seem to have those guys pegged without any documentation. I don't need your time or your insight so badly that I'm about to make any deals with a disappearing act."

"That's too bad. I might have something to show and tell, but first I need to check some things out."

"Who's the cop here?"

He smiled. "You are, Lieutenant, as close-minded a hard-nosed dick as I've ever seen in a velvet glove."

"Don't let this getup fool you."

"I won't, if you won't."

She was silent as she contemplated the conversation thus far. Elusive was his middle name, as if he didn't have enough of them already. She might have to deal for her long-wanted interrogation, but he was capable of taking the info and running. He was even capable, she suspected, of breaking into headquarters to get it.

"If I decide to let you take a look at these guys, it will have to be downtown. And I'll want some answers about the Goliath."

His mobile face soured with a doubt-curdled expression. "I don't want that high a profile. Much as I enjoy chatting with you, this clandestine tête-à-tête will have to do for now. You're right, Lieutenant; I do have a thing or two to tell you. Meanwhile, just remember that it's not Temple that you're after."

He was at the door so fast the fact seemed supernatural.

She nearly knocked over the light bench as she stood.

"I'm not through with you," she warned him in the dead serious tones she would use with any suspect.

Kinsella paused, his hand on the battered doorknob, looked over his shoulder, turned.

She knew enough to approach him deliberately, her face an authoritarian mask. Still, she felt she was wading through Jell-O, aware of the long, soft skirt brushing her calves, of the lightweight holster gartering her ankle. No cop was ever off duty.

He waited, wary but curious. "Do you think you can arrest me?" he asked when she reached him.

That issue had both legal and physical implications, especially in a confrontation that had become an exercise in domination. They faced off, not moving, neither giving an inch in determina-

tion. She was not a small woman; in her vintage shoes she sur-
passed six feet, so he had a scant two or three inches on her. And
probably only thirty pounds, she estimated expertly.

She sensed imminent movement on his part—street sense—
and her right arm lifted to stop his escape.

He caught her wrist, a weak tactic, but a canny move. That
token counterforce allowed her to test his mettle. His upper body
strength was surprising for one so lean, and his expression was now
amused, which angered her, as he meant it to. Resistance did not
dismay her. She knew some moves, but better yet, she had spent
four years as a patrol officer doing take-downs in South Central
L.A.

For the moment they remained paralyzed, exerting equal
counter-strength, balanced like arm wrestlers before they get serious. Her will was as adamant as his. Besides, the real battle
wouldn't begin until she slipped his wrist-grip to work some surprises of her own.

The balance held for frozen seconds.

Suddenly, without relaxing his grip, he leaned close and spoke
in a deep whisper. "Don't." His vibrant baritone at her ear almost
made the silk dahlia at her temple tremble. "Don't ruin the start
of a beautiful . . . pursuit."

Irony and intimacy were concealed weapons she hadn't expected. Her wrist was now free, but so was he, eeling through the
barely open door like a second-story man.

For a split second she debated pulling out her own concealed
weapon and chasing him through the Blue Dahlia. No. Not yet.
She wanted publicity no more than he, because she had so damn
little probable cause for pursuing him, just the terminal itch of instinct.

Furious, she turned and slammed the door shut with her back.
The grand gesture forced her to face herself in the tacky mirror
across the room. C. R. Molina shut her eyes. Whatever her professional annoyance at anyone's—any suspect's—manipulation,
she had to analyze the personal flaw that had surprised and paralyzed her for the vital instant he had used to leave without resistance. It wasn't pretty, but it was pretty obvious.

She allowed herself to replay the bolt of sheer sexual heat lightning that had riveted her from head to toe. His swift, alarming closeness, the warm, ironic voice, the physical tension of resistance, his and hers, suddenly altered into something else.

She hadn't allowed herself, hadn't had a hope in hell of experiencing anything like it in . . . years. She had felt as if an elevator she rode daily and indifferently had suddenly plunged three stories, and would the elevator operator do it again, please.

Calculated, of course, down to the second. Manipulative. Cocky. Effective. Part of her despised any woman's vulnerability for that ancient sexual domination game, always stacked against women. Part of her wanted to play it again, Sam.

Carmen leaned against the closed door, bracing her hands on the cool, smooth wood. She felt as if Bacall had just met Bogart. And he was good.

He was very, very good.

Lieutenant C. R. Molina pushed herself away from the door's support, from the past, from dispensible trivialities like libido.

So was she.

Chapter 12

Hearse and Rehearsal

"Cheyenne invited us," Temple told the man in the knit shirt who paused beside the seats she, Kit and Electra occupied in the Peacock Theater the next morning.

The man glanced at his beeper, nodded and rushed on.

"Whew." Kit slid onto her tailbone until her head was barely above the seatback. "No New York theater would let onlookers camp out like this during rehearsal."

"This is Las Vegas," Temple explained. "Everybody knows or owes somebody. People are always dropping in. As long as you have the right name to drop—and apparently we do—no problem."

Electra had not bothered to shrink into her seat; with her hair moussed and sprayed papaya pink, what was the point? She gazed mistily toward the stage.

"Kind of brings back my uncovered, undercover assignment as Moll Philanders. Golly, that Hesketh Vampire made a dynamite stage prop, though."

"Huh?" The string of confusing allusions brought Kit upright again. "I know what a vampire is, but what's a 'Hesketh' vampire? One with a lisp?"

"A big mean, screamin' machine," Electra intoned with fond and unfaded memory. "One thousand cee-cees of silver-streak 'cycle."

"I don't even know what a 'cee-cee' is. Max's vintage British motorcycle," Temple translated for Kit's benefit. "Electra got it as a downpayment on our condo. She used it in her gig as a senior citizen stripper when I was doing PR for the stripper contest."

Kit blinked. "Senior citizen strippers? I knew Las Vegas had a loyal elderly clientele, but—"

"It's a long story," Temple said, "and rather rowdy."

Kit gave up for the moment to look around. "Pretty ordinary theater and house, without the turquoise and violet velvet curtains. So. What if you hadn't had Cheyenne's name to drop? Would we still be persona grata?"

"Sure." Temple grinned. "I work for the Crystal Phoenix now, so I could always use my position here."

"Hey!" came a deep booming shout from the back of the house.

"Yeah!" came its cousin.

"Ta-rah-rah boom-de-ay," came a lusty male chorus of at least six.

Temple turned, looked, cringed and tried to shrink in her seat.

"Temple's back, and guess who's got her?"

The bearers of this untimely news came charging down the center aisle en masse, or so it sounded. Temple couldn't bear to look, but she could smell them at fifty paces: a phalanx of English and Russian Leather intermixed with a soupçon of Brüt.

Temple peered between her fanned fingers, trying for a body count. To her best estimate, she was viewing the complete Fontana, Inc. All nine brothers—except Nicky, who didn't travel in packs—at once. Nicky, owner of the Crystal Phoenix and husband to hotel manager Van von Rhine, was the White Sheep of a large family more noted for its wool of blacker hue. The other brothers were bachelors—attractive, genially oblivious to all but the finer vices in life (like gats, gambling and gams) and prone to preen. But now their image had taken a one-hundred-and-eighty-degree turn.

Gone were the Italian ice-cream suits; also gone was the discreet bulge of Beretta here and there. No, now it was skin-tight designer jeans and bulging muscle shirts. Ralph not only had a ponytail, but it wasn't one anymore. Instead, his unbound hair, moussed into a tangle from a figure on a Cretan frieze, dusted his shoulders. The presence of so many feral Mediterranean males made Temple feel like an extra on the set of "West Side Story."

"These guys look like they should be on Hesketh vampires," Kit commented, not without appreciation. "Friends of yours?"

"Business associates." Temple smiled gamely up at the assembly. "What are you fellows doing here?" she asked before they could ask her. "Security detail?"

"Naw," said one, "we're in the Hunky Hero contest."

"Is there a group category?"

"Nope," said another. "We compete separately, but we make our public appearances all together, if that makes sense."

"Yeah, if the six Goat Guys from Elbow Grease, Indiana, can rack up modeling contracts, we figure the nine Fontana Fellows from Las Vegas, Nevada, can do twice as good."

"Who are 'the Goat Guys'?" Electra asked.

"Sextuplet bodybuilders from Indiana," Aldo—or maybe Armando—said disdainfully. "Genuine hayseeds. They raise fainting goats; the kind that up and fall down when they hear a loud noise. That's probably what makes them so good at holding up all those swooning women on romance bookcovers. Practice."

Rico frowned in disagreement. "The way I heard it, they raised pygmy and dwarf goats, for little people, I guess. You know, those hairy suckers with the pig's feet and devil horns."

"Forget the details," Julio—or maybe Giuseppe, sometimes known as Pepe—said. "The bottom line is that the Goat Guys made it into the big time at last year's Incredible Hunk competition. They went straight from the slop pail to the media trough. Big-time modeling, acting, even recording contracts."

"Do you do any of that?" Kit asked.

"Raise goats? Hell, no."

"Model, act and record," she specified.

"Oh, that." Ralph was blasé as he gave his locks a finger-fluff. "Any fool can do that stuff. You just gotta have the look. We're not the bodybuilder type, but we have other advantages."

"Yes," Electra and Kit agreed a bit too quickly for credibility's sake.

"So is there a talent segment?" Temple wanted to know. She really wanted to know.

"Yeah."

"There is?"

Ernesto—or possibly Eduardo—nodded soberly. "Yeah. Wearing clothes."

"And *not* wearing clothes," Emilio put in.

"Actually, the pageant is mostly about changing clothes," Ralph said eagerly. "First we all come on in clothes. Next we don't wear much clothes; then more clothes; then less clothes; then we all come back out in clothes and wait to see who gets to wear no clothes on a book cover."

"It's a big strain, let me tell you," Julio complained, "keeping track of all those costumes and what to take off and put on. Plus, they give us no time flat."

"And loo room."

"And no private dressing rooms. The smell is like the locker rooms of the Rams after a playoff."

"But we don't mind personal hardship if it pays off big," Rico added with a grin.

"Doesn't it bother you to parade around onstage undressed?" Temple wondered. "What happened to the totally tailored Fontana brothers?"

"Fame."

"Fortune."

"An audience of adoring babes."

"But I do kinda feel a little naked sometimes," Ralph said with a doubtful frown.

"You do?" the amazed other brothers asked as one.

"Yeah." Ralph looked down and seemed, for a moment, as

sheepish as one would imagine a Goat Guy would look if his faint-ing goat refused to swoon. "I kinda miss my Beretta."

"Ahh!" His siblings pounded him consolingly on the back, in the time-honored gesture of male sympathy. "You can't pursue a career in the arts without some sacrifices," Armando consoled him grandly.

Ralph nodded, then brightened. "On the other hand, I can add to my earring collection. Earrings are really hot among the con-testants."

"We gotta go," Aldo urged. "Hit the backstage before we miss our cueball."

"*Cue*," Temple and Kit corrected in tandem.

"Wait'll you see us in our competition getups," Pepe bragged. "This is even better than our surprise appearance in the Gridiron show."

"I'm sure," Temple said, not at all sure that the world was ready for an intentional Fontana Brothers stage appearance.

"Tally ho!" said one.

"One for the money," said another.

"Two for the show."

"Three to get Freddy—"

"And four to go!"

They were off like Italian greyhounds, sleek, single-minded and born to win.

"Whew." Kit was suitably dazed. "Who was the chorus line from 'Guys and Dolls'?"

"The hotel owner's brothers, all nine of them."

"For a girl with romantic troubles, you certainly know a lot of eligible males; most, unfortunately, are on the young side."

"The Fontana brothers are bachelors, all right, but they're about as eligible as gigolos."

"Such darling brothers," Electra put in. "Look at Ralph's charm-ingly boyish attachment to his Bearetta. I had no idea young men nowadays were into stuffed animals. I'm sure they'll grow up and settle down in time. Do you think these Goat Guys will show up this year? Swashbuckling sextuplets. They sound absolutely fasci-nating."

Temple shook her head without comment. She knew she had risen too early this morning for a person in a fragile emotional state.

"There she is," sang out another male voice, a baritone mimicking the Miss America theme song.

Temple stiffened. Apparently the world had nothing better to do this morning than to draw attention to her.

"Our ideeeeeal," the singer finished in perfect pitch, arriving beside their row of seats with a flourish. "Show us the tootsies," he ordered Temple. "What are our little tiny toes wearing today?"

Temple surrendered and lifted a foot into the aisle.

"Fabulous," he pronounced. "Yellow is your color. Is the ankle stronger than sheet metal again?"

"It's the other ankle and, yes, at least as firm as tinfoil. How are you, Danny?"

"In my element, ducks." Danny Dove cast a theatrically languishing glance over his shoulder at the stage thronging with wandering, bare-muscled, bawling hunks in search of stardom, not Stella.

Danny wore vintage Gene Kelly today: tight black T-shirt, jeans and sockless loafers. Gene would have worn the socks—dorky white sweat-socks—but that had been forty years ago, before the birth of Contemporary Cool.

"Are you coordinating the pageant?" Temple asked hopefully.

" 'Coordinate' is more word than most of these guys can manage. Some have modeling and acting experience, if you count blue movies, but theatrically, the majority are barbarians. Three days to turn these sows' ears into silk tuxedos. Still, I do love a big, juicy challenge."

Danny stiffened his shoulders and marched up the aisle toward the milling contestants.

Temple glared at Kit before she could say anything. "He is *not* an eligible man."

"Not to us, perhaps. But everybody is eligible to somebody. Who is he?"

"Local choreographer. I would have introduced you, but his heart was in the Highlands." Temple jerked her head toward the stage, where a tow-headed giant wearing a red tartan kilt and little else was striding over the boards, broadsword in hand. "Danny Dove is a pretty big name in this town."

"Danny Dove? No kidding?" Kit leaned forward in her seat to watch the wiry director instantly whip milling hunks into something resembling a chorus line.

"You've heard of him?"

"He made his name on the Manhattan bathhouse circuit back when Bette Midler was making hers in the same venue. So he ended up in Vegas. I'd bet he makes bucks."

"You'd win."

Electra frowned. "Then why is he doing this little show?"

"Kid in a chocolate factory." Temple nodded at the stage. "Men in tights. Ambiance."

Electra was not assuaged. "Is it . . . safe for these young men—?"

Kit laughed. "Golly, Electra, guys who look like that have learned to encourage or fend off either sex since high school. They're the ones who take advantage of—they take advantage of their looks and other people's longing. Beautiful people learn the drill early, and if they choose to make a career of it, they're usually the least vulnerable of anyone in the dating game."

"I'm old-fashioned," Electra confessed. "I married all of my husbands."

"All?" Kit was shocked.

Electra nodded demurely. "Let's watch the rehearsal, girls. Isn't that what we're here for?"

They sank back into their seats in unison, but Electra's question lingered in Temple's eternal inner monologue.

What were they themselves here for? Kit was the professional. A writer, imagine that. Her aunt the romance novelist. To Kit this pageant was a mere promotional circus, and the men on stage were the attractive animal acts that lured the public to buy her popcorn.

Electra was the ardent amateur, a reader yearning to break into print. She saw these rather overwhelming men as symbols of lost youth and late-life renewal.

Temple was an escapee from reality. Along for the ride, evading the angst at home, dodging her personal responsibilities. Fleeing to an environment she barely understood, and wasn't sure she liked or even approved of.

Women frankly ogling men as a role reversal had a certain kinky appeal, but was as silly and immature as men ogling women. And, at the moment, Temple wasn't in the mood for either option. Had Hamlet showed up instead of Danny Dove, and barked "Get thee to a nunnery," she might have gone, gratefully.

Kit, actress-author extraordinaire, gestured to the proscenium. "This is set up more like a fashion runway."

Temple nodded as she examined the temporary tongue of stage covered in garish red cloth with cellophane blades like trampled grass, sticking out at the audience in tacky audacity.

Onstage, Danny's hands were slapping out amazingly loud claps.

"Attention, Romper Roommates. You all have your order of appearance, God bless us, everyone. Walk it on down, one by one, and show me the shtick you came in with. Then I'll give you something that works. Go!"

They came down the runway, as obedient as lambs who would be lions. Shoulder blade–long manes streamed (though some men were post-Delilah Samsons, conventionally shorn); sculpted muscles flexed in four-four time in shoulders, thighs and washboard stomachs (though some were less muscle-bound than others); all flashed bleached-to-bone-white teeth (though any audience was absent except for Temple and associates, and a mixed-sex cadre of stage crew and costume volunteers).

"Oooh!" Electra exclaimed as one candidate performed several handstands down the runway.

The next produced a wavy dagger with a jeweled hilt, then held it pointing floorward between his legs as he executed a slow split, letting the metal blade suggestively lift skyward as his riven thighs neared full contact with the stage.

"Whew!" Kit fanned herself with one hand. "A night at the Laddie's Lair."

A rogueish sort with short curly hair sashayed downstage, a workman's leather tool belt clattering around his hips like a gunbelt. At the runway's very tip he took a wide stance, then drew a metal measuring tape from its center-hung housing in the twelve o'clock low position.

"Danny Dove is right," Temple muttered. "Everybody has a gimmick."

"Just like the strippers in 'Gypsy,' " Kit agreed, rising. "I've got to visit the ladies' room. Let no hunk do anything he shouldn't do before I get back." She bustled up the aisle.

Onstage, Danny Dove had collapsed into a cross-legged position at stage right, rubbing his corrugated forehead with his hands. His dancer's eloquent body conveyed what words did not: the contestants' preplanned shticks were as corny as anticipated.

"What a disappointment." Electra spoke loudly enough to carry to the stage apron, just as Mr. Tape Measure's nine extended inches snapped back into its holster. "I mean . . . I expected more, more savoir faire."

"More dash and less trash," Temple said. "I hope Cheyenne doesn't embarrass himself, though I shudder to imagine what the Fontana Boys will come up with."

Electra nodded bleakly. "Kit isn't missing anything."

"Maybe we can sneak out discreetly," Temple suggested, rising.

"Imagine, a front-row preview parade of Incredible Hunks and we're bored. Let's catch Kit coming out of the ladies' room."

A lull in the lineup of male pulchritude created a perfect escape hatch. Temple and Electra were tip-toeing rather ostentatiously up the plush-carpeted aisle when rustles and whispers erupted behind them.

Yell bloody murder and no one will look. Whisper a little and they'll stand transfixed. The two turned to the stage just as a bare leg thrust out from behind the side curtain.

It was well-formed, and hairy enough to be masculine, but also decidedly equine.

Temple raised an auburn eyebrow.

Another leg—or, rather, foreleg—followed.

Edging nervously onstage was a horse of mottled gray color daubed with white, an Appaloosa famed for the pale scatter of melting "snow" spots on its hindquarters.

But no one in the audience could see its hindquarters yet, and who would even worry about it, given the tawny, sinewy, naked male figure of an Indian—Native American, in politically correct terms—on its back?

"Well!" Electra stopped so sharply Temple caromed off her suddenly solid form. "Wait. I once considered using an Indian hero in my romance entry. Wish I'd seen this guy sooner. This is more like it."

"It's theater, all right," Temple agreed, watching horse and rider amble downstage. "Will that makeshift ramp hold a near-ton of horseflesh and hunk?"

Each hoof struck stage with the muffled thump of a drumbeat. Though the rider looked naked, Temple soon spotted the thongs over each hip that supported a buckskin loincloth. The brave's long dark hair was braided in front, and no smile fractured his chiseled features. A small deerskin pouch on a leather string lay on his bare breastbone. The leather strap slashing diagonally across his well-developed chest led the eye to a beaded quiver and three feather-tipped arrows peeking over his right shoulder. He carried a pale bow of antler or bone, with a two-foot-long arrow nocked on the string, though his arms were slowly lowering the weapon as the horse moved toward the audience.

Very sensible, Temple approved. Safety before sensation.

The horse paused at center stage. It wore no bridle, Temple realized, no reins, no saddle, but was trained to respond to rider signals only. *What a magnificent creature!* she thought, although most (less romantically burned-out) women would apply that praise to the rider rather than the ridden.

The horse held its noble position for long seconds, then turned its head over its shoulder and whinnied inquiringly. Temple didn't know much about horses and whinnies, but she knew a lot about greenhorn performers wondering 'what next,' whether in plain English or plaintive horse.

The rider did nothing. Did not so much as move.

Good call; his stoic bearing added to the mystery and the moment. Cheyenne—for Cheyenne it was—had created a show-stopper. Even Danny Dove sat immobile and rapt, captivated by a true stage suspense as everyone present was, by a breathless wondering *What will he—they—do next?*

"Bravo," Temple whispered under her breath. "But don't milk it too long—"

Even as she spoke the rider moved. The warrior's lean torso shifted left, as if to dismount, the bare left leg slid sideways along the horse's gray belly, the bow and arrow pointed downward, to the floor. Every motion was as elegant as ballet, blessed with a lingering, sure sensuality that only intensified the effect. The onlooker didn't want the slow-motion poetry of man and horse to end, but knew that—at any instant—the moccasined feet would spring lightly to the stage, for the horse couldn't walk on the temporary runway.

But the anticipated dismount didn't happen. Instead, the man's body kept tipping sideways, like a tin figure struck by a lucky shot at a shooting gallery. Temple expected such a figure to flip upright and move on. It didn't.

Cheyenne's feet touched the stage floor only an instant before his entire length did, collapsing like a straw man. Bow and arrow fell to one side.

Everyone watched, motionless, waiting for the drama's next act. Surely something not yet seen would explain this turn of events.

Temple saw the unthinkable reason first.

"No!" she shouted at someone, spurred to action, wanting to roll the film backwards. She sprinted down the long aisle and up the five or six steps to the runway.

Every eye wrenched to her. She could sense annoyance on the accusing faces of watching stage crew members in the wings. But she had her glasses on, all the better to see the heroes on parade strut their stuff. She had spotted something else in the spotlit glare . . . something other than naked horse and nearly naked man.

Blood dappling the snow of an Apaloosa's hindquarters.

No one—nothing—was moving but her and the gently side-stepping horse, except time. The horse whinnied again, this time in obvious distress. It minced away, as magnificently bare as its fallen rider, turning to display a thin crimson stream that meandered down the sleek, swelling belly.

Now everyone was running for the same spot, but Temple was already there. She paused at the foot of Cheyenne's figure, studying his open, unseeing eye, his slack mouth. Then she saw the feathered haft of an arrow bracing his back, keeping it from sinking flat to the floor.

Or was *he* sinking to the floor, driving the shaft in deeper?

Temple knelt to seize his ebbing shoulder with both hands.

"Help me! We've got to keep him from falling on it—"

Someone crouched beside her. "Hang on, dear heart!" Danny Dove.

Even greater force checked the body's fall. A Fontana brother knelt at Cheyenne's head, his bent knee helping prop up the torso.

Temple sensed legs crowding around them.

"Lay him forward," someone suggested.

"Has he got a pulse?" Another voice.

"I've done some nursing—" A man knelt beside them, then pressed two fingers to Cheyenne's carotid artery.

After a second, his fingers moved to another site. And another. Temple sensed rather than saw the headshake that accompanied his spoken verdict. "Nothing. No pulse."

A nondescript costume woman brought rolled-up towels daubed with suntan-shade makeup anyway, pushing them under Cheyenne's back to keep . . . the body . . . from rolling onto the arrow.

An arrow. A stage prop gone awry? Or a murder weapon, first and last? Temple stared into Cheyenne's dead face, remembered its charming yet oddly diffident animation the previous night, when he'd invited her to today's rehearsal . . . for death.

No! He had first asked her to go somewhere else last night. With him. For a drink. To talk. She had considered the invitation frivolous and insincere; he was just another ambitious hunk winning women's favor and influencing votes. Kit and Electra wanted to assume that he was attracted to her, thought that she should accept any flattering invitations. She had brushed off both assumptions. She had said no. She had no time for games.

But maybe Cheyenne *was* interested in her, for reasons other tnan the eternal he/she. Maybe he had a problem and knew about her role in uncovering the Stripper Strangler.

She had said no.

Nobody would ever say no to him again.

People were edging away from tragedy, stepping back from death. There was nothing they could do.

Nothing she could do.

"Come on," someone above her urged, a hand on her shoulder, as she had laid hands on Cheyenne's shoulder only moments before.

Temple remained crouched beside the body, dumb as a dog. Danny caught her elbow in his wiry grip and pushed her upright despite herself. She teetered on her high heels like someone on a cliff. The sudden change in position made her senses swim. Beside her, the horse minced nearer, a great gray wall of muscle and hide.

"Someone get the bleedin' 'orse outta 'ere!" a disconcertingly Cockney voice ordered.

"No," Temple said. "The police will want it kept as close to the scene of the crime as possible. It's evidence."

"Some blighter's supposed to stand 'ere and 'old the big bugger by his nose hairs?"

Temple glanced at the speaker. He was almost as tall as the horse, a chestnut-maned hunk with an artistically broken nose and piercing hazel eyes. He was obviously not volunteering for groom duty.

"I'll . . . hold it," she said. "And we should keep people away from here until the police come." .

Temple had never held a horse in her life, much less one bare of bridle and rein. So she stepped near its huge head and caught a fistful of mane, stroking its long nose.

Everyone but Danny Dove and the anonymous Fontana had backed away. Violent death did that to people: first attracted and then repelled them.

"The police have been called?" she asked.

"I sincerely hope so, Miss Annie," Danny said, his face ashen.

"Annie?"

Danny grinned from under his angelic coil of grizzled blond hair. "Annie Oakley, that is. Don't worry, I'll keep an eye on our friend Flicka there with you."

The offer was welcome.

Temple didn't know which she would have more difficulty handling in the long run: the live horse she didn't know how to hold, or the dead man she hadn't known how to help.

Murder on the Hoof

Death had taken the stage of the Peacock Theater, demanded the attention of everyone in the house, and then had bowed out, leaving only the props from a vanishing act behind.

A fallen man. A riderless horse. A deadly, never-shot arrow. And one sound effect: silence.

Forty-some mute, pallid-faced people sat scattered like whitecaps on empty waves of blue-green velvet seats in the theater's empty house, waiting, not for Godot, but for Clouseau.

Temple and Danny Dove were not among those lackluster islands of people. They sat alone together on the runway's top step in matching poses: glum faces on fists, elbows on knees, like Debbie Reynolds and Donald O'Connor poised to jump up to sing and dance in a movie musical of forty years ago. These two weren't in the mood for a melody.

The stage itself was deserted except for Cheyenne's crumpled form and the heavy-set girl who had finally volunteered to manage the horse. She stroked its long muzzle now, down to the sensitive, flaring nostrils, all the while whispering sweet equine noth-ings into the nervous, mobile ears.

The auditorium's double entrance doors sprang open with a echoing clank that startled humans and horse alike. The animal whinnied—an eerie, anguished scream that carried like crazy in the semi-deserted house. The people managed to keep silent.

"Is it the police?" Temple asked Danny, not lifting her eyes from their fixed consideration of the thousand-eyed peacock-feather pattern carpeting the aisles.

"How should I know? Two strangers in town, for sure—"

"One of them a woman?"

"The light's at their backs, love, as it is for all good strangers in town. They're both awfully damn tall to be female, though, unless one is a showgirl."

Temple's lips twitched at the notion of applying that word to Lieutenant C. R. Molina. Her gaze lifted to the pair moving down the spectacular carpeting toward them like a bridal couple in civvies on a gaudy magic carpet.

The newcomers paused at the foot of the steps, where Lieu-tenant Molina didn't even bother saying something witty like "You again."

Mute yet still in tandem, Temple and Danny stood, then parted to reveal the scene behind them.

"What's going on here?" Molina asked Temple after a cursory glance at the body, the horse and the horse-holder.

Temple knew she wanted terse talk. "Rehearsal for the In-credible Hunk contest sponsored by a romance convention meet-ing in the hotel."

"Incredible Hunk?" Molina's tone was more than incredible.

"Male cover models for romance novels. You know, pirates, Vikings, Indian chiefs. Thirty-some guys competing. One keeled over after riding onstage."

"That's the horse he rode in on?"

What other horse would it be?—Temple nodded.

"And the woman with it?"

"A volunteer handler. The horse has no saddle or bridle, and no union hand would object to an outsider taking care of it, I bet.

But I figured you'd want the crime scene as undisturbed as possible, so it made sense to keep the horse nearby."

"You consider the horse a witness? Did it happen to make a plaintive wail?"

"Only a plaintive whinny," Temple answered, stung by Molina's eternal sarcasm, "but it does have some of the victim's blood on its rump. Won't you need photos and samples?"

"Unfortunately, yes. And probably videotape at five, thanks to the Dream Team." Molina mounted the steps, clumping loudly in her low-heeled loafers, her partner behind her.

Temple had never seen him before: a dapper man with a neat salt-and-pepper moustache. He murmured an apology as he cut a swath between Temple and Danny.

Danny sighed loudly when the officers paused mid-runway to survey the damage.

"Just what I need when I've only got a few piddling hours to mount a show." Danny answered Temple's unspoken question in a hoarse stage whisper. "The police camping out on stage for who-knows-how-long. You've had experience with murders; how many hours will it take them to do their little dust 'n' bust routine?"

Temple surveyed the desultory clots of people. "The cast of witnesses and possible suspects would fill a Cecil B. DeMille crowd scene. Interviews could last all day. The physical crime scene is fairly limited, but the whole backstage area will have to be gone over with a blusher brush, of course. Ask Lieutenant Molina what can be arranged. The Las Vegas police understand about working around public places, crowds and deadlines."

"Lieutenant Molina's the hard-boiled dame in the Hush Puppies? The one you were afraid was coming?"

"You got it, Danny."

"I'd rather ask one of the guys on Mount Rushmore for something."

"Hey, better you than me. She really hates my guts."

"She must have as poor taste in people as she does in footwear."

He grinned an impish farewell before bounding down the stairs to round up his cast and crew for the inevitable police questions. Choreographers always bounded, Temple observed wistfully, as if they had inner-springs in their ankles. Where did they get the energy?

She suddenly had a mental image of Mount Rushmore looming behind her and turned back to the stage. Lieutenant Molina had approached on sneaky Hush Puppy feet and was watching her with the usual disconcerting deadpan before speaking.

"The Amazon with the horse said that you instructed everybody present at the time of the murder to stay put."

"I did."

"Good thinking, but can you be sure someone backstage didn't skulk off unseen?"

"No. I guess that's your job."

"But no one has left, that you know of?"

"Well   "

"Who?"

"Just Electra Lark, my landlady."

"I half-expected you to be here, God help me, knowing that you're working for the Crystal Phoenix, but what brought Mrs. Lark to this convention of weight lifters?" She nodded at assorted, half-attired hunks lounging in the seats. Sober faces went oddly with their luxuriant manes of well-tended hair.

"She had to attend a romance-writing class she signed up for."

"That sort of thing can be taught?"

"Apparently. And—"

"Who else has left?"

"My . . . Aunt Ursula. Well, actually, her name is Kit. Nickname, that is . . . when she doesn't go by Sulah Savage."

"Your Aunt Ursula." Molina repeated in numb, computerized tones. "Explain."

"I ran into her at the hotel yesterday. Didn't even know she was in town, and she didn't know I lived here. She's a famous romance writer."

"Sulah Savage," Molina repeated, her voice cold enough to flash-freeze a fish.

"Well, famous to some. Her given name was Ursula, you see, but she couldn't stand it, obviously, so her friends call her Kit."

"Kit what?"

"Er, Kit Carlson."

"Kit Carlson." Molina thought. "She ride horses?"

"Oh, I'm sure not. She knows absolutely nothing about horses and, and arrows. She's from Minnesota, you know, but she's lived in New York City for years."

"That clears her, all right."

"Anyway, Electra and Kit were sitting with me two-thirds of the way up the aisle. They couldn't have done it."

"We don't even know how the man was killed yet, so don't rule them out."

"With the arrow, isn't it obvious?"

"Perhaps, but was the victim shot . . . or stabbed? Tell me what you saw. You're the closest thing to an expert observer I've got."

Temple didn't know whether to be flattered or insulted. She certainly knew enough to comply.

"His animal act was a surprise. Only a few people backstage must have seen the horse brought in; the rest would be dressing or undressing, or helping the guys dress or undress, as the case may have been. He had arranged for a girl to help him with the horse—"

"Yon dainty wench." Molina jerked a thumb over her shoulder at the buxom lass by the Appaloosa. "Her name is Camellia Stubbins and she gave her reason for being here as 'groupie.' Apparently it was her self-appointed task to stand and wait upon these strapping he-men at large."

"Anyway, the . . . rider emerged slowly from the stage left wings—our right as we look toward the proscenium—bareback and bare a lot else, on the Appaloosa.

"He really milked the moment," Temple went on in appreciative remembrance and review. "It was a pretty stunning presentation: the bare horse and the almost-naked warrior atop it. The horse headed for stage center and the runway. I don't know if he was guiding it at that point, because any signals he'd have given would have been imperceptible, a mere tightening of leg muscles."

"You ride?"

"No, but I was a teenage girl once, and we go horse-crazy for a time. We learn these things, you know."

Molina's professional facade fractured into a wry smile. "I do know. I'm supposed to somehow fit a horse on a city lot, never mind the codes."

Temple guessed the horse fancier was the lieutenant's awkward preteen daughter, Mariah.

"Have you ever considered miniature donkeys?" Temple asked in all seriousness.

"I meet enough of them in my work," the policewoman answered pointedly, her cobalt eyes flashing blue steel.

Temple swallowed and accepted the admonition in silence. Back to storytime, although she hated reliving those awful moments when Cheyenne's act was revealed as an act of violence. She recalled the so-short moments when she assumed Cheyenne was doing exactly what he wanted to be doing, instead of dying.

"A fabulous entrance, as I said. He looked magnificent, except I thought he was drawing out the strong, silent type image a bit too long." She grimaced. "Then he slipped sideways, and before we all could see it wasn't a dismount but something more . . . deadly, I saw paint, red paint on the Appaloosa's snow-white hindquarters, red paint running down its gray side. War paint, I thought at first. What a great dramatic touch, I thought. Then I realized . . . what it must really be."

"The folks smoking in the foyer said you were the first to notice that something was wrong, that you ran right for the body. 'The little red-headed gal,' they said. I knew that was you even before we walked into the theater."

"I didn't run to 'a body.' I ran to help someone who looked ill. I didn't see the arrow until I got there, and by then he was falling back on it." She winced again, picturing Cheyenne's own weight driving death more deeply into his body.

Molina was less dramatic and more practical. "Too late by then. The wound was probably mortal before he even appeared on stage."

"You mean we were all watching a dead man?"

"Deep stab wound can do that: turn the walking wounded into a walking corpse for a few seconds. In this case a riding one."

"The worst part," Temple said, almost to herself, "is that

Cheyenne wanted to talk to me about something last night, and I . . . I brushed him off."

"Cheyenne? You knew the deceased?" The last sentence was a definite accusation.

"Knew him? Not really. I did meet him, once, when I was doing PR for the stripper competition a few weeks ago, that's all. He said hello last night."

"And wanted to talk to you?"

"Don't sound so incredulous, Lieutenant. According to Electra and my Aunt Kit, I'm surrounded by a sea of eligible men all panting to get me off on a desert island. They thought he was hitting on me."

"An Incredible Hunk candidate? And you didn't make time for him?"

"I don't like to be hit on; I was busy; I didn't believe them anyway. Besides, I think he may be—have been—bisexual."

Molina's eyebrows rose. Such a juicy detail, if true, increased the pool of possible suspects and the range of motives considerably. "Any basis for this insight on the late Cheyenne's sexual preferences?"

"Female intuition, but I must admit that my instincts about men have been a little off-kilter lately."

"Funny, I thought that condition was chronic."

Temple refused to rise to that bait.

"Did you ever get the gentleman's full, or real, name?"

"No. I just met him for a few minutes both times. I'm sure the pageant organizers have stat sheets on the entrants."

"And exitor." Molina eyed the crime scene again over her shoulder. "A horse. Of course. And I *will* want to question Electra Lark and your aunt Kit Carlson later. Who are those women over there?"

Temple twisted her neck around to look. Perhaps sixteen well-dressed, middle-aged women sat in a whispering cluster, looking like the ladies' garden society transplanted to a murder mystery set.

"Danny might know."

"Danny?"

"Dove. Danny Dove."

"Of course," Molina said with the same fatalistic politesse. Her blue eyes focused on Temple as if wondering if a concentrated stare could set her red hair on fire. "Are you sure that there isn't something else you want to tell me?"

"About the murder?"

"About any little recent event worth noting."

"The only recent event in my life isn't little," Temple said. "Unless witnessing a man die counts as a triviality."

"I was thinking more of witnessing a man coming back from the dead," Molina said cryptically. She twisted her head over her shoulder. "Not him, that's certain. He was . . . beautiful. I wonder if he would have won?"

"Somebody killed him over the pageant?"

"Certainly did stop his act cold. You can go now. Just tell your errant chums to stop by later. I'll deal with you then. We'll be here all day."

"Danny will have a fit. He literally has only days to put the show together."

"The show must go on, but only after my murder investigation." She pointed a forefinger in Danny's direction.

Temple didn't argue; she figured Danny would be doing plenty of that very soon. She passed him in the aisle as he came forward.

"Who are the Babes in Boyland?" Temple whispered, tilting her head to the ladies on the aisle as they crossed paths like doomed ships in the night.

"Author escorts for the boychicks. They were supposed to rehearse their walk down the runway."

No more could be said in flight, but Temple eyed some of the Reigning Heads of Romance as she skated past. A thoroughly respectable lot, most the farther side of forty or fifty. That didn't surprise her. From what she had learned of the publishing industry during the American Booksellers Convention last spring, any author under seventy was lucky to be well-established, so slow and frustrating was the climb to even moderate success.

And Electra was a newcomer at sixty-something! Better that Temple herself should try her hand at becoming the next . . . Cella Savage. At least she had a few decades to burn, and from the suspended state of her love life at the moment, she would probably be better off writing about romance than attempting to commit it.

Wait! How about writing about murder committed at a romance convention? No, death and desire didn't mix, except in real life.

Lieutenant Molina was amazing. By five-thirty, when Temple returned with an excited Electra and Kit in tow, she looked no different than she had that morning.

The trio sat in some front row seats. Most of the people were gone, except for a few union stagehands who were being interviewed up front by another pair of plainclothes detectives.

Yellow crime scene tape made a crazy-quilt pattern from stage left, down to a music stand set on the runway solely to serve as a turning point for the tape, and up to center stage again.

All that garish tape marked off an absence now: no horse, no corpse. Temple suspected the crime scene technicians had come and gone, along with the body bag brigade. She wondered if the horse had been dusted for prints.

"He fell there?" Kit's eager contralto could carry all the way up to the stage flies, and did.

"No, farther back. Upstage, they call it." Molina followed her voice out from the wings, stage right, of course, and walked along the tape and down the runway. Her height, weight of office and slow, flat-footed tread made her progression seem more of a dirge-like drag than a walk. Certainly it was not the high-spirited romp the runway had been erected to sponsor.

Molina stopped at the elevated edge and stared down, looking a little like Mount Rushmore's Jefferson, if stone faces could outweigh gender.

"I assume you're the famous aunt," she told Kit, "with the migrating name."

What was Kit to say? Nothing, and she did it well.

"Nice to see you again, Lieutenant," Electra chirped like a Technicolor cricket.

She had worn raspberry and violet for her writing class, and accessorized the usual muumuu with matching bangles, shoulder-dusting earrings and fingernail polish, raspberry and violet on alternating nails. Her hair was a monotone, tasteful shag of unnatural silver today.

Molina came down the steps, then leaned against the runway lip behind her, crossing her arms. Her maroon wool pantsuit gave her olive skin a darker cast. Temple wondered where her gun was: under her arm, at the back of her waist, around her ankle. Hard to tell, which was the idea. Her partner materialized from somewhere behind them, sat on the chair arm across the aisle and flipped a long, narrow reporter's notebook to the back section.

"First your names and addresses."

This they gave, in turn, as Molina's partner wrote it down.

"You"—she eyed only Electra and Kit, in turn, like a mama eagle deciding which of two offspring should get the gory little mouse goodie next—"are attending the romance convention." Nods. "You"—Kit only—"write romance novels under the alias of Suelah Savitch?"

"Sulah Savage," Kit said in her demurest voice. "I once considered using the pseudonym of Vernah Verandah—alliteration is critical—but decided that esses are more sensual." She pronounced the last word in the British fashion, without a "sh," slowly: "sen-sue-al." Slowly and sen-sue-al-lee. The male detective behind her choked back a laugh.

"Kit is a published author," Electra explained in awed tones.

"And you are here—?"

"I'm aspiring. An aspiring . . . author. Like Kit. Or aspiring to be like Kit. Published."

"That's why you left this morning to attend a romance writing class?"

"Yes."

"Did you learn anything?" Molina inquired pleasantly.

"Oh, yes. All about alpha males and pacing and sexual tension—"

"But you both were with Miss Barr this morning when the victim came on stage?" Molina interrupted.

"No," Kit said. "I'd already left for the ladies' room. By the time I came back, it was curtains."

Electra spoke. "Temple and I were leaving when we heard the horse come on stage. We were standing halfway up the aisle, awestruck."

"You both had the same view?"

Electra nodded.

"Why did only Miss Barr go up on stage when the man fell?"

A silence held as they regarded each other.

"Temple works here," Electra said. "I was . . . a visitor."

"And Temple's pretty at home on a stage, anyway," Kit put in. "Besides, Electra, you hadn't figured out yet that something was going wrong, right?"

"Right. I couldn't imagine why Temple was hotfooting up that runway . . . unless she couldn't keep her hands off that darling Cheyenne a moment longer—"

"Oh, please!" Temple cast a beseeching glance at the unnamed detective whose moving pencil would write and move on, putting her in that ridiculous light forever. He was quashing a smile under cover of his mustache.

"I simply realized that the man was sick," Temple said, "that he was sliding off the horse, not dismounting. Gallopin' Gertie, I even knew him a little. I didn't think about interrupting the act, just getting to the scene of the . . . the problem."

"A true PR person down to her press kit." Kit's pixieish smile would get nowhere with Molina.

"So . . ." Molina turned to Kit. "Tell me about your meeting with the victim in the hotel bar last night?"

"What 'meeting'?" Temple interrupted with a trace of huff. "Aunt Kit and I were sitting there chatting when he walked by. Pure chance."

"Well, I don't know—" Kit began.

Molina pushed her long frame away from the support of the runway. "What do you mean?"

"Hard to miss that man. Looked to me like he had spotted Temple, then hung around until our conversation paused and he could slide in there suavely."

"No . . ." came Temple's modest, disbelieving drawl.

Kit nodded soberly. "He was after you, Temple. And then when he asked you to have a private drink with him—"

Temple found it high time to state the obvious. "This is a police detective, Aunt Kit. She is looking for likely suspects. You being such a congenital matchmaker could establish me as knowing the victim, or him as knowing me. In simple terms, you are marching me down to storewide services and setting me up for what is known in the trade as a murder wrap, with satin bows on it. I didn't go with him, did I?"

"Not then . . ." Kit's tone was pure, puzzled honesty.

"Not ever! We all three went to the MGM Grand to sightsee after that, returned to the Phoenix for dinner, then went to our rooms and to bed. Electra and I were roommates! We were there all night."

"Well—" Now Electra was looking uncertain.

"Yes, Mrs. Lark?" Molina's voice cracked like a whip.

"She . . ."—Electra gave Temple a hangdog look—"I woke up and you weren't in your bed, dear."

"Aargh!"

Kit cleared her throat in a warning. "Was that a confession, Temple dear?"

"No. I didn't sleep in my bed. I slept in the bathtub."

"Oh?" Molina was really interested now.

"Actually, I mostly read in the bathtub, where the light wouldn't disturb Electra. All those books you gave me to study, remember, Auntie darling?"

Kit nodded sagely.

"But I did sleep finally, yes, Lieutenant, in the bathtub. And, believe me, Cheyenne was not there. So that's where Electra found me in the morning. Alone."

"But you could have been *not* there," Molina observed. "Mrs. Lark had no way of knowing if you left and returned sometime in the night."

"Okay. I've got the books. You can give me a surprise quiz on any of the contents."

"That's hardly necessary, although it might be fascinating."

Molina nodded at her partner to close his notebook. "At this point you are not a suspect, despite your ardent attempts to implicate yourself."

Temple strangled another inarticulate cry of protest.

"But don't leave the hotel," she added, as if Temple were about to.

"Ladies." She dismissed the other two with a nod.

Temple was planning to scram with them, despite their betraying ways, when Molina caught her eye. Temple bowed to fate and stayed behind. Molina nodded her partner away.

They were standing nose to nose, if you could count Temple's nose reaching Molina's third blouse-button level.

Molina lowered her voice. "You know how I hate these particular murder cases."

"Ones with me in the vicinity?"

"That, too. But especially ones that occur where large groups of out-of-state people convene for a few precious days and then skedaddle. Ones where the victim and about—oh, two to twenty thousand other strangers—share some common, outré interest, where someone kills someone, and then they all leave town en masse. Except for the victim, of course."

"And maybe the murderer," Temple said brightly.

"And maybe the murderer." Molina crossed her arms again, never a good sign. "I want you to do something for me."

"I'm leaving. I'm leaving now. Not the hotel—just the . . . vicinity. I swear I'll stick with Electra and Kit all week and weekend. I'll go to the convention events, I'll keep my mouth shut and my eyes closed. I will hear no evil, see no evil, speak no evil. I just wanted a nice, relaxing time away from the home office. You won't even know that I'm here."

"No."

"No?"

"No. I *want* you to play amateur sleuth. I *want* you up to your anklebones in romance writers, and readers, and especially in Incredible Hulks."

"Hunks."

"Incredible Hunks. I want you to notice everything, talk to

everyone, bother everyone, annoy everyone. I want your little pug nose sniffing about the premises and the programming."

"I do not have a pug nose!"

"I do physical descriptions in my job. Trust me."

"It's retroussé."

"Retro-what?"

"Retroussé. That is French for turned up. Piquant. Pointed. A pug nose is thick and bulbous. Ugh. Mine is narrow and refined."

"And French, apparently. All right, Miss Barr, stick your narrow, piquant little nose wherever you like, but if you smell anything suspicious, report it to me."

"You're . . . deputizing me?"

"Please. I'm offering you a deal. I will not report your liaison with the victim to any interested parties at the Circle Ritz you might not want to know about it, on the condition that any results of your congenital nosiness come home to me? Got it?"

"Absolutely."

Temple had never received so clear an assignment to meddle.

Chapter 14

Every Little
Breeze . . .

I stand inside the Crystal Phoenix, bothered, bewildered and be-
witched. Everywhere I see women scurrying somewhere, tote
bags like Miss Temple carries swinging on their arms. Every bag
bears an animal warning sign: G.R.O.W.L.

Luckily, the sentiment is written, not articulated.

I am also bemused by the presence of several large gentleman
who appear to be hard up for clothing, such as shirts, and for
grooming assistance, such as barbers. I like to consider myself
the hairiest dude on any scene (in both senses of the word). I am
mightily miffed that these ponderous dudes are attracting all the
attention, not to mention that they are often in danger of squash-
ing me underfoot like a rug.

Given that Miss Van von Rhine has gone to the trouble to in-
stall a magnificent carpet of golden phoenixes on a navy background—which reminds me of carp afloat on a true-blue sea—it
is most inconsiderate of these overblown dudes to keep their
noses in the air and ignore it, particularly when I am on it.

Although I overheard news of bloody murder on my arrival, crime is not foremost on my mind for once. Dead bodies, particularly the human kind, are a ducat a dozen here in Las Vegas, but the living presence of the Divine Yvette is a true rarity.

From the first, one fact has not escaped me: Miss Savannah Ashleigh, such as she is, will be involved in the conference. Thus I have a priceless opportunity to pay my respects to my lost love. However, this opportunity is looking more like an obstacle. Through relentless eavesdropping, I discover that Miss Savannah Ashleigh will not be required to honor the premises until the date of the actual pageant, four long days and nights away.

Yet the redoubtable (and poutable) Miss Savannah had checked in two days ago. (In plenty of time, I note, to kill the Hiawatha on horseback. Talk about a late entrance!) I would like nothing so much as for Miss Savannah Ashleigh to be found suspect of a small murder or two, as she stands in the path of my true love and I. The Divine Yvette would not dream of forsaking her spoiled and selfish mistress so long as breath still stirs the movie star's formidable frontage. Although I do not wish to see the Divine Yvette disappointed in her human, who is all that she knows of the species, I *would* like to see Miss Savannah Ashleigh all alone on a slow boat to China with a bad case of ptomaine poisoning.

Of this ignoble desire I must not breathe the tiniest meow to the Divine Yvette. She is most solicitous of her mistress, which I find commendable but wrong-headed.

When on the trail of a human, I must use all my wit and wisdom. When I hunt one of my own ilk, I need only the sensitive services of my olfactory apparatus. This is not as fancy a device as it sounds. I merely apply nose to the toes and sniff along the floor until I catch whiff of an appealing scent. In a hotel full of human beings, this is a rarer phenomenon than one would think.

I decide to search the hotel's public areas first. Knowing Miss Savannah Ashleigh, she may not be required to perform her duties until later, but she is sure to loll about in case an idle spotlight should turn her way. I have never seen such a camera-ready woman in my nine lives.

This is what finally leads me to the back of the hotel, where I find an army of photographers and videotapers shooting a chorus line of unarmed (and even unclad) dudes by the swimming pool.

I wrinkle my nose against the overbearing scent of body oil and tanning lotions. Beneath the obnoxious fumes I do detect the signature odor of Miss Savannah Ashleigh, which is heavy on the spice and light on the nice. Then, as I trail unnoticed among the greenery caressing the hotel walls, a vagrant breeze (is there any other kind?) wafts my nostrils with the near presence of my dear departed.

A few eager wiggles through the canna lilies, a brief belly-crawl along the sandy dirt in which they are planted, and I find myself nose-to-Naugahyde trim with the Divine Yvette's pink canvas carrier. This portable habitation sits beside a director's chair with matching pink canvas seat and back. The name emblazoned on the chair is MISS SAVANNAH ASHLEIGH.

No Miss Savannah Ashleigh is about, however, and the chair is empty. I hope that is not the case with the carrier, but there is only one way to find out: basic detective work, i.e., I must see for myself.

I cautiously lift my head to the mesh screen and inhale the soft, powdery scent of my lady fair. As in a mirror, on the other side of the screen I see a dainty head rise. Then I am the beneficiary of a sharp swat across the kisser.

"Hey! What is the meaning of that?"

Silvery whisker tips pierce the mesh. "Do I know you?" a female voice demands in a low, throaty growl.

Well, this is a fine how-do-you-do . . . not! I trouble to make myself into a feline welcome mat and I get stepped on. Could I have the wrong carrier?

"How soon they forget," I lament under my breath.

"They?" The occupant sounds as miffed as a celibate mink in mating season. "You dare to include me with others of your acquaintance?"

"I did not lump you in with the hoi polloi when I rescued you from the Stripper Killer," I remind her.

A genteel sniff tells me the Divine Yvette is beginning to take herself too seriously. "I believe that you were most interested in saving your roommate in that instance. I was perfectly safe in my carrier in the other dressing room."

"We can debate the past later. Are you not glad to see me?"

"I have not 'seen' you yet. Come closer."

"No more swats."

"Certainly not! A person in my position must be careful, especially when my mistress is thoughtless enough to leave my carrier on the ground, where just anybody might stroll up. I was not sure of your identity . . . it is Midnight Louie?"

"In purrson," I reply in my best Bogart rumble.

This time she looks before she leaps to conclusions and puts her delicate pink nose to the mesh. I gaze into her long-lashed, half-closed eyes as we go nose-to-nose for a few stolen sniffs.

"You have still been filching carp, I notice," the Divine Yvette comments, wrinkling her nose.

Dames! A dude cannot do guy things without being called to task for unpleasant smells. The female of the species will eat the fish when it is presented to her already filleted, just don't let her see too much of the capture and processing.

"Not recently," I say.

"Hmmm," she answers skeptically. (Dames are also loath to believe a dude when he speaks the truth about his whereabouts and activities.) "Perhaps I notice because I eat only one type—and brand—of food exclusively."

"And what is that?" I ask pleasantly. I would not be surprised to hear that it is truffles, an expensive delicacy rooted out by French pigs. Most French culinary delicacies would be best given to French pigs, in my experience. I do not care for tripe, brains, eel or ox tongue. Yet I know that the easily impressed will swallow any such nonsense if it is introduced as French in origin. I am afraid that the Divine One is a victim of her mistress's snobbery. "What is the tidbit of your choice?"

"Free-to-be-Feline," she announces.

I blanche. The Divine Yvette should be nibbling curled baby shrimp on jellied flounder, oysters Rockefeller, scallops on the half-shell—not those Army-green pellets full of organically grown, vitamin-enhanced pre-processed health food!

"You like that stuff?" I demand. I may have to revise my opinion of my darling's divinity.

She shrugs, a gesture that charmingly ruffles the luxurious collar of silver fur covering her neck and shoulders. "I have to like it, *mon ami.* I am the Free-to-be-Feline spokescat."

I hardly hear her answer. That *"mon ami"* has sped straight to my heart. I can hardly hear over its wild beating. Or did she say "bon ami"? "Good friend" is not as intimate as "my friend." Also, "bon ami" is the name of a common household cleanser. Does she mean that I am only fit to wipe up the dirt that she has walked in? These pedigreed dames are a pain in the neck to interpret.

"You said something, *ma cherie*?" Let her wonder what I really mean by that!

"I said that I have an exclusive contract with Free-to-be-Feline. My mistress came to the Crystal Phoenix early so that I could shoot my first commercial. They say that I will be a household name."

Now the wax is out of my ears and the ice is forming on my heart. "You are going to be a television star?"

"So they say. Frankly, I abhor the spotlight. It is hot, noisy work, Louie. But my mistress can obtain no film work lately, and someone must earn the upkeep on her Malibu beach house. You do not think that Miss Savannah Ashleigh would stoop to hostessing an Incredible Hunk pageant unless matters were serious, do you?"

Actually, I think that Miss Savannah Ashleigh would stoop to a good deal in the pursuit of a spotlight, and probably has, if rumors of her early blue-movie days are true. But I do not wish to disabuse the Divine Yvette of her commendable loyalty to her less-than-commendable mistress.

"I am sorry that you are forced to labor for a living," I say. "Especially when it means chowing down quantities of that awful Free-to-be-Feline. Can you not employ a body double to do the dirty work?"

"Alas, no one can be found that precisely duplicates my coloration and bearing."

Amen, say I, and I have seen a few.

"Also," she goes on, "I like Free-to-be-Feline."

"You like it! But it is dreck!"

"What is 'dreck,' Louie? I am not familiar with the term."

In my amazement, I have allowed a crass street expression to pass my lips, and I do my best to repair the damage to the Divine Yvette's sheltered little ears. "Dreck is . . . distasteful stuff, like" —I cannot think of anything one could cite in polite company that would convey how awful Free-to-be-Feline tastes—"like lizard droppings."

"Oh! What a vulgar thought. I will do my best to forget it. I have other things on my mind today, anyway. I am soon to meet my co-star."

"Co-star? Oh, you mean the human who pours the drool . . . that is, the culinary delicacy, into your bowl. Usually only the feet and hands are visible. Perhaps your mistress could land that part. You could refuse to cooperate with any other pourer until the producers get the idea."

"How ingenious you are, Louie! It is true, now that I am to be a star, that I should show some temperament. However, my co-star is not human."

"Not human? Is this an advertisement where an alien descends and deposits a wad of Free-to-be-Feline before your very nose? I find that appropriate."

"No, no UFOs, Louie. Just the spokescat from the company's other line of food products."

"Other line?" An awful suspicion stirs my soul.

Just then I hear approaching feet and dive back into the canna lilies. The Divine Yvette is no dummy. She curls up in her carrier as if nothing had happened, and indeed it has not.

My midday naps in Miss Temple Barr's closet have made me an expert in the styles and scents of human shoes. A jazzy high-heeled gold lamé pair can only shod the feet of Miss Savannah Ashleigh. Beyond a second, hard-shelled carrier that has been deposited beside the Divine Yvette's home-away-from-home, I spy some stodgy men's wingtips that speak of points east, like Chicago or New York.

All these feet are shuffling around, except Miss Savannah Ashleigh's, which are doing tricks, such as arching the foot and rubbing a toe on the back of her shapely calf or on the calf of one of the wingtip wearers. Again her breathy voice is wafted down to me on a passing breeze.

"We must keep Yvette in the shade. I do not want her getting a freckle on her nose, although I suppose we could consider it a beauty mark. It was good enough for Marilyn. . . . Is this the other animal?"

The words, "other animal," are pronounced in a distasteful tone I cannot quarrel with, for I suspect the identity of the Divine Yvette's performing partner sight unseen. Sometimes it is most depressing to be able to put two and two together. One comes up the odd man out. I have no doubt that I will momentarily be in this most unhappy position.

"Yes, Ma'am," answers a fellow whose voice has all the manly resonance of a hornpipe.

"Well, remove him from that . . . box. I want to keep Yvette protected in her carrier until we know he is reliable."

"He is very well trained, Miss Ashleigh."

"Still, I don't want that brute attacking Yvette for some reason. She is very sensitive."

"Perhaps she will not work out for the commercial, then."

"Nonsense. My Yvette always rises to an occasion. Still, I intend to see that nothing disturbs her. She is not some trickster cat bailed out of an animal shelter at the eleventh hour and kept by an animal trainer. She is a personal pet, as well as the result of decades of the most persnickety breeding."

"Yes, Ma'am," says Mr. Macho.

So I see him bend down to unleash the fate I fear awaits the Divine Yvette. The carrier's metal grill (how well I remember the other side of that noxious barrier a time or two when Miss Temple got carried away and carted me off to the House of Dr. Death for some unfortunate procedure or the other) opens. I see a garden-variety pink nose poke through. This is not the delicate shell-pink that adorns the Divine Yvette's face. This is a big, bold tongue-colored nose in a big, bold face of yellow stripes, which clashes with the nose. Pink and yellow. Ick! A long, horizontally striped leg thrusts from the carrier. Then another. Soon all of the Divine Yvette's co-star is catching rays.

"He is so big," Miss Savannah Ashleigh complains. "And . . . yellow. And . . . striped. I had hoped for a more elegant cat."

"He makes a hundred-fifty thou a year," Yes-man answers, with feeling. "I guess he does all right. He has his own fan club, calendar and video. We plan to release a 'Cat Carols' cassette for Christmas, featuring his meows and a chorus of sleigh bells. Your Yvette will be lucky if she tickles the public fancy like our plain old alleycat Maurice here."

I am still toting up the probable dimensions of the fellow's financial empire when out slips the name I love to loathe. Maurice. Of course it is he. What other commercial cat is so infamous? That lolling-about, unemployed camera-hog who represents Yummy Tum-tum-tummy feline food. Have you ever heard a more obnoxious brand-name? All this, plus a singing career. It is enough to make an ordinary alley-serenader, well . . . spit hairballs from here to Needles.

Maurice stretches until his belly touches concrete, then ambles past Miss Savannah Ashleigh's trim ankles (though they are not so well-turned as my roommate's). He gives her the brush-past, then sways over to the main event: the Divine Yvette's carrier. After an initial sniff along the side seams, he pokes his big mug up against the screen.

The Divine Yvette peeks through. I see the blue-green glimmer of her gemlike orbs.

She reaches up a silver velvet paw.

Then she swats Maurice across the intrusive nose, and follows up with a savage hiss.

That is my girl!

Chapter 15

Hocus Focus

Temple came to a dead stop just inside the hotel lobby, her mind in public-relations brochure mode:

Picture this.

Picture walking into a Las Vegas hotel and casino.

Picture twinkling lights and clinking slot machines.

Picture Frank Sinatra leaning over a lobby balcony to greet the clientele.

Caesars Palace, you say? The new MGM Grand? Some other high-profile Strip hostelry?

No.

This is the only Las Vegas establishment to bear a woman's name, a woman whose forty years of film, song and dance put the E in entertainment of the old school: glitz before grunge, talent before attitude.

Aha! Shirley MacLaine, you think.

No, it isn't that Rat Pack token woman of yesteryear turned New Age guru. It's—

"Debbie Reynolds's Hotel and Hollywood Museum," Temple mused aloud as she and Kit gazed up at Frank, who gazed right back without blinking a blue glass eye. "Why are we meeting your author friends so far from the Crystal Phoenix?" she asked her aunt.

"Security," Kit said. "This hotel is off the Strip, so convention-goers aren't as likely to wander over here. We want our instant little focus group to feel free to dish dirt. Besides, the group will adore touring the hotel's Hollywood costume museum after our little café-au-lait conference."

"I see," Temple said, though she didn't, "but here, even the walls have ears." She gestured to other celebrities lining the upper level.

"But *deaf* ears." Kit glanced at the well-attired mannequins. "Isn't that the Duke? In a tux? He really didn't have to dress for us."

"This is neat." After gazing up at the celebrity mannequins lit by a triad of massive crystal chandeliers, Temple returned her attention to the first floor, wading through a moat of slot machines toward a hallway guarded by Mae West in full feather. "Hollywood Walk of Fame," a light-bedazzled marquee above their heads announced. At the hall's opposite end, the glitz was multiplied by a theater marquee whose round flashing lights beckoned like Broadway on a Saturday night. Cardboard cutouts of Laurel and Hardy on the left wall welcomed them with hats in hand.

"I knew you'd like it." Kit hurried after. "I was only guessing what it would be like, though. You haven't been here before, really? And you a resident!"

"I can't keep up with everything in this town. When's lunch?"

Kit squinted at the thin, elegant watch decorating her wrist. "The others are coming in three different cabs, so as not to stir suspicion. Should be along any minute."

"You're sure these security measures are required?"

"Absolutely. The Phoenix is crawling with media and other eager ears ready to overhear and report. You can't expect our . . . expert witnesses to spill their guts when they might end up on Candid Camera, or—even worse—that tacky tabloid TV show *Hot Heads.*"

Temple shook her own hot head of blistering red hair. "I can't believe that romance writing is such a dangerous game."

"A day ago, who would have thought cover modeling could be so lethal?" Kit demanded.

Temple nodded, ambling down a memory lane of memorabilia. The film-strip design carpeting detoured to a rest room alcove, where signatures of the kitsch and famous covered the walls. A cardboard-cutout Ann Miller lurked on a stairway landing, wearing mostly fishnet hose and a mile-wide smile.

"So these are all authentic props and costumes," Temple noted. "I always wondered where that stuff ended up."

"Sold at auction and separated," Kit said. "The idea here is to bring it all back together. I bet you're really aching to see Dorothy's ruby red slippers. A pair is on display here."

"Truly?" Temple brightened. "The ones on the MGM mannequin are contemporary copies, because the actual shoes used in the movie are too valuable to set out to steal. Poor Toto was dognapped a few months ago."

"Somebody nipped Toto?" Kit's deep voice reached a soprano squeak of indignation. "Is there no respect?"

"Not in Las Vegas, and not in New York City either, I bet."

Kit shrugged, then looked past the rail dividing the hallway from the restaurant, a low-lit cavern whose dark walls showcased black-and-white photos of famous film faces of the forties.

"Perfect!" Kit clapped her hands with delight. "We can snag that huge back-corner banquette, then conspire in utter privacy. Maybe Humphrey Bogart will stop by our table and ask Sam to play 'As Time Goes By.' "

"And maybe Ingrid Bergman will ask us the way to the ladies' room."

"Oh, pooh, Temple. You have no romance in your soul. Sometime this weekend I'll have to find out why over a mai tai or another equally tongue-loosening concoction."

"If we want that booth, we had better sit down."

"Right."

They made for the entrance and its waiting hostess, but Temple stopped before they could be seated.

"Is that really Tallulah Bankhead's trunk?" she asked.

"Absolutely," the attractive blond cashier confirmed from behind her glass case of sundries.

Despite the initials T.B. emblazoned on its brown side—"My initials," Temple whispered to Kit—the trunk was a low-profile prop compared to the glamorous babes atop it. Suspended in gaudy gowns like a pair of lifesize puppets, which they were, were Jim Henson's imperious Miss Piggy and Wayland Flowers's brass-mouthed Madame, both in hot pink and ostrich plumes. Behind them was a wall mural of a 1930s Hollywood studio "class photo," filled with famous faces named Astaire and Gable and Garland.

"I Iiiiiii," Temple said, the windmills of her mind visibly churning in double time.

"We need to be seated." Kit dragged her away from the exhibit as if she were a dawdling child.

"Yes, mother," Temple mocked as they wove through the intervening tables to the gigantic corner booth of tufted red leather.

"The rest of our party should be along shortly," Kit told the hostess, who left the requested six menus before returning to her post. "Temple! What is it?"

"Just a wicked idea. Maybe your focus group can help me with it after lunch."

"I need to fill you in on who we'll be seeing."

"Right." Temple set the menu aside and folded her hands on her lap like a good child.

"You wanted a crash course in who's who and what's what in the romance world, so I've recruited—not the best and the brightest—but the nicest and the knowingest. The stars are on a plane of their own and may be nice enough, but simply no longer share the common interests of the rest of us grunion struggling for our places on the sand. The raw beginners are eager, but naive as newts. What I've assembled is a panel of midlist experts. You do know what midlist is?"

"Not yet bestselling, name-brand authors; steady performers with potential."

"Very good, my dear. Doing PR for the American Booksellers Association convention was an instant education."

"Actually, I learned all that stuff from meddling in the murder investigation."

"We do not ask how, just how much. Anyway, what you'll meet here is a cross-section of the heart of the romance industry, pardon the expression. I know them from other conventions. We've all been around the publishing track a few times, and we're not about to be pushed off the merry-go-round. Still, we're not megastars. We have concerns about the field and what's happening in it, and to us."

"Sound like experts to me." Temple lifted her water glass in a toast.

Kit chinked rims with her own water goblet. "Just don't be surprised to find that feelings run high. For many of these women, this is their livelihood."

"Is that enough to kill for, do you think?"

"You mean . . . one of us might have murdered Cheyenne?" Kit looked truly shocked.

"Suspects come in all shapes, sizes and sexes."

"I believe that there are only two sexes, niece."

"Not in Las Vegas," Temple said firmly. Her blue-gray eyes intensified to the color of navy slate. "Say, do you suppose those prize shoes might be on a drag queen at Gays 'n' Dolls downtown? Who would ever think to look for them on a size twelve foot?"

"A transvestite revue? Not on your life. Those shoes would no more deign to dance to the wrong number than Dorothy's ruby slippers would shoe the tin woodman. Now, get your mind off fancy footwear and on the murder case at hand, because here come my body of experts."

Temple looked across the dim room. A clot of colorful convention-going garb ranging from linen blazers to cotton print dresses to hand-painted jersey sweat suits were milling beside Miss Piggy and Madame. If they were hoping to disguise their origin, they were off to a bad start. Each clutched a black canvas bag emblazoned with G.R.O.W.L. and hot-pink hearts.

In moments the hostess had led the four newcomers to the

banquette. All one could hear was the squeak of cushions as they slid behind the table on both sides of Temple and Kit.

Temple felt like a kid trapped mid-seat in a carnival thrill ride. On the one hand, she was cushioned from all exterior shocks; on the other, she was in danger of being crushed by her human shock absorbers.

They accomplished the business of ordering by calling for two large pizzas and ice tea. The waitress bustled away after warning them the pizzas would take twenty minutes.

"No problem," Kit said. "We have lots to talk about." She began with introductions. "Temple is my niece and totally trustworthy." (Temple thought that was a nice thing to say, especially since they had just met.) "The lady on the far left is Doctor Susan Schuler." (Temple paused as she worried her glasses from the squashed tote bag beside her. A doctor—that was interesting. What kind?)

"Do you mind if I take notes?" Temple asked. "Not for . . . evidence or anything, but simply because I won't be able to tell you apart for a while."

"Hey, that's easy." A woman wearing a red, black and white flowered dress with puffed sleeves reached into the tiny patent leather bag trailing from a thin shoulder strap. "Slap on our convention badges, people, for Temple. We can remove them again in transit."

Soon Temple was gratefully studying the group's left shoulders.

"What kind of doctor are you?" she asked the woman named Susan, a low-key type who wore no makeup and whose short, permanent-waved hair was a greige Brillo pad.

"A gyn-ecologist," said a younger woman in a yellow linen blazer, with a teasing laugh.

"Not a medical doctor," Susan said tolerantly.

"Ph.D?" Temple asked with the awe of a lowly B.A.

"Right, in anthropology."

"Susan's written a book on the roots of romance fiction," Kit said. "*Alpha Men and Omega Women.*"

"Any relation to that bestseller, *Men Are from Mars, Women Are from Venus?*"

Everybody but Temple laughed. Susan reached into her canvas convention bag to extract a trade paperback with a plain-Jane cover.

" 'Fraid not, Temple. This is a scholarly tome from a university press, with a minuscule print run. Even persuading a university press to publish a book on a topic as despised as romance novels was a triumph."

Temple pulled over the book to riffle the pages. Chapter titles like "He Tarzan, You Jane" leaped out as they flashed by. Also "Wild West vs. Nest."

"It's yours." Susan's smile would melt nails and certainly dissolved any dry academic air clinging to her. "Instant background, and we academic press authors are pathetically happy to have people read our books, even if we have to give them away."

"Thanks. It looks fascinating—no, really! This chapter, "Hawks and Doves"—it sounds like a political thesis."

"Bless you! God knows I'd get more respect for analyzing dull matters like politics." Susan shook her curlicued head. "Hawks and doves are opposites, as they are in real life, but in romance novels the battle is the war between the sexes."

A jolly-looking woman with airy blond curls, wearing a nice, comfy knit pants outfit to disguise her nice, comfy expansive body, lifted a finger to pronounce: "*The Flame and the Flower*. Let us all bow our heads for a moment of silence."

Temple neither bowed nor kept the peace. "What does that mean?" she asked the blond grandmotherly type, whose nametag read LaDonna Morgan.

The other women laughed.

"It's a title," explained a sleek black woman of forty named Vivian Brown.

"*The* title," LaDonna corrected.

Even Kit had something to say on the subject. "The title that launched a thousand hips, so to speak. The first sexually explicit historical romance written by a woman."

"What about *Forever Amber*?" a woman named Lori asked. She had shining, long brown hair and a teenager's fresh-cream complexion, though she must have been Temple's age. Or more.

"A forerunner," Susan declared, "but not the true revolutionary work that Kathleen Woodiwiss's book was."

Temple watched the discussion, feeling that she was watching a tennis match from the much-confused point-of-view of the net.

"What do flames and flowers have to do with hawks and doves?" she wanted, very sensibly, to know.

"Titles," Susan explained. "The ever-important titles. The uninitiated sneer at what they see as stereotypical romance titles, not realizing the art of it. Oxymorons are *all* in the romance field."

"Oxymoron . . ." Temple was sure she had once known what that word meant, long ago and far away, in a college communications class in Minnesota. "Not something I put on an untimely zit, is it?"

"Nor is it an idiotic castrated bovine." Kit's overarticulated, prissy diction made everybody giggle.

"I think Kit is referring to what we call a plain bull with no balls in Missouri," LaDonna said.

"Is that why they call it the 'Show Me' state?" Lori threw in with a wicked grin.

"Oh, lawdy, we're gettin' bawdy." Vivian sighed. "Temple will think we're awful."

"You can't write about the world's most hilarious subjects— love, sex and marriage—without a sense of humor," Kit said. "And Temple has been in the thea-tuh, dahlings. Nothing shocks her."

"Not true," Temple objected. "I've just learned not to show it. Right now, I *am* shocked that, with so many writers present, no one has explained 'oxymoron' yet in a clear, one-syllable manner."

"We bow to academe." Kit nodded at Susan, who had watched the byplay with a smile.

"The textbook definition is more confusing than Kit's, believe it or not: an oxymoron is 'a rhetorical figure in which an epigrammatic effect is created by the conjunction of incongruous or contradictory terms,' for example, 'a mournful optimist.' "

"Get that woman a copy editor! Simplify, simplify." LaDonna hooted, then put her hands on her ample hips. "I've always wanted a rhetorical figure, though."

"Not to mention an epigrammatic effect," Vivian added.

"That would be LaDonna in a Wonderbra," Lori teased her full-figured senior.

"Seriously." Susan smothered laughter in the stiffening corners of her mouth. "Seriously speaking, romance novels heighten the differences between the sexes before they resolve them. If literal oxymorons aren't used in titles, certainly suggestive opposites are employed. In these metaphors—we do all know what that means?—the man is the wild, untamed, consuming masculine element and the woman is the fragile, lovely, preserving or enduring element. Flame. Flower. *The Flame and the Flower.*"

A moment's silence held as each recalled a favorite, illustrative title.

"*The Leopard and the Lark,*" Sylvia put in.

"*The Hawk and the Dove,*" said Lori, nodding.

" 'The Tiger and the Titwillow,' " Temple interjected. "Or, with a bow to our new friend the oxymoron, 'The Bull and the Buttercup.' I get the picture, ladies."

"That's just one pattern of title." Susan was still grinning at Temple's impudent images.

Temple frowned in suspicion. "Why does the symbol representing the man always come first?"

"Because he gets his in the end," LaDonna said.

"What does he get?"

"He gets the girl," said Kit.

"He gets domesticated. Tamed." Susan sounded fully academic now. "That's why the titles exaggerate gender differences. That's where the oft-satirized 'Sweet, Savage' school of romance titles came from, and phrases like 'devil's angel' or 'steel and silk.' Don't let the namby-pamby female symbols fool you. Romances ultimately empower the woman. By succumbing to the force of masculine passion, swaying with the sensual storm, the heroine subdues the hero's lone-wolf ways and transforms him from demon lover into loving husband, helpmate and, ultimately, father."

" 'The Wolf and the Willow,' " Temple summed up sourly. She

wasn't in the mood for the male-female gavotte or happy endings. "Okay. Granted that romance novels are complex blends of mythological models and pop culture, where do the cover guys fit in?"

"Between the sheets," impish Lori suggested, dimpling like a Regency Miss.

"Off the cover!" Vivian's fist pounded the tabletop.

"Hear, hear!" came from Kit.

"Now that's an interesting phenomenon," Susan began. "In the beginning—"

"In the beginning the heroine was the cover focus, and the hero was just a handsome prop," Vivian noted. "That was the heyday of the 'bodice ripper' covers that gave the genre such a bad name. Remember the heroine with her hair flowing over her shoulders and her front falling out of her dress?"

"The *Love Is a Wild Assault* days," Susan agreed. "Don't look askance at me, Temple, there really was a romance novel titled that. As women readers became more open about what they wanted in romance novels, the heroine went from a passive, reluctant object of unwanted masculine onslaught to—"

"An adoring, willing, ogling prop at the feet of the new romance cover star—the mighty hero." Kit shook her head.

Temple smiled. "I take it some of you dislike the new hero-central covers."

"Some of us," Vivian said, "have loathed the old clinch covers and the intermediate 'dueling cleavage' covers of bare-chested hero and half bare-breasted heroine all along. Now we loath the newest wrinkle: he alone in all his muscular, hairy glory, although he can't have hair on his face or his chest, for God's sake. Male models are waxed and air-brushed into unreality just like female ones. And, in the process, somehow women have been pushed off center stage in what's considered a women's genre, written by women for women."

"Oh, Viv, you're just griping because you have a master's degree in history to protect you from intimations of sleaze."

LaDonna's face beamed as the waitress wafted a large round pizza tray onto her end of the table. "Face it, honey. Hunks are in, so we writers might as well enjoy the view. Besides, it's liberating to have men as sex objects for a change."

"What do you think?" Temple asked Susan as the second pizza tray hovered and then descended like an aluminum UFO in their midst.

The group separated their chosen slices from the artery-clotting herd and installed them on bread plates. Discussion stalled as cheese extended into thin strings and knives excised edible bites.

Susan thoughtfully nibbled a sauce-gored slice. "The new covers offer positives and negatives. Lots of romance covers nowadays have beautifully embossed and foiled fronts with more mainstream and neutral subject matter: flowers, fabric, precious objects. The front cover opens to an interior step-back painting: the old clinching couple—or the man alone in a few cases."

"Now *those* you could take on the subway, or a bus." Sophisticated Vivian, with her black blunt-cut bob, managed to fit her comment in between swallows. She was attacking her pizza like Attila the Hun.

"But hunks sell books," LaDonna insisted between bites.

"Do they?" Kit was breaking her pizza slice into tiny pieces with fork and knife. "Sure, Fabio was a twelve-day wonder, but will anyone pull down the attention and the money the first and most famous male cover model did?"

"Even if they don't match his take, so what?" LaDonna answered. "The Incredible Hunk contest is a big chance for these guys. Most are models who wanna be actors, or actors who wanna be models. Not only is there a little barbell money in cover modeling, but the hunk contest itself is fodder for tabloid TV, so whoever is named Incredible Hunk gets a lot of exposure."

"I guess." Kit rolled her eyes at the unconscious double entendre. "Possible calendars, game show appearances, film jobs, syndicated TV show parts, maybe even a stab at the America's most famous houseguest/hostile witness title."

"Ooh, what a great idea!" Lori's eyes were shining to match her glossy hair. "Kato as an IH contestant."

"Which one do you have in mind?" Vivian asked in an indifferent drawl. "The dude or the dog?"

Temple wanted the talk back on track. "Is that kind of media exposure worth killing for?"

That stilled knives and forks and mouths. Kit leaned close to mouth dramatically: "Motive Number One: Model Competition."

"Fame and fortune is always a worthy motive," Vivian said.

"So a rival hunk could have killed Cheyenne?"

"Sure." LaDonna shrugged. "Except one dead dude wouldn't guarantee another the title. The judging is honest, as far as I know."

"There are early favorites," Vivian objected. "You know that, LaDonna. You've seen the guys chat up the convention-goers. Prince Charmings by the pack. They charm them, then sweep them off their feet—"

"Is that what it's called?" Temple interjected. "Charming!"

"Temple was 'swept' by Fabrizio in the registration line," Kit explained.

"That Fabrizio." Lori sounded disgusted. "The original Mr. Unoriginal. He comes on as all muscle-man, but he only picks up the petite women. What a wimp! Fabio should sue."

"What makes Fabio king of the Prince Charmings?" Temple asked.

"He was the first romance cover model to emerge as a personality in his own right. Then he won the first cover-hunk contest, parlaying it into international celebrity," Susan pointed out. "Is his career so different from what Arnold Schwarzenegger or any other muscle man since and before Johnny Weissmuller did? Only nowadays, a media muscleman can have his own profitable 900 line, his romantic music cassettes, etcetera, ad nauseum. Thanks to romance novels selling forty-nine percent of all paperback book titles, he can be marketed directly to women without making a single Hollywood film."

"Whoa!" Temple's attention had really caught fire. "Forty-nine percent of all paperback books? Does that include nonfiction?"

"You bet." LaDonna crumpled her paper napkin into a lump like a bloody tomato and threw it onto the empty pizza platter.

"Why aren't you all rich then? Or are you?"

Amid hoots of laughter, Kit leaned close to whisper: "Motive Number Two: the Woman Scorned."

"Many are called, but few are chosen," Vivian quoted acidly. "Women writing romances have always been the most exploited group in publishing. Our royalty percentages are often lower than those of other writers. Sometimes our very pen names are not our own to take to another publisher. We have been production-line workers expected to toil forever for minor rewards. And, of course, as the icing on our very plain cake, we get no respect for what we do. Romance novels are just silly women nattering on, especially embarrassing when we write about sex without using the clinical, unemotional prose male writers have institutionalized since Hemingway was immortalized, to make men feel good about being afraid to feel anything." She paused to catch an indignant breath. " 'The earth moved.' Really captures the moment, doesn't it, ladies? Hell, Hemingway was just too uncertain of his masculinity to convey more than terse little nothings about sex."

"My land o' Dixie!" Kit fanned a hand before her face, a swooning southern belle in intonation as well as gesture. "Our little Vivian is shorely all fired up about that most unsuitable topic!"

"Kit's got it," Susan said. "What really makes the male-oriented world of publishing and criticism uneasy about romances is that they present a female quest in female terms. Every young girl who enters the dating game perceives that it's one she can lose terribly. She bears the greatest consequences of sexual activity: pregnancy and loss of reputation, ergo self-esteem. How can she learn to be sexual without being betrayed by her body and the society that demands such an impossible role of her? Virginal but desirable. Sexuality without experience. Eternal love discovered without trial and error."

"Too true," Temple said.

"And now," Vivian put in, "romance novels are the focus of national media attention, and do we get a more enlightened, less sexist, revised view of their underlying issues? No, we get swooning features on cover hunks, which makes our work look even less socially relevant."

LaDonna put down her ice tea with emphasis. "What's even worse, and what drives me nuts, is that quarter-of-a-million deal Fabrizio made to 'write' a series of books. Makes it look like there's nothing to writing a romance. And we all know who's really writing those Fabrizio books—an underpaid, unsung female romance writer. I wonder how Sidney Sheldon would like it if the cover models for his heroines made oodles more money than he did. Wouldn't put up with it for a nanosecond."

"Celebrity authors have always been part of publishing," Kit interjected a little more coolly. "I saw an old book tie-in to Mary Pickford. Gypsy Rose Lee wrote a couple of ghosted mysteries decades ago, and we all know that some celebrity names on mystery and science fiction novels are fronts for the anonymous real writer who produces them."

"Those unsung writers get more ghostwriting than they do for their own books, or they wouldn't take on the work," Lori pointed out.

"And they'll continue getting less money for their work if publishers keep hiring the rich and famous as fronts instead of nurturing real writers' careers." Vivian sat back with an indignant whoosh of the padded vinyl banquette seat for punctuation.

"Oh, please!" LaDonna's eyes rolled over the tops of her half-glasses. "When have writers ever been nurtured? We have to fight for our books, our careers and our survival. If you wanted nurturing, you should have enrolled in kindergarten."

"So . . . who's angriest about the new prominence of cover hunks?" Temple asked.

A moment's silence while mental wheels turned.

"Sometimes even the biggies aren't too fond of the trend." Lori said. "I heard that Mary Ann Trenarry threatened to leave Bard Books when they signed up Fabrizio for all of her future and re-issue covers."

"At her career stage, it doesn't matter what they put on her books."

"It does to her. She's been a vocal spokeswoman for the redeeming social value of romance novels, and of her books in particular. This Fabrizio deal has her chewing royalty statements."

"What about the husbands?" LaDonna asked suddenly.

"Huh?" everyone said.

"Temple asked who was angry about the cover hunks. What about the husbands who have to hear about the 'Tantastic Fabrizio' and his ilk?"

"Whose husbands?" Kit wanted to know. "Readers' or writers'?"

"Both, I suppose," LaDonna said. "Maybe especially the husbands of prominent fans, the ones who organize the hunks' fan clubs. They sometimes get to work with them one on one. Most husbands aren't used to competing with perfect media models like women are."

"I did hear something." Lori looked both eager and reluctant.

"Tell us!" several urged.

"That's what we're here for," Vivian pointed out. "To pass secrets."

"And to keep them to ourselves." Lori fidgeted with her dark hair, twirling a long, straight tress on the instant roller of her forefinger. She sighed. "Remember that Ravenna Rivers went on that long book tour with the West Wind imprint's Homestead Man? I heard that afterwards she called him the 'Homestud Man.' "

Kit turned to Temple. "Romance publishers will hire a male model as an image/spokesman for a line of books nowadays. As a marketing tool, he gives all the authors' books a signature look; as a media draw on tours, he packs in readers who'd never show up for poor, unexciting us. West Wind's Homestead Man is Dwayne Rand, a Texas frontier type."

"That reminds me," Lori interjected with a giggle. "Ravenna also called Dwayne 'The Amazing Randy' after that tour. Do you think she was trying to hint at something?"

Kit ignored the gossip to further educate Temple on current romance-marketing ploys. "Picture Tom Selleck with Wild Bill

Cody lovelocks, but without the moustache. That's the Homestead Man."

"That's a tough assignment," Temple admitted, recalling her amazement at Max's rather understated ponytail. "And Tom Selleck without a moustache would be roast beef without mustard."

"No moustache," Kit said. "Sorry. Damn few moustaches for cover hunks; same reason newscasters don't wear them. Considered too ethnic."

"That Homestead Man!" Lori was continuing to gush. "He's a Dreamboat with a capital *D* as in Dishy. The rumor is that interviewers on Ravenna's tour assumed they were sleeping together. Her husband heard something and came running with his forty-five. For sure the tour was abruptly cancelled."

"I heard she had a book deadline to meet." Vivian looked troubled.

"The deadline was her husband's ultimatum, believe me," LaDonna added. "No more gadding about with good-looking guys."

"I don't know why Mr. Ravenna Rivers's so worried," Vivian put in. "Half of these guys could be allergic to women. Do you know how high the percentage of gay men is among bodybuilders, dancers, actors and models, ladies? Enough that straight men in those fields get a bit defensive about their occupations."

"Sexual preference doesn't matter," Dr. Susan said authoritatively. "It's the fantasy image that counts. Look, most of these women who go crazy over the male models know it's all show and no go. They're not expecting a relationship. It's an escape at a romance conference weekend, a goal to get an autograph or a photo taken with a cover man. Consider it a scavenger hunt."

"Hunting implies a prey," Temple pointed out. "What about Cheyenne? Any rumors about him?"

"Oh, that's such a shame!" LaDonna looked genuinely grieved. "Such a nice young guy. He was a favorite for the G.R.O.W.L. award at this year's pageant. That's the popular vote. And from what I heard, his routine would have been spectacular."

"He competed at a previous pageant?" Temple was surprised. She had figured Cheyenne for a local male stripper who was moonlighting, not a cover hunk wannabe of any seriousness.

"Sure. Last year in Atlanta."

"So some of the cover model contestants repeat from year to year?"

Lori nodded. "Just like in women's beauty pageants. It takes experience to win. Why? You don't look too happy."

"I'm not. If contestants repeat from year to year, then I assume conference attendees come back too?" They all nodded. "So we've got more potential here for relationships than I thought."

"What's so wrong about that?" LaDonna was defensive. "Sure, there are regulars, both onstage and off. Most of the same authors return every year too. It's our annual chance to chat and back-pat. This is a very mutually supportive field."

"And mostly female," Temple said. "Except for a few good men. And a very few tagalong husbands. Yet the authors are rivals as well as colleagues. Then add the heightened competition of the pageant. Like I said, this isn't just an annual convention, it's a traveling carnival of relationships. And I don't have to tell you romance writers what relationships can be in real life as well as in fiction."

"Murder," Vivian said slowly, nodding her head. "They can be murder."

The four conspirators left two by two, apparently convinced that there was less reason to hide their joint outing on the return cab ride.

"We'll say we were doing the Strip," Lori said.

Temple was reflective as Kit bid each one good-bye with thanks and promises of getting together later at the conference.

"Well?" her aunt demanded, scrambling to dig out and light a Virginia Slim. "Hey, don't look at me like that. This is a smoking section. I just refrained while the others were here."

"Why do people do to their relatives what they wouldn't to friends?"

"They expect relatives to understand." Kit's hands had frozen midway to her mouth, slender cigarette in one and upright, poised lighter in the other. "I can wait."

"No, go ahead. I owe you something for gathering the clan."

"What did you think of them?" Kit muttered through the act of inhaling.

"Great sources—do all writers gossip so much?"

"It's not gossip, it's networking in self-defense. Writers are isolated, yet we live and die by the publishing industry. So we grapevine like mad. Writers are also proud, so we tend not to reveal what we get for our books when the pay is squinky. When the advances get to the big time, everybody knows."

"It looks like I should talk to some of these writers with axes to grind. Any advice?"

"Just pass yourself off as a national media person and they'll slit their writers' wrists and let the ink run out. Not even bestsellers get enough attention."

"You were quiet during the gossip session."

"I listen, but I don't dote. We need to know what's going on for our own protection, but I don't enjoy hearing about other people's woes and throes. I can do all that stuff to the characters in my books. I did notice something when I came in a couple days ago, though."

"Did it involve Cheyenne?"

"How did you guess?"

"I listen, but I don't dote."

Kit stabbed her half-smoked cigarette out in the ashtray. "I did notice some cozy conferences between the deceased, as we say on the Perry Mason set, and the pageant hostess."

"The pageant hostess?"

"Yup, an anchor team of he/she emcees the event, reading unrehearsed witticisms with iffy timing. The host team changes from year to year, depending on where the conference is held, so there's no ongoing relationship between hosts and contestants to worry about. But I could have sworn that there was history between Cheyenne and this babe."

"Do you have the name, rank and serial number of the 'babe'?"

"A Hollywood type, naturally, Los Angeles being just a hop, skip and plane trip over the state line. So-called actress, once. You probably never heard of her, or saw her in anything, and can count yourself lucky. A real B-movie mama. One Savannah Ashleigh."

Ah, Sweet Mystery of Hystery

A laptop computer was such a tidy, nonthreatening machine.

Its small, empty screen seemed especially easy to fill. This made writing like walking—one step, one word, at a time, and you could see yourself getting somewhere. The reward . . . ah, maybe an award. Maybe a fat book contract and a river of royalties.

Anybody could write a romance.

The writer lifted poised hands above the keyboard like a musician about to throttle the Lost Chord out of an organ's resisting throat—it helped knowing how to type—and glanced at a stack of paperback novels on the hotel desk. The well-thumbed covers curled, making the hero's hands seem to rest audaciously higher than usual on the heroine's bared thighs.

That was the image to keep! All those steamy covers to inspire the all-important "sensual scene" that the Love's Leading Amateur contest required as the test of true romance.

Any idiot could write a romance.

As for the historical details, a few could be dropped in later. Details didn't matter, except in the "sensual scene."

The writer paused, then typed two words.

SAVAGE SURRENDER

The cursor sat blinking just beyond the final "R," a twinkling Tinkerbell of the keyboard. Did that title have fairy dust? Would it drive the contest judges to their knees? It was alliterative; it had sinuous initial esses, it implied torrid sex.

Now, what about the pseudonym? Every romance writer worth her salt had a catchy pseudonym. Watch this, cursor!

BY FELICITY FEVER

No. Too phony-sounding. And not "hot" enough, despite the last name. Another name. Something hot-sounding. Hot . . . something, hot . . . hot . . .

BY TAMALE TOWER

Naw. Somebody would probably pronounce the first name Ta-mail.

BY TEMPEST TOWER

There we go. Nothing to it. Writing these things is so easy it should be prosecutable. Big bucks, here I come!

Okay. Him. Think hunk. Highwaymen are always hot.

It was a bright and moonlit night.

Good start. Classic.

The road was a ribbon of moonlight over the purple moors.

Golly, this is easy. The words come flowing out like red-hot lava. People. Better get the people in there fast.

The

Captain? Too ordinary, too low on the totem pole. The Masked Avenger. The Maroon Mask. Not virile and dangerous enough. The . . . Demon of Devonshire. The Demon Dagger of Devonshire. There we go!

The man known as the Demon Dagger of Devonshire drew his namesake weapon while he waited for the carriage to arrive.

He didn't know which of the two treasures the vehicle carried was the more tempting: the five hundred thousand pounds for the Earl of Eddington's daughter's dowry, or the Earl's adored only daughter herself.

He could hardly wait to get his hands on them both.

An entire itty bitty, teeny weeny screen full, but, hey, War and Peace wasn't written in a day. Maybe we need some sort of detail here. Remember the tip sheets, hero is central.

He lifted his pistol barrel to brush the long, golden hair from his forehead as the wind rippled against his body like the expert fingers of his latest tart. Soon he would be back at the

Bow and Bottom . . . Bow and Bum . . . Bow and Arrow. Hell, forget bow. At the Bottle and Bun.

Bottle and Bun with his booty. And perhaps also with his beauty, if he deigned to despoil the lovely wench before shipping her back to her dastardly *dad . . .* father.

Long had the man known only as the Demon Dagger of Devonshire waited for this moment of revenge on the wicked Baron who had ruined all his relatives, turned the family estate into a sheep farm and stolen their famous and fabulous jewel, the

Pigeon's-blood . . . naw, too ordinary.

Peacock's-blood Blue Diamond of the Punjab!

Getting the hang of it, excuse the expression, Mr. Demon Dagger, you. Oops, that's right, mention danger, always sexy. Something like:

If the Crown captured the Demon Dagger of Devonshire, his long, trademark tresses should serve as his hangman's noose.

Huh? What does this mean? Dunno. Sounds good. Nobody reads these things for sense, anyway.

But the beautiful

Oh, boy. Beautiful . . . Hazel. Sounds like a witch. Ariania. There we go, just a bunch of vowels and a couple consonants. Good thing I've pounded out a few good lines in my day job.

Ariania was worth the price.

Dagger reined his coal-black steed to a stop in front of the carriage.

178 • Carole Nelson Douglas

"Stop!" he shouted at the shrouded coachman, waving his

Pistol? Were they used then? Just when is this? Horses, highwaymen. Somewhere in the seventeenth or eighteenth century, I guess. Check it later. Besides, this guy is Mack the Knife in a ponytail.

waving his long, silver dagger in the moonlight.

Great! And that big knife is a phallic symbol, too. What a genius. I should have done this years ago. Don't forget about that moonlight. Terrific detail.

"John, what is it?" trilled a melodious female voice.

The coachman huddled in his cloak, saying nothing.

That's the kind of minor character I like. Minds his own business and stays out of the way.

The Dagger nudged his powerful steed toward the coach

What the hell does a coach have, a door? Door will have to do.

door. The fair Airiania . . . Araniana

What the hell was that stupid name?

Araniana shook her long, coal-black hair as she pushed her head through the window in the door of the coach.

"Who are you?" she quavered, her eyes glistening in the moonlight as she gazed up at the tall, dark figure on the huge black horse with the long, flowing golden mane.

"You will never know my name," he spat in the dark. "But you will come to know me well. Where are the jewels?"

Yeah, where are they?

Chapter 16

Bugged Out

"Thanks for humoring me," Temple said as she and Kit headed for the checkout counter. "Now comes reason number two for being here. You pay the bill and distract the cashier while I do my undercover work."

Kit rolled her eyes, but accepted the two twenty-dollar bills Temple had pushed upon her and buried them in her handbag. By the time they reached the exit, she was digging for them again, apparently to no avail.

"Oh, dear." She slapped her purse atop the cashier's glass case and began rummaging frantically. "Do I have my glasses on?" she asked the fiftyish blonde behind the counter. "Maybe I'm blind and don't know it. I could swear I'd taken the bills out and—"

While Kit distracted the cashier with her blithering idiot act, Temple did the unthinkable and edged over to the helpless puppets. Both Miss Piggy and Madame were much bigger than they looked on TV, virtually life-size. Temple eased up Madame's ostrich-feather hem, then peered into the darkened tent within. No feet, ergo no hidden Austrian crystal-covered shoes.

Casting a glance around the restaurant, Temple ignored Kit's exasperated huffings and puffings behind her—her aunt was now systematically emptying the considerable contents of her purse on the countertop, managing to leave the money hidden inside. Madame was positioned higher than Miss Piggy, so Temple had to bend down to peer up the glamorous pig's skirt. Some might take her curiosity for evidence of a perverted act, but faint heart never won fair shoes.

"Wonderful, aren't they?" a woman's voice boomed behind her.

It wasn't Kit's or the cashier's.

Temple straightened in double time, quashing a shriek. "Yes, fabulous. And so . . . big. I was just wondering if they had . . . feet."

The restaurant hostess nodded. "Miss Piggy does. You can look if you like."

Well, thank you! Temple liked and did so. She unveiled pale, shapeless stuffed-cotton stumps, incapable of holding any article as exquisitely shaped as a Weitzman Austrian crystal slipper.

The hostess misinterpreted her disappointed sigh. "How sad that both of the men who created these wonderful characters died so young. That's why this hotel is also a show business museum, to keep the costumes and artifacts of these entertainment milestones alive. Have you seen the museum presentation yet?"

"No." Behind her, Temple heard the sound of twenty-dollar bills being rung up. The charade was over. "What's it like?"

"Wonderful! A multimedia experience in the theater section, with a tour of an adjacent costume display area. And, of course, other costumes are on display throughout the hotel."

Kit was jamming her goods back into her purse when Temple caught up to her in the hall.

"Hear that? We have to see the museum."

"Why?"

"Well, the shoes might be secreted in the show somehow."

"Honestly, Temple. You have a finder's fixation. If it isn't murderers, it's migrating shoes."

"It'll just take another half hour or so. Please!"

"Yes, dear child. But ever-practical auntie suggests we eyeball the free exhibits before we pop for the price of two tickets."

"You should love this, too. Costumes used to be your business."

"No, they used to be my props. What have we here?"

"Oh, lordy, I'm in love."

"Now, Temple, you know that shoes are your thing."

"My addiction has just expanded to black velvet evening capes covered in star-shaped rhinestones."

"Julie Andrews." Kit smiled nostalgically at the well-dressed mannequin in a glass case decorated with floating silver stars. "I saw her in *Camelot* when I first came to New York. Not Burton, though. He had already left the show and was off in Rome making headlines with Elizabeth Taylor during the *Cleopatra* filming."

"That was *eons* ago. I wasn't even born yet."

"I know. *Now* look at you. A woman grown and engaged in a madcap scavenger hunt for some Cinderella shoes."

Temple shrugged off her aunt's point. "At least I'm seeing parts of Vegas I might have missed otherwise. That's always good for business. Oh, look. Yummy red velvet."

Another mannequin, another era, another vintage film under glass.

"Betty Grable. She was old even before my time," Kit said pointedly.

"That's some long-barreled pistol in her hand. The MGM Grand pirates could have used it."

"And that's some holster on her hip. Kind of clashes with the thigh-high slit in her skirt."

"And here!" Temple had found an entire tableau under glass further down the hallway, and another spectacular red velvet gown. Mannequins of Debbie Reynolds and leading man Harve Presnell from *The Unsinkable Molly Brown* occupied a Victorian setting, backed by a portrait of them in their roles of Molly and her silver-striking husband.

In the upper reaches of the glass, the theater at the end of the tunnel cast reflections of its twinkling marquee lights, as it had all along the hallway.

"THE STAR THEATER." Temple turned to read the illuminated

sign, staring into a Milky Way of tiny lights. The entrance was a mini-Broadway theater front with all of its lights and action. " 'The Debbie Reynolds Show.' Smart to buy your own hotel/casino and perform there."

Kit, who had seen plenty of Broadway in the flesh and flash, was already heading back down the hall's other side. "Here's another classic."

"She was thin," Temple marvelled as she examined the street-length, copper-colored jacket-dress light and glittery enough to tap dance like a dream. "Eleanor Powell, *Broadway Melody of 1940.* Look at the military-style cap."

"War already."

Another forties-era tap dancing outfit, this one long-sleeved and short-skirted, clothed the next solo mannequin. Then came a full vignette of Tudor costumes, appropriately modeled by headless mannequins, since that was the time of Henry the Eighth, although the setting for this film had been France.

"*Diane,*" Kit read from the placard. "Must be Diane de Poitiers, a famous mistress of a French king. Don't remember the movie."

"No wonder you write historical romances! You certainly know the odd historic fact. These costumes are gorgeous. Imagine sewing on all those tiny pearls on velvet."

"Imagine gluing on all those tiny Austrian crystals on your mythical shoes."

"They're not mythical. That reminds me. We passed the Movie Museum marquee. Want to see? I'll treat."

They came out blinking, like all people who spend time in the dark looking at magical things. That was the underlying purpose behind the stupefying magic shows and chorus lines, behind the entire circus of magicians and the high-wire acts and the big cats. Las Vegas liked its visitors to come out blinking . . . and reel right into the oh-so-near gaming area, still believing in whatever magic they have seen. Call it Las Vegas Architectural Principles 101. No one can reach a hotel theater without walking through a gaming area.

Beyond the Hollywood Hall of Fame, only fifty feet away, waiting slot machines were wailing their metallic song. Temple and Kit paused in the hallway, getting their bearings.

"Wonderful stuff," Kit said. "It's even more wonderful to know we were seeing the real thing, that these artifacts are being preserved as well as presented. What did you think of the ruby slippers? They make the pussycat shoes pale by comparison."

"They're fabulous, but I never wanted to go home, like Dorothy did. I want to stay in Oz, thank you, and the pussycat shoes fit the territory better."

"That's a nice operation," Kit said in a theater insider's tone. "Not massive, but classy, the gray flannel surroundings and then lights up on the exhibits. High tech."

"High tech for what some might call old dreck."

"Not for long. People today realize that the labor that went into those long-ago costumes and props would be priceless now."

They were passing the restaurant area when Temple suddenly stopped and pointed to a glass case they had missed.

"Oh! It's the Santa suit from *Miracle on Thirty-Fourth Street*. Wine-red velvet and white fur. I had no idea Edmund Gwenn was so small! I mean, this costume really isn't big enough for a traditionally fat, jolly Santa."

"The camera probably did the rest of the costuming job for him. They all add twenty pounds."

"Is that really true?"

"Swear to Santa."

"Look!" Temple crouched at the foot of the glass case. "The carpeting is that white cotton Christmas batting that's sprinkled with silver glitter."

"Nice touch."

"No, don't you get it? It's all *lumpy* and *rumpled*. Suspiciously so. This would be a perfect place to hide the shoes! Could it be more apropos? Right at Santa's feet, get it? Merry Christmas."

"It's not anywhere near Christmas yet, Temple."

"Heck, department-store Christmas decorations go up after Halloween nowadays, and the ghosts and goblins are just around the corner. How can I get in that case?"

"This is one time you're stymied. You can't get through solid glass."

Temple pressed her lips together. "There's got to be a way." Suddenly she stood up and screamed.

Kit clutched her chest in the area of her heart, her eyes widening behind her glasses. Riveted passersby stopped to stare. And the nice cashier from the restaurant across the hall came racing over.

"Oh, my god," Temple was saying in a shaky voice.

"Are you okay?" the cashier asked.

Temple moved to support herself against the wall. Kit and the cashier crowded around, faces concerned.

"I don't want the . . . customers to hear," Temple told the cashier in hushed tones. "Is there any way to get in that Santa case?"

"Well, yes . . . but it's locked."

"You've got to get in there. I was looking at that wonderful costume and right there on the white stuff at the bottom was this horrible, huge cockroach. Crawling. Waving its feelers. They must have been two inches long." Temple shuddered. "It . . . crawled back under the batting, but it's going to give some other unlucky tourist a heart attack. Anyone older than I is in severe jeopardy." Given that Hollywood memorabilia attracted an older clientele, this was serious news.

"Cockroach?" The cashier glanced over her shoulder at the nearby restaurant. "I can't imagine . . . we've never had anything like that. I'll call the office immediately and they'll send someone to take care of it."

"I'll wait," Temple said in a tone of self-sacrificing heroism. "My conscience won't rest until I know that hideous bug is gone. Besides, I need to sit down and compose myself." The women followed her like Mary's little lambs to a hall bench. "Maybe you should make sure whoever comes doesn't kill it," she whispered to the cashier on second thought. "Someone sponsors a 'World's Largest Cockroach' contest, you know, and the hotel might win big if it entered that one."

The cashier grew even paler. The moment Temple and a solicitous Kit had been seated, she raced to the phone at her stand.

"Temple, that was outrageous," Kit said as soon as they were alone. "There was no cockroach."

"What will it hurt?"

"You really are amoral when it comes to a pair of shoes. Perhaps you need a twelve-step program."

"The only twelve steps I need are the ones I take in those shoes."

The cashier was back, leaning over Temple with a glass of lemonade.

"Thank you so much. Will it be . . . long?"

"No, no. They're sending a security guard to take care of it."

"Good thinking, given its size," Temple said, nodding somberly. She shuddered again, taking care not to spill any lemonade.

Not long after a new clink came from the slot machine area, toward them. It was accompanied by squeaking leather and the jingle of keys. The security guard, in medium blue uniform pants and shirt, billed cap and a utility belt hung with a beeper, walkie-talkie and a holstered gun, walked up to them.

"You the ladies who saw the . . . er, insect?" she asked.

Temple nodded, while Kit committed truth by doing and saying nothing.

"Don't you worry now. I'll get rid of it."

"You're not . . . squeamish?"

"Heavens to Betsy, no." The tall, solid, sandy-haired woman looked as if she could have driven a cab or even handled twenty-six three-year-olds on an outing.

She singled out a key tiny enough to open a suitcase from the riches on her crowded ring and bent down. The case unlocked at the rear of its base.

Temple edged over to watch.

The guard hesitated. "Now you won't faint, ma'am, if we find it?"

"Oh, no. I want to see that bug gone! It was right there, near that big lump of cotton." Temple crouched down, reached into the case and depressed the lump. It flattened instantly.

"Careful, ma'am! Better leave this to me."

Rising, Temple wobbled on her high heels, fell against the case and grabbed the bottom edge for support. In doing so, she managed to flatten the rest of the rumpled cotton batting, until it couldn't even conceal a toothpick.

"Here now." The guard took Temple's arm and firmly steered her away from the case. "I'll handle this."

Madame Security Guard then proceeded to shake, rattle and roll the abused fabric until a needle couldn't hide in its folds.

No shoes. Boo hoo.

"I can't understand it! The roach was right there." Temple pointed, now so entranced by her story that she almost believed it herself.

"Those big bugs are sneaky," the guard said. "They can slip in and out of places we'd never even notice. I'll spray the case." She viewed the deflated cotton batting, which looked more like stomped-on cotton candy than fluffy fake snow. "I suppose the exhibition director will be right irritated with my housekeeping talents."

She poked and prodded the batting back into place, managing to make it look like oatmeal.

"Anything else I can do, ma'am?" she inquired in a tone that implied additional pointless tasks were not welcome.

"Nothing at all." Temple's thanks were profusely enthusiastic. "Thanks ever so much for trying to nail that horrible bug!"

Kit, who had observed the entire scene from the bench, clapped slowly as Temple returned. "Brava. Even I was beginning to believe in that bug. You could probably develop a profitable sideline winning nuisance suits by claiming to see roaches in the radicchio."

"I don't want ill-gotten gains. I just want those fabulous shoes, darn it! At least we've ruled this place out."

"Oh, we're not swinging up on the balcony like Tarzan to check out the Duke's footwear? After all, you can't see his feet from here—whoa, never mind, Temple! I was just kidding."

"I'm not." Temple looked ready to storm the upper level, now that Kit had drawn her attention to it. "What the plate of petunias is Eightball O'Rourke doing up there?"

"That old guy next to Liza Minnelli? It's not Jimmy Durante? It's alive?"

"Not for long." Temple was pushing her sleeves up. "Maybe he's some maintenance person."

"Liza Minnelli's feet! That would be so perfect, since her mother wore the ruby slippers! Let's go."

Temple charged the stairs near the ladies' room, almost knocking the Ann Miller cardboard cutout into an unpremeditated tap-dance down the steps.

The second floor was a maze. Finding the entrance to the balcony meant opening many false doors: one to a room where a maid was cleaning; one to a closet where the maid that was cleaning the room got her cleaning supplies; one to a service stair that brought the cleaning supplies to the closet where the maid got them before going to the room that she was cleaning . . .

"Sorry." "Oops." "Wrong door." Temple sang out the appropriate formula for whatever false lead she followed, until she opened a fourth door.

"Aha!"

"Temple!" Kit warned her from the hallway. "Everybody can see you. It's like being in a department store window."

Temple peered over the balcony wall. "Luckily, nobody is curious enough to look up, like me. Drat. I'm in the wrong balcony section, and there's a solid wall. Is there another likely door in the hall?"

"Dozens," her aunt sang back. "And I'm not going to barge into a damn one of them."

"Then I'll just have to—" Temple brushed by Sammy Davis, Jr. to peer around the narrow wall separating her from the next balcony compartment. "Eightball!" she whispered hoarsely.

His startled face (Temple would have described it as a "guilty mug") peered around John Wayne's broad shoulder.

"What are you doing to Liza?" she demanded.

"Nothing."

"Then why are you up here?"

"Uh . . . for the view." He leaned over the balcony wall, spotted a security guard who seemed about to look up and ducked behind John Wayne.

Temple did likewise with Ol' Blue Eyes. Then she scraped her back along the wall until she was at the hallway door, and slipped through it.

Kit, and Eightball, were waiting for her.

"What's Liza got on those famous feet?" she asked him.

Eightball's well-seamed features screwed into chagrin. "Nothin'. Guess they figure no one sees them from below."

"You were looking for shoes, weren't you?" Temple said.

He shuffled, drawing attention to the battered penny loafers on his feet, which boasted shiny new dimes.

"Can't say," he answered. His faded straw fedora turned in his hands like an anoretic Frisbee.

"Why not? It's transparent as Plexiglas! You're hunting the Stuart Weitzman prize shoes. Why?"

"Goddakleyent," he mumbled.

"Once more, with articulation," she demanded.

"Gotta client."

Temple, shocked, leaned against the wall behind her. Actually, it was the door to the balcony, which eased open under her weight. She saved herself from falling over backwards, then tilted onto the balls of her feet and came out swinging, at least verbally.

"A client? You've actually been hired to hunt for the shoes? By whom?"

"Can't say."

"Can't say?"

"Client privilege."

"Someone has hired a private detective to find the shoes and win the contest? Such a person hardly qualifies as a 'client.' That is . . . that is low! Despicable. Beneath contempt. Like hiring a pro to take tootsie rolls from a tyke." Temple paced. "Besides, who has that kind of money to throw around? Someone who could afford to *buy* the shoes, that's who. Eightball, you have sold your soul for a pair of designer spikes! You are overturning the balance of power in the footwear world. You are lending your abilities and your name to the shoddiest scheme ever to come parading down the Las Vegas Strip, and that's going some! I can't believe it." Temple stopped pacing.

"A client's a client."

"Don't be so stubborn. What kind of a P.I. slinks around town eyeballing the feet on lady mannequins? Are you following *me*, hoping I'll lead you to them?"

He shrugged. "You might have a better instinct."

"You bet I do. And if I find you snooping in my tracks again, I'll . . . I'll call the police and charge you with something disgusting. Like shoe-sniffing."

Eightball put up a defensive hand. "It's just a job."

"A dirty job. The whole idea of a contest is to have fun, is for someone to find and win the shoes, not engage some hired gun."

"I ain't armed, and I'm getting damn tired of hunting high and low for a pair of fancy shoes. It's not like it's a significant assignment. And it sure ain't worth the wrath of a redhead."

A pause followed this cranky confession. Temple thought about calming down.

Kit lifted her hand palm out, first two fingers spread to make a peace symbol. "Remember," she told Eightball, "I'm just Temple's even-tempered, fading-redhead aunt Kit."

"Eightball O'Rourke." He nodded sourly, and suspiciously. "You ain't interested in those damn shoes, are you?"

"Only as an innocent bystander. As such"—she included Temple in her glance—"I suggest we adjourn to the Crystal Phoenix. Whatever side you two are on, there are no shoes here for you to bicker over, except the ones we walked in on. Thank Thom McAnn!"

Putting shoes into their proper place, they all walked back to the Strip and caught a cab to the Crystal Phoenix.

Chapter 17

. . . Seems to Whisper Louise

It is not long before the sophisticated brains, eyes, nose and vibrissae (whiskers to you less educated folk) of Midnight Louie find
their way to the lower-level dressing room that has been claimed
by Miss Savannah Ashleigh.

I could say that I had used my sensitive nose to trail whatever
Rodeo Drive scent of the month Miss Savannah is using now, but
that would be misleading. I could have done so, but did not need
to, as I have a good idea of where she is to be found. This is, in
fact, the same site that she commandeered on her most recent
visit to the Crystal Phoenix when she had some ceremonial duties at the Rhinestone G-string competition. In fact, it is old home-
away-from-home week. Not only is the Divine Yvette present in
the pink carrier that serves as her portable residence, but our re-
union is marked by an event similar to our last encounter: a murder of a human person who makes a living by wearing as few
clothes as the law will allow.

I am all for it. Not murder, but wearing as few clothes as the law allows.

You will notice that one does not have to tell the truly superior species to bring warm clothing: they arrive with all the outerwear that they will need—warm, durable, full-length coats of fur or hair or feathers or scales. It is only humankind that arrives on the scene wearing nothing more than a fragile layer of skin. (I can attest to just how fragile that skin is, having accidentally peeled off a fine line of it now and then.) But humans are not totally ignorant. Taking instructions from the humble spider, they have evolved numerous and complicated ways to weave, spin and construct suitable clothing.

Then, having overcome their natural inferiority complex, they move up to a level of idiocy that one would think they made up, did one not know the species intimately.

They split into two mutually exclusive camps. Some become skinophiles and can be found in nudist camps. Others, the vast majority, become skinophobes and can be found in Bible camps. I wish that they would make up their minds, but that seems to be the last thing that humankind is capable of.

A very few humans learn to exploit the druthers of the skinophiles by performing in their natural state (which skinophobes find filthy and disgusting), wearing a few skimpy accessories that skirt the laws on such actions. What is really brain-boggling is that when naked humans invent little nothings to give the lie to total nudity, they usually feel obliged to shroud the only site where they can boast a smattering of fur anyway! This is why human beings see psychiatrists and animal companions run away from home.

I myself see nothing to crow about in the unclothed human state, but feel, philosophically, that all species should continue in their natural condition. For one thing, in making an art of clothing themselves, humans have an unfortunate tendency to covet the skin, fur, scales and feathers of other species, most of which cannot give up their outerwear without losing their lives, not that most people show any remorse for their ill-gotten garb.

Ah, well, as long as I am not forced to wear pantaloons and vest, I suppose it is no skin off of my nose. But it would most definitely be skin off of your nose if you ever tried to take my epidermis for a muff. Luckily, muffs are history nowadays.

And, luckily, the curled muff of silver fur that is the Divine Yvette is sleeping safely in her carrier, alone. At last! I pad near the mesh window to my darling and gaze fondly on her snoozing form for several seconds. Frankly, the Divine Yvette is sweetest when she sleeps. When she is awake, she is likely to ask awkward questions, and sometimes, even show the front of her fangs (which are supernaturally white and well maintained, but are fangs nevertheless).

So I am standing in rapt regard of my sleeping innocent, watching the tips of her vibrissae tremble with each breath, when somebody behind me whispers, "Hsst."

Usually I am not one to be surprised by the stealthy approach. I turn in alarm, expecting that odious Maurice. I am no less alarmed when I see who confronts me from under the long row of garments hanging on Miss Savannah Ashleigh's costume rack: the vulpine Louise.

"What are you doing down here, Pops?" she asks. I can tell that her form of address, rather than being a respectful bow to my paternal status, is an expression she uses to address gents of a certain age. The implication is that I am a geezer.

I never pick up an implication if I can let it lie there and ferment. So I lift a casual mitt to my face and rub my whiskers contemplatively.

"Just looking over the scene of the last crime," I say, incidentally reminding her who really cracked the Stripper Killer case and nailed the perp. "Now that Miss Temple Barr is busy with another show here, I do not want any unfortunate reruns of the breaking, entering and murder both attempted and accomplished that we had before."

"Oh, your old war stories," she huffs, rolling over to admonish an ear, apparently for the crime of even hearing about my exploits. "I have the account now. Everything is under control."

"Indeed? I suppose you consider the murder of an Incredible Hunk too trivial an event for your notice."

"I noticed, daddio. These human hunk types are too large to overlook. In fact, I made the murder scene before the police, if not before your nosy roommate. That woman is a regular Typhoon Mary."

"I believe you refer to a historical personage known as Typhoid Malaria, who brought a dread disease with her everywhere she went. Miss Temple Barr is nothing like that. She is merely quick to notice that things are amiss. Now, you," I go on, yawning a little, "probably were so disinterested that you could not even remember the color of the dead dude's hair."

"Burmese brown," she snaps back, barely missing the tips of my whiskers. I smell the odious reek of Free-to-be-Feline on her breath. "Eyes of watered-down green. Hawk feather on the arrow that brought him down. His own weapon, ironically."

I now know, of course, exactly what I wanted to learn.

"What was this dead dude doing with a live arrow?"

"Wearing it . . . and not much else." Midnight Louise wrinkles her little black nose, which is rather cute, if I do say so myself. "Whew! What a lot of skin to smell, along with the equally unpleasant scent of death. I do not know why these hunks insist on sharing so much of their body odor with the rest of us."

"It is their way of being provocative."

"Consider me provoked." She frowns until the short, satiny fur on her brow wrinkles like a throw rug. "I had to slink away pronto, though, before anyone spotted me. I tried to interrogate the horse, but it was too spooked to speak."

"The horse? You mean tall as a two-story building, with hooves?"

"Yeah, a big bruiser with knobby knees and a forelock. And it wore iron shoes. Mere size does not intimidate me." Louise's round gold eyes give me a once-over that is not a compliment. "Anyway, the equine was in shock. Could only whinny about a slap on the rump. Later, I jumped up in the flies and got a bird's-eye view of its rump, and it deserved slapping. Had all these white spots on it, like it had been caught in a bleach rainfall. Silly-looking creature."

"I believe you refer to a valued birthmark that indicates a breed known as the Appaloosa."

"Appaloosa, applesalsa, it ain't talking."

I cringe at my reputed offspring's grammar. Not only ain't, but a contraction. She misreads my body language, which is not unusual.

"So what would you have done different, Pops? All I know is that this fallen hunk was masquerading as an Indian warrior when someone stuck him in the back with an unbroken arrow. Goodbye, Cheyenne."

"Cheyenne?" I sit up and take notice of my chest hairs, which I proceed to groom with some agitation. Not only are they a trifle mussed, but my mind is also a little ragged around the edges as I realize I have heard that name before, in this hotel.

"Cheyenne," she repeats, narrowing her eyes to horizontal slits you could not see out of a tank through. "What of it?"

I cannot decide whether to take her into my confidence or not, for I know the name from Miss Temple's association with the stripper contest. Could this murder have its roots in the last slaughter at the Crystal Phoenix? While I am making up my mind, the Divine Yvette is waking up in her carrier, emitting a series of soft, sleepy mews that are sweet and charming and loud enough for the vulpine Louise to hear even with her ears flattened.

She—the vulpine Louise, not the Divine Yvette—perks her ears, elongates her neck, then rises and trots over to inspect the carrier.

I can only hope that she does not notice it is occupied, but that is extremely unlikely.

"Mew," the Divine Yvette murmurs in greeting the black feline face peering through her mesh. "Louie?"

"I might have known!" The vulpine Louise whirls to face me, inadvertently smacking my chops with her tail. At least I prefer to think that it is inadvertent. "This pose of slinking about the premises to protect poor Miss Temple, when you are visiting some sleazy showcat! And my mother was not good enough to occupy your attention for more than a one-night stand. Males! You are all alike, no matter the species."

I spit out some stray black hairs and maintain my dignity. "You are sadly mistaken, my dear girl. The Divine Yvette and I have a purely platonic relationship."

"The Divine Yvette? What a pushover for some overbreeding and a pedigree, along with a phony French name!" Midnight Louise turns on the drowsy Divine Yvette to snarl, "Parlay voo French, chérée? Translate this."

With that, Midnight Louise smacks the mesh so it collapses like an expired balloon.

I am paralyzed by horror. And I am even more horrified when I see the mesh bounce back as the Divine Yvette lets loose with a flurry of ungloved jabs, claws out.

"Civet!" she hisses. "Rank roadside runaway! Nameless hussy! Fatherless floozy! Ungroomed hairball! Alley scum. Your mother is a glove liner and your father's tail is a rearview-mirror trophy."

Midnight Louise sits back to let the abuse unfold, casting a brief glance in my direction.

"Not exactly," she interjects when the Divine Yvette takes a deep, heaving breath before expanding on her charges further. "Daddy dearest is a friend of yours, I believe."

"Impossible," the Divine Yvette hisses in righteous indignation.

I am, of course, caught between two irresistible forces of feline nature. I can only sit still, cringe and wait for the storm to pass.

"That is what I call him, too," Midnight Louise spits. "And they call me Midnight Louise."

"Oh!" The Divine Yvette's fury has subsided suddenly.

"I will let you chew upon that fact," Louise says, de-arching her back and shaking out her tail, "as I bid you adieu. Just remember that this is my turf nowadays, and I demand a certain respect, even from visiting aristocrats. Do not count on my old man having any influence whatsoever with me."

She stalks off, stiff-legged, her tail kinked and still twitching.

The Divine Yvette's carrier is worrisomely quiet. I inch nearer and peek in.

The Divine One is busy licking her silver coat into fresh-minted condition, rolling out her long rosy tongue with skillful regularity. She glances up with her deep blue-green eyes.

"You did not tell me that you were married, Louie," she rebukes me in sad, calm tones.

I swallow. "It was an informal affair. And we are divorced now. Hey, Las Vegas is the capital of the quickie marriage and divorce. That was a long time ago."

"Oh? I detect zat zee dainty Midnight Louise cannot be more than a year or so old. I am nevair wrong about zee age of anozzair female."

Is it possible that the Divine Yvette has developed a French accent since Midnight Louise accused her of being French? Talk about a suggestible sensibility!

"I am sorry, dear lady, that my miscreant daughter was so rude to you."

"I am sorree, Louie, that you have such a rude offspring. And now I must nap. My beauty sleep was interrupted."

"You will not hold my relatives against me?" I inquire more anxiously than I would like.

The Divine Yvette sighs as she rests her soft gray triangle of a face on her silken paws. "I cannot say. I have always known that we exist on two different planes—"

"You are not leaving already?"

"But I try very hard not to be a—how you say? A snob. Perhaps your daughter could benefit from obedience school."

"That is for dogs!" I reply, horrified.

The Divine Yvette shrugs and shows the pearly tips of her two exquisite fangs. "If the shoe fits, the foot should wear it. *Au revoir, mon ami.*"

I withdraw, not knowing what to blame Midnight Louise for more: betraying my past lovelife to my current amour, or giving the Divine Yvette the idea that she is French.

Chapter 18

Every Large
Breezy . . .

Temple and Kit returned to the Crystal Phoenix to find the lobby packed with registering G.R.O.W.L.ers.

"Oh, no!"

"What?" Kit asked, scanning the mob.

"Fabrizio again. Does he stake out the registration line, or what?"

"Of course he wants to catch them coming in. This is his business, Temple, and these women are his fans."

"At least we registered early and can sneak past."

"But we're not going to." Kit corralled Temple's arm as she tried to eel away. "Here's an ideal opportunity to practice your new undercover persona."

"What new undercover persona?"

"Remember? I told you at lunch. Trot out your old reporting skills and become officially nosy. This crowd expects the media to be out in force, and it's dying to get noticed."

"Dying is the operative word around here lately."

Temple frowned as Kit pulled her toward Fabrizio's knot of women. "I really don't want another close encounter with Fabrizio. He's so bold, so blond . . . so bigger than life. I feel like I'm going to be stomped by Trigger when I'm around him."

"Ah! But you are Media now. Breezy will be a pushover, and you'll do the pushing. Mention a major show, and he'll trot over quietly for a lump of sugar, I promise. Now, here's the notepad and pen from my registration packet. Remember, he's probably got the inside scoop on all the pageant personalities. He might even be the killer. Go, girl!"

Kit pushed Temple into the charmed circle surrounding the cover model. It made an odd sight: the squat cluster of women swarming the towering blond-maned man like a ring of enchanted mushrooms. He was it. The pinnacle of power, the Viking god with oiled muscles, sun-streaked blond hair and a twenty-four-karat Personality with a capital Pow.

Temple felt like an ambivalent bobby-soxer on the edge of the Elvis phenomenon, but ole Breezy zeroed right in on her, probably because she was, as usual, the most liftable female present.

"La Rossa!" He greeted her like an old fling.

His tanned face beamed, his Mediterranean-blue eyes twinkled, his impossibly white teeth flashed. This guy was a one-man weather report: clear and sunny and shining only for you, lucky woman. Just you and another two-and-a-half million females on the planet. His . . . oh! . . . huge, grasping hands were stretching for her.

Temple let out a big breath, as Matt had instructed her to do when confronted with a superior force, barked, "Stop!" in English, then "Basta!" in Italian, and held her palm up like a school-crossing guard.

David could not have gotten Goliath to so much as blink with this tactic, but Temple's routine halted the oncoming action figure in mid-stride. Maybe the Italian word for "enough" had done it. A cloud of uncertainty shadowed Fabrizio's relentlessly upbeat features.

"You do not like to be picked up by Fabrizio? But why?" His hands spread wider, both to question . . . and to prepare to pounce.

The encircling women grew quiet, like jackals waiting for the lordly lion to finish off the prey before they tore the leavings apart.

Temple swallowed, but her voice was firm when she answered. "Because I can't take notes when I'm off the ground, and notes are very important to a field producer for *Hot Heads*."

The fans' faces transformed from suspicion to rapture. Breezy was no less blissful. *Hot Heads* was the moment's most torrid tabloid TV entertainment show. The *Heads* was short for headlines, but the contraction was apt: famous faces and talking heads telling all made the show so hypnotizing to viewers.

"Why did you not say so earlier, dear *signorina*? I would never want to interfere with your working. And what do you wish?"

"Ah, just a few minutes of your time while I take preliminary notes for our on-camera personalities."

"You have them, these minutes. You have all of me." His arms spread wide, his open shirt gaping to strain across rippling chest muscles. Temple found the effect rather creepy. She could see her mythical tabloid headline now: "Fabrizio possessed by sentient muscles from Mars!"

Temple backed away from the oncoming Fabrizio and his train of silent, intent, gap-mouthed watchers, then led him to one of Van von Rhine's cream Italian leather seating pieces that dotted the lobby. Van had designed the Crystal Phoenix with such personal pains that every piece seemed a favorite of the hostess.

Temple perched on the cushy seat's edge, her heels planted on the lobby's navy and gold carpeting. Experience had taught her that sinking into down-stuffed furniture could entrap her. Fabrizio leaned expansively into a shirred leather corner, like a very rich milk chocolate in a luxurious box, spreading his arms over the backrest and his legs until one askew knee almost nudged Temple's. And she taking so pathetically little space on her best days!

She laid her notebook on her crunched-together knees—she felt like a novice in a Spanish cloister, but Breezy was such a territory-hogging guy that she had no other choice, unless she wished to be annexed.

The fans had withdrawn to a decent distance, just barely, and hovered, hoping to overhear any scintilla of stray sound.

Fabrizio smiled at her, steadily, knowingly, intimately. "Why you not like picking up, eh? Every woman"—he pronounced it "woo-mahn"—"likes man to take charge, to carry her away from the everyday. This is what Fabrizio do. Why you not like?" His piercing gaze, honed under hot studio spotlights hundreds of times at $3,000 a pop, she had read, focused on Temple like a lascivious Latin laser beam.

The three-grand ogle did not impress her. They all had that smug invasive look, the professional ladykillers, implying that the woman was some uptight ignoramus resisting the Sultan of Sex. And just underneath the romantic schmaltz lay an implicit threat of superior masculine knowledge, if not force, of knowing what was best for her. Temple was too polite to tell Fabrizio that the whole manner repelled her because it was so perfectly professional.

"I have a phobia of heights," she said shortly.

"Oh, yes." He nodded. A neurotic weakness was perhaps understandable, and not unexpected. "So you say before. I will not let you fall. You would no longer be afraid with Fabrizio."

"I'm, ah, afraid I would be. Now, about the show—"

His body and features clicked into another mode: rapt attention.

"Everyone, of course, knows your story, Fabrizio."

"Ah, yes. How Fabrizio is simple Italiano boy. Always I want to be model, travel, always I build body and want to go to America. Like Arnold. But then I model for romance covers, and the woo-mahn is ecstatic. I now am multi-media personality. I have workout book and tapes, calendars, romantic advice line, cologne for men."

"Do you model for romance covers anymore?"

"No, too busy." His smile again showcased the Teflon teeth.

"Or . . . there are so many other male cover models competing now."

Fabrizio shook his head until his split ends whipped the sofa back. "No. Covers are start, not end. Small fries for international multimedia personality. I only come to do walk-through for pageant because G.R.O.W.L. was a good start for me. But I do not need this audience. Fabrizio is for whole world now."

"Then you don't feel threatened by all the up-and-comers?"

He shook his golden mane again, his distant watchers shivering with delight. "Fabrizio not threatened by anybody." The lothario's smirk was back. "Except lovely woo-mahn who believes she is afraid of height. This makes Breezy feel very bad, that she does not think he is strong enough to hold her."

"So you're not even threatened by a murderer?"

The last word froze the look on his face, but the intimacy had left it.

"You think a murderer would want to kill Breezy? No. This dead model, this Cheyenne. He was new to this, and he did not have the physique of Fabrizio, no?"

"Still, he apparently had done some modeling abroad. That's usually a sign of a rising career."

"Peanuts, how you say? Little stuff. Fabrizio does all the big stuff, leaves that small fries to the others now. He would be no threat to what I do, what I am. No man is."

"We may assume that you are not a suspect, then, since you had no motive?"

"Suspect? For small woo-mahn you play big games. Why should Fabrizio wish anyone ill? He is rich, famous, happy. Many woo-mahns wish to be picked up by Fabrizio, all over the world!"

The massively muscled arms spread wide again, the better to display his firm, rounded, fully packed pectorals. Funny, Temple thought, that used to be a female secondary sexual characteristic. Breezy's thigh pressed into hers, hot and hard. It reminded her of an encroaching Christmas ham.

She slapped the notebook shut. "As the second Incredible Hunk winner, you can't compete again anyway, can you?"

"No. But there is no need. Fabrizio has won every heart, because he speaks from the heart." A ham-sized hand pounded the tan-gilded breastbone, in case Temple had overlooked a part of his anatomy. "Sincere, that is the secret of Fabrizio. And we do very well with that."

How odd that he referred to himself in both the third person and the royal "we," when mentioning his business enterprises. Temple supposed that he was a one-man conglomerate of sorts. Pneumatic Man, able to spread himself into million-dollar multimedia areas with a single muscle flex.

Temple stood. "Thank you. This will help ground my anchors."

Fabrizio snapped his fingers. A harried-looking woo-mahn trotted over, tote bag in hand. "This is Cindee, my publicist. She has press kit."

A glossy folder with a color image of a hip-up naked Fabrizio was thrust into Temple's hand. The photo was so lifelike that Temple expected her palm to suffer an oil slick.

Fabrizio stood, too, towering over her as he had loomed over countless swooning, swept-away cover models. His eyes, already too close together, narrowed horizontally as well. "You will one day like to be picked up by Fabrizio."

On that threat and promise, he strode back into the mob of woo-mahns, who closed on him like eager antibodies surrounding an infection.

"See!" Kit had materialized from somewhere, and was as happy as hell's bells. "He doesn't bite. Learn anything relevant?"

"Only that there is no justice in who gets rich and famous, and how."

"Pshaw, we knew that already."

"He's not worried about being a victim," Temple said thoughtfully. "Either he hasn't thought about the possibility, or . . . he knows why Cheyenne was killed."

"Maybe we could waylay him late at night and interrogate him."

"Aunt Kit! You don't find that bloated hunk of overdeveloped ego attractive?"

She shrugged, shameless.

Temple headed for the elevators, Kit by her side.

"You were right, though," she told her aunt. "Pretending to work with tabloid TV is an open sesame. Works much better than legitimately being employed by a local TV station years ago."

They were edging into the chiming slot machine area, for no

one can go anywhere in a Las Vegas Hotel without passing these garish coin-catchers for the eternally hopeful.

Temple suddenly grabbed Kit's arm, jerked her into an aisle and sat them both down on two adjoining stools—hard.

"I can't believe it!" she said indignantly. "Keep your head down."

"Why? Is Fabrizio trolling for redheads again? I fear I'm a bit faded—"

Temple's red head was bobbing up and down like a dunking apple on Halloween. "Shhhh!" she ordered, her fierce eyes focusing over the top of the slot machine. "What are *they* doing . . . together! Of all the nerve."

"Who?" Kit cautiously peered over the machine in the direction that Temple was staring. "Those two cover models?"

"They are *not* cover models!" Temple was almost rabid with rage. "They have no business being here. Especially together."

"Temple! Who are they? They look innocuous enough."

"That was *my* first mistake. One is the Mystifying Max—"

"Your ex?"

"So to speak. And the other is Matt Devine."

"Oh. Your . . . maybe current." Kit tilted her head almost horizontal to the floor to sneak another look. "Which is which?"

"Who cares? What are they up to?"

"I would say about six-three, if you're looking at the tall one. Hmm, not bad, Niece. Either one could compete in the pageant. If you don't need both, I'm available."

Kit was summarily jerked back down to her stool.

"Fine, if you're in the market for traitors!" Temple was still fuming.

"What have they done?"

"Well, the last time I saw them together, you could carve the hostility into chunk-size pieces and feed it to the sharks. Now they're strolling around the Crystal Phoenix like buddies. And Max claimed he needed to keep out of sight! Sure. Of *me*!"

Kit ventured to stretch her neck up again. "And so he is. Now. Matt too. Pity. I'd sure like to see them closer up."

Temple stood slowly, ready to duck again. "I don't know whether they make me more nervous when I can see them, or when I can't."

"That's men for you, every time." Kit yawned. "Well, now that I've had my daily dose of excitement, I'll pop up to my room for a beauty rest before dinner." She patted Temple's hand. "Don't let this worry you. I'm sure that there's a very simple explanation."

"There isn't," Temple said grimly.

Clutching her Fabrizio folder until the glossy paper squeaked, she ventured to the elevator with her aunt. She kept scanning the area for another sighting.

And never saw hide nor hair nor pectoral nor tempestuous mane of anything that resembled a cover hunk the entire way back to her room.

Electra was lounging on the bed when she got there, studying a folder full of papers.

"How did the writing class go?" Temple asked, tossing Fabrizio facedown on her bed's coverlet.

"Terrific. We had a two-hour lunch break, so I dashed up and began my contest entry. That little machine is so adorable and petite, just like you!" She didn't notice Temple grinding her teeth. "It makes such cute little words, all prancing across the itty-bitty screen. So much more interesting than a typewriter. I'm glad you brought it."

"So am I. I'm going to have to punch some notes in tonight. The cast of characters at this circus is larger than the extras roster in a Hollywood epic. Speaking of epic, I had another close encounter with the scrumptious Fabrizio."

"Oh." Electra was so intent on her class papers she hardly reacted.

"And guess who I just saw strolling through the lobby? Max Kinsella and Matt Devine."

"That's nice, dear. I've got to concentrate on my scene-and-sequel writing exercise."

Temple held her arms up, wide, Fabrizio-style. Didn't anyone want to be swept off their feet anymore? Not even by a hot news flash?

"I'm going to jump in the shower with Fabrizio," Temple said, gathering her gear.

"That's nice, dear. Don't let the water get too hot."

"And with Norman Bates's mother!" Temple shouted from around the bathroom corner.

"Um hmm. Say hello for me."

Chapter 19

Ship of Jewels

Entering the Treasure Island Hotel and Casino was like diving into the chill of a grotto formed from tarnished brass. Despite the elegantly orchestrated atmosphere, Temple heard the same old Musak playing the same old sweet song. This was a cabaret, my friend, and the theme song was "Money, Money, Money." Coins tumbled into slot machine tills like pieces of eight pouring out of bottomless, upended treasure chests.

Though the decor was dark and dignified, it had a macabre bent. Large antiqued brass skulls on the door handles split lengthwise as they opened, and the tastefully beige massive chandeliers, on second look, were composed entirely of human skulls and garlands of dangling bones.

Temple, however, was indifferent to the mock-morbid; she'd seen death's true, bare-faced presence close-up at the Crystal Phoenix all too recently. No, the boisterous slot machine area intrigued her, and not because of the sporadic, seductive clink of crashing quarters.

Like many blasé Las Vegas residents, she had neglected to tour the new behemoths grazing along the Strip's Jurassic Park of hotel-casinos. She had read about them, but had not yet gone to see the architectural elephants in person. So she was only guessing when it came to what evil (or delights) might lurk inside the Treasure Island, but . . . yes!

Temple clasped hands to breastbone and went up on tippy-toes, despite the three-inch heels on her Evan Picone pumps, all the better to see her quarry.

She smiled sappily—not at the garish blinking and clinking slot machines—but at the ceiling above them. A pirate's ransom of brass, silver and real gilt paint, of pearls and cut-glass gemstones, tumbled from niches set under the ceiling. Enough treasure cheats hung above the gamblers below to hide a hundred crystal shoes.

Temple cruised toward the glitzy black-and-gold island of a bar that was ringed with sky-high treasure troves. Of course the displays were temptingly out of reach—just. Certainly that seemed un*just*. If she were *just* six feet tall. Or had Alice's little bottle that made her bigger. If she *just* had a stepping stool, or a pogo stick or stilts!

If hotel security personnel *just* weren't cruising these black-gold waters like uniformed barracudas, looking for people who were behaving oddly. People like Temple herself, who was watching the ceiling, which was probably watching her back. She snagged the nearest stool and sat before a machine decorated with a grinning buccaneer, dagger in teeth.

She dug into her tote bag for her wallet, then scraped some quarters out of the zippered compartment. While she idly consigned the coins to swift perdition inside Long John Silver's ravenous metal mouth, she eyed the surroundings.

Men in sharkskin suits, wires from discreet communication devices attached like some naturalist's tracking mechanism to their ears, floated through colorful schools of oblivious tourists nibbling at instant fortune. The uniformed guards were more obvious, for a reason, but their eyes constantly scanned for potential trouble.

The Midnight Louie shoes were not to be seized, like common pirate booty, but seen and reported, Temple reminded herself.

Nothing in the contest rules required her to take them into actual possession. The numerous treasure troves dangling from the casino ceiling like so many jewel-encrusted tongues made perfect hiding places. All she'd have to do was walk by and eyeball each one for signs of the elusive slippers.

Except. Her height, or lack of it, was a disadvantage, which was no news to her. The hidden shoes might only be visible to a taller person. Nothing in the contest rules said that they would be placed in plain view of a shrimp, either. Children were obviously not competing for this particular prize. She could only make the rounds of the various troves at enough distance to get a panoramic view of the contents. *I am a camera* for the vertically challenged, in Cinemascope.

So Temple sneaked up on her quarry, throwing away quarters like worthless coppers of old as she hopscotched from slot to slot, choosing positions that would allow a wide view of the nearest trove.

It was neck-spraining work. Her eyes could hardly focus on the assembled glitter as she squinted through her glasses. And she didn't dare look up for too long, or she might attract unwanted attention.

She had worked her way around the bar area and was scouting the area's fringes when someone tapped her on the shoulder just as she was sacrificing another quarter to the slot-machine gods.

"I see what you're doing," a voice behind her announced.

Luckily, it was not an authoritarian voice, nor male, so that eliminated the Iranian secret police in the somber suits as well as most of the security guards.

Temple turned to look, nearly giving herself whiplash.

"What's your game, honey?" a woman asked.

She was thinner than a wire clothes hanger. The clothes she so feebly supported were a peach polyester pantsuit over a violet floral polyester blouse. A thin fleece of taffy-blond ringlets surrounded her face like an elaborately decorated 1950s bathing cap. Time and desert sun had folded, spindled and mutilated her face into a brown frill of wrinkles, from which her pale eyes peered like water chestnuts. Time had also embedded her in the amber of another era, encouraging her to draw harsh dark-brown eyebrows and a tangerine mouth on the well-tracked mask of her face.

Temple recognized her instantly, though they had never spoken before: legendary casino slot-shot Hester Polyester, who in another place and another time (and another outfit) might have been known by a more common surname like Brown. Or Smith.

A coral canvas fanny pack sat dead center of her flowered, concave middle. No watch circled her freckled wrist; dedicated slot players never sleep, or go anywhere else. Schools of wooden tropical fish dangled from Hester's overtaxed earlobes. Temple was so shocked to meet the Minnesota Fats of slot machines that she didn't check out Hester Polyester's footwear until last: gold metallic tennis shoes.

"What's your system?" Hester was asking with narrowed eyes. "I never seen a player run this kind of pattern before. Can't figure it out. You're not hitting the aisle machines that are supposedly looser, to attract the tourists. You're not moving on 'cuz a machine's gone cold. What the heck are you doing?"

"Losing," Temple said promptly.

Laughter made Hester's face wrinkle like a paper bag someone's fist had suddenly squeezed shut. "Hell, girl! That's not a system. That's nuts." She sobered at once. "Unless you got some deeper strategy."

"None at all. I don't want to win."

"Don't want to win? That's not . . . legal in Las Vegas."

"It's the opposite of positive thinking, don't you see?"

"Opposite?"

"Yeah. Kind of like . . . zen and the art of slot machine selection. I don't *want* to win."

"And, by not wanting to win, the law of averages works in your favor and you do?"

"Nope. Not yet. But that's okay. I don't *want* to win. So I win when I don't, get it?"

"What happens if you actually do win?"

"I lose."

Hester shook her blowsy head.

"That's crazy. But I guess I said that." She hefted her cardboard bucket, so quarters chimed like a belly dancer in full shimmy. "Guess I won't wish you luck, dearie."

"Thank you. I appreciate that."

Shaking her head and her bucket, Hester Polyester resumed her pursuit of the elusive jackpot.

Temple's sigh was loud enough to make several nearby heads turn, and it was hard to interrupt a slot player. She was tired of inspecting the usual bulbous brass lamps, the predictable swags of pearls, the gleaming Aladdin's lamps and seeing nothing but flashy trash. She prowled the slot machine aisles, eyeing the row of treasure chests along the casino's far wall.

What she had told Hester Polyester wasn't so wrong. She must not really *want* to find the shoes for some deep psychological reason. Maybe she felt she didn't deserve the shoes, or good luck. Maybe she was hooked on heels. (That last word could cut two ways, given at least one man in her life.) Maybe she was codependent on cool shoes and in denial about even cooler dudes. Maybe she was just a lousy treasure hunter. . . .

As she passed the second-to-the-last niche, something glittered white and bright, like a snowflake in sunlight. Temple paused. She craned her neck and went up on her toes like a vigilant meerkat again.

Silver lamé fabric bunched into the corners of this display, and something in it sparkled. Star stuff. Maybe . . . a glitter that went yesteryear's rhinestones one better. Rhinestones had been named for Germany's river Rhine because they were first made there, but today's upscale Austrian crystals—made from real lead crystal rather than mere glass—had fiercer fire.

Before she thought about it, Temple had dragged a stool from a vacant slot machine and had hopped atop it. Now she was teetering on it. Now she was *just* high enough to lose sight of the trove's big picture, like a kid climbing for the cookie jar on the top shelf. Her nose nudged the shelf-lip. Drat, she could see the tops of everything, but nothing more.

Oops. Now her balance was going. Her fingertips curled over the ledge as she felt the stool wobble. Temple grabbed for some of the star stuff, which was like catching at clouds. The fabric was airy, fragile, it was barely there . . . it was pulling toward her as she wavered on the stool, and all the pirate plunder that rested atop it was oozing like gravid, luxurious lava to the shelf-rim above her head.

Temple's eyes winced shut, her shoulders hunched, anticipating the forthcoming downpour.

"Let go!" someone ordered her, and she did. Any port in a storm.

She felt herself tip off the stool, but someone caught her. After a little kicking and striving, she was standing on her own two Evan Picones on the floor. Her rescuer was no hoop-earred pirate bold. If she were a collector of salt and pepper shakers, she'd pair him with Hester Polyester, but she knew better.

"Eightball O'Rourke! What are you doing here?"

"I'm not doing nothing. You're the one who was assaulting the Treasure Island's ceiling. What's up?"

"That's right! I must have shifted the contents." Temple scrambled backwards, gazing up, until she could see the entire vignette again.

The treasure, looking more like junk now that it balanced on the brink, had pulled away from the silver-white material, now flat instead of fluffy. No shoelike shapes lurked behind or under it. Slack, it drooped over the trove lip, flashing a single star-shape of silver glitter.

Eightball was dragging the stool back into place. "Lucky for you security is on a rum break," he grumbled. "Messing with casino decorations is mighty suspicious behavior. You're probably on tape, closeup. Let's get out of here before they make you walk the plank."

Temple did not argue.

She could barely keep up with Eightball's blue-jeaned and booted legs as he wove through the gaming area. They were soon dodging tourists through the lobby toward the building's main entrance.

"You still didn't say what you were doing here," Temple said when she caught up to him.

"Same case," he said shortly. "Only I found my way here on my own."

Temple could hardly complain, given her uncommon luck. Only two people had noticed her studying the treasure chests: Hester Polyester and Eightball. Neither was fond of hotel security. Maybe there was something to zen gambling, after all.

They broke into fading daylight through another set of skull-handled doors, reminding Temple that it was past 7:00 P.M. She glimpsed a hillside of quaint architecture and exotic landscaping to her left. Before them a wooden walkway thronged with coming-and-going people all the long way to the Strip. Something large loomed on her right. She looked up at yet another dinosaur of the new Las Vegas Strip—an eighteenth-century sailing ship, its sails rolled up like windowshades, tucked into snug harbor against the towering cliffside of the Treasure Island Hotel. People four-deep crowded the railings on both sides.

She stopped to gawk.

"Ain't you seen the show yet?" Eightball asked.

"You mean the battling pirate ships?"

"Well, that one there's the pirate. The other one's the Royal Navy, and that comes along later."

"Who wins?"

"Wouldn't be fair telling if you ain't seen it yet."

"Is that why those rope barriers divide the bridge? To keep show-watchers separate from the traffic in and out of the Treasure Island?"

"What a gumshoe! Exactly."

"When's the next show?"

"Anytime between now and forty minutes from now." Eightball edged over to the left wooden railing to gaze down on an expanse of water lapping at the walkway's piers. "Everything's peaceful now, which means they're setting up for the next sail-bashing."

Temple joined him at the rail, which came up to her collarbones. Across the way, a large bay window framed a glint of cutlery and metal lamps. The diners at table were strictly contemporary, so she was peeking into one of several hotel eateries. But the exterior scene made a course of a far less formal flavor. Cables and barrels littered the landscape. A presumably stuffed parrot roosted on a post. A ship's female figurehead thrust out from a second story, busty enough to give the one on Caesars Palace's Cleopatra's barge an inferiority complex and a yen for a Wonderbra.

The scene was obviously a pirates' rookerie on some uncharted island.

Water licked at the bridge's support structures and lapped at the artificial lagoon's faraway edge near the Strip, where more people lined up. The scene, the water, the distant diners instilled peace in a place more noted for haste and hustle.

Temple lay her forcarms on the sun-warmed wood, joining the waiters and watchers.

"Quite a show," Eightball observed. "Worth the wait."

"I suppose I'm obligated to see it, being a PR person."

He nodded.

The crowd had that air of mass expectancy found in theaters and sports arenas. What a perfect place to murder someone, Temple thought. One quick stab and away into the mob. No! Her mind was not on murder. No hunks lurked here as victim or perpetrator (unless some manned the ship), and the Treasure Island sat next to the Mirage, far from the Crystal Phoenix.

Temple noticed that the waves kissing the distant pilings were now administering slaps. Yet there was no wind, only the long slow sunset simmering at their backs.

"If we're lucky, it'll be twilight by showtime," Eightball said. "Enough light to see by, but more dangerous in the dark."

Temple shivered as she felt an imaginary breeze and watched its ghost riffle the cool water below, in which the nearby lamp reflection twinkled like a falling star. Fair wind, fiery star. Yes, the water was making waves now, small ones that snapped at the pilings, fell back and grew bigger. Was that possible in an artificial lake with little wind present? True, Las Vegas would try anything for a special effect. Did some eggbeater-like machine lurk beneath the waterline? Creepy!

Temple suddenly noticed a small wooden boat on the water,

two men rowing like mad toward the bridge. Voices from the anchored pirate ship behind her urged them on. The men rowed
under the bridge and vanished. Their voices ebbed.

Eightball was right. The day was dimming. A candle-glow
brightened the faraway restaurant window, reflecting from knives
and forks that rose and fell like waves. . . . The lagoon water was
really heaving against the pilings now. How . . . and more puz-
zlingly, why?

"See there!" Eightball pointed like a lookout.

Temple stared where directed and saw the diners gazing back
at her. Then something moved. To the right. A high black prow
nudged into her line of sight, sharp as a dagger shearing the fading sky in two.

How amazing . . . A huge, gliding full-sailed ship edged into view
on a toy lagoon. The ruffled waves had been silent emissaries of
the unseen yet approaching ship. The silence ended. Music, or-
chestral and ominous, welled up all around them.

Voices called behind them again.

Turning, Temple watched the buccaneers swarm up the rigging,
the pirate ship now lit by hidden spotlights like a stage set. Crew
called each other to readiness.

Then British barks of orders boomed from the oncoming ship.
Temple switched her attention to the left. And so it went, the
Royal Navy ship sliding around the point to furl its sails and take
up a firing position, the pirate ship behind them all loud chaos as
the surprised buccaneers readied for battle.

Temple felt as she had at the authors' lunch at the Debbie
Reynolds hotel: like a spectator at a tennis game who was seated
along the net. Voices bounced back and forth above her head, ex-
changing volleys of priggish British demands and lusty pirate defiance.

"I'm getting dizzy," she complained to Eightball over the hullabaloo.

"Worth it," he answered with a grin. "The folks along the Strip
get a wider view, but we're right in mid-action."

"I could use a seat right now." Temple shifted her weight from right to left foot. High heels didn't bother her, unless she was forced to stand in the same place for a long while.

The British captain was bawling orders to his navvies: open the gun ports. A row of tiny doors in the ship's keel popped ajar. The ship's cannons made their politically incorrect appearance, thrusting out en masse in a phallic salute.

Instantly a red, booming burst exploded at the gun ports. Whipping around, Temple saw the pirate ship's masts bloom like fireworks, all flame and outward-flying flotsam. A screaming sailor plunged headfirst from crow's nest to deck, checked only a few feet before impact by the rope tied around one ankle. A perfectly timed stunt.

"Shiver me timbers," Eightball observed with a chuckle.

"You've seen this before. Who wins?"

"Who do you want to win?"

"Well, the pirates were lazy and off-guard—"

"So you're for the forces of law and order?"

"But the British are such bloody martinets—"

Barroom! The martinets fired again on relentless, crystal-clear command. And again.

On the pirate ship, masts and men tumbled deckward together. The light and heat of the disintegrating ship flickered on Temple's and Eightball's faces. Around them, people hooted in excited disbelief.

Another round hit the ruined privateer. The former theater flack in Temple cringed to watch a great set smashed to smithereens. Something else plunged to deck on a rigging-top rope, too bulky to be an acrobatic sailor.

Temple squinted through the smoke, wishing for a spy-glass. Could it be—? Was it possible—? How had she forgotten something so vital? So far she had spied no treasure chest, but now a massive example swung to and fro above the battered deck, its lid agape and its contents glittering.

She might as well be in China, Temple thought in despair. The chest dangled at least two sailors' height from the deck. The ship itself sat ten feet from the bridge's right railing, which was crammed with onlookers and therefore witnesses. The ship was also systematically being shattered down to its skeleton, and who was to say that the treasure chest was not the next target?

Perhaps the propmaster was to say, because if the special effects folks destroyed the chest for the show, a fresh one would have to replace it at every performance. Propmasters, Temple knew, hate replacing big, complicated props like fully loaded treasure chests.

So the chest was safe, which meant that it could very well house the prize pumps . . . safely.

While Temple tried to follow her thread of logic to the gravity-defying act of somehow swinging aboard the pirate ship to rummage in its fallen chest, the British had not been idle.

An articulate order of "Fire!" came once more.

This time the order was taken literally. The pirate ship exploded from mast-top to main deck in searing flames. On the structure behind the ship, where the pirates presumably stored their powder in a mighty magazine, the entire wall expelled a massive black cloud haloed with a fiery nimbus. Blast-furnace heat flushed Temple's face as people around her screamed their delight at tasting danger so close. She herself wondered how the attraction dared barbecue its audience. What if something went wrong?

Meanwhile, pirates were deserting the ship like rats, diving headfirst into the dark waters. Even then their valiant captain exhorted his remaining men to return fire one last time.

Speaking of rats . . . ugh, what a touch of ghastly realism! One particularly large specimen clung to the treasure chest's drooping lip, back legs churning as its forelegs hung on for dear life. At first she took it for an animated machine, but no robotic tail could thrash so fluidly. Amazing what animal trainers could do these days, Temple marveled. The rat's silhouette was as sharp as etched glass against the fiery magazine wall beyond it, and its frantic struggles made the treasure chest twist on its rope, turning its open maw toward her.

She could see inside! If she could only really *see!*

Temple elbowed, kneed and toed her way through the upward-staring crowd, trying to keep her head (and line of sight) above bald spots and sunvisors. She was soon pressed against the opposite railing, thisclose to the heat and the hectic activity . . . and to the treasure chest twisting slowly in the wind, with no one paying it any mind.

Contents, she thought. Something red and sparkly, like rubies . . . no, crinkled red cellophane, an old stage trick. Something silver that shone . . . Shoes?

Drat that rat, it was interfering with her view, with its big black head and its thick black tail. Rats don't have big heads. Nor furry tails. And rats aren't black, are they? Not even trained rats.

"A *cat*," Temple whispered.

Who did she fear would hear her in that crowd? Eightball was across the way. Only she saw what she saw.

A black cat.

The animal continued to claw the trunk as if trying to scramble inside. Finally, its grip loosened and it fell—Temple winced but did not shut her eyes—it fell, pulling the chest contents after it in a tumble of crumpled tinfoil, cellophane, metallic plastic beads and . . . no shoes.

Where was the cat?

Temple's gaze raked the deck just in time to see a last craven figure catapult from the rail into the water below.

"Louie," she whispered. She knew it was Midnight Louie.

Pitch-black in the ship's shadow, the water still rippled from the recent explosion, but nothing living moved in it. Temple pushed back across the bridge, where she stood and searched the brackish waves for survivors.

Nothing. Not a sailor, not a ship's cat. Eightball was still raptly staring at the British ship, which suddenly erupted in flames from the pirate ship's last volley.

"Louie," Temple murmured disconsolately into a sea of triumphant shouts. Nobody liked Captain Spit-and-Polish.

The British ship began to sink. The captain ordered his crew to swim for it while he remained ramrod-rigid at the splintered mast, clinging to his doomed position as stoutly as the shredded sails clung to the masts. The entire ship slowly slipped down, down, down into the briny deep.

Is that where Louie was now?

Temple leaned her head over the railing and watched the

British crew thrash toward the bridge. When they were almost under it, she shouted, "Is there a cat down there?"

Two men looked up, treading water.

"A cat!" she mouthed, hoping they could read lips. She made pathetic little paddling motions with her hands.

They read her distressed face, looked under the bridge, then shook their sopping heads. Then they swam on to some hidden exit under the bridge.

Maybe Louie had found it.

Music swelled around her, but Temple was too worried to heed it. Eightball grabbed her arm.

"Look. Look there! The ship's rising again."

Would Louie rise again?

Temple saw the Royal Navy's mast-tops pricking the water's thin skin and then rising more and more, until the Captain's bare head appeared. There was the bloody prig now, still standing at attention as "Rule, Britannia, Britannia Rule the Waves" pounded over the speaker system and his battle-battered ship lifted to ride normally on the waves.

The crowd, laughing and applauding, thinned into a moving stream of indistinguishable people with pressing places to go, like craps tables. Solemnly, the British ship retreated around the point, to be restored to spanking, white-sailed condition by the next show.

Temple wandered back to the pirate-ship side, where all was broken and charred. She assumed the technical crew would have it shipshape again in forty minutes.

Could she find someone from the crew? Beg them to check the ship, the water, the staging area for Louie? Would they believe her?

"Kind of hard to believe," Eightball ruminated beside her.

She glanced at the elderly man. He was discussing the programmed destruction and resurrection of the dueling ships, but he had inadvertently answered her unspoken question. No one would believe a cat had jumped into the midst of battle to claw open a treasure chest so his human roommate could find a pair of bejeweled shoes.

Temple sadly eyed the fallen treasure, as tawdry and deceptive as any dream of riches from El Dorado to Indiana Jones's Temple of Doom.

Midnight Louie was her real treasure, not some rare shoes bearing an image she had decided was him, and not simply an anonymous black cat. Perhaps the shoes would be his memorial.

For he had slipped aboard on purpose to inspect the chest; she knew that. Somehow, he had picked up the trail of her quest and had boldly gone where she could not go.

A tear meandered down her cheek to her throat.

"Hey." Eightball jerked on her sleeve. "That's funny. Never noticed that detail before."

"What?" she asked listlessly.

"Over there by the houses, next to the parrot. Look, atop that buxom figurehead."

Temple finally did look. It would be too hard to explain the unrehearsed show that she had seen unfolding amidst the advertised attraction: the end of Midnight Louie.

The parrot still sat there in its gaudy glory, head forever cocked. The figurehead still thrust her chin and bosom into the distance. And crouching atop her tilted-back head, eyeing the parrot, was a cat. A black cat. A wet black cat.

Temple opened her mouth but said nothing.

The cat's green eyes blinked, then the left one closed as it began licking a spiky forepaw.

Chapter 20

Long John Louie

Greater love hath no cat for his human, than that he should get wet in her service.

Wet? I am waterlogged in the first degree.

At least it is an artificial body of water, so my own torso is not subject to fish-nips, leeches and other things that go glub in the deeps.

Much as I like to give my finned friends the occasional love-nip, the truth is that they do bite and my terminal member looks much like a black caterpiller fallen on hard times.

So I sit in the semi-dark atop this somewhat wooden, naked and truncated lady known as a figurehead (why a head when her most prominent figure feature is somewhat lower, I do not know), tending to my grooming. I am relieved that Miss Temple has finally gotten her wits about her and noticed both my heroic actions on her behalf, and my long, slow recuperation afterward.

How I got here and did what I did is simple. When Miss Temple Barr leaves the scene of the crime these days—and these days the scene of the crime is my beloved alma mater, the Crystal Phoenix, sad to say—she is off on errands of a peculiarly repellent nature: looking for love in all the wrong places, such as a shoe store.

I do not know what the big deal is all about with my little doll and the two dudes at the Circle Ritz. The solution is simple, as my old friend Sassasfras would say to her many suitors: You got the dime, I got the time.

I do not understand why humans are so addicted to the notion of exclusivity. If we felines followed that creed, we would be on the verge of extinction. True, I have been wounded by the darts of that Persian enchantress, the lissome Yvette. But this does not mean that Midnight Louie is off the romance shelf and stamped "Expired." No, siree. I am free to come and go, and do a good bit of both.

It seems to my beknighted mind that Miss Temple would do better in her relationships with the opposite sex if she would adopt a feline point of view. Obviously, the Mystifying Max is a roamer who should be taken on his own terms and enjoyed when he is in town. Mr. Matt Devine is more domesticated, although he is unaccountably persnickety about the rules and regulations for activities that are best pursued in an improvisational frame of mind. So Miss Temple can have her cupcake and eat it too, if she would only see that it takes two to tango, and they are often both asking her to dance.

However, I am not about to meddle in these complex human hormonal matters. Where I hope to lend a helping hand, so to speak, is in a smaller area of operation: Miss Temple's devotion to footwear. Although I myself eschew decorative accessories, far be it from me to sneer at another's obsession, especially when it is a leather fetish. Yum-yum. I like nothing better than a good chew now and then, a long-standing masculine pleasure, and Miss Temple has the leather goods to keep my habit humming. (Although she does wax indignant when I slobber on her suede.)

Now that I know that a master of the shoemaker's art has been enlightened enough to use an image reminiscent of me on some of his creations, I can only extend all the powers at my command in assisting Miss Temple to obtain these rare objects.

This is why I followed her from the Crystal Phoenix, this is why my lightning-swift brain immediately surmised that her interest in things nautical had more to do with greed (as is usual with pirates then and now) than with wanderlust. This is why I risked body and soul by boarding the pirate ship. Who else could run so neatly over the rigging? Could cling so doggedly to the treasure chest, until all its tawdry contents had been exposed and dropped to deck?

Who else could face the burning deck without getting his whiskers singed? Who could be the last man ... male ... to desert ship? Who could paddle through the dark, disgusting water until he made shore safely, then find a high and dry refuge in plain sight of my distraught roommate, who by then had, to her credit but my underestimation, presumed me dead?

Only Midnight Louie is equipped to handle these kinds of crises. Please do not try these feats in your own home. There could be consequences and an investigation by the Federal Communications Commission.

Chapter 21

Opening Knights

"Here."

Kit thrust a fistful of printed matter into Temple's hand when she opened the door to her hotel room.

"What are these? Membership papers for the Hare Krishnas?"

"Mug shots."

"They are not." Temple shuffled through the array. "They're . . . the back covers torn off romance novels! I suppose the prose is provocative: 'He was wild as the wind, a whip-lean man of uncommon strength and fierce independence who would bow to no beauty's way, but whose proud heart longed for the sweet torment of the right woman's love.' Several titles right there: *Wild as the Wind . . . Bow to No Beauty . . . Beauty's Way . . . Proud Heart . . . Sweet Torment . . . The Right Woman's Love*. The whole blurb is a series of bloody titles!"

"Now she's getting it." Electra looked up from the dressing-table mirror, where she was performing curious rituals with mousse, an electric brush and cans of washable hair color.

Kit shook her head. "*Bow to No Beauty* and *The Right Woman's Love* are too mainstream, kid. But I didn't rip the backs off perfectly good paperbacks just so you could wax cynical about the copywriters who blurb our books. Turn over the covers and you'll see your lady rogue's gallery of author suspects."

Doing as instructed, Temple inspected the smiling faces of several naturally (or unnaturally) attractive middle-aged women. "They look like accountants' wives dressed up for New Year's!"

Kit's face squinched up. "Ooh, unkindest cut of all! We dump our eyeglasses, buy some ritzy outfit we can't afford and a new hairdo, *even* go to Glamour Shots to get that soft-focus, wrinkle-erasing look for our book cover photos, and *you* compare us gloriously dramatic romance writers to *accountants' wives*? I take exception. I am not married."

"You and I *are* exceptions," Electra murmured from the mirror, where she was frowning at the green and blue stripes in her hair.

"What does she mean?" Temple asked.

"She's right," Kit said. "Most romance writers are disgustingly married. For years and years. To the same man. I could honestly describe them as an unprovocative lot, despite their spicy reputation in the press, which is inaccurate, as usual. We are middle-aged, middle-America, middle-of-the-road."

"And sometimes Middle-Earth," Electra added while spritzing lavender into her elfin coiffure.

"Hmmm." Temple nodded at the black-and-white faces fanned in her fingers like a hand of playing cards, all queens. "That could mean that these women all have straight-arrow husbands who might take violent exception to macho models, especially now that women authors are touring with them."

"An arrow does seem like a man's weapon," Kit agreed.

"Why?" Electra stepped away from her hair preparations, looking like an interrupted rainbow. "Anybody can stab something, and women get lots of practice with the Sunday pork roast."

"Unless," Temple pointed out, "these are modern households where hubby does the chef work. That's a good question, though; why an arrow?"

"It was there?" Kit looked pleased with herself.

"Yup, the arrow indeed came from Cheyenne's own quiver, but this murder must have been premeditated. Was using Cheyenne's arrow more than just handy? Was it symbolic?"

Kit's glance consulted Electra. "Is she always so existential about murders?"

"I think Temple is asking, did someone really want to stick it to him? Was it personal?"

"Murders usually are, aren't they?" Kit said. "What else would they be?" She looked shocked, which was a shame, since the expression clashed with the ultra-chic, silk-faille dinner suit she was wearing.

Temple hesitated. "Let's see. The murders I've seen were definitely done by personally involved killers, though in more than one case the murderer had never met the victim until he zeroed in for the kill."

"Then why kill them?" Kit looked even more shocked by Temple's calm dissection of a murderer's modus operandi.

"Revenge for ancient wrongs. It was good enough for the Greeks."

"I'll say. Enough to spawn dozens of endlessly long tragedies, some of which I had to appear in. On stage. In front of people."

Temple studied the photographic faces again. "Not one of these ladies looks mean enough to stab a Thanksgiving turkey with a thermometer."

"Looks are deceiving. That's why these lovely ladies are suspects." Kit plucked a cover from the crowd and held it up for Temple's closer inspection.

This woman, Temple decided, was the torchiest-looking: acres of curly blond hair like a cloudy halo, a dab of decolletage, mouth ajar in the professional model's about-to-suck-a-persimmon pose.

Kit tilted her head at the photo. "Some romance writers— usually the younger ones who have the most natural qualifications—cultivate a sensual image. They want you to think that they could pose as the heroine of their own book covers. Maybe they occasionally delude themselves into playing that part. This is Ravenna Rivers, the one rumored to have cozied up with the Homestead Man on tour last winter. Her husband always escorts her at conventions, and should be here. So should the Homestead Man. By the way, her books are the 'spiciest' of the lot, with a bit much S&M for my taste."

"How much is a bit much?" Temple wanted to know.

"Any at all. Sado-masochism was more common when the sexy historical romance got hot in the seventies. A lot of overprotected women in those days didn't know what was sexy unless it came home with their husbands in a brown paper wrapper, and a lot of male pornography depicts S&M. There's less of that stuff now in historical romances, but the underground appetite for kink, and for one's own worst interests, still keeps some practitioners of the art selling lots of books."

Kit tapped another author photo, a sixtyish woman with over-styled suspiciously raven hair. "This one is rabidly opposed to the hunkification of romance cover art. Mary Ann Trenarry. She started a letter-writing campaign against model-author contracts to the publishers involved and the media. I admire her guts, because the backlash could hurt her book sales. The rumor is that she can't sell her new books to anyone. Maybe a crusader scorned would want to sabotage the pageant."

Kit selected another photo with an odd smile. "And here we have Sharon Rose, a simple woman she would have you think, who just happens to be the Rasputin of the romance industry."

"This moon-faced, grinning woman in the dated bubble cut? Mrs. Girl Scout Mother incarnate?"

Kit nodded. "Makes Shannon Little look like Cruella de Vil, doesn't she? I told you appearances were deceiving. Her books are sentimental melodramas, and her fans adore her, but in real life she's a piranha in polyester. Also the biggest bestseller in the bunch. She had her own sister, a new author at the time, drummed out of her publishing house because she didn't like the competition. Poor woman didn't sell anywhere else, either. No one has heard of Jessica Rose since."

"If this woman is that filthy rich, why on earth does she wear polyester?"

"Because it doesn't wrinkle when she travels, dummy!"

Temple eyed her aunt's smashingly simple, simply smashing

dinner suit. "Yours will wrinkle like a prune. That's silk shantung, probably designer."

"Indeed. Bought off-price, of course. We poorer souls have to dress for where we want to be. Some of the folks already there wouldn't know silk if the worm came up and mugged them. There is no justice. All the people you know who get rich never spend their money the way you would."

"At least you don't have to pine over what they've got," Electra said briskly. She turned her Technicolor head from side to side. "What do you think? As an aspiring writer, I want to get noticed at the opening ceremony, but is this too much?" Before either Temple or Kit could reply, Electra posed her real question: not if, but how much. "Should I blend the edges or go for the shock effect?"

"Blend the edges," Temple and Kit replied as one.

Nobody organized special events like the Crystal Phoenix. Fantasy potted palms of white metal and brass ringed the ballroom. The convention decorating committee had taken the decor—eighteenth-century French palatial, with pale-painted wood paneling and discreet touches of gilt—and swagged it with such airy, fairy fabrics as iridescent netting and metallic lace. Temple definitely felt that a troop of fairy godmothers should assemble soon to inspect the royal newborn and confer good wishes.

But somewhere around this hotel, if not in this crowd, lurked a wicked fairy whose wand had been a fatal arrow. Cheyenne's sleeping beauty would not awaken at the kiss of a lovely princess. Interesting, Temple mused, had anyone tried writing a role-reversal romance version of *Sleeping Beauty*? Eeek! She had been reading too many romances for homework lately; she was getting ideas. Her mind should be on mayhem and murder, not tulle and roses and . . . *hissss* . . . men.

"Those are some shoes." In the hustle of separating Electra from the hair sprays, Kit had not noticed Temple's feet. "They could double as a weapon."

"Steel heels, Weitzman. Clawed cousins to Louie's shoes." Temple spun to show off the wavy prongs of pewter-colored metal on which she balanced. They added kick to her primly styled sixties platinum-metallic suit.

"Where did you get that outfit?"

"A resale shop called Reprize. Some of this ancient stuff is actually neat."

"Some of this ancient stuff, baby, was neat, and new, when *I* wore it." Kit's wry expression as she viewed the resurrected fashion ghosts of her youth turned into a smile. "I really had concluded that all that stuff from my era was absolutely horrid, but you look so cute in it."

"Don't call me 'cute,' " Temple warned. "That's one of my button-pushing words."

"Oh." Kit grinned. "I see, as in your 'cute, button nose'?"

"Were you always mean?"

"Only since I left Minnesota."

"The real show-stealer to swoon over is Electra."

They turned to their companion, who was obliviously craning her neck to see the crowd as the crowd craned its necks to study her hair.

Instead of wearing her usual muumuu, Electra was swathed in an electric-blue lamé pantsuit, and wore shoulder-dusting, pink-fluorescent flamingo earrings.

"She's really serious about this romance-writing bug, isn't she?" Kit asked in a whisper.

"I guess so. Any hope of real money in it for newcomers?"

"Virgins, you mean? Sure. As there is in anything. It's just that so few get it. Why?" Kit cocked her a shrewd look. "Are you thinking of turning your personal woes into bestselling fiction?"

"Except that my story would be sold as 'true horror.' Is there such a category?"

"Not . . . yet," Kit said. "Although paranormal, or what we call New-Age themes, are hot in romances now."

"What sort of books are those?"

"Oh, vampire heroes, angel heroines, time-travel and futuristics, which are set in space."

Electra's flamingo earrings jangled in their direction as she heard her own trigger words. "New Age! Right up my Ouija board," she said gleefully. "But I'm confining myself to a simple historical romance for the contest. Nothing fancy to distract the judges."

"Good idea." Kit was searching the crowd now. "Keep it simple when you're starting out."

"Maybe it is simple," Temple mused. "Even I had an idea for a romance novel just now."

"Watch out!" Kit made like a goblin, startling Temple into jumping to look behind her. "The big-time romance-writing blues are gonna get you."

"No," Temple said, reassembling her dignity. "I don't think that's my strong point."

A new voice, masculine, insinuated itself into their threesome. "You seem to be standing on your strong points, Red."

Temple whirled. No one called her "Red."

Oh. Of course.

"These shoes were made for kicking," she told Crawford Buchanan, who had changed into an evening vest and jacket, both black to match his oil-slick hair. "And if you don't step back a bit, that's what they're gonna do."

"Tsk-tsk." He minced backward. "And here I was going to get a closeup for *Hot Heads*." He had to lean closer to whisper, "These romance broads aren't half as photogenic as you, T.B. Most of them fill up the camera and then some."

"Maybe they're fed up with you," she suggested. "Haven't you got anything better to do than hang around and harass women?"

"Hey, it's my job." His long, thick eyelashes flickered. "I get paid to do this."

"That's what is wrong with this country," Temple said, turning her back on both him and the camera.

That didn't stop Crawford Buchanan. Temple watched Kit and Electra bloom in an aura of light as the cameraman panned down Temple's head to her shoes.

"If I had the Midnight Louie shoes," she muttered under her breath, "the Austrian crystal kick would burn out the camera sensor."

"You were saying something about sensuality," Buchanan

purred in her ear. Or maybe he growled. Men did that a lot in some romance novels.

Temple would have loved to G.R.O.W.L. back, but instead she did the mature thing and ignored him, until finally the bright lights drew away and faded.

"Is he gone?" Temple asked her companions.

They nodded.

"Next time he comes around," Electra said, "I'll tell you when he's leaning close again so you can stomp his instep with your steel heel."

"You need to meet a better class of men." Kit focused like a very chic Doberman on a nearby group of people. "Ah. There stands an abandoned husband. Husbands, and men in general, are rare in this crowd; isolation is an occupation for them. Want to do some sleuthing on the sly? Follow me."

Throwing her hands up at Electra, Temple did so. All too soon she found herself confronting one tall man standing like a lonesome pine in a sea of overdressed shrubs.

"Hello," Kit said warmly. "Haven't seen you in ages! Remember the G.R.O.W.L. reception in New York at the romance writers' convention a couple of years ago? Kit Carlson, better known, I devoutly hope, as Sulah Savage."

"Oh, yes," the man said with relief.

Besides being tall, he was pleasant-looking in a low-key way, nice but not exciting, the perfect man to be somebody else's husband. Although he was doing a good impression of a man happily alone in a world of women and content with doing nothing but gawking, he was clearly glad to see a possibly familiar face. He gazed uneasily at Temple, as if he should know her too.

"My, ah, cousin," Kit extemporized, deftly erasing their age difference, and thus enhancing hers. "Temple Barr. She writes for *Women's Work* magazine, you know, the mag about rags-to-riches women entrepreneurs. Their circulation is massive. I'm sure they'd love to do a story on your darling wife."

Kit glanced toward an animated knot of women who were either in a feeding frenzy around the chip and dip table, or gathered to worship a face familiar only lately to Temple from the ripped-off back of a paperback book.

"Quite the popular girl," Kit said in her blatantly artificial social voice. A woman would have instantly heard the underlying satire; a man, or at least this man, merely nodded politely. "Temple, this is the man behind the woman behind the bestsellers, Sharon Rose. I know your last name is different . . . Herbert—?"

"Harvey," he said.

"Oh, sorry! Harvey—?"

His shook his head with a smile. "No. Herbert Harvey."

"Oh."

How unfortunate, Temple thought, to have two first names.

Herbert Harvey nodded shyly at her. "I'm sure my wife would be delighted to have another national magazine article. She was featured in Martha Stewart's celebrity holidays issue. Quite a spread. She had the down-home Fourth of July picnic with old-fashioned bottles of Coca-cola on ice in a washtub and country ham on a checkered tablecloth."

This was not the sort of upscale entertaining Temple expected from a filthy rich, bestselling author. Then she remembered Kit describing Sharon Rose's books as "nauseatingly" homey and sentimental.

Having been assigned her role and then handed her cue by Kit, Temple wrote and recited her first speech, which was not brilliant.

"Do you often attend these conferences, Mr. Herbert . . . I mean, Harvey?"

"That's all right. Everybody's always getting my names mixed up. Just call me Herbert." He sighed and looked over the animated crowd, whose dominant female voices were going a mile a minute. "I just come now and again, when it's convenient. I'm on my way to do some hunting in western Canada."

Now that was more like lifestyles of the rich and famous! Canadian hunting trips, with guide, cost a bundle.

"Where do you and Mrs. Herbert live?"

"Muncie, Indiana. I was an assistant school superintendent there." He looked somewhat lost for a moment. "I'm retired now.

No need to work." He glanced again toward his wife's charmed circle, as if worried.

Temple guessed that Hervey Harbert, or whatever, was still in his forties. His wife's fame and fortune had made his entire career redundant. He stuck his hands in his pockets and smiled expectantly at Temple, waiting for her to toss back the conversational ball. She figured she'd learn more by letting him take the lead, which he did.

"Tell me about your job. Interviewing all those successful women must be interesting work."

"It is." Temple nodded brightly. "Sometimes annoying."

"Annoying?"

"Well, they're so rich and busy, and I'm just a freelance writer. I wish I could write one of these romances—"

"The pay isn't good at the beginning," he warned her. "And it's a lot of hard work in a pretty cutthroat business. Sharon has had to fight for every inch of progress she's made. She travels more than she writes."

"I don't think I'm cut out for romance writing anyway. Crime writing, now's there's an area I might go for. You did hear about the cover model murder?"

Herbert frowned and cleared his throat. "I guess they have to put those guys on the covers to sell books, but it's kind of hokey, don't you think—these prima donna musclemen? Oh, some of them seem decent enough fellows, but the women sure make idiots of themselves swooning over them."

Temple smiled conspiratorially. "I agree! It's embarrassing to see all these middle-aged women chasing the nearest pretty pectoral as if they were mainlining hormones. Shallow and silly. Pure ego-building."

Herbert blinked. He couldn't tell if Temple was putting him on or not. But he laughed, nervously, and that's when a short, plump woman with a really overcooked permanent in a shade of not-*too*-blond brown materialized by his side, her arm possessively through his. She was smiling, but through her teeth, and she made no effort to conceal her intense annoyance with them both.

"Thank you," she told Temple in steel-wool tones meant to rub her raw. "Thank you, miss, a mere stranger, for keeping *my Herb* busy while I was chatting with all my fans."

With that she jerked her entwined arm and led Herbert Harvey away like a delinquent labrador retriever brought to heel. He lumbered off faithfully.

Temple felt herself flushing, not for her masquerade, but for Sharon Rose's awful behavior to both of them. The nerve, as if Temple were some vamp trying to lure away a lawfully wedded husband just by talking to the man! As if he couldn't be trusted to be away from her uxorial claws for one minute. Why hadn't wifeypooh bothered to include Herbert in her adoring circle, if she feared that he couldn't talk to another woman without imminent danger of seduction?

Kit cruised up, both hands brimming with goblets of white wine. "She just *writes* romance, remember? She doesn't necessarily know a thing about men, or marriage."

"I suppose that's an expert speaking." Temple took a glass and sipped before she forgot herself and spit. "What a— Too bad I don't use those words about other women."

"Oh, make an exception. I know just what you mean." Kit turned to beam on the new, adjusted scene: Sharon Rose in bloom amid her admiring wreath of fans, ignored by nearby husband Herbert, who was sticking up like a transplanted stalk of hollyhock desperately in need of water, or something much stronger.

"*Her* Herb," Temple repeated in the same pointed, treacly tone of voice.

"Are you stuttering, dear?"

"No, I'm trying to fathom that paranoid, possessive mentality. She must be insecure."

"Brilliant deduction."

"Still, why me? A stranger. What does she do to women who actually know her?"

"Grinds them into the ground with teeth-gritted pronouncements about how they should do everything from family rearing to writing a sex scene. And she smiles every moment. She'll go after men like a pit bull, too. I've seen her trotting around conventions with a whipped-dog male agent on one side and a hu-

miliated female editor on the other, both two steps behind. That
lady has a genius for dysfunctional living, actually. That's the
book she should write: *How to Whip Ass and Stomp Egos for Fun
and Profit.*"

"I could see someone murdering *her.*"

"No such luck. Nor does her husband strike me as the type to
knock off a cover hunk, do you think?"

"Never! Why?"

"Oh, I happened to see the sales cover flat of Sharon Rose's new
book before I left New York, *Satin and Sagebrush.* And it was
Cheyenne's last, best moment, believe me. A smashing painting
of him in cowboy gear, minus shirt and pants. Her 'personal pen
pal' notes on the inside back bubbled about how fun it was to witness a cover shoot with a rising star."

"Then you came here and recognized him?"

"When I saw him dead. And undressed. He was reclining on
the cover."

"That's a new angle. I suppose you didn't want to tell me until
I had experienced the Rose of Sharon personality close up and personal. Ouch! Do you suppose I'll have the stomach to approach
her later and ask some pointed questions?"

"It depends on how badly you want to know the answers."

While they talked quietly, Temple had been vaguely aware of
a civilian, a woman in a modest knit top and slacks, standing two
or three feet away, out of earshot but clearly waiting.

"Yes?" Temple said.

She approached diffidently. "I saw you talking to Miss Rose. She
seems awful nice."

"Hmm," said Temple in that politely noncommittal way the
British have mastered since the time of the Norman invasion.

"I'm much too nervous to ask her for an autograph. Maybe I
can just ask you about her. Is she as wonderful as her books?"

The woman's eyes were shining, as was her unpowdered nose.
She would never be a bestselling novelist who touted down-home
virtues while she ran roughshod over other people with a cattle
prod. How do you tell hero-worshipers that their idol has feet of
corrugated steel?

Temple didn't. "She was lovely, just lovely." Temple smiled.
The woman nodded and floated off to the fringes of Sharon
Rose's admirers.

"A legend is born," Kit muttered. "We all know what she's really like, having felt her bite as well as her bark, but we have to
hear readers coo over her as if she were a plaster saint. And she
doesn't write worth a damn, either. That's show biz. No justice."

"It would be nice if Sharon Rose had murdered Cheyenne."

"Nice, but pure fiction I fear. She doesn't need to kill anyone;
she shrivels their spirits while they're still living, like her poor husband."

"Opposites do attract," Temple mused as they cruised through
the mob looking for the blue-green neon of Electra's hair.

"Or maybe you're attracted to opposites. Your two guys look
pretty diametrically different."

"I wish you wouldn't call them 'my two guys' as if I had a harem!
Everything's on hold, at the moment, with everyone. Nobody is
nobody's anything."

"Maybe you had better not try writing a romance. You don't
make sense when you get excited, and that's fatal in the sex
scenes."

"Fine," said Temple. "I'm more interested in fatalities than sex
at the moment, anyway. Now let's find Electra so we can watch
this show get on the road."

Kit kept meek silence as they do-si-doed around the room,
stopping whenever someone recognized Kit or, more likely, the
pseudonym on her name badge.

"Sulah Savage! I love your books!" the typical greeting would
begin, an approach guaranteed to put a seraphic smile on the face
of the hailed author. "When's the next 'Love's Inquisition' book
coming out? I loved Reynaldo's story."

"My Spanish epic," Kit murmured modestly to Temple as they
moved on, leaving an excited fan in their wake flashing Kit's
phony signature at all her friends.

"Doesn't it feel funny to sign a made-up name?" Temple asked.

"Heavens no! I made it up myself. Besides, it's like playing a role.

When I appear as Sulah Savage, I'm in character as Sulah Savage. It's liberating to have an official alter ego."

"This is all about role-playing, isn't it?" Temple said.

"I told you, this is bookselling. Hype. Theater."

"Maybe the murderer was playing a role too. Or Cheyenne was. One he hadn't counted on playing."

"Of course Cheyenne was playing a role. That was his job."

"His job." Temple thought about that too. "I need to see more of what a cover hunk's job is like."

"Well, forget that for now and grab a chair, because Electra has been nice enough to save a couple seats at that table just ahead, and I hear the podium mike being tested by amateurs." A horrible screeching momentarily froze the assemblage before fading. "Showtime!"

"I've got to work on a good pseudonym," Electra said as soon as they sat down. "I've been talking to readers and they all say the name is very important."

"Electra Lark is a fabulous pen name!" Kit argued indignantly. "Not so long it will run off a book cover, but different as well as pretty."

"Everybody says it sounds like a pseudonym." Electra took a heartfelt slurp through the straw in her Blue Hawaii. "Besides, it isn't alliterative."

"All that alliteration is regarded as hokey today," Kit said. "You forget that I've been doing this for ages. I'd never use Sulah Savage now, but it's too late."

"What were you thinking of using?" Temple asked Electra.

"I've always wanted to be a Vivian."

"Well," Kit said, "we all know I didn't want to be an Ursula." She eyed Temple. "Did you ever cherish visions of another name?"

Since Temple Kinsella was the only speculating Temple had ever done in that area, and it was hardly a harmonious name, or appropriate to mention now, she kept quiet. Then some imp of unconscious invention put the name Temple Devine in her head. She swallowed her wine wrong, laughing the entire time as Kit and Electra pounded her on the back.

On the low, long staging area, spotlights were brightening.

"I think I'd keep Temple Barr," she whispered when she could talk again.

They both nodded, no longer interested, eyes focused on the narrow area of light in the darkened ballroom.

There followed the usual opening ceremony rituals at conferences everywhere, only with a romance novel twist. The president of G.R.O.W.L. welcomed the authors and readers. The president of Fabrizio's fan club came up and presented him with a sterling flacon for his new cologne, "Macho Man."

"Temple's been picked up by him," Kit leaned across her to tell Electra.

"No!" Electra leaned across Temple from the other side. "I've heard that he accosts women in elevators." She frowned. "I've also heard that he really doesn't care for women at all. So I guess both rumors can't be true."

By the time the two had finished hashing over Breezy's inclinations and/or lack of them, the model himself was gone, golden locks, silver flacon and all that muscle.

By the time Temple had realized that there was something very different about this opening ceremony—all the officials at the mike were women—the few obligatory speeches were over.

Another woman bathed in the spotlight, only she had the Barbie-doll hair for it. Temple blinked, and then a breathy monotone hyperventilated into the microphone.

"Ladies and . . . ladies. And laddies." She glanced coyly to her left. Temple could just see the shining crowns of a long line of male models.

"Oh, no," Temple moaned to her wine glass.

"My official duties don't begin until the pageant Saturday night, but I'm proud and pleased to introduce the contestants." A furious rustling of papers came over the mike.

"Who is she?" Kit was asking, dumbfounded.

"Looks like we didn't listen to the introduction. That has to be Las Vegas's version of Norma Desmond, the film star Savannah Ashleigh."

Beside her, Electra jolted into life from a long reverie. "That's it. My pseudonym. Great name."

"You can't use it, Electra. It's already *her* pseudonym, whatever her real name was."

"And besides," Kit put in consolingly, "it's much too long for a book cover. I've never heard of her," she added.

"You're lucky. I had to interview her during the Stripper Killer case. I would have gotten more, and more sensible information, out of her cat Yvette."

"Yvette? For a cat?"

"You should see it. A Persian, of course, a silver thistledown with tiny little teeth and claws. She keeps it in a pink canvas carrier."

"Savannah Ashleigh did what in a pink canvas carrier?" Electra demanded.

"Never mind. We better hush up while she's talking. I guess that's what you call it."

With another wicked giggle, this time shared with Kit, Temple settled down to serious listening. A clue might pop out from the mouths of babes. It was possible.

The mouth of this babe, though, continued to stumble over the models' names and vital statistics. Perhaps Savannah needed reading glasses and was too vain to use them. Or perhaps she had never been able to read and talk at the same time.

Once called, the men bounded onto stage with the same eagerness as if they were about to be introduced to Sharon Stone. Confident, charming, each with a prepared off-the-cuff comment, they made Savannah Ashleigh look like the aspiring performer.

Female heads nodded approval all over the room, and each contestant was ushered off with enthusiastic applause, especially the blond-white-haired surfer male nurse who flung heart-shaped wrapped candies into the audience.

While the audience was sizing up the men for the coming contest, Temple was watching and listening with different criteria in mind. Any bit of background suggestive? Any link to Cheyenne? No one's biography mentioned the stripper contest, but that wouldn't be something they'd emphasize. Although most of them were professional or aspiring models and actors, they didn't want to project too raunchy an image before this house of middle-American women.

Temple contemplated the fact that these men walked a fine line. Yes, they were sex objects. Yes, they had to court and charm convention attendees in order to succeed and win followings. But they also had taken care not to cross over into any behavior that could be considered sexual harassment.

That was a charge that female sex objects didn't have to worry about.

Not all the men were pros. Some were dedicated amateurs. Those with everyday professions were particularly applauded: chiropractor, car salesman and lawyer (he was hissed first and then applauded). Those with perceived sexy job descriptions, cop and forest ranger, were hailed with roof-raising hoots and applause.

"It's nice they have under-forty and over-forty age categories," Electra commented between introductions.

"Thirty-three," Temple said contemplatively.

"No, dear. Thirty-three isn't the break point, though it would be as good a place as any."

"I meant thirty-three contestants. Cheyenne would have made thirty-four. That's a lot of potential victims, and suspects. Poor Lieutenant Molina!"

"You feel sorry for Molina? This is a first."

"It doesn't make sense to kill Cheyenne over the contest. There are just too many contestants to fix the outcome with one death."

"Oh, goodie. Now you're going to tell us we have a serial killer at large," Kit said.

"No, we don't. Not yet, anyway. I've got to get closer to the contest."

"You mean the contestants," her aunt said. "You think you can stand the heat?"

"They're just a bunch of nice guys trying to finish first."

"Right," said Kit skeptically.

"Without getting finished off."

"Well, I'll look into your wish, Pinocchio, and you may prove to be made of wood, even with all those sparks around. But if your nose starts growing, I'll yank you out of there."

"Don't worry. I told you. I'm off men. I'm immune."

"With that attitude, you are not a good candidate for a reader of mine. At least you're not entering the Love's Leading Amateur writing contest."

"Contest," Temple repeated dreamily. "People coming from all over to compete for a prize. And then they die. Why?"

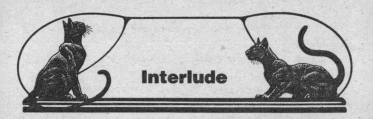

Interlude

Hysterical Again

Great to escape the hullabaloo of the crowd. A writer needs quiet to create. Now where was I? The jewels. Where could I hide them in a carriage? Maybe in the tire. Or weren't they inflatable then? Does it have a trunk? Hard to say. I know—

"The jewels?" Even in the moonlight, the lovely Amaianariala's skin was seen to pale. "My good sir, I have no jewels. My carriage was a ruse to divert dastardly robbers from the real treasure trove. The jewels are on their way to

Timbuktu. Was there a Timbuktu then? If not, where?
to Sicily."

"Cecily? Is this your sister?" he gruffed, brandishing his dagger.

The fair Aananamiklia was seen to blush. "I have no sister. Sicily is an island in the Mediterrean Sea."

"And I have no ship, so I am in no position to pursue the jewels by sea. I see. . . . Then—" The Demon Dagger of Devonshire grinned and leaped off his steed into the roadway.

In a moment the carriage door was jerked open so quickly that the lovely Amslslisdfnkdl

Dammit! Rotten, stupid name. Never comes out the same twice. Oh, well, fix it later.

tumbled to the road and right into the arms of the Demon Dagger of Devonshire.

"Aghhh!" she screamed. "Would you mind not brandishing your dagger, sir? It pricked me."

" 'Twill do more than prick you, madam, do you not do as I say you should do."

Hey, I'm really getting the hang of this flowery language. And that repeated use of "prick" isn't too shabby. A little subliminal sex never hurt anyone. Now what?

The duke's daughter swooned, so the Demon Dagger tossed her back into the carriage, ordered the driver to move on without any tricks and tied his faithful steed's reins to a

Carriage wheel. Oops, that might strangle the damn, inconvenient horse. Ah!

lantern (thingamajiggy at the top, find word later).

Then he leaped into the carriage, his dagger between his teeth. The comely Arianainla cowered in a corner.

Sex, remember, sexual tension.

The Demon Dagger thrust his dagger in

in . . . in . . . his (belt? too modern) . . . sash!

his scarlet sash, and took out his

Finial!

That's the damn word I wanted to tie the reins to.

moneybag.

"I have no money," shrilled the lass.

"Luckily, I do," he rasped. "I don't want your money, I want justice."

"And for you, justice is—?" she inquired spiritedly.

"Whatever of the Baron's possessions I can take," he snarled, as he looked her lush, recumbant form up and down.

"What has my father ever done to you?" she cried.

"He has transported my brother to the wilds of Australia, my other brother to the coal mines of Wales, my eldest sister to the gin mills and my youngest sister to the streets of San Francisco (check for time). And he has made a wanted man of me."

"You sound a thoroughly degenerate lot, sir. No doubt you deserved my father's treatment."

"But you will not deserve mine," he swore, sitting beside her on the seat of the carriage.

"What do you intend?" she said faintly.

Okay. Got to get down to the hard stuff. Where's that section in this one book? I can kind of . . . echo it. In my own original way, of course.

Moonlight washed through the casement carriage window like midnight lace, and painted the face of ~~Lady Hester~~ lovely Arianaina soft silver. Moonlight shone from the white silk shirt of the Demon Dagger, emphasizing his broad shoulders and narrow hips, his long limbs and pale long hair, his hairless face, his washboard stomach and rain barrel chest.

Say, rain barrel goes pretty well with washboard. Wonder if this is what the tipsheet meant when it said to avoid "laundry lists" of physical description? Maybe I'd better cut that washday analogy; save it for a rainy day. Heh-heh. Look at me! I can write wringers around these dumb romance hacks. Bet I win.

Chapter 22

Morning, Moon and Molina

"Charlie Moon."

"Charlie Moon?"

"Cheyenne's real name."

"Really?"

"Would I kid you?"

Temple looked up into Molina's ice-blue eyes and knew that would be the day.

The lieutenant didn't seem happy about conveying information to Temple, but in her profession she must have to deal with snitches, and one does not get unless one gives.

"That's a charming name," Temple said after a moment. "Why did he change it?"

"I suspect other kids used to laugh at it when he was a child. On the reservation and off of it."

"So he did have Native American blood!"

"Some. Enough to bounce between relatives on the reservation and in Phoenix when he was growing up. The usual 'troubled youth' clashes with the law. Petty stuff. We can't find any next of kin to claim the body."

"No one to claim him? That's ridiculous. This guy could have been a celebrity, if he'd won. He would have been on *Hard Copy* and *Hot Heads*."

"Even then no one might have claimed him. Family is a forgotten concept for some of these kids growing up today. Charlie Moon never had much, except his looks. Now they're on ice at the medical examiner's, and the show goes on."

Temple followed Molina's glance to the stage, with its ramp, stairs and partial set.

"Somebody even showed up to claim the horse." Temple knew she looked as disgusted as she sounded.

Molina cocked her head like a hungry robin who had heard worm stirrings. "That's right. The horse. Getting an animal that big into—and out of—a hotel can't be that easy. How did he manage it?"

"Don't ask me, Lieutenant. I never had a horse, unfortunately. I just know that Danny Dove said one of those horse-haulers whisked it away. He was big-time nervous about horse droppings on his stage."

"Where's Danny Dove?"

"Backstage." Temple pointed. She could hardly wait to see Molina and Dove go one-on-one.

"And what are you doing around here anyway?"

"Ah, I'm helping with the show."

Molina nodded, slipping her narrow notebook into her sage-green jacket side-pocket. "You're practically on staff here now," she noted.

Temple said nothing. She wanted Molina to think that duty kept Temple around the crime scene. Temple knew that it was a different kind of duty than her employment at the Crystal Phoenix: guilt over Cheyenne's death.

"Any fingerprints on the arrow?" she only remembered to ask as Molina turned away.

Molina turned back and her dark head shook. "Not a one. The killer was clever enough to think of that. Probably used a cloth, snatched up just before he, or she, grabbed the arrow from Cheyenne's quiver, and struck. The backstage area is cluttered with odd pieces of costuming and such. If you can call it costuming! The victim had nothing on but a flesh-colored jockstrap, a loincloth, and the quiver and bow case. And a medicine pouch with a bone and a feather and a few crystals," she added. "Not much material for evidence."

"If Cheyenne was struck backstage, how could he ride out and continue his act?"

"He didn't." Molina indicated the ceiling above the audience. "The routine called for him to shoot an arrow through the balloon."

Temple searched the dim heights, puzzled until she spotted a huge, heart-shaped red-foil balloon attached to a lighting fixture. "Pretty spectacular trick. I suppose a spotlight would hit the heart for the actual pageant."

Molina nodded grimly. "With the stage crew's concerned with the heart's placement and lighting, nobody backstage paid attention to what riveted the people in the audience: the victim and his horse. Whoever stabbed him backstage with the arrow, a broad-head steel-tipped one more than sufficient for the job, knew that the shock of the blow, directed at a man who was keyed up for a performance, would virtually immobilize Cheyenne until the horse took him out on stage. There, massive internal bleeding enervated him, and he tumbled to the stage, the arrow in his bow never released. He was dead before anybody reached him."

Temple felt a chill. "So I'm not a suspect."

"Not if you were standing mid-aisle, gawking, in the presence of a witness."

"And Cheyenne was as good as dead the moment he passed the teaser curtains?"

"Exactly. A very clever attack, but risky. I have to hope that someone saw the perpetrator doing something out of character."

Temple nodded, then watched the policewoman plod up the stairs and down the long runway toward the stage proper. Molina always moved like a military tank. Maybe Temple wasn't used to large women. Or maybe Molina lacked grace. Temple favored the latter explanation.

"Don't stand and gawk when you can sit," a voice urged from the empty seats.

She didn't like being reminded of what she was doing when Cheyenne was dying, and turned with irritation to the empty auditorium seats behind her. Not all empty.

A hunk sprawled on a fifth-row seat, long blue-jeaned legs and cowboy boots thrust into the aisle. His western shirt was cut close and buttoned tight where it wasn't open to the chest hairs at their most profuse. No wonder they called this the Incredible Hunk pageant; all the entrants looked as imminently ready to split their seams as the comic books' Incredible Hulk himself.

A long, narrow woman wearing the same western uniform sat beside this particular edition of hunkdom like a feminine twin.

Temple took his suggestion—especially since she was wearing her smashing, red but uncomfortable, resale-shop Charles Jourdans—by perching on the seat-arm across the center aisle from the Deadwood duo.

"Troy Tucker." The man's hand extended for a hearty shake. "This here's my wife Nance."

Nance just nodded. She had a long, frizzy palomino ponytail and a face born to be freckled.

"I work for the hotel," Temple said, adding several yards of hemp to Molina's rope of misconception. "I'm trying to get a feel for the contest. PR, you know."

Both of them unconsciously tensed, as if suddenly on stage.

"This is our third," Nance said in the same soft country drawl as her husband.

"Great! You can fill me in on everything. What's it like?"

They exchanged glances. He spoke. "Wahl, it's mighty like a rodeo, ma'am. Standin' around behind the scenes, gettin' in line, gettin' the adrenaline up for your few seconds in the spotlight and hopin' that nothin' out there throws ya. At least here you don't get horse hockey in yer bootheels."

Temple laughed, as she was meant to, and kicked up a high heel to indicate just how deeply she might sink in the stuff if it were around. "Maybe I would have been in deep doodoo . . . if I'd been around when Charlie Moon was killed."

A new tension coiled both figures.

"How'd he get that huge horse in here anyway?" she went on.

"Simple as cow pies, ma'am," Troy said. "Unload 'im out back, at the hotel loading dock. Take 'im down in the freight elevator and bring 'im back up in the stage elevator, the one behind the scenes."

"How do you know all this?"

"Shoot, ma'am. I helped with the critter."

"Then you knew Charlie."

Husband and wife consulted glances again. Both their eyes seemed permanently narrowed, maybe from regarding distant, bright Western horizons, maybe from natural skepticism.

"We did," Nance said at last. "From the previous pageant. And he had done some rodeo, too."

"Rodeo! Really?"

"Naw, not really. Local kid stuff, years ago," Troy said. "Just enough to ride that pony on stage and look like Cochise. Sharp shtick."

"So was the arrow that stabbed him."

Nance winced, but Troy never stirred, his thumbs hooked in his hip-hugging belt, fingers arrowed toward the tight crotch of his jeans.

"Real thing, too," he said.

Given his pose, Temple had to resist a double take as well as a double entendre. "What do you mean 'real'?"

Troy ducked his curly cowboy head. "Shoot, it was an old arrow, that's all. Artifact, you could say. Charlie got the whole getup from a place out on the highway that deals in genuine Indian gear. Not so old it would be in a museum, but collectors' stuff."

"Why do you think he was killed?"

"Who knows? Could have been jest about any reason. I figure it for an impulse thing. Somebody saw him alone backstage waiting to go on and grabbed the arrow, then, whoomph." Troy's fist made an effective, thrusting gesture.

"But if Cheyenne was on the horse, the killer would have to be eight feet tall."

"Hey, the police know all that angle-of-entry stuff. Anyway, there's a whole elevated ramp section backstage. Anyone standing on it would be in great shape to do in ole Charlie."

Temple let her expression curdle. "How awful to think of him riding out on stage, already wounded. And his career . . . I hear he had done some work in Europe even."

Troy shifted in the seat, creating a scrape of denim and creak of leather belt. "Yeah, well, Charlie Moon's look does okay in Europe. He could do greased-back hair and Armani suits. Me, I'm too all-American to get much work overseas. It might mean good money, but that there jet set is an unhealthy crowd, kind of corrupt. Nance is just as glad I do my modeling at home."

She nodded seriously.

"You don't mind your husband up on stage, getting ogled by hundreds of women?"

"Honey, that's fine with me. We're married. He's been around both loose and hitched, an' I figure he knows enough to keep away from anything too sticky. This pageant is pretty harmless stuff. These ladies jest like to look. Most of 'em would faint dead away if one of these guys put a real move on 'em."

"Most?"

Nance shrugged. Temple noticed that her shoulders were broad for a woman. If a raised walkway had run alongside where Cheyenne sat astride his horse, his attention focused on controlling the animal and his imminent entrance, anyone—including a woman—could have struck down at his bare back with the assistance of gravity.

"Are you so sure all of these women are so innocent? Really?" Temple pushed for an answer. "Have you never heard of any hanky-panky between the cover models and the women, whether fans or authors?"

"Hey, stuff happens," Troy said. "We don't know for sure, and we don't want to know. We just do our thing."

"How bad can it be? Some of the guys bring their wives along."

Nance's fingers toyed with the pearlized buttons on her half-open shirt front.

She wasn't a shy sort of filly, either, Temple thought. The Tuckers were two of a kind: above-average attractive and used to showing, using, enjoying it. Their behavior wouldn't threaten each other.

Nance said as much. "Why would the guys bring wives along if they were up to anything special?"

"Especially murder." Temple rose suddenly, dropping her weight to her feet.

The pair jumped as if she had snapped a whip.

"This murder stuff does make us skittish." Troy's earnest true-blue eyes looked out from under sun-whitened eyebrows.

He was a real appealing galoot, all right. "What about a rival?" Temple asked abruptly.

"You mean some other contestant?" Troy demanded incredulously.

"That's who's back there." Temple's thumb jerked toward the stage and its behind-the-curtain labyrinth.

"And a whole lot more," Nance said quickly, with emphasis. "There are the technical guys, the stage crew, and a whole lot of lady volunteers eager to lace some he-man into his open shirt or his tight leather pants that open all down the sides. And"—her eyes, a muddy green, were flicking Temple up and down—"there are a whole lot of lady authors hanging around checking out the contestants, supposedly eager to get the lay of the land for their walk-ons with the guys."

"What walk-on with the guys?"

"Every contestant comes out first on the arm of what they call 'a romance industry professional,'" Troy explained. "That could be a cover artist or even an editor, not jest a book-writer."

Nance grinned. "Gives the ladies a chance to get all gussied up and get their names and their book titles or whatever called out," Nance said. "They do put on the pooch."

Troy frowned. "Speaking of dogs, I sure hope I don't get one for my escort this year," Troy said.

"Honey, that batch of ladies are worrying the same thing about you guys right now, don't you fret." Nance was laughing.

"So the matchups aren't announced yet?" Temple asked.

"Naw, we do that on pageant day," Troy said. "It don't keep the ladies from coming around, though. They want to know what the setup is, and what they have to do. 'Course, they gotta wear high heels and those long dresses, and this runway is pretty dicey. They're in and out of here all of the time."

"Speaking of which, I have to check on something backstage."

Temple excused herself to follow Molina's route up to the stage, her mind churning. It sounded like everybody and anybody at the convention could find an excuse to be backstage, and as if no one would be noticed. Temple hoped Molina had somehow found her way out. She arrived behind the curtain, relieved to spot no familiar face, although she recognized the various portions of male anatomy hustling to and fro in an undressed condition. She'd just think of England and forget about it.

But where was Danny Dove?

She asked that question of a guy nailing down a section of the raised backstage ramp Troy had mentioned. He gestured left, so she edged into the wings to find Danny consulting with the sound man.

"Let's set a level and keep it," Danny was saying, "no matter what. I hate it when the sound goes up and down like a see-saw. So unprofessional."

He turned away and saw Temple waiting.

"Hello, Miss Muffett. What can I do for you?"

Temple edged nearer the wall, for more privacy. "I need a favor."

"You need only ask."

"I want to get closer to the pageant. I need a reason to hang around."

"You can be my assistant and carry my clipboard." Danny slapped this everpresent artifact against his blue-jeaned leg.

"Something that gets me in greater contact with the contestants."

Danny's lowered blond eyebrows forced his forehead into corrugations of worry. "I thought we had a boyfriend."

"I did, too. Had, past tense. And that has nothing to do with my request. My aunt Kit said the best way to get acquainted with the contestants was to be a model in the pose-down."

Danny's eyebrows seemed to be leaving the planet.

"Who is your aunt? The Mayflower Madam? Do you know what the pose-down is?"

"It sounds like something in wrestling."

His laugh was loud, long and delighted. "So it is, in a way." He pulled her deeper into the shadows and lowered his voice. "Dear girl, do you have any idea of what you're putting yourself in for? No, of course not. The pose-down is the pageant's third and final tier. First the boys come out in evening clothes with authoresses and other interesting and interested females on their arms. Piece of cake. Then they come out solo and introduce themselves. Then they come out bareback."

"Everybody rides a horse?"

"I was speaking literally. It's the equivalent of the swimsuit competitions in women's beauty pageants, except that too many hairy legs might offend the refined sensibilities of this particular audience, so our boys wear tight jeans, or less, and a broad smile."

Temple nodded. She was not surprised that, with the amount of upper body development on some of these guys, inspecting their progress would serve everybody's mutual interest.

"The third, and final, heat—if you'll excuse the expression under these circumstances—is the pose-down."

Temple nodded seriously.

"That's when the men come out in costumes fit for a historical romance cover and assume cover poses with young lady models."

"That doesn't sound too hard."

"Oh, my dear. I have tossed a ballerina or two around a stage in my time, but that is nothing compared to this. You must be prepared to be nuzzled, nibbled, smooched and pawed by almost-nude savages who are seeking a like degree of dishabille from you. You must expect to have your skirt pushed up and your bodice pushed down. You will suffer from tickling hairs, particularly from these pre-Delilah Samson types. You will be bent backward like a bow. You may be thrown belly-down over a shoulder like a feed sack. You may even be, horror of horrors, 'dipped.' "

"What is . . . dipped?"

"You have done the tango?"

"Not in this lifetime."

" 'Dipping' is similar, but much deeper and it should be performed by an expert, 'else the dippee, that is to say the lady, could suffer permanent back injury."

As he spoke, Danny took Temple's hand, then whirled and tilted her until her torso was horizontal to the floor. She had a swirling impression of the wires and flats in the flies above. She had a sense of bending over backward until she broke. She had a tummy-churning fear that she would fall or be dropped much farther than the distance to the wooden backstage floor.

"You see?" Danny brought her up slowly, with perfect control, but she could feel his arm muscles trembling with strain. "And I am a professional. I have done this for a living. These guys are, on the whole, untrained amateurs."

"Do I have to get dipped?" Temple inquired in a small voice.

"It won't be your choice, believe me." Danny threw his hands up. "That's all these unoriginal bozos know to do with a woman. They want to come out, show their muscles and dip the nearest female. When you are dipped, you must *not* try to hold your head up. It creates too much strain, and besides you want a long, vulnerable throat line so the gentleman can go for your jugular like Dracula, and then you will have to try not to sneeze when his languishing locks tickle your nose."

Temple blinked.

"In addition," said Danny, "you must keep on your face at all times a vacant, simpering expression that says you find the proceedings so impossibly exciting that you can hardly wait for the next gentleman caller and the next nauseating dip."

"That really doesn't sound *too* much different than the high school prom," Temple said. Still, she knew the secret terror of someone who announces that she will go on a really big roller-coaster ride and then wishes she hadn't. "I've had some acting experience. And in high school, I even played the shrew in Shakespeare's *The Taming of.*"

"Hah! In that play Katarina gets to knock the men around. In these vignettes, they will be pouncing on you. And imagine how two-hundred-and-twenty pounds of unfeeling muscle feels when it pounces in its own clumsy, oafish way."

Temple didn't have to imagine. She recalled the dubious benefits of having been uplifted by the adorable Fabrizio. For one of her petite size, these muscle men seemed abnormally huge and hazardous to her health. Still, a pose-down model would have a golden opportunity to get to know the contestants, and to find out what the contestants knew about Cheyenne's death.

"I appreciate the warning, Danny, but I'm afraid I have to do it."

"You are inserting yourself into another life-and-death situation." He was speaking of more than the pose-down. "Why?"

"Lieutenant Molina asked me to tell her the lay of the land."

"Lieutenant Molina did not mean undercover investigation."

Temple sighed. "Cheyenne wanted to talk to me the night before he died. I didn't take him seriously, but I think he had suspicions."

"Why would he come to you?"

"I'm good at figuring things out. Except I didn't figure out that he wanted to speak to me about something important. He never got another chance."

Danny shook his head. "I'll try to assign you the contestants with the least resemblance to King Kong, but I can't control everything." He thought. "And I don't want another murder. Especially yours."

"You think that there might be one?"

"Don't you?"

"I don't even have a full suspect list for this one yet." That reminded her that Danny was the perfect person to ask about something that had been bothering her, if only she had the nerve.

"Was Cheyenne bisexual?" Temple asked bluntly.

Danny hesitated for a long time. "Sexual preferences aside, I'd say he had a universal soul. He was soft inside, if you know what

I mean, with a very thin protective shell. He meant well. He had charisma, but it was built on deference. He wanted to be . . . useful to people. Maybe that was all kinds of people in all kinds of ways. Maybe that meant being used at times. He wasn't a user, though."

"You liked him."

Danny nodded. "I thought he was too nice for this game. I guess I was right." He glanced at Temple. "What do you think of these Incredible Hunks? As a woman, I mean."

"Me? I'm the undercover investigator. I don't have an opinion."

"Sure you do." Danny crossed his arms and grinned.

"I don't even read romance novels. Well, I didn't until I got here and had a few thrust upon me. There's such a range in the books, from embarrassing adolescent drivel to extremely sophisticated literary sagas. I notice the same range in the cover models. Some seem all muscle on the outside, the equivalent of the ever-popular female bimbo, with hair mousse for brains and the sensitivity of a moose—north woods variety. Others are accomplished, attractive, well-rounded performers. They all have a public persona, though, that one would do well not to take too seriously."

She sighed and joined Danny in leaning against the wall. "I did that with Cheyenne. He approached me for a drink the night before he died, and I brushed him off. My friends were teasing me, and I didn't want to be taken for a vain, silly woman with a flattery threshold of zero. I think he wanted to talk to me because he was worried about something. He was on the scene when I meddled in the stripper killings. You know, I underestimated him because he looked too good to be true. And now he's dead."

"Hey!" Danny shook her arm. "You're not superwoman. One chat wouldn't have stopped a murderer." He looked amused suddenly. "Are you always so contrary with the opposite sex?"

"You mean Matt. That's right, you met him. He's too good looking to be true, too, but he is. It's me I distrust, not them. I don't want to be hooked by the shallow."

"Then move out of Las Vegas, honey! Nothing on the Strip is more than skin deep, not even the skin."

"You didn't answer my original question. Was Cheyenne bisexual? I'm not just being nosy. If true, it would enlarge the cast of suspects, and the range of motives. Lieutenant Molina asked me to background her."

"The Dragon Lady of the Las Vegas Metropolitan Police Department is taking hints from amateurs?"

"She's keeping an open mind. What about Cheyenne, bisexual or no?"

"Probably." Danny shrugged. "I didn't pay much attention to the daily do-si-do. Some people—gay and heterosexual—do like the edge of being with someone who cuts both ways."

"Even in the age of AIDS?"

"Especially in the age of AIDS. You forget that gays aren't the only ones who run on self-loathing. The promiscuous lifestyle isn't 'gay' in the old sense, or glamorous and knowing, or even smart. If being gay can be hell, I imagine that being bisexual nowadays can be purgatory."

"I'm surprised. I would have thought you, of all people, would be comfortable with your orientation."

He laughed, as if to say, "Oh, you kid!"

"Look, darling girl. The flagrant act is a kind of bravado, and a kind of defiance. Even straight theater people spread around the easy affection, because we all graduated from the same Odd Duck School. We're family, all of us in the sweetie, dearie, darling set, who assemble and disperse for temporary shows, temporary togetherness. There's both an intimacy and an eternal isolation.

"High school was hell, and being openly gay was suicide in my day. You barely begin to guess who you are at that age, sexual preferences aside, except that you know you don't fit in a thousand ways."

"Who does fit?" Temple wondered suddenly. "Do all the supposedly cool kids really feel so sure behind the facade?"

"A few are cursed with no self-doubts. That's why the supercool kids in high school never amount to much afterward. That was it. Their peak. At least the ugly ducklings are still waddling toward swanhood later in life."

Danny leaned against the homely concrete wall by the backstage phone. With its graffiti of phone numbers, it reminded Temple of a set from *West Side Story*.

"Anyway," he went on. "I knew as soon as I hit high school that my social life was going to be non-existent. I was already being called queer for taking dance lessons, then I realized that I wasn't going to be any Adonis, or any taller than five and a half feet. Kids like me back then usually found an older guy outside high school who would use us, or we might use them. Which was which wasn't always clear. But I still had to ask some poor girl to the high school prom, and sweat it that she'd turn me down, or—worse—think that my invitation meant something. After I got out, I stumbled into the underground gay scene. And then I did it all, took all those risks, too soon and too long. And I developed my front-fag, my swish and bravado just so everybody would know where I was coming from, especially me. Hey, it keeps women from getting the wrong idea, heaven forbid. Well, I guess heaven wouldn't want to forbid that, a gender-preference conversion, but it ain't gonna happen. I'm so gay that I don't understand bisexuals."

"Me neither," Temple agreed. "Sometimes I think celibacy is the simplest answer."

"You?" Danny mocked her. "Miss Hot Redhead of the nineties? Besides, do you know any happy celibates?"

"Maybe. At least they're disease-free."

"And emotionally empty, I've got to believe. At least I was when I was celibate. I don't believe in taking physical risks, but emotional risks are always necessary."

He paused, regarding Temple with a stark serious face that made carefree Danny Dove look like his own worried older brother. Even his happy, curly hair seemed to have straightened.

"I'm not the gadabout gay you think. I have a partner," he said, still in a sober mood. "We've been together—monogamous—for seven years. He had HIV when we met, but he's hanging in there. Safe sex, of course, which is a bore but better than regret after the ball is over, so to speak." Danny's bawdy laugh deliberately broke the mood. Temple suspected he seldom allowed anyone to see his serious side.

"Seven years. That's . . . great." Like all supportive murmurs, hers was vague and somehow inadequate. Even Temple wasn't sure whether she referred to the duration of Danny's relationship or the duration of his partner's survival. But Danny didn't care about the quality of her cue lines; he was reciting from his life story.

"He's a landscaper. Really into xeroscape—native water-sparing plants. I worry about melanoma, out in this hot sun so much. I make him wear sunscreen, nag him about hats. He hates hats."

She nodded. She hated hats, too, almost as much as she loved shoes.

"And then I think—" Danny made a self-deprecating face. "Hey, at least what he does has a life beyond a few hours on stage. If he dies—when he dies—there won't only be a grave to visit. There'll be all those scrubby little, ecology-saving cactus corners to drive by every day. . . ."

"I'm sorry," Temple said, voice breaking and eyes welling. She disguised her emotional downfall by hugging Danny.

His reciprocal hug nearly cracked her ribs. "You've got heart, girl." His voice was raw. "Don't you let anybody break it."

Easier said than done, Temple thought, especially when she herself seemed bent on imperiling it.

Chapter 23

Catfood vs. Dogmeat

I like to consider myself a pretty liberated guy, despite the usual hoots at that idea from the Midnight Louise corner. (And why, do you suppose, would such a liberated little doll keep a name that is a rip-off of her unesteemed *pater famillas fellnus?*)

Still, I must admit that some modern-day scenarios are enough to turn a few of my muzzle hairs gray, and I do not need any artificial assistance in that area nowadays.

Scenario is exactly the word to describe the situation that has made a successful takeover bid on my mind these days, to the exclusion of such usually distracting and juicy subjects as Chef Song's koi pond and Miss Temple Barr's latest murder victim. (Although she and I share living quarters, we also share a penchant for dead bodies; we differ only in how they arrive in that state and what we desire to do with them afterward. Miss Temple is consumed by the cause and effects of said dead condition; I cause the condition and consume the effects. Except for these wee differences, we have much in common.) In the case of human

demise, I can confine myself to pure curiosity: death as an intel-
lectual exercise. This is why I have been so useful to Miss Temple during her homicidal adventures.

But these days I have little appetite for the quick or the dead of
any species, even the slow of paw and fin. I suffer from emotional
indigestion, and the reason is simple: the ladylove of my life, the
Divine Yvette, is pussyfooting up the stairway to stardom with
some other dude.

That he is a well-known media figure is yet another claw in my
coffin.

So while Miss Temple noses around below-stage, having put
herself into the unenviable position of Incredible Hunk playmate,
I play games of a different sort in a sequestered ballroom at the
Crystal Phoenix. There the Divine Yvette is going for the animal
acting Oscar by waxing enthusiastic over the latest Incredible
Gunk designed to catch the feline fancy.

If the script calls for her to throw cat fits over co-star Maurice,
she will be a natural for the Incredible Acting award.

I find my way onto the closed set by braving the kitchen during breakfast hour, under the cover of every stainless steel cart
in sight. Should Chef Song spy me eeling beneath these low-
lying islands of safety and concealment, I would lose more than
a few loose hairs. His meat cleaver would give my coat a center-
part so deep that I would develop a permanently split personality. And my nine lives would be down to four and a half and
counting.

But in the kitchen at rush hour, omelets and pancakes are siz-
zling off the stovetops faster than hundred-dollar bills off the wad
of a Texas poker player. All the white-coated figures are flying
around looking up, not down.

"A hair!" Chef Song suddenly solos like a demented Barber of
Seville, bending over the yellow fluff of an omelet. "Short and
black. A moustache hair. Who has not shave?"

I has not shave . . . and I has not stayed long enough for the
lone hair to come home to me. I am through the swinging door
into the back service halls that connect with every hotel ballroom

and restaurant. Via the same hip variety of door, I am into the Lalique Ballroom and under a floor-length tablecloth before you can spell Esiuol Tghindim frontward.

Only my nose and eyes peek through a tea rose–pink linen tent. I view the expected horrors: the blackened spaghetti of thick electrical cables; the restless, high-heeled feet of Miss Savannah Ashleigh; the pungent sneaker-clad tootsies of the camera crew; the Italian loafers of the director; the wingtips of the watching catfood muckety-mucks; and the pink canvas carrier of the Divine Yvette.

I see no sign of transport for the loathsome Maurice, but I know he is lurking somewhere.

Meanwhile, I shimmy from tablecloth tent to tablecloth tent until I am within whisker-distance of Miss Savannah Ashleigh's ankles. These are not the dainty appendages of my own little doll. Miss Savannah Ashleigh is no tenderfoot. Her ankles are tanned to within an inch of their epidermis, but the varicose tracks of blue veins deface the landscape nevertheless. I know Miss Temple would want a full description of Miss Savannah Ashleigh's footwear, were she here, so I overcome my distaste to examine the area further. There is no doubt that Miss Savannah Ashleigh has a taste for flashy shoes. The current pair are oil-slick patent leather that zip up the back of the heel and the so-called throat of the vamp. Given that her spike heels tower at least an inch higher than Miss Temple's most elevated pair, the bony, blue-veined Ashleigh feet look forced into the shoes. Her insteps bulge like Cinderella's stepsisters' feet. All in all, a most unappetizing sight, normally unworthy of comment, did I not have a moral obligation to consider my roommate's interests before I focus on my own.

Speaking of which, Miss Savannah Ashleigh does. Speak, that is. Of the Divine Yvette.

"What are you doing with that stick?" she demands in a voice both low and breathy.

Mr. Italian Loafers spins on the soft carpeting. "It is a toy to encourage your cat to perform for the camera."

"Yvette does not play with such cheap diversions. They do not interest her."

I see a turquoise ostrich plume spin near the carpeting. I agree that the color is cheap and obnoxious, and that I would much prefer the natural feather, attached, in fact, to its natural ostrich. Size is not a factor for Midnight Louie. However, it is all I can do to restrain myself from dashing out of cover and clawing that feather flat.

Apparently I am not alone. A silver shape vaults out of nowhere to clutch for the feather. The Divine Yvette, despite pedigree and petite size, is quite a stalker. In fact, she is adorable when she is mad. I watch her fierce face bare tiny fangs as her dainty velvet mitts swat the feather-on-a-stick to smithereens. Well, perhaps feathers cannot smash into smithereens, but turquoise curls fly like emigrees from a Ginger Rogers ballgown.

It is all I can do not to sneeze, which would be disastrous.

"Tacky, tacky," frets Miss Savannah Ashleigh.

I am surprised that she is not looking at her feet instead of the Divine Yvette. She rises and moves nearer the camera.

"And what are those . . . grass clippings on the rug?" she wants to know next.

Mr. Italian Loafers shuffles. "Ah, something to make kitty happy. Catnip."

"Catnip? You are supplying my Yvette with a mind-altering substance? Get rid of it at once! She has never had anything herbal other than a bit of organically grown rye grass now and then, and my Boston ferns."

"It is just a little nip, Miss Ashleigh." The loafers do a soft shoe of irritation on Miss Van von Rhine's finest broadloom. "It relaxes them. I have done dozens of animal commercials—"

"That is obviously your problem," Miss Savannah Ashleigh interrupts. "Yvette is not an animal."

"Animal companion commercials," he revises through gritted teeth, trying for a more politically correct term.

Politically correct oils no hinges with Miss Savannah Ashleigh. "She is not an animal!"

"Cat?"

"Hmmph." Miss Savannah Ashleigh swivels on the ball of her

high heels to turn her back on the Italian loafers and the unenlightened person in them.

"She is not a cat? The manufacturer will be pretty upset to hear that."

Miss Savannah Ashleigh bows low without bending her knees, a maneuver that keeps her posterior high in the air like a lady cat's in heat, which presents the director with much more to think about than the precise nature of the Divine Yvette.

The Divine One snarls prettily as her mistress wrests her from the feather into her arms and next to her face. She straightens—the mistress, not the questionable Yvette.

"Mommy's 'ittle sweetums is not a nasty old animal! She is a little fairy princess yummy-nummums with an ancient, wise soul. She does not chase foolish toys or need hallucinatory substances to perform. She is a natural star, like Mommums."

If that is truly the case, the Divine Yvette, the Italian Loafers and the catglop commercial are in trouble-wubble.

The director suddenly decides to direct. He plucks Mommy's yummy-nummums (I do have to agree with Miss Savannah Ashleigh's besotted estimation, for vastly different reasons) from the vicinity of Mommy's facey-wacey.

"Sit down, Miss Ashleigh," he says. "It will be over much more quickly if you let us do our jobs." Moving to a set surrounded by a convocation of tripods and cameras, he plunks the Divine Yvette down on a Plexiglas balustrade. A crystal chandelier has been lowered from the high ceiling to twinkle and flash above the Divine Yvette's perch like a diamond waterfall. Nearby sits a long banquet table covered in the tea rose–pink damask that matches the pale pink pads of the Divine One's silver-velvet feet and the center of her tiny triangular nose set like a rosy pearl in a thin bezel of black enamel. She looks adorable, and she is still mad, thanks to sequential bouts of feather-sniffing, catnip-licking and Mommy-mauling.

"Where is the other cat?" The director turns to the crew while Miss Savannah Ashleigh settles back in the pink canvas director's chair that matches the Divine Yvette's carrier and apparently accompanies her everywhere as well.

"Yvette does not need a costar," Miss Savannah Ashleigh sniffs in a soft, injured tone.

Did she not need the dough from this venture, one can be sure that Miss Savannah Ashleigh would not be here. In fact, she gasps as a woman on the staff darts toward the Divine Yvette and backs away to reveal a pink-ice cubic zirconium collar circling my beloved's delicate neck.

Miss Savannah Ashleigh sits up indignantly. "I hope that I . . . that *she* will be able to keep that after the shoot."

The director rolls his eyes and curls his toes in butter-soft, and colored, Italian leather. "I am certain that can be arranged, Miss Ashleigh."

It is obvious to both him and me that the trinket will be adorning the Ashleigh wrist rather than the Divine Yvette throat from now on.

My poor lady love! Forced to labor under the influence wearing confining gems destined for her greedy mistress. There should be laws against this sort of thing. And the alien, intrusive male has not even made an appearance yet. This entire scene begins to smack of a forced mating, with my captured darling decked out for the harem.

"All right." At the director's nod, the same woman who had collared my lady love waves the feathered lash before the Divine One's pink pearl of a nose.

The Divine Yvette's blue-green eyes widen to perfect, baby-doll circles as her platinum whiskers tremble. She leaps along the balustrade, balancing like a Chinese acrobat, as airborne as a prima ballerina performing *Swan Lake*. (Speaking of *Swan Lake*, I wonder if that is an upscale version of *Duck Pond*. I have enjoyed games of cat-and-mouse in such vicinities.)

Despite the weight of the alien collar, the Divine One floats like a butterfly . . . and stings like Ali, fiercely boxing tiny turquoise curls from the plume that catch in her silver neck ruff like falling stars. Miss Savannah Ashleigh is right about one thing: the Divine Yvette is a born performer. A catfood manufacturer could sell worm-steak with this pussums!

In a few airy hops, she has lofted atop the pink damask tablecloth, the camera dollying in the feathery wake of her pendulum tail. Now her sensitive nose detects the point of the exercise. A fresh dollop of Á La Cat fills a footed, cut-crystal dessert dish at a place setting fit for the Queen, or at least her first cousin.

Yet while the camera captures the Divine Yvette's cavorting, I notice sinister background preparations. A mullioned window stands alone, propped up by wooden supports. A black curtain behind it signifies deepest night, and also black intentions, for I see a familiar mug poking out of a familiar carrying case.

It is yellow, as are the two slitted-pupil eyes in that notorious face. Maurice, the Yummy Tum-tum-tummy cat, is about to make his entrance.

I watch as he is pulled from the carrier and his big, splayed mitts are posed on the supposed windowsill. With a little prodding from behind and another plumed stick waving like a turquoise carrot before him, he leaps atop the narrow sill and teeters for a moment.

I turn to see the Divine Yvette in closeup, sampling the proffered catfood in innocent cooperation. Little does she know she is about to be accosted by a gate-crashing camera hog.

A gentle push from behind encourages Maurice to take his mighty leap to join the Divine Yvette on the tabletop. I launch myself from beneath that very table like twenty pounds of avenging hellhound.

We meet in midair, claws out, tails curled, camera rolling. Maurice's surprised yowl is drowned out by my superb battle cry. After batting him down like a butterfly, I turn (with my best side to the camera) and jump up to join the Divine Yvette atop the table.

"Louie!" she greets me, pausing to lick her whiskers feline-clean.

We sniff noses to insure that a body double has not been slipped in somewhere. She is not unduly upset, but the vanquished Maurice and the director are livid, I notice.

"Ahhhh!" Miss Savannah Ashleigh has risen to the occasion, but is shocked motionless. She clutches her purse to her breast like a baby, and wails.

Maurice growls fiercely from the floor and tries to jump up. I do not even have to biff him again. The Divine Yvette watches with contempt, then bats at him when his whiskers are within striking distance. The blow is anemic, but enough to startle Maurice out of his stripes. He lands like a sack of soggy potatoes, and stays there. The Divine Yvette sure is cute when she is mad, which I tell her.

"I am not mad, Louie," she says with a dainty shrug. "I am eating."

At that, she resumes to consume, as is her duty. What a pro!

I sniff the edge of her bowl, then back off. I have just gotten a good whiff of the muck she is eating. *What a pro!*

By then the director, the collar lady, the cameramen and Miss Savannah Ashleigh are all converging on me with contorted faces and unintelligible growls, howls and yowls.

I leap for my life, spinning a gold-rimmed plate to the floor along with some silverware that feels as heavy as a Buccalatti service for twelve. The crash and clang of the falling place setting muffles the humans' naughty words, so my darling does not have to hear them.

The last I see of the Divine Yvette is her piquant little kisser buried to the nostrils in Á La Cat.

The last I see of Maurice the rum-tum tiger, Yummy Tum-tum-tummy cat is his yellow-striped hindquarters being stuffed unceremoniously into a portable plastic cubicle like so much dog-meat. Too bad it is not a Dumpster.

Chapter 24

Jake of All Trades

"Cheyenne's dressing room? Sure thing." He jerked his head in a forward direction to indicate Temple was to follow him.

With thirty-three guys making five costume changes en masse somewhere in the Crystal Phoenix basement, Temple felt more secure asking a passing stranger for guidance than blundering around on her own.

Her guide was amiable, and also tall, but more lanky than hunky. In fact, he reminded her of Tiny Tim's cuter younger brother, which wasn't saying much for his looks.

But Temple followed his long legs as fast as she could without her high heels clicketying like a typewriter on the harsh concrete floors. She soon discovered that the pageant contestants had been given a vast, empty storage space as a dressing room. Long rows of imported folding chairs and tables topped with plug-in makeup mirrors had been curtained into two-person cubicles. Still, with thirty-plus contestants, any real privacy was—as always in theatrical ventures—a snare and a delusion.

Now that she had seen the dressing rooms, killing Cheyenne in the dark confusion of the spacious stage wings made much more sense than trying to do the deed discreetly in one of these cramped, confessional-sized, cloth-walled booths.

Temple's anonymous guide stopped by the burgundy entrance curtain to one cubicle and swagged it back, bowing with a sweeping gesture for her to enter.

She saw nothing inside she didn't expect to see . . . and smell. Theatrical makeup never hid behind floral additives; it broadcast a strong, oily-waxy odor. Temple eyed open tins of bronze body makeup, a much-fingered clear plastic bottle of some kind of oil, and an upstanding chorus line of mousses and other modern hair shapers and bodifiers necessary for long tresses, no matter the sex. That was one of the two adjacent tables. The other tabletop suffered from a neatness verging on abandonment, except for a blue folder, a box of tissue and a lone tin containing a pallid golden sun of makeup.

"Mine," the man said, noticing her surprise at the lack of cosmetics.

Temple turned, even more surprised. "You're a contestant?"

"Over forty." The man slumped onto his metal folding chair to gaze into a tilted makeup mirror rimmed with unlit theatrical bulbs, like the matching unit on Cheyenne's cluttered tabletop. The overhead fluorescent cast a sunken, sallow visage into the mirror. He made a deprecatory face. "More over forty than most. Jake Gotshall. And you are—?"

"Temple Barr. I work for the Crystal Phoenix."

"I guess I'm what you would call a wild card contestant." Jake smiled at his ghastly reflection.

He reminded Temple of Gumby, another elastic, vague figure dating from a few decades ago. Call it aging hippie. Jake's hair was long, but thin, lackluster and graying. From an ebbing hairline it dwindled into a limp ponytail that thinned into split ends before reaching his shoulder blades. His features were Gumby-soft too: no overshot ledge of jaw and chin to cast a shadow on massive pectorals; no lush eyebrows shading deep-set eyes. After a few days of seeing Incredible Hunks, Temple was amazed to realize that Jake looked completely masculine while claiming not a single characteristic that could be termed "hunkish."

He smiled at her expression.

"No doubt you're wondering why I called you all together here. Actually"—he looked carefully around Temple for signs of other people—"you're alone." His voice assumed an Alan Alda self-mockery. "No doubt you're wondering why I called you here alone?" His straggling eyebrows quirked upward in patented ogling villain style.

"I wanted to come here," Temple pointed out. "I took you for a stagehand."

"Oh, cruel fate! Does this indicate that my chances for this year's Incredible Hunk are not hunky-dory? Don't I look like the late hunk's dressing-room mate?"

Temple sat, gingerly, on Cheyenne's empty folding chair. "Apparently you are, whether you're sure about it or not. I knew Cheyenne, very casually. I wondered what had happened before he went on stage. Maybe you can tell me."

Jake leaned his elbows on the makeup table, hands cupping his amiable, if not particularly attractive face. "You're being too polite. You know you're dying to ask what I'm doing in an Incredible Hunk contest. Instead of inquiring about my late mirror-mate, you should wonder how I got past the contest doormen, in this case doorwomen."

"Enlighten me."

He grinned and leaned closer, revealing rather gray and crooked teeth. "I know a terrific photographer. Besides, I do some stand-up comedy, and figured this gig would give me an unlikely new shtick. Here's my photo." He slipped an eight-by-ten from the blue folder and spun it toward Temple.

"You *do* have a helluva photographer." Lots of shadow and tricky highlighting had given Jake an intense, aging Hamlet look. Too bad the man in person completely contradicted the image. He more resembled an aging ham-actor, period. From the stamp on the back, the photo wizard was a woman. Temple would have to look her up if she ever needed a really flattering portrait. "Is that all it took to enter? A good photograph?"

He nodded. "And some bio sheets, with vital statistics." When Jake flexed his arm, as he did now, his plaid shirtsleeve remained loose and unimpressive. "Of course I lied a lot." He peeked, like Tiny Tim, from behind a strand of graying hair that had escaped the rubber band at his nape.

Temple started laughing. "You're a shill. A walking lampoon! What did the pageant organizers do when they actually saw you?"

"Screamed bloody murder until they realized that ejecting a pre-accepted candidate would be bad press. So they made the best of it. I'd showed up, hadn't I? Paid my money and they took a chance. Besides, I'm warm and breathing, and they were really short of entrants in the over-forty category this year. I, as you can see, am tall, and about as over forty as you can get."

"Forty-nine?" Temple guessed.

"And three-quarters. That's what I put down as my chest measurement."

"Three-quarters?"

"Forty-nine and three-quarters."

"So you're more of an outside observer than the other contestants," Temple said thoughtfully, still smiling.

"Yeah. I mean, who'd watch me? So I watch them. And, boy, do they watch themselves a lot. A few of these guys are so hooked on mirrors that they can't even look at who they're talking to. Beauty is a consuming business, isn't it?"

"Don't ask me. So the contestants are pretty self-absorbed, but the people-watching must be enlightening."

"Fascinating," he responded Mr. Spock style, with cocked eyebrow and aloof tone. When he saw that Temple had recognized the delivery, he added a wry smile. "*He* wouldn't have stood a chance here either. Not with those Mickey-Mouse-on-Mars ears."

"What have you concluded so far?"

"Besides that I don't have a chance in Hairspray Hell of taking that super-Hunk title? Okay. Most of these guys are pros with attitude, ambitious models or actors hoping to catch one more eye, one more camera, one more big rolling wave of media attention. Some are fun-loving off-camera types, regular guys good-looking enough to enter on a dare from their girlfriends. These guys usually have expectations as ordinary as a day job. Only one other jokester like me slipped in for fun and self-humiliation." Jake spun his makeup tin.

"Why do it? Couldn't you have imagined a male beauty pageant to put in your comedy act?"

Jake shrugged. "A *Current Affair*, *Hard Copy* and *Hot Heads* don't show up, cameras running, for any exercises in imagination that I've dreamed up. Look at Pat Paulsen, the comic who regularly runs for president. He's not so nuts. He gets loads of coverage, and even a nanosecond on national TV can jump-start a career. Hey, *regardez* Kato Kaelin." Only he pronounced the name of the world's most hyphenated man, the live-in hanger-on in the O.J. Simpson case, "Ka-*toe* Kae-*lin*," in a *tres*, *tres* phoney French accent.

"A world did, and you know what? He didn't have anything there to boost."

"Whatever. Maybe me and the other dud—as opposed to stud—just want to say . . . hey, regular guys can be romantic too."

"What about Cheyenne? Was he a prime contender? Was he going to win?"

Jake's shaggy head shook. "Who knows? He had all the right stuff—and seemed hip enough, but . . . he never gave me a clue about himself. He came storming in, one of the last contestants to arrive, fresh off some transatlantic flight, smelling of first class. I hated his washboard guts."

"What does first class smell like?"

"Leather and champagne and stewardess. He plunked down a couple of duffle bags—as you saw from his costume, there wasn't much of it; all he needed otherwise was a tux, jeans, spray mousse and his Evian water. What a guy!"

"Knowing a murder victim should enliven your act."

"Sure. I can say all the cover hunks were knocking each other dead."

"You really think the murder is going plural?"

Jake's genial, flaccid face—he had a good old gray gelding

look—tightened with alarm. "Shit, I hope not! I didn't enlist for hazardous duty with no pay. Waggling your tush for a few hundred screaming women shouldn't be a terminal offense."

Temple sat at Cheyenne's vacant place, lost against the mirror's reflected burgundy curtains. Even traveling light, Cheyenne carried more hair accessories than Temple kept on her whole cosmetics shelf at home. She picked up a small sleek aluminum canister of mousse, as compactly packaged as Mace. It felt full. She set it down quickly, imagining how many times a living Cheyenne could have still used it.

"Nobody came for his things but the police," Jake noted. "The duffle bags with his clothes and stuff. I glimpsed an electric shaver, a fancy blow dryer, some foreign magazine, French or Italian. They left the glop."

He nodded at the slick array of bottles and canisters. "Maybe someone killed him for single-hairedly doing in the ozone layer."

Temple touched another of the aluminum soldiers on parade. "These are pump-sprays, not aerosol containers. All politically correct. He wasn't hurting anything."

"He must have been hurting somebody's chances, or why kill him?"

"It doesn't have to be a pageant rival. Take your pick of possible killers: a jealous lover; an ex-lover of a new lover; a would-be lover spurned. Maybe even a terminally irritated author who hates cover hunks getting all the attention and the money."

"The *authors* hate these guys?"

"Maybe I exaggerate, but many of these women have labored for peanuts book after book. To see some pretty boy walk off with big bucks for standing around buck naked for an hour might be a trifle aggravating. It's a theory."

"Holy hair-mousse!" Jake flattened his hands on his dressing table top, as if about to spring himself into orbit. "It's bad enough to sashay out in your skivvies in front of hundreds of screaming women, but to think that some of them might be screaming for your blood—! That's gruesome."

"Cheyenne was killed at the first rehearsal, not at the pageant, but all sorts of suspects were around that morning: fellow contestants—"

"I didn't do it," he screamed melodramatically, going down on his knees. "You know I'd never win no matter who I eliminated. I could off the entire lot and still lose. I'm innocent, I tell you, innocent."

Temple refused to be distracted by theatrics. Comics were always on, always improvising. It didn't make them the world's most astute witnesses. She wondered what Molina had made of this guy, while continuing to tick off suspects on her autopsy-red fingernails.

"And stage crew. Then don't forget the fans . . . you know, those pudgy, eminently overlookable sweet midlife ladies who volunteer to help you hunks shake your tushies into those skin-tight pants. Demented fans are not unknown in the entertainment biz. Several lady authors were milling around too, trying to figure out who they'd escort on the big night."

"None were milling around me," Jake reported glumly, pushing himself back into the folding chair.

"Listen." Temple leaned forward on her chair—Cheyenne's chair—and nailed him with a dead-serious look. "I know life is a cabaret, my friend, but even a professional jokester must occasionally notice more than how his jokes are going over. Cheyenne was worried enough about something to want a tête-à-tête with me the night before he died. Why? Because I'm a PR person? Because I work the hotels and conventions, know the scene? Or because I've been involved in solving a few murders."

"You? Cute little cheerleader-type you?" Jake's naturally pallid face had turned a lighter shade of gray. "Involved in murders?"

"Only indirectly."

"I should hope so!"

"So tell me something that will help me understand what Cheyenne tried to tell me and couldn't. Because I wasn't listening to him that night. You shared this cramped space for what, twenty-four hours? You must have heard, seen something significant."

Jake shrugged and made a face. "Just the usual. He came in,

fighting jet-lag with that kind of show-biz energy you can call on to keep going no matter what."

"Not drugs?" Temple thought of another motivation: a new, exciting jet-set lifestyle running on speed and sex appeal . . . maybe even smuggling.

Jake's headshake was final. "Naw. I can tell the difference between a two-hundred-dollar high, a java jag and Mother Nature's freebies. I've done it, run on the dead certainty of performing. That's what he was high on: doing this pageant and coming out good." Jake's serious voice sank into a Brando drone. "He coulda been a contendah—"

Interviewing a professional comic was like opening a bag filled with cartoon characters all screaming to get out at once. Temple nodded, encouraging Jake to say more.

"Man, he had energy, though. Made me feel my age, and I don't like to get that personal with myself. You should have seen him, dashing out to handle last-minute details. He got that horse here without tipping anybody off but a pal or two. He wanted to surprise the other contestants, too. He wanted 'em all to know he had a leg up on them. Get it? 'Leg up'? Horse?"

"I get it. So he *did* have business to take care of once he got here. He could have left the hotel and seen—or been seen by—almost anybody."

Jake nodded solemnly. "He did act . . . abstracted, though, rehearsal morning. He dashed out with one of his duffle bags, and when he came back, he kinda threw it in a corner as if he didn't like what was in it. Like it wasn't really part of him. Now that you nag me to death about it, he acted a little schizy. Even asked me to run out and get him a Pepsi, when he'd been guzzling nothing but Evian water. He was—"

"Worried?"

"Maybe. Or maybe he wanted to get rid of me for a while. When I came back, he didn't say much. Just grabbed his stage kit, stood up in that skimpy outfit, what would you call it—teeny weeny loincloth and itty bitty medicine bag and great big quiver on his back, which come to think of it, was a hell of a phallic symbol. Lord, that would make the ladies quiver! I guess, looking at him as Navaho Joe, I knew my chances had been shot in the heart." Jake's arms spread wide to display his unremarkable body in its unremarkable clothes. "What's to say?"

"You've got nerve," Temple admitted. "I bet the ladies will love you, especially the hunky-cover-model haters."

"The ladies, God bless 'em, love a lot of guys like me. These studly types with mammoth muscles are just window dressing. For looking at, not into."

"Perfect Kens," Temple mused. "As in Ken and Barbie." She recalled Matt's dislike of his own good looks for the superficial attention they brought him. "Still, beautiful people have real feelings. And fears. Somebody must have feared Cheyenne—Charlie Moon—enough to kill him."

"You think that was the motive? Not jealousy?"

"What kind of jealousy, that's the question."

"And a good question. Was it a maddened contestant, afraid he'd lose the crown to a hot contender?" Jake donned a guilty, hang-dog look. "Or was it some red-hot lover afraid of losing Cheyenne, period?" Jake twirled an imaginary mustache.

"Did you glimpse any romantic hunky-panky around here?"

"In less than two days? Hardly likely." His face flickered with sudden remembrance. "Say, I did see Cheyenne holding cocktail glasses with an author in the hotel bar, pretty late the first night we got in."

"Who?"

He shrugged. "Haven't seen her again. Not one of the pageant participants, for sure. Classy lady. I was gonna say 'older,' but I bet she's only a few years older than me, so I better watch it. Still a looker. Your size. Red hair, too, but hers isn't as bright."

Temple's blood froze. She recognized a spot-on description of her aunt Kit when she heard it.

"What time Wednesday night?"

"Time I saw them? Oh, say around eleven. She was old enough to be his mother, but Cheyenne seemed like a cosmic kind of guy. I bet details like age, gender and national origin didn't phase him one bit."

Temple, though still in shock about Kit, was not surprised to have her bisexual suspicions confirmed by an impartial source.

"Don't look so shocked, sweet thing." Jake sounded like a counseling older brother, but he misread what had really shocked her. "Consenting adults try all sorts of combinations nowadays. But I doubt anything is going on at this convention. Too much performance pressure for the boys. Everybody's way too stressed out by the pageant to have time for *romance!*"

Jake, sprawled against the dressing table, then assumed a maniacally suave expression that ludicrously altered his homely face, and not for the better. "Unless you aren't doing anything tonight, ba-bee?"

"Sorry, Fabrizio Junior." Temple stood, patience and interview ended. "All booked up."

Chapter 25

True Confessions

C. R. Molina cruised the Crystal Phoenix hotel lobby, cursing casino floor plans that always forced people to pass gaming attractions on the way in or out.

She disliked the constant clatter of slot machines, especially when she was trying to think. Not that she had much to think about: only the inevitable end of the romance convention, and with it the exit of all likely suspects in the Charlie Moon murder.

She knew that the odds on solving the case by Monday were longer than the odds on a nickel slot machine payoff. So the chug-chug-chug of doomed coins down mechanical gullets sounded like the Failure Machine engine revving up before running her over. This annoying convention murder case particularly rankled, coming, as it did, on the heels of her unexpected and spectacularly unproductive encounter at the Blue Dahlia the very night before the morning of Charlie Moon's demise.

Recalling the frustrating skirmish with Max Kinsella brought to mind her always-annoying head-to-heads with a known associate of the elusive magician: Temple Barr. Molina could not believe she had encouraged the woman's nosiness on this case. But in some instances, any sort of information was worth the effort.

Even as she mentally stalked the thin grungy line of her remaining options during a swift passage through the gaming area, Molina's professional eye was on automatic record. One anomaly pricked her consciousness: a pit boss engaged in deep discussion. Pit bosses watched, they did not talk. Especially not to rank casino amateurs like . . .

Molina stopped in her tracks, letting tourists jostle her as they scurried for their slot machines of choice. The stance of the person with the pit boss was even more naggingly out of place than the becalmed supervisor.

She spun into a different direction and quietly circled the pair beside the inactive craps table, approaching so she faced the pit boss.

Spike Saltzer was a casino veteran, a seventyish man with supernaturally shiny, full black hair and a perpetual tan. The tan was his only Las Vegas vice; Spike didn't smoke, drink or do drugs. Sometimes she even wondered if he slept. He had been married since Bugsy Siegel had died, to the same woman, and attended the Golden Light Church. Despite all that, or perhaps because of it, he missed no abnormal action on a gaming floor, so he had spotted Molina almost as soon as she had him. He didn't show it, except to back off from his conversation partner.

Pit bosses were the casino ringmasters, captains of the Good Ship Fun (yours) and Fortune (theirs). They kept the action constant and clean, weather eye always alert for fraudulent patrons—or employees, which was more often the case. That's why pit bosses seldom stood around to chitchat with—Molina was close enough to the blond man to confirm her first impression—Matt Devine. Well, well.

She managed to materialize beside both men before Devine, at least, knew what was happening.

"So how long could—" He glanced at the nearing motion and saw her. Conversation stopped.

She enjoyed the confused, possibly guilty, expression on his striking face.

"I got no more time," Spike announced in a voice fogged by decades of second-hand smoke. His hooded eyes paused on Molina for a split second, then he was back cruising the tables like the seasoned land-shark he was.

"Lieutenant," Devine greeted her, his face still slack with surprise.

"Too bad I can't return a title," she said, smiling as his confusion deepened into wariness, if not resentment. "So. What were you and Spike talking about?"

"Nothing . . . important. Nothing of interest. To you."

"Everything is of interest to me, especially when it's adjacent to a murder scene."

If anything, Devine looked even more guilty. It was almost mean of her to prolong his misery and confusion, but her current need for the upper hand was probably a reaction to her split decision set-to with Max Kinsella the other night. Yes, it was mean of her, she decided, to transfer her rage toward a more expert opponent to a lesser quarry.

"Miss Barr is backstage or downstairs, I believe," she said brusquely, assuming Temple was the reason he had come to the Crystal Phoenix. "Why did you stop to pester Saltzer?"

"I was curious about how this place is run, that's all. Temple is here? Alone?"

Devine looked even more puzzled, and more worried, if possible.

"Alone? Not if she can help it. I believe about thirty paperback heroes are flitting about her general vicinity."

"Paperback heroes?"

"Cover hunks. Models. Male models. Romance-novel cover hunks. You do know about the romance conference?"

Devine shook his head.

"Isn't that why you're here? Because she is, yes, once more dead center of a murder investigation. Or are you here to protect the officers of the law from the patented brand of Barr interference, dare I hope?"

"The murder is . . . old news," he said cautiously.

"How blasé you amateurs become. Yeah, the guy died a whole thirty hours ago, but the case file has hardly grown cobwebs." Molina studied his still-blank face and took mercy, in her own way.

"Did you know that a certain someone is back in town, by the way?"

"Did you?" he replied warily.

"Would I ask otherwise?"

"How did you—?"

"The power of the police," she answered, her tone self-mocking. "I suppose that this bodes quite a change of weather for you."

"What do you mean?"

"Well, you *were* the escort of record, and now 'Max is back.' " She was paraphrasing a line from "Mac the Knife," but it was lost on Devine.

"That's between Temple and . . . him."

"Is it? I think not. It's between him and the law."

"Have you arrested him?"

"Don't get your hopes up."

Devine flushed slightly. She really was vile to pick on someone so ill-suited for performing the courtship gavotte. She smiled again, this time nicely.

"I'm afraid I can't discuss the details, but the Mystifying Max will most certainly be arrested as soon as I can get ahold of him."

"What for?"

"Irritating an officer? Don't worry, there will be something I can pin on his ponytail one day soon."

She watched his face tauten with the belief that she really had seen Kinsella. That's why she had added the telling detail of the ponytail. And now she knew that Devine had seen this "demmed elusive" creature as well.

"What did you think of him?" she asked next.

"Funny. I was going to ask you that."

She shrugged. With a wary soul like Devine, going first often meant getting what you want last. "How would they say it in the old days? 'A smooth customer.' But mine is a professional evaluation. I'm not interested in the personal."

"My summation is professional too," he said coolly enough, finally relaxing into their verbal fencing match. "A complex personality. Charming, of course. Alarmingly bright, but . . . somehow uneasy. And dark. A deep, dark streak, quintessentially Celtic."

"Celtic. Not the usual word you find on police blotters, Mr. Devine. I'll have to take it into consideration."

"Why are you baiting me?"

"Oh, because I have nothing better to do, or because I'm frustrated with the current case and it's more amusing to worry at old ones."

"Current case? *Another* murder?"

"Which murder did you think I meant? Or is there one I don't know about?"

"There have been so many since—"

"Since you met Miss Barr. I know. Well, now there's another. One of the competing cover hunks. Arrow through the back seconds before a dramatic entrance—and exit—at an onstage rehearsal. Didn't she tell you about it?"

"I haven't seen Temple in a while."

"So she doesn't know you're here?"

"No. And I didn't—"

"Know she was here. Where did you think she had gone?"

"I—I don't know. I didn't want to ask. I figured—"

"No. No, my son. She is *not* with the Mystifying Max, at least not that I can tell. I would expect her to be less interested in the cover model murder, if that were the case, and no such luck. However, I wouldn't get too complacent, if I were you. She's with thirty-some half-clad muscular male models."

He frowned, ignoring her jibes. "Temple shouldn't be involving herself in that."

"I agree, but she does not. This time *she* has a guilty conscience."

"Guilty? Temple?" He sounded more alarmed by the latest murder than by Max's return, Molina noted.

"The victim had asked to speak to her alone the night before the murder. She knew him—slightly, she says—from the stripper competition a few months ago."

"I didn't know much about that," Devine muttered, distracted.

Molina suddenly realized why he was so disoriented. *"That's* why you were talking to Saltzer! You knew nothing about the latest murder, you were inquiring about the Effinger death. Oh, great, another amateur detective on the loose."

"Not an amateur anything." He flushed again, a victim of the ex-priest's innocence of ordinary social give-and-take beyond the charmed circle of a clerical collar. "I'm a concerned party in that case. Effinger was my stepfather. Or was the dead man really Effinger?"

Molina reared back, ambushed by an astute question. "What do you mean?"

"What do *you* mean, Lieutenant?" he added more softly. "You misled me. Why? I finally . . . realized that there was no need for me to trek to the morgue and view the remains. Effinger had a police record. His fingerprints would be available here, and in Chicago. Why did you put me through that identification mummery? For fun? Is that what you learned in Catholic schools, Carmen?"

Molina discovered that she had inherited the Catholic flush of guilt, too, especially when an ex-priest had caught her being officially devious and then used her hated baptismal name to bring the venial sin home.

"I needed your input," she said stiffly.

"Input?" His tone made the word an epithet. "Is that what you call it? I didn't have much input. Standing in that vacant place, with those vacant corpses in various stages of dissection, with that . . . smell like bitter orange blossoms strewn atop a cesspool, waiting for the beige curtain to be drawn so I can look down on some still, beige body under a white sheet. Death warmed over posing as cold oatmeal. Why, when you already knew—*knew*—who he was?"

"But I didn't," she confessed in a low voice. "I still don't, since even you couldn't be certain."

"But the fingerprints—!"

"Don't match," Molina admitted, hearing the bitterness in her own voice. The failure.

"Don't match?"

He stared into her face, a handsome man her own height, who couldn't, wouldn't dream of intimidating her except with the moral indignation he had rightfully leveled at her. Using him without telling him why was part of her job. Most parts of her job were not nice.

Matt Devine settled into his own uneasy speculations, his emotions finally as readable as faceup playing cards. He was starting to learn the game of self-defense. She frowned. Using someone as undefendedly honest as Devine was more than mean; it was rotten. She suspected that his family history was tortured, now she could see the proof of that.

"It's a good thing I didn't call my mother—" He thought aloud, making her kick herself again for good measure.

Yet the reflex of official suspicion would not be denied. If the Devine/Effinger family history was so tormented, Matt Devine *could* have killed the man who called himself Cliff Effinger, not knowing any better than she who he really was.

"Thanks for finally telling the truth," he said, looking up.

She wished she could be sure enough to say the same.

Chapter 26

Another Opening, Another Shoe

Shades of the late, great Gridiron Show! Temple was once again racing through the theatrical underbelly of the Crystal Phoenix, thinking about skits, costumes and crime. This time she was in cover-model costume, so she had long, heavy lavender brocade skirts to drag along. Good thing she had packed her Guthrie costume.

Off-the-shoulder necklines may be tailor-made to drive historical romance heroes crazy. They are also designed, she found, to drive anyone who wears them—except a broad-shouldered linebacker—insane. She shrugged as she ran, wanting the material either on or off. It persisted in riding her shoulder rim like a gargoyle clinging to a cathedral ledge.

Her ice-cold fingers jerked up one brocade shoulder . . . what self-respecting romance heroine wouldn't have cold fingers when she was about to rehearse a pose-down with a cover hunk? Heavy on the hunk, no doubt, and light on the rehearsal. She'd heard the author escorts buzzing about a contestant who'd tried to goose any passing female last year.

Though Danny had promised to steer obstreperous sorts away from her, he wasn't God and couldn't control everything. And with Crawford Buchanan's stepdaughter Quincey, a not-so-sweet sixteen, among the cover models, Temple was bound to inherit some of the lusty overflow directed away from Quincey. Temple could hardly plead maidenly qualms at thirty.

She circled her neck to ease a cramp, rebelling against a fall of hot, heavy red hair, also part of the compleat covergirl's costume. The hairpiece still felt prone to ebb down her back like an auburn sun sinking slowly in the West, so she jabbed oversize bobby pins into her coiffure as she went, hoping to hit hair, wig or something anchorable, even scalp would do in a pinch. . . .

Of course she had to wear extremely flat-footed satin slippers, so naturally she slipped on the slick concrete and went skating ahead of herself until she caught a costume rack pole, tilting it to perform a fancy circle-stop against the wall.

Temple leaned against the concrete blocks and panted. Running in this heavy, theatrical getup did her composure no good. At least she hadn't damaged the "real" costumes. She eyed a frothy row of still-swaying sequins, pearls and feathers from the Phoenix's nightly revue. The pageant people, of which she was now one, were transients, mere borrowers of this space and these facilities. Interfering with the true show people would be a professional discourtesy.

Righting herself and the rack, her glance was caught by something underneath it that twinkled. She couldn't have stumbled upon another entrance to the underground tunnels, because those were all sealed. What she saw was a shoe, no doubt.

A shoe in fact. It lay toppled. Only the sole was visible, as smooth and untouched as fresh-laid linoleum. But a tiny rim of glitter visible around the toe beckoned like a tinfoil smile, and Temple found herself smiling back. Some people smiled at babies. She smiled at shoes. So sue her!

Oh, what the heck! She could at least see what it looked liked. That was her eternal quest, after all.

She sank into airy layers of her costume's velvet and brocade skirts, then crouched by the rack and bent forward despite the strict disinclination of her corset. She finally managed, with a few grunts, to touch her fingertips to the shoe.

The difficulty made her all the more set on seeing the hidden shoe. That rim of glitz looked mighty like solid silver-white rhinestones. Wouldn't it be wild if this was it? *The* shoe! Maybe a showgirl (shoegirl?) wore it onstage nightly.

By inching the sole closer with her fingernails, Temple was finally able to pinch her fingers on the toe and work the shoe close enough to pick up.

Except it was . . . a boot. And what a boot! She stared, stunned, like a Cinderella with an absolute klutz for a fairy godmother.

Oh, it was a fancy boot: inlaid flame-patterns of silver leather, with rhinestones scattered hither and thither like glitzy exclamation points. Though flashy enough to be a women's boot—it was like a size . . . Bigfoot. And all the rhinestones did glitter, but most were big and clunky. In a word, crude. Sorry, fairy godmother, you aren't klutzy, but your taste in boots sure as shootin' is! Of course showgirls, being almost six feet tall, usually wear fairly large-size shoes. Maybe this was an escapee from a Western routine. Rhinestone Clementine. The old California folk song ran through Temple's mind, with new words. *In a basement, in a ho-tel, excavaaaating for a crime, toiled a miner, old-boot-finder and her name was Ne'er-on-time. Light she was and like a fairy, but her boots were number nine. Big old bootsies, for giant tootsies, not the shoes she'd hoped to find.*

Temple stood up, painfully, the big, bad boot in hand, and puzzled. Here she was, hunting the prize designer pumps and here she had found—instead—a crude rhinestone boot that Trigger wouldn't wear on a bad mane day. Surely this ghastly thing had a mate! She couldn't bear to bend over again, so she tried to sweep the long costumes up from the floor with her slipper-clad foot. All right, she kicked the hems into a froth. No other boot lay revealed under the rack. Yippee cayaaaa! This was a lonesome boot.

So a boot had been forgotten under the costume rack. Discarded, or deliberately ditched? Why? Temple was expected onstage right now for some serious hunk-hugging. What to do? She tapped the boot's virgin sole against one palm, undecided. Why was it unworn and abandoned? She would have to contemplate that mystery later.

She bolted back down the empty hallway, back to the two-mirror cubicle she shared with the sullen Quincey. There she dumped the boot in her canvas totebag. She would worry about it later. Right now, she had more pressing matters, like two hundred and twenty pounds of bare, muscled serial hunk to contend with.

Fabrizio stood, wide-stanced, hands on hips (what big hands, what lean hips!), hair tossed back over his shoulders (what luxuriant hair, what broad shoulders!) facing the stage.

That was where his audience was, at the moment. The house seats were empty, but the stage teemed with testosterone and its most spectacular by-products. Thirty-three handsome heroes, restless as a wayward wind, wandered the risers, which squeaked for mercy under their conjoined weight. Fontana brothers roved in a restless pack, all clad in tight black-denim jeans.

Danny Dove sat cross-legged on the stage floor like a power-mad elf, facing the models—frowning, pointing and projecting his voice to the wings.

"You. Three feet to the left. Not you with the three left feet! Come to think of it, don't move a muscle. We haven't got accident insurance. Just kidding, gang. And you in the tape-measure suspenders. Down a riser, big boy, your head will be hitting the boom mike. Yes, Mr. Fontana the Fifth or whoever, edge that boyishly lean bod over just . . . a . . . tad."

Temple felt small and vulnerable as she huddled with the other two pose-down girls in the stage-left wings. She would have liked to stay there. Her two sister models were dallying with their costumes, jerking them down from the top and up from the bottom, exactly the opposite approach Temple was inclined to take.

Quincey was gowned as an Old West saloon girl. Whether she had a heart of gold was unclear, but her deck-of-cards bustier featured the jacks of hearts and diamonds front and provocatively centered. Her knee-length red-satin skirt was edged in black maribou feathers, which she was hiking up to high heaven on one hip and fastening there with a safety pin.

"Don't you have any underwear on?" Temple asked, following the diamondback-rattlesnake pattern of Quincey's fishnet pantyhose all the way to ground zero.

"Of course not." Quincey's tone was pure teenage disdain. "You never know what will show during one of these things, Danny said. Would you want someone out there in the audience seeing your groady old underwear?"

"Well, it might be better than the alternative." Temple tugged at her receding dress shoulders again. "Darn. This outfit will not stay put!"

"Your boobs are supposed to hold it up," Quincey explained, rolling heavily made-up eyes.

"Oh, that's the problem." Temple regarded the gown's gaping neckline. "I don't have any."

"Sure you do. Just lean way forward into the dress, then stand up again."

Quincey demonstrated with limber enthusiasm, thus revealing the tiny tattoo of a bulldog smoking a cigar that had hitherto hidden coyly behind the jack of hearts. Her mild exercise had increased her bra size by at least a letter of the alphabet. Bras were the only subject where getting Cs was better than Bs or As.

Temple, impressed despite herself, bent over, nearly cutting off the circulation in her torso, and rose again. Quincey was right, the bodice felt tighter and—oh, my—much more of her had come out to look around.

"What keeps us from falling out of these getups during the action onstage?" she wondered next.

"Nothing," said the girl on her other side, a brunette named Lacey with authentically long, burnished hair. These were mere girls so slight and young that there was no point in calling them women and looking ridiculous. "This is exactly like a real cover shoot, you know: the more provocative the better."

Oh, my ripping bodice! Temple thought. *I didn't sign on to be provocative, just to snoop.*

"Luckily," Lacey added, "most of these guys are pretty good, and have their own, like, routines. We'll just get together and decide whether we go horizontal or vertical, like where we wrap our legs and arms and all that stuff. You know, consult before trying it."

Did she say "*consult before dying?*"

"So you've done this before?" Temple said aloud.

"Naw, I talked to a girl who did it last year. She's running the bookstore this time."

"Why isn't she modeling again?"

"Oh, she did this reeeally hot, super-steamy number with the guy who won last year, you know, an' her folks saw it on tabloid TV, an' *Skintight* magazine called an' wanted her to do a, you know, really sexy photo layout and her, like, Stone-Age folks got totally bent out of shape and almost didn't let her come at all this year." Lacey's snapped gum, transmitting a tooth-decaying aroma of fruit-flavor, put a period to her endless sentence.

On Temple's other side, Quincey bent to pull a red satin garter up her thigh and snapped it into place.

Temple thought that she would do something different and simply snap. Like a twig. An overaged twig in a tempest not of her own making. But their attention was again drawn to the unknown horrors to come onstage.

"Now," Fabrizio announced during a lull. "I volunteer for sample pose-down, in case any of you guys are feeling shy."

None of the guys onstage looked the least bit shy, Temple noticed, with the possible exception of Jake Gotshall. And even he was looking, frankly, pretty hot to trot.

Nor were any of the assembled hunks swooning with enthusiasm at Breezy's self-sacrificing suggestion. Danny's head had turned to fix the Dallyin' Italian with the basilisk eye of a director sensing a mutineer.

No one directs a macho man, though, but his own ego. "Who will be Breezy's little woo-mahn for a run-through, eh?" he asked.

"Oh, this is too awesome!" Quincey murmured. "Just like one of those historical romance scenes where the women are captured and rounded up to be sold as love slaves and the handsome pirate captain picks one out. Me, me, me!"

"Wrong period, kid," Lacey said. "You need John Wayne or somebody else dead. Leave the live ones to me."

She undulated in front of Temple and Quincey to strike a pose in a harem costume apparently made from Salome's original seven veils after the moths had gotten through with it. A hand that jingle-jangled with seventeen or so thin brass bangles waved to and fro. "I'll do it, Fabrizio!"

But that would have been too easy. *Too easy for Breezy,* Temple muttered in her mind.

She knew what was coming. He knew from experience that she was easy to pick up. She was a marked woo-mahn. Quincey was right. Temple was beginning to feel like the much-put-upon heroine of a historical romance.

Time froze. Temple's mind beat birdlike against the confining cage bars of reality, seeking refuge in memories of a moment so like this one: a scene from one, or ten, of the historical romances she had speed-read in the past few days. She stood there, on that sandy, forgotten shore, in her disheveled finery.

"Who will be Breezy's little woo-mahn? I will run through anyone who says me nay, eh?" he demanded. Rasped. G.R.O.W.L.ed.

Captain B̶r̶e̶e̶z̶y̶ Beelzebub "Blast" Slaughter's intense eyes, bluer than all the seven seas churned together into one seething, intemperate tidal wave, raked over the captured prey, frightened booty of the good ship Windswept.

Then they paused on the frozen form of dismayed Tempest Storm, proud, Titan-haired daughter of planter Gust Storm and his lovely but frail aristocratic wife Gale, and sister of the darling baby boy Squall . . . who would do exactly that, were he to understand his sister's vile predicament.

Stunned, Tempest heard Captain Blast's seven-league boots stomping over the s̶t̶a̶g̶e̶ sand toward her. Her fate lay in this hard but handsome man's hands, and his intentions lay in the hot, burning flames of his ice-blue eyes.

She desperately tried to . . .

look tempestuously disdainful, yet knowing that she must endure all that the pirate captain might do to her before a leering crew of thirty-three tall, broad men cut from the same bold, rapacious sailcloth . . .

. . . RUN!

But first . . .

she desperately decided to . . .

de-bend her dress bodice.

Like all gravity-defying acts, this one looked easier to do than to undo. Drat, her pose-down debut would be a sight to remember. Where was the sweet retreat of fiction when she needed it?

"Hah!" Captain Breezy stopped, took a wide stance that emphasized thighs the size of Easter Island hams, and pointed imperiously to Temple, whose only relation to any kind of Storm was as a licensed driver. Life had returned to Real Time, no matter how bizarre.

"*La Rossa.*" He smiled. Showed his teeth. Leered. Licked his lips. Ate her grandmother. "We are already experts at the pose, no?"

Before Temple could shake her head, or shrug her gown back on her shoulders, Fabrizio strode over and caught Temple's itty-bitty hand in his great big paw.

He led—dragged—her to center stage, not her idea of undercover work.

Apparently, it wasn't Danny Dove's idea of how to run a rehearsal either.

Danny jumped up and spun Temple out of Fabrizio's ham-handed grip before either of them could blink.

Now Danny pointed imperiously. "You. To the risers with the rest of the chorus line." He turned to the assembled hunks.

"If you must have a demonstration of the finer points of a pose-down, I will give it. Now, you must remember that although you are dealing with a person who may weigh as little as half your own poundage, she is liable to feel heavier than you think, especially if you try too-heroic maneuvers without a careful rehearsal. For instance, no *Taming-of-the-Shrew* sack of potatoes over the shoulder shtick . . . unless you've rehearsed it."

Danny demonstrated by bending and rising with Temple draped

over one shoulder, his arm around her knees the only thing that kept her from tumbling to the hard stage floor.

Temple tried to gasp, but the corset ruled out all emergency breathing techniques. Danny had spun so she faced the empty house, and a good thing, too; gravity was pulling her bodice to depths that Quincey and company could not dare dream of. She crossed her arms over her gaping decollétage (and crossed her fingers on her shoulders) while eavesdropping on Danny's crisp lecture on her rear . . . er, at her rear.

"In this position, the woman's weight is mostly over my shoulder, but gravity makes even the lightest one like lead. Let go of her legs, and you drop her. Lean back too far, and you drop her. My advice is: don't try it. If she ends up on her ass, you end up looking like one. Not very romantic."

Temple felt her world shake as Danny bent and she once again touched terra firma, feet-first.

Not for long.

"I know, gentlemen, that during pose-downs you are fond of executing a maneuver known as a 'dip.' " Danny's scathingly precise enunciation made the act of a dip sound like . . . well, the act of a dip.

"Bear in mind that the female torso bends, but it does not break."

Danny turned and bent again. Temple suddenly was staring at the hems of curtains suspended in the flies. She felt she was lying head down on the grounded half of a teeter-totter. Speaking of totter, she felt that she was going to slide headfirst and backwards off the edge of the known world . . . which-did-too-have-one!

"Not to worry." Danny's reassuring tone soothed as he maintained their difficult position and continued his lecture.

"This looks easier than it is. Notice that my supporting arm is lengthwise as much as possible beneath the lady's spine. Notice, too, that I leaned *back* a bit as I bent her and myself over, so her feet are not churning to keep braced on the floor. You do not wish to make your lady fair look like a hyperactive gerbil. If you must dip, and I do not recommend that you try this in your own home, practice slowly and safely. Get it right. Otherwise, you will have her flailing in your arms . . . or falling to the floor. Then the only dip you have to take is your farewell curtsy as you are hooted off-stage as an unromantic boor."

Danny pulled Temple upright as if she weighed six pounds and dropped custody of her hand. "Any questions?"

Temple had one. She knew she had been heaved around like a side of beef, but she had never really felt out of control, despite her fears. And Danny probably weighed a hundred and forty pounds with his hair wet.

A slow, ponderous wave of clapping bestirred the becalmed hunks, who understood the weight problem, if nothing else. Danny took Temple's hand and stepped away. She recovered fast enough to take a shallow (due to the dress) bow, and smile like a trouper.

"My hero," she whispered wryly as Danny bowed and kissed her hand.

"Better than being a hero sandwich," he muttered, rolling his eyes at the risers, where Breezy pouted like the world's largest five-year-old.

Danny's angelic grin as he regarded Fabrizio sobered to a director's sternness. Temple ambled offstage, trying not to feel dizzy.

"Spotlight-hog," Lacey greeted her. "Too bad you got stuck with the wimpy director."

"I'll tell him you said that," Temple answered sweetly. "I know he'll make sure that you get all the dorkiest guys as pose-down partners."

"Right on, Batgirl!" Quincey grinned at Temple.

Together they watched Lacey slink away to wave at the guys on the risers.

"You did okay," the sixteen-year-old told Temple in a hurried, hoarse whisper. "But don't be such a nerd about the damn neckline."

It was, Temple realized sadly, excellent advice.

Since the worst, for now, was over, she realized her subconscious had been playing tricks during her mental sojourn in Historical Romance Heaven. The least of them was the unlikely handle of Tempest Storm: it had come to mind so quickly because it was the stage name of an infamous stripper.

Did this fact offer an omen for Temple's fate during the real, live dress rehearsal and actual performance still to come?

Temple decided to distract herself from forthcoming indignities with another shoe hunt.

Chapter 27

Witch Switch

I am more than somewhat worried about Miss Temple Barr.

After witnessing her odd behavior the other day at the MGM Grand theme park, which resulted in her being swept off her tootsies not once, but twice, by dirty, greasy pirates, I fear that her recent emotional upsets have also swept off her sanity.

So I resolve to keep a weather eye on her (in keeping with the nautical theme of her recent expedition).

And what do you know? The very next time I find her slipping away from the Crystal Phoenix for a little R&R (Wrest and Wreck-reation) it is the dark of evening, and where do her size-fives head but back for a return engagement with the Big Guy at the MGM Grand? Does she not get the picture? She is not safe on these nasty, neon streets.

I amble after her, wondering what sort of aerial antics she is up to tonight.

Once again I risk life and lateral limb nipping through the awe-some glass doors, which would like nothing better than to snap shut on any part of my anatomy in arrears. These casino doors are hungrier than a loan shark on a diet.

On this occasion, Miss Temple appears to be playing the role of innocent tourist. She immediately heads for the quaint little kiosk with the cabbage-size Technicolor flowers blooming all around it at the back of the "Wizard of Oz" enclosure just inside Leo's welcoming paws. I note that an admission fee is charged, so I slink into the ersatz greenery and belly-crawl on the skimpy dirt until I am a mere whisker away from the Yellow Brick Road.

(By the way, do you have any idea of why the Yellow Brick Road is yellow? This is real insider stuff, so listen up. Toto. Yup. For a pipsqueak, he was mighty powerful in the elimination department. Dogs will do it anywhere, you know. And that goes for other matters, as well. An inferior species from start to finish, but they do have their occasional uses.)

I wait impatiently for Miss Temple to catch up to me. There are many disadvantages to being human, but having to pay admission must be one of the worst. Not only does Miss Temple have to slam down five bucks for this insider tour of the Haunted Forest and the Emerald City at its center, but she has to wait until showtime while a mob of tourists jostles and stomps behind her.

According to a sign on the gingerbread kiosk, the Emerald City houses a magic show. I could show her some real magic: just belly-crawl under the fence and you are in free of charge. Of course Miss Temple might claim to find the notion of crawling into an attraction rather undignified, but—given her recent shenanigans in the rigging with the pirate scum and her new role as wench—she is hardly one to plead dignity as an excuse for not doing something.

So I hunker down in the so-called woods and wait, trying not to let the artificial smells of plastic and putty put me off the scent. Soon I pin my ears back as a gaggling crowd of tourists and their jabbering offspring stumble down the Yellow Brick Road that weaves through this movie-set woods like a center highway line painted by a drunken sailor with Montezuma's revenge. An awesome assortment of tennis shoes parades by, but nowhere do I spot my little doll's high-heeled sneakers. Okay, they are not really sneakers. They are black denim with a rubber-clad sole and heel made to resemble maple, so they are easy on the ears.

The babbling gawkers hunt and peck down the Yellow Brick Road while I shimmy my way near, sniffing for Toto. Luckily, this setting is so artificial that nothing natural has been permitted to permeate the pathway. At last! I spot Miss Temple's dainty spikes hushing down the lane. She is tailing the sightseers, but pauses by the first solo act in this compact scenario, little Miss Dorothy Gale with her Red Riding Hood basket and her red-sequined shoes.

Miss Temple Barr has no time to dally with picnic baskets and checked pinafores. She squats down by Miss Dorothy and studies the sequined pumps. She doesn't even look up when the mannequin cranks into life and begins declaiming a pre-recorded message. I can tell what Miss Temple is thinking, even from the rear (hers, not mine). She is mooning over the ruby red slippers, though she knows that they are a copy of a reproduction. She is never one to overlook a snazzy pair of shoes.

But she rises with an audible sigh and makes a face at Miss Dorothy Gale. It is not really her shoes Miss Temple covets in her high-heeled sole. Too low, too dowdy, too dusty for my little Rustilocks. She minces on, eerily silent for once in her new snooping shoes.

What can a fellow do but follow?

Not forty feet farther down the YBR, she stops cold. Or perhaps she stops hot. Either way, she is as still as one of these overdressed, over-chatty statues. I slither closer to discover the object of her attention.

I am soon sorry.

Someone has escaped the gingerbread kiosk, and it is no ticket-seller. In fact, this figure could not sell flying monkeys to a circus. There she stands—tall and green and thin and unlovely—no girl from Impanema, but the Wicked Witch of the West, a sight designed to give even an anteater an upset stomach. Her clawed hands are clutching her glassy spy-globe while her sharp nose and chin try to touch warts as she cackles about what she will do to Miss Dorothy Gale "and the little dog, too."

Actually, maybe the Wicked Witch is not such a bad sort, after all.

Miss Temple must have come to the same conclusion, for she stands mesmerized by the animated performance, which is good, but not earth-stopping. I am somewhat taken aback—in fact, I am forced to scoot under a scraggly spreading plant of some sort—when Miss Temple bends down and begins examining the ground around the witch.

She keeps an eye over her shoulder for wandering tourists, but seems to be looking for something. Not five feet away she finds it. A genuine tree branch, about three feet long. Scrawny, like the witch. And leafless and loose for the taking, which she does. My poor little doll. I have been neglecting her for the siren call of my kind. Can her state in life be so barren that she must resort to collecting dead branches as a hobby? What happened to her hankering for shoes?

Whatever the answer, I am not about to get it now.

Miss Temple discreetly brandishes her branch with a triumphant expression, then returns to confront the witch. Hey, I do not cotton to the old grouch, but there is no need to take a switch to her animated effigy!

Yet Miss Temple does not seem to have corporeal punishment in mind. No, it is something even more outré, and possibly . . . depraved.

Leaning over the low wooden fence separating her from the witch, Miss Temple stretches her petite frame, extending the homely wand of the branch, stretching and grunting and possibly even perspiring (an ugly and distasteful human process I prefer not to discuss in detail) in her quest to reach the witch's figure.

When the overhand approach does not work, she crouches down by the fence, thrusts her stick through and again gropes to span the five feet that separate viewer from wound-up witch.

I hold my breath as well as my tongue. For one thing, the witch is timed to break into odious motion any time again, thus attracting undue attention to my dear roommate's bizarre behavior. For another, someone besides my subtle self might be watching this shameful pantomime of a mind gone ga-ga even now. Someone like a security person. For a third . . . well, I cannot imagine yet another dire possibility.

An instant later, I doubt the witness of my own eyes.

Miss Temple has finally maneuvered the stick under the witch's skirt and is carefully drawing it up. I am horrified. Do witches wear skivvies, and would anyone want to know if they did or did not? What is Miss Temple thinking of? She has gone papayas! Or am I confusing my fruitcakes?

Even as I doubt the evidence of my eyes, the green sky above the Emerald City shifts with lightning. Thunder rumbles and glowers. I anticipate the arrival of a gaggle of security guards while the message "Surrender Temple" is etched across the dreadful lime sky above.

Miss Temple Barr, of course, is oblivious to all but her weird task. With a last lunge forward and a terrific jerk upward on her stick, she manages to dislodge the witch's long black skirt from the ground. Beyond it I glimpse shadow and no substance—the witch has nothing left to stand on! No wonder she melted like liquified rubber at the film's end. I also finally understand the object of Miss Temple's machinations. The witch has no feet, and therefore no shoes.

Oh, what a clever, inventive girl my little doll is! I confess that I have utterly underestimated her for once. Of course she would suspect a pair of black-cat Halloween shoes of being hidden under the Wicked Witch of the West! Not only did the ruby slippers originally bedeck the witch's feet (when she had these useful appendages, which her stand-in does not), but black cats and witches go together in the popular imagination like white doves and peace. Not in this instance, alas, but good try Miss Temple!

Even as I transmit waves of support and approval, I notice that someone human has sneaked up on Miss Temple. A blond young woman in a short skirt and a vest. She is frowning.

"Pardon me, ma'am," says this Goldilocks in the wrong world.

Oh, Miss Temple must hate that "ma'am." She straightens so fast her precious branch snaps into two skimpy pieces, and she knocks her shin on the fence rail.

"Did you lose something?" The babe in the woods regards my dear roommate with a solicitous smile that is most denigrating.

Never let it be said that Midnight Louie associates with those overburdened by the heavy weight of literal truth.

"Uh . . . yes," Miss Temple extemporizes in a wide-eyed Dorothy way. "A . . . cat. Not a real cat. A little black cat figure I keep on my keychain. I think it rolled into the woods right here."

"I don't see anything," the helpful girl guide says.

Meanwhile, Miss Temple has noticed the uniform nature of the girl's attire and realizes that she has been caught by someone official.

"Maybe I lost it getting out of the car. I'll check there. Am I too late for the show?"

"Almost," the young woman answers. "Better hurry."

And so Miss Temple Barr does: right past the blathering animated tin woodman and scarecrow and into the towering green domes of the Emerald City itself. The young woman watches her retreat so closely that I cannot follow, although I am dying to see the magic act inside the fabled viridian metropolis.

Instead I make my hidden way to the Emerald City's other side, observing that it is constructed of particle board and glitter. Illusions. Life is a magic act and this time I am in the last row. But I am waiting in the fake greenery when Miss Temple emerges from the structure, blinking. Above us, thunder grumbles and the Wizard exhorts the masses from the podium of his balloon gondola.

The more things are different, the more they are the same—here or over the rainbow. And where are the purported bluebirds, anyway? I could use a snack even more than Miss Temple Barr could use another pair of shoes.

Chapter 28

Romantic Rendezvous

"Where have you been all morning?" Kit demanded the next day, sounding mighty like Temple's mother.

"Out. *Hun-ting.*" Temple echoed Bela Lugosi's fiendish intonation when he had played Dr. Frankenstein's hunchbacked assistant; he didn't always get to be Dracula.

"Okay, Igor," said Kit, proving herself well up on vintage horror movies. "Shoe business again, huh?"

Temple nodded, not eager to relay her indignities at Fabrizio's hands. She was also wondering where *Kit* had been all morning, given Jake's disturbing new information about her aunt's late-night assignations. And Electra hadn't been too evident this morning, either, come to think of it!

Oblivious to Temple's mental reservations, Kit verbally careened on. "Whilst you were off tracking the wild Weitzman, I arranged for a high-powered coven of romance writers to assemble. A murderer may be among them. Need I say more?"

Temple shook her head.

"All right." Kit went on, talking a mile a minute. "The setup is you're a producer for *Prime Time*—"

"*Prime Time?* You don't mean the network news show?"

"Right." Kit shoved a slippery stack of author press-kit folders into Temple's arms. "I grabbed these in the press room, so it looks like you've done your homework."

"Thanks for the big promotion, but I really can't pose as a *Prime Time* producer. That's . . . actionable if anyone finds out. Impersonating a tabloid TV producer with intent to trap a murderer doesn't carry the same risks. Nobody in tabloid TV has much reputation to protect, but masquerading as *network*—"

"Cool it, kid. I admitted that you're my niece, so these authors probably assume you're just a lowly producer-in-training-wheels. And so young for such an important position, too."

She patted Temple's unruly curls into place, like a mommy readying her offspring for the garden club.

"*Aunt* Kit! You are the senior member here. First you suggest I offer myself up to some mysterious pageant ritual called a posedown; now you arrange an audience with the queens of romance under childishly false pretenses. You said these women were megabestsellers. They'll be much too sophisticated to fall for me extorting information under cover of media blitz."

"Don't count on it." Kit was now patting her own unruly redgray curls. "They'll cut you slack because you're a relative of a colleague. Besides, we poor romance writers have been the national media's whipping girls for so long that we've developed the pathetic optimism a single woman feels about another blind date. Maybe this time it won't be so bad."

"And maybe tomorrow is another day, Scarlett."

"*Scarlett.*" Kit's eyes squinched shut behind the sparkling picture windows of her glasses. "God, I wish, I wish I'd gotten *that* writing assignment! I'd have done a helluva better job, and I'd be squalidly rich by now."

" 'Squalidly rich' is an oxymoron, Auntie, as you well know from our earlier buzz session at the Debbie Reynolds' Hotel. What is it nowadays, with everyone and their first cousin writing sequels to classics by long-gone authors?"

"A dastardly trend," Kit said with a snarl. "Here's what it is: publishers . . . and agents . . . and heirs so remote they're almost invisible, all making easy money from dead writers by exploiting live writers as work-for-hire, sweat-shop labor to continue the 'sure thing' of the past. Forget about today's writers, and their present and future. Who are they gonna rip off forty years down the road if they don't let us writers get anywhere significant, huh?"

Temple seized an opportunity to segue into a touchy subject. "You feel strongly about these publishing issues."

"I should. It's my livelihood."

"And you aren't crazy hot about the cover trend to feature semi-nude hunks."

"True." Kit, being an actress, had immediately read the underlying seriousness in Temple's voice. She was waiting for the real question to surface.

Temple decided to end the suspense for them both. "Then why did *you* meet Cheyenne for a drink Wednesday night after I turned him down, and why didn't you mention that after he was murdered?"

Kit eschewed Jake's theatrics.

"Because I may not need hunks on my covers to sell my books, but I'm not opposed to admiring them in person," she said deadpan. "And then, of course, if I had murdered him, I wouldn't want to draw attention to our association."

"You had an 'association'?" Temple hadn't meant for her voice to rise an octave.

"Now, Niece, don't interrogate your old auntie." Kit smiled. "I didn't mention it because I was so damn embarrassed. I ran into the guy in the lobby bar after our expedition to the MGM Grand and dinner—and after you and Electra had gone to bed with visions of pirates swooping out of crows' nests in your heads. We chatted and that led to a drink. I wondered why he'd wanted to talk to you, but I never found out anything, except that he was as charming as hell."

"Nothing happened?" Temple demanded.

"Don't be so maternally vague. Spit it out. No, we did not go to bed. We did not even pass 'Go.' We talked. We flirted a little.

I *am* single and past twenty-one. We said good-bye. Permanently, as it turned out. But I didn't want to look as if I'd grabbed your guy."

"As I recall, you liked the look of them, too," Temple noted suspiciously.

"Call it a post-menopausal speculation." Kit smiled again. "Once a woman reaches a certain age, she can get away with things men have been doing all along. Very liberating, really, and fairly harmless."

"Most of the author suspects are your age, or a decade younger." Temple, relieved, returned to her trail of *pre*-menopausal speculation. "Could one of them have actually done it?"

"Murdered Cheyenne?"

"Ultimately. But first, slept with him?"

"Anything is possible and maybe even probable. That's why I set up this interview, Niece. So you could study the prime suspects. Want to know if their position on cover hunks is righteously upright, or sleazily horizontal? Ask 'em in your own subtle way. Thanks to the cover controversy, they'll be so busy frothing at the mouth that they won't notice when you pose any not-really for-*Prime-Time* questions. And I know you'll pull off your impersonation with pizzazz. Not only do you have a legitimate news background, but you have the famous Carlson acting genes!"

Temple shook her head. "Name one famous acting Carlson."

Kit was stumped. "Well, since I retired from the stage—" Then she screeched out, "Richard!"

"Who is . . . or was . . . that?"

"Lord, give me patience with the child. Richard Carlson did some great grade-B sci-fi movies and lots of TV in the fifties. *I Led Three Lives.*" Temple's expression remained unenlightened. "About the Communist menace in America." Temple didn't bat a press release. "Oh, and all those neat kiddie educational films for Bell Telephone Company, too, that we saw in grade school." When Temple still looked as blank as a ream of fresh twenty-pound bond, Kit added wistfully, "You have at least heard of Ma Bell, haven't you?"

"Just barely. Rings a bell. Okay, where am I to meet this posse of grand dames?"

"Electra said she'd arrange a private room with the hotel. In fact, she's seeing to the food and everything."

"Food?"

"You can't expect a major network show to buttonhole people in the corridors, can you?" Kit fumbled in her purse, then squinted at the neon pink Post-It note that emerged sticking to her forefinger. "Here it is. Room seven-eleven."

"Okay." Temple gamely turned toward the hotel elevators, then stopped. "Isn't that the . . . Ghost Suite?"

"The Ghost Sweet?"

"Never mind."

Temple trotted briskly for the elevators, as if she wasn't lugging six pounds of press kits. The seventh floor was purely residential, so it was quiet as a tomb when she stepped out of the elevator alone.

She advanced down the lush, recarpeted hall. Yup, 711 was the infamous Ghost Suite all right. Temple paused to listen at the door. Faint laughter, but a clink of silver and crystal indicated corporeal life behind the sturdy wood door. Ghosts may snicker, but they don't eat. Although, Temple recalled, Jersey Joe Jackson's shade had shown a certain fondness for drinking champagne on one not-so-distant occasion. . . .

Temple shuddered and put her hand on the cold brass doorknob. Then she decided to knock, just in case any lively ectoplasm wanted to do some last-minute tidying.

"Come in!" Electra stood there, resplendent in a solid yellow muumuu, her hair a curled halo of reassuringly plain, past-sixty silver. "The boys have already delivered the first cart."

"Boys?" Temple muttered uneasily as she edged past Electra.

"You'll see. Meanwhile, your guests await."

Did they ever! Temple had never seen the Ghost Suite so definitely occupied. A flock of prosperous-looking middle-aged women perched on the authentic 1940s furniture. All were sampling hors d'oeuvres from glass and silver trays. A brass bar cart glittered with Baccarat crystal and decanters glowed with amber, topaz or diamond-clear liquors.

Temple immediately glanced to the end tables, but each one was protected by coasters.

"It's all under control, dear," Electra said beneath her breath, which smelled of . . . Johnny Walker Black. "Trust me. Would you like something?" She waggled her eyebrows at the bar.

"Not when I'm working," Temple said through her teeth, and under her breath as well. "Where did you get all this?"

"Restaurant. Van. Chef Song. The boys."

Boys? "Free, I hope?"

"Of course. You know they'd all do anything for you."

"I just wish it was something I knew about."

"I'll be right back," Electra said, slipping into the hall. "Go to it, girl!"

Temple pulled the light chair away from the desk beside the door. She put the heavy press kits on the desk, where they immediately slid into avalanche mode. She contained them as best she could, then smiled at her . . . guests.

"I'm impressed." The slender woman Temple had seen pointed out as megastar Misty Meadows nibbled cream cheese and caviar. "The network really knows how to put on the ritz."

Temple smiled broadly. Very broadly. She would say not one word that could be interpreted as misrepresentation. She shuffled press kits on her lap and beamed at the assembly.

"I'm sorry to be late, so much to do! And I just grabbed your press kits, so I'm afraid I haven't done my homework yet."

"No problem," said a heavyset woman in hot-pink linen, making inroads on three celery sticks and a radish. "We're used to improvising."

"We're also used to abuse." Another woman's voice came clear and challenging from the chartreuse-upholstered loveseat that Midnight Louie so liked to lounge upon, who knows with whom . . . or what? "I hope you won't hand the on-camera personality a script that says we romance writers 'crank out' these bestsellers in an effort to 'put a little sexual fantasy' in our lackluster, overweight, middle-aged women's lives."

Temple's upraised hands fanned in a plea for peace. "I understand your problem, and hope to be part of the solution. In fact, that's my first question. About these so-called cover hunks . . . "

They groaned as one, which was more than she had hoped for. While they tossed disparaging comments about current cover trends back and forth, Temple made a quick study of the press kits, matching photographs to the actual persons.

The lineup was: Sharon Rose on the chartreuse satin loveseat; Misty Meadows on the armchair. The solemn woman in glasses beside Sharon Rose was the outspoken Mary Ann Trenarry, who had carried the banner against the cover-hunk trend, although she had said nothing significant yet. Maybe she regretted her strong position, as Kit had suggested.

Temple glanced to her left, nearly jumping to see the immense purple mountain of Shannon Little capped by a tilted straw hat with several snowy white feathers, from beneath which the romance doyenne icily glared down at Temple. A glass plate of hors d'oeuvres in her lap was as mountainously heaped as her person. But Shannon kept silent because she was devouring the goodies with mechanical efficiency, too-tight rings glittering as her fingers moved delicately to and from her mouth.

Though she had to admit that Shannon Little was a Purple Presence, Temple found the other authors disappointingly ordinary. Misty Meadows, seen close up, was one of those monotoned women from a sixties youth who wore no makeup. They all looked as if a wire brush had scrubbed their faces of all vivacity, a look that made the drama of Misty Meadows's hip-length hair seem like a forgotten adolescent cause without a rebel to wear it.

Sharon Rose's pink floral blouse and A-line skirt would have caused Hester Polyester to drool with envy. Her housewive's bubble-perm was as crisp as her apparel, and she had accessorized the casual outfit with a heavy gold necklace and earrings dripping diamond chips. All her taste was obviously concentrated on her plate, which was modestly filled with one of everything on the trays. Mary Ann Trenarry, a well-preserved woman well into her sixties, wore an exquisitely tailored coral silk suit with a single strand of pearls.

Only one woman in the room qualified as what Temple would call a glamour girl. Ravenna Rivers, likely a pseudonym. The thirty-something (and-wouldn't-*you*-like-to-know-exactly what?) woman perched on a Sheraton side chair, her short, narrow black skirt showing lots of expertly crossed, exposed and hosed legs ending in red Manolo Blahnik heels. A white linen jacket vulgarized her aggressively tanned skin, and its vee neckline dipped way below the cocktail-hour zone. Unbelievably profuse, elbow-length blonde tendrils framed an angular face made up to Joan Collins standards. Temple expected to hear the theme-music of some late-night soap opera playing "Enter the Vixen."

Temple didn't need a convenient musical cue to recall that Ravenna Rivers was rumored to have cozied up with the Homestead Man on her recent book tour. Apparently, this urban she-devil named Ravenna Rivers wrote frontier historical romances full of home fires and patchwork quilts, would wonders never cease?

"How do you authors vote on the cover man question?" Temple began.

"My position is plain." Mary Ann Trenarry set her glass of club soda on a coaster and sat forward. "I think the focus on male cover models distracts the public, and the publicity machine, from our books. Romance novels, when written by women—"

"Good point!" Misty Meadows interrupted, bouncing on her chair like a cheerleader. "Decades ago when books like ours were written by men like Thomas B. Costain, they were 'historical novels' and considered serious fiction."

"Costain never wrote novels like ours," Shannon Little interrupted imperiously, so inflamed that she temporarily returned a bacon-wrapped chestnut to her plate. "Women put the sex in historical novels."

"What about Frank Yerby?" Misty Meadows asked with raised eyebrows.

The women rolled their eyes.

"Please, you're talking pulp fiction," said Mary Ann Trenarry. "As I was saying, when women revived the historical novel in the seventies, with the new wrinkle of a female point of view—and, admittedly, something really new, explicit sexual frankness—their books were classed as trash. The urge to merge in full color and detail was a sociological reaction to women becoming liberated enough to reclaim their own sexuality. The result was what always happens to what women do: the books were belittled and only the sexual content attracted attention. Ravenna, who else besides women romance writers are keeping the Western novel tradition alive in these days when Louis Lamour is that last big-name male Western writer, and he's dead?"

Ravenna Rivers uncrossed her knees high on the thigh. Then she recrossed them, angling them smartly in the opposite direction. Imagine that, Temple thought enviously, ambidextrous crossed legs!

No plate occupied Ravenna Rivers lap, what little there was of it, but a lowball glass on the table beside her brimmed with straight Scotch, the color ale-dark.

"That's true. The Western romance keeps frontier stories alive. But this whole debate is so boring; what sells, sells, and that's why romance novels are here, why we are here now, why cover hunks are hot." Having said her piece, she took a swig of her Scotch.

Temple had been swiftly scanning the press-kit materials during the debate.

"Men certainly are a much more visible presence on covers," she said, holding up a handful of paperback bookcover flats, over half of them featuring a bare-chested man, period. "Isn't this Cheyenne, the one who was killed?"

Temple could have been holding up the queen of spades, the way all eyes riveted to the cover in question.

"That's him," Misty Meadows agreed. "He was getting lots of work. Isn't he on your latest, too, Sharon?"

"Well, my books don't have semi-naked hunks on the cover," she said primly, "because I bother to insist that my publishers do them differently. My newest will have an embossed white tablecloth lace front cover, with a step-back painting of a charming picnic scene. I supervised the cover shoot myself in New York. I always do, so no lapses in taste occur. Cheyenne was quite handsome in a plaid shirt and jeans, and the heroine wore dimity. Of course, he did fashion work as well lately."

"Oh, yes." Ravenna smiled significantly. "Cheyenne was exceedingly versatile. He could do country or pop. He and Fabrizio made *Vanity Fair* at the Milan design expo, when they both wore aluminum-riveted space-age silver jeans. It's still the same old story, ladies. Skin sells. Sex sells. You're fooling yourselves if you think anything different."

An unhappy silence ensued, during which Ravenna Rivers worked on her Scotch and Temple hunted for a question she wanted answered.

A knock at the door made them freeze like stalked rabbits.

Electra entered. "Ready for more?"

And in came carts of finger sandwiches, salad, fruits and pastries, wheeled by various brothers Fontana, all clad in the hunk uniform: tight blue jeans and form-fitting shirts with a closing problem. And all in author-charming public relations mode.

"Here comes the champagne, ladies," sang out Rico, pouring and passing glasses as fast as he could. "Compliments of Fontana, Inc."

Temple put away her press kits, and tabled her curiosity with them. She would get nothing more out of these authors now. But she had two curious crumbs to consider. Ravenna Rivers obviously had known Cheyenne very well, as she did many cover models, and almost every author present had their names across a book cover featuring the dead man, even Sharon Rose, who publicly disdained the cover-hunk craze.

"Champagne, miss?" Rico asked, bowing and pretending to not know her. He was undercover, too, you know.

She took the stem in her hand and sipped.

Rico winked.

Chapter 29

Four Queens Get the Boot

"Hi!" Temple stuck her nose into the Four Queens' dressing room. She wasn't visiting the downtown hotel of that name, but rather the Crystal Phoenix's quartet of showgirls known by the same name.

Darcy, Midge, Jo and Trish were all present that evening in various states of dress and undress, depending on how you viewed the process of preparing for a Las Vegas revue.

"Can I ask you guys a question?" she continued.

Calling the quartet "guys" was akin to calling Eskimos Fiji Islanders, but none of the four showgirls took offense. All were too busy taking off what few articles of clothing remained on them.

"What's up?" Darcy asked, adjusting the ride of her rhinestone g-string.

Temple produced Exhibit A from behind her back. "This."

All four women glanced up, defying gravity and the double sets of long false eyelashes glued to their lashlines.

"Bitchin' boot." Trish, a big-boned blonde, swung an extra-long leg over a wooden chair back, then flexed her knee and stamped her taps down hard on the seat while she adjusted a marabou garter.

Each dancer's fishnet hose bore the symbols of a different suite of playing cards: tiny red hearts for Darcy and diamonds for Midge, teeny black spades for Jo and clubs for Trish.

Jo, a statuesque redhead whose purple-mahogany locks made Temple's brighter curls seem garish, laughed as she applied a crystal earring that brushed her collarbone to her left earlobe.

"Temple, you cute thang. Your two feet could go in that big ol' boot and you'd still have room to swing a cat."

"Speaking of swinging cats," Temple said, "has anybody seen Midnight Louie around here lately?"

Darcy stepped back from her dressing table to reveal Himself sprawled on a red velvet pillow, one forepaw sweetly curled against his black velvet chest.

Someone had put a red satin bowtie around his neck, which he had managed to scratch off-center until it sat rakishly under one ear.

"Lord, he looks wounded . . . or decorated!" Temple shook her head. "What's the big attraction for him down here?"

"Besides Trish's smoked oysters?" Darcy grinned, then nodded at the boot. "So when is Big Tex coming to town?"

"That's what I'm here to ask. I found this stuffed under a costume rack in the hall and wondered if it was from a floorshow costume. I'm, um, sort of involved in the cover model pageant, and didn't want any of your essential costumes getting mixed up with theirs."

"Nice thought." Jo twanged the side elastic on her g-string. "But none of *our* costumes are exactly essential."

"Actually," Temple corrected, "they're the *only* essential things you're wearing. So. Nobody owns up to the boot."

"Let's give it a once-over," Darcy suggested. "It sure isn't ordinary streetwear."

They gathered around, their tap cleats ringing on the concrete dressing-room floor like horseshoes. Temple experienced a rare attack of claustrophobia as the showgirls closed in. With their heel-abetted height six feet-something, their plumed headdresses and the glitzy sway and clatter of their scanty harnessry, they reminded her of elegantly caparisoned circus steeds. She didn't know whether she felt more in danger of being crushed—or dazzled to death.

Since her Crystal Phoenix association had begun, she had often glimpsed these women from a distance, knew them by sight, had waved and smiled. Now, in their glamorous midst, they overwhelmed her as much as the equally large, bare and blatantly sexy male cover models. Why must erotic symbols always come in the Large, Economy Size, like the Wizard of Oz's false, inflated head? Great and powerful might seduce at a distance—and Temple was no subscriber to Dorothy, the meek and humble—but what was wrong with small and subtle?

"Nothing subtle about this here boot." Jo took it from Temple to turn this way and that. "Talk about your Rhinestone Cowboy! Will you gander at these zit-size rhinestones caking the heel?"

"Gross!" Darcy's moan commented on both the rhinestones and Jo's inelegant comparison. "But this is all custom work, and that silver-leather flame design has been hand-applied. The tragedy is that someone paid major money for this pair, when it was a pair."

"Why did you think this gunboat might be ours?" Jo surrendered the boot with a wrinkled nose.

"It's pretty big, but then so are you."

"Not *that* big." Trish peered down the boot's tall sides as if hunting hidden treasure. "No size stamped anywhere. Odd. But I'd call it a fourteen or fifteen, at least. Who's been hotfooting it through our corridors—Bigfoot?" She nodded authoritatively at Temple. "That there's a galoot's boot."

Temple sighed heavily. "I didn't want to hear that."

"Besides," Trish hefted her foot back onto the chair seat to display her size-ten silver pump. "All of us hoofers wear these regulation character shoes with two-inch Cuban heels and the Mary Jane straps. If we tried to tippety-tap onstage in those rhinestone galoshes, we'd break our necks. Check with the boys in the Incredible Hunk contest."

Temple watched them disperse to their makeup stations with a sense of relief. "You know about that?"

She hadn't expected them to notice. Showgirls were night creatures and birds of passage as well, with lives of their own far from the madding Las Vegas Strip. They did their grocery shopping at 3:00 A.M. and their nails at noon. They rarely had time or inclination to notice the gaudy male of the species Show Biz.

"Who could miss a convention of Conan the Barbarians?" Midge asked. "Especially when one of them gets knocked off so spectacularly. Died in the saddle, I heard."

"Not quite." Temple absently wrapped her arms around the boot and clutched it to her chest. It was less heavy that way. "He rode Native American–style. Bareback."

Trish shook her plumed head in mock mourning. "Dead so soon, half-naked on a naked horse."

"I knew him," Temple began.

"Oh, gosh! Sorry." Trish smiled an apology. "We get a little melodramatic down here."

"That's all right." Temple sat on an empty chair near the door, still clutching the boot like a stuffed toy. She rested her chin on the conveniently notched tops. "It's funny. I've been running all over town in search of a Cinderella shoe, and I end up with a glitzy, mystery cowboy boot on my own home turf."

"You want some great shoes, cheap?" Midge asked, enthusiastically spraying the only part of her hair that wasn't covered by a begemmed headpiece—her bangs. "Try the Shoes Galore Discount Emporium."

"Not just any shoes," Temple explained glumly. "The new Stuart Weitzman store in the Forum Shops at Caesars is offering a free pair of custom Austrian crystal–covered high heels to whoever can spot a similar shoe somewhere in Las Vegas."

"They used rhinestone shoes in the Tropicana show a few years ago. Like to blind the sun."

"Not rhinestones," Temple explained patiently. "Genuine Austrian crystals."

"What's the diff?"

"The same as between a jam jar and a brandy snifter. Crystal has more fire, and costs more."

"These shoes must be worth a fortune."

"To me, they would be. And the worst part is, he's on them." Temple pointed at Midnight Louie.

"Louie? He's always on shoes, on makeup tables, on g-strings—" Darcy laughed as she pulled a string of pearls from under Louie's red velvet pillow.

He batted lethargically as the pearls swung past, then yawned.

"It's nice to have him calling on us again," Darcy said.

"That's because Louie has a lady cat to visit on the premises."

"That little black one we see around all the time?"

"Heavens no." Temple was shocked. "Midnight Louise is his namesake. She's like his daughter. Besides, she's fixed. Louie's ladyfriend is an out-of-towner who breezes in now and again."

"I bet he's been keeping 'midnight' hours," Midge speculated. "Now that he's back, we have to box our tap shoes again, or he'd gnaw their straps off."

Not even mention of Louie's past misdeeds could rouse Temple from her vision of shoe-heaven lost. "Oh, I suppose it isn't Louie, in person, pictured on those prize pumps, but these shoes are sooo wonderful, and just made for me! Black-cat figures on each heel. For Halloween. I just know that's Louie."

"For you, it's Louie. For me, it's bad luck." Trish's shudder set her costume swaying in all the best places. "I'd never wear black cat shoes; everyone I'd walk in front of would panic. This is Las Vegas, children, where gamblers are so superstitious that they wear crossed suspenders."

"If you only saw these shoes," Temple keened softly. "You'd love them."

"Not really," Jo said. "I don't wear heels off the job."

"Me, neither," added Trish.

"You should discuss your lost shoes with Savannah, the vamp of Ipana; she's up to her ankles in oddball shoes," Darcy suggested.

"Savannah, the vamp of Ipana?"

"La Ashleigh with the bleached overbite. What a pain-a! She's emceeing the hunk pageant, and demanded her 'old' dressing room. Even though this area is off-limits to pageant people, she got it. All the prima donnas aren't in the opera."

Temple stared at Midnight Louie, who stared right back.

"Savannah Ashleigh . . . shoes. Of course! Not only is she back in town—with her cat Yvette, I bet, which explains the return presence of your G-string warmer"—she nodded at Midnight Louie nodding off again on the pillow—"but she's going after my shoes!"

Temple leaped to her feet.

Four sets of double false lashes blinked at her in the mirror, then dipped as they glanced as one to her feet.

"Not *these* shoes I'm wearing, the prize shoes. Have you seen Eightball O'Rourke around lately?"

The queens of diamonds, clubs and spades shrugged their naked shoulders, but Darcy's frown ended the group gesture.

"Little guy, wiry. About seventy," Temple prompted.

Darcy turned from the mirror. "I *have* seen Eightball down here a couple of times. I figured he was visiting Jill and Johnny Diamond."

"He was working, the rat! He was after the black-cat shoes for that Hollywood has-been. If Savannah Ashleigh can afford to hire a private detective to find them, she can afford to buy them!"

"I hear Savannah's been on her last uppers for some time," Midge noted with a cocked eyebrow.

"Well, she can keep her greedy hands off *my* last uppers! Look at me. I hunted up and down the Strip, risked drowning and pirates and breaking my neck and being arrested for getting fresh with a witch, yet all I've got to show for it is one odd boot with a virgin sole and rundown rhinestone heels. Life is not fair."

"Temple?" Darcy clopped over on her silver tap shoes, sounding remarkably like Cheyenne's Appaloosa. "Are you all right?"

Temple sat again, knowing the answer was no, and knowing that she didn't want to explain why finding the Midnight Louie shoes seemed like the only sane act in a world gone mad, a world of murdered models (one, so far) . . . dueling boyfriends (two, so far) ... and undercover pose-downs with a herd of handsome hunks (one dreaded dress rehearsal coming up).

"I've been working pretty hard," she said, "between the pageant and the shoe hunt, that's all." She hefted the boot. "I just hope this thing isn't an essential part of somebody's costume and they're missing it."

"So what part do you play in the pageant?" Darcy returned to the mirror to powder her makeup.

"Wench."

"What?"

"Wench of all work, with neckline down to here. They need warm bodies for the cover pose-down."

"Pose-down. That's a new term."

"They photograph embracing romance-novel cover models for the cover artist. The Incredible Hunk candidates need willing females to pose with them for the pageant's last competition: serial, live-action lusting."

"You volunteered for this?" Trish sounded incredulous.

"Let's say I was drafted by a relative."

Midge shrugged and grinned. "It could be kind of fun."

"So," said Temple, taking up her boot and preparing to walk, "could acupuncture."

Temple returned to her dressing room, a cubicle identicle to the one Jake Gotshall and the late Charlie Moon had shared. She stored the odd boot—odd both for being only one of a pair, and for its garish decoration—deep in her costume duffel bag. One never knew what someone else would mistake for a valuable.

Her costume hung from one of the curtain-draped pipes that defined the limits of each dressing area. According to her wristwatch, in only half an hour she'd have to change for the pose-down dress rehearsal.

Still, half an hour was longer than the absent Quincey was going to spend dolling herself up for the main event. Temple plucked her wallet from the duffel bag and moved into the aisles between the dressing rooms.

The Incredible Hunk candidates themselves were not about to skimp on preparation time; not one was to be seen, since all were closeted in their cubicles, primping. Voices murmured and curtains bulged here and there with sudden movements as Temple passed.

The aisles were filled with anonymous scooting forms, though— the hunks' lady-volunteer dressers. Most were safely past middle age, like priests' housekeepers. Unlike priests' housekeepers, they weren't automatically indifferent to their charges' boyish charms. With the outstanding exception of Matt Devine, most priests weren't blessed with looks gorgeous enough to pose for a romance novel cover.

Thinking of Matt had made Temple think of Max, which was an awkward juxtaposition in any event. What had brought these two strangers together, besides her? That mystery was more aggravating than the conundrum of Charlie Moon's dramatic death, if not as serious.

Think about Charlie Moon, Temple advised herself. Then think of England.

Moon first. Alone in the wings. Preoccupied with his entrance, mentally a million miles away from what was happening around him. Temple could believe that. Nothing was as isolated as the stage wings in the few, nervous moments before an entrance, especially if you were trying to manage almost a ton of horseflesh in an alien situation. The animal would be mincing around, its hooves slapping the wooden stage floor, making a racket, distracting the rider.

Temple could see how the numbing impact of an arrowhead in the back would hardly penetrate the adrenaline-driven concentration of a performer about to go onstage. She'd badly stubbed her toes on a metal plate backstage while rushing to make an entrance once. She'd gone on anyway, declaimed two pages' worth of light-comedy lines, and swept off laughing . . . only to collapse writhing and cursing *sotto voce* in the opposite wings, finally feeling the injury, or allowing herself to feel it.

And no fingerprints on the weapon. Whoever had snatched the arrow had thought to grab a makeshift hotpad to hold it. Picturing an actual oven mitt on the killer's upraised fist was such a laughable image that she chuckled.

She was still chuckling when she ran straight into another person.

"Oh, sorry!" Temple said.

"Goodness, girl, you ran right into my clipboard. You could have flattened yourself permanently," the woman added, frowning at Temple's bosom. "That would never do for a pose-down girl."

"You know who I am?"

"Not who, what. The only females your age back here before dress rehearsal are the lucky skinny young things who get to play cover model. Otherwise, only old bags like me hang around here."

"You're not an old bag!" Temple had always hated the term. "What's the clipboard for?"

"Oh, I don't even get to push, pull, prod and lace the laddies into their tight-fitting costumes. I'm the List Lady. Paperwork, not pantwork, that's my specialty."

Temple laughed, but she was also thinking furiously. Her new acquaintance was a raw-boned woman in her late sixties wearing baggy jeans and a grass-stained Ohio U sweatshirt she had no doubt inherited from a grandson.

"Then you know who's paired with who for the pose-down?"

"Haven't you checked yet?" She raised eyebrows as wild and wispy as a cat's.

"I've been . . . busy elsewhere. I'm wearing an off-the-shoulder, lavender brocade gown."

"You must be Miss Melisande, then, the Medieval/Renaissance model. We give everyone quickie code names. You sure can't be Miss Kitty, that's the Wild West outfit, and that minx Lacey is Miss Odalisque."

Temple tried to peer over the top of the clipboard the woman was consulting, but she whisked it out of view.

"If you haven't bothered to find out," she said sternly, "it's too late now."

"No, it isn't. Look, can't I just see what costumes the guys might be wearing, so I could figure who I'm likely to work with?"

Her white hair, cropped close to her head, shimmied as she indicated no, but Temple edged to the side to read the paper clipped on top anyway.

"Oh, all the guys have little titles too," Temple cooed. "Such a clever idea."

"I can't have great long lines of costume description, can I, and still end up with one sheet for thirty-three guys? Here's one you might be a match for: Mr. Romeo."

"Renaissance Italy," Temple said, nodding. She peeked further down the roster. "And Mr. Lancelot, that's mine. I imagine that some of these guys must be wearing gloves."

"Gloves? Whatever for?"

"Accurate period costume."

"In all my days as a pageant Wardrobe Witch, I have never heard anything so funny." She put her head back and roared, displaying a filling-free mouthscape of false teeth.

"No . . . gloves?"

"No, my dear. They'd get in the way during the pose-down—and, besides, the audience wants to see as much of the contestants as the law allows. Gloves don't quite fit the bill."

"Oh. I suppose mail gloves would be a little chilly." Temple shivered daintily.

"Don't you worry, Miss Melisande. No gloves, no gauntlets." The woman ran an expert eye up and down the two-column list. Then she frowned. "Except—"

"Except?"

"Well, he's way ahead of your period anyway, so I wouldn't worry."

"What period is he?"

"Viking raider. He goes with that ferrety girl in the see-through chiffon."

"But he wears gloves?"

"The only one, and only one glove, like Michael."

"Michael, that's his name?"

"No! Like Michael Jackson." The woman held up a fist, spread her fingers and pantomimed pulling on a glove. "Only his glove isn't white, it's black. Black leather. Because of the bird."

"The bird." Temple was really lost now.

"The bird. He's supposed to come on with this hawk on his wrist. So he needs the glove. Keeps it backstage, or rather that PR girl of his does, all hooded. Not her, the hawk. Kind of creepy. Haven't you noticed the cage?"

Temple shook her head numbly.

The costume lady smiled, certain and satisfied. "That's the only guy with a glove. The Birdman, so to speak. And he won't be in your vignette, not unless you move back a century or two, or he moves forward, and the pageant isn't a time-travel novel."

"Who?" Temple asked patiently.

"Who? Who what?"

"Who," she repeated, beginning to sound like another bird of prey, an owl, "who is dressing for pose-down as a Viking raider?"

"Why the big blond, of course. Fabrizio."

Fabrizio. Of course.

It's Hystery!

Deadlines, deadlines.

That word is so appropriate for this convention of happy, dancing G.R.O.W.L.ers, now that someone has knocked one of those over-advertised hunks out of the running.

But murder is not my game; romance is. I'll give those contest judges something to growl about. Now it's time to pull out all the stops and make some organ music here. Sensual scene, coming up! Millions, here I come. Ye old Demon Dagger had better get to it.

The Demon Dagger of Devonshire leaped into the carriage and ordered the bound and gagged driver to make haste to

Can that driver drive bound and gagged? Sure. Reins aren't much to hold, just some leather straps. Where to? Ah . . .

Dover by morning!

"My relatives will hunt you down, Sir," the fair Arianiola warned, "for this impertinence."

"You will be sorry if they do."

"Oh, and why is that?"

"Because, my charming renegade, I am about to change your life, to sweep you to the stars."

With that, he

Just how far can we go here? Better scan a couple more sex scenes from some of these hot numbers over here. Let's see . . . talk, talk, talk . . . escape . . . more talk . . . servants talking—hey, where's the boudoir business when you need it? You're falling down on the job, ladies. Come on, inspire me. A kiss, for three paragraphs? Get real. Okay, I'll show you how to do it.

With that, he grasped Ariania's shoulder and smashed her into his manly arms. Instantly she responded to the awesome masculine charisma that radiated from the muscular form of the Demon Dagger of Devonshire. She was a wildcat. She began purring and spitting in pretended disgust, but the Demon Dagger knew what effect his physique had on women of all kinds, from tavern wench to top-drawer duchess.

Soon she was gasping and undoing the buttons on his

Is it doublet in this period? Why not?

doublet. Meanwhile the Dagger thrust his powerful tongue into her mouth, causing her to moan.

And still the carriage driven by the bound and gagged driver drove on through the night, as lightning snarled in the sky and fireworks exploded on the cushions within.

Ariana had no chance. She was putty

Did they have putty then? Don't want to strain the judges' credulity here.

in his maddeningly sensuous hands, and soon he had worked her clothes into a lumpy pile on the carriage floor, as his own soon joined them, and they were joined in a jolting, mad dash over the moors.

Finally he had mercy on her and revealed the mightiest weapon in his arsenal. She seemed much impressed, if not surprised. And so the wild ride went, in a hurtle of two hearts through the night, two bodies twined by impetuous desire and true love found on the floor of the Baron's best carriage. . . .

When the moon was a pale an albino pumpkin in the dawn, the carriage rested at the brink of the white cliffs of Dover, the steeds weary and drooping, the sweet Arianail weary, the Demon Dagger of Dover drooping. The confiscated coachman had long since tumbled to some wayside rest, and the lovers lay happy and satisfied in each other's arms.

Bluebirds swept up into the clouds as the waves crashed on the shore below, and the Demon Dagger's vengeful heart knew peace for the first time in years, now that the carriage had stopped, the impetuous passion had lulled, and the lovely Ariania was safe in his arms. She was forever safe from his vengeance now, if not from his charms.

How do I end one of these scenes? Or a so-called "proposal," for that matter? Hey, the dawn is good enough. The next chapter can always start with tomorrow. Now to run it through spellcheck, and make sure the dumb broad's name is spelled the same way twice. Think I'll do the next one in real time.

Chapter 30

Undressed Rehearsal

From the wings, the Incredible Hunk pageant set looked almost as imposing as the MGM Grand's Emerald City layout.

White pillars recalling the glory that was Rome towered over a squat medieval arch of rough gray stone. Next to Gothicland stood Westernworld, represented by the crude wooden supports of a livery stable, complete with haystack. The late Cheyenne's pageant getup, and his horse, would have been in clover here.

Temple studied the construction from the rear, then promptly nicknamed the three pose-down settings "the Good, the Bad and the Ugly" from left to right: first the vaguely celestial soaring white columns; the definitely down and dirty gray stone keep; and finally a barn scene about as romantic as a roll in the barbed wire.

Temple saw that her vaguely medieval costume (and the lamb-to-the-slaughter in it) doomed her to the creepy Gothic dungeon. Lacey's sleazy harem silks fit the schizophrenic associations of faux white marble: classical purity versus the decadence that was ancient Rome. Quincey, the gilt-edged saloon girl, would inherit the haymow. Temple didn't envy her comfort quotient.

Studying the scene of the imminent forthcoming crime—a dress rehearsal for the pageant pose-down—Temple shuddered. The architecturally eclectic set resembled a Hollywood back lot awaiting an invasion of Barbarian hordes. Or perhaps invading accountants.

She tiptoed closer in her costume's odious flat-heeled stretch slippers (discount store glitz in bronze-metallic fabric). Yup, as she had feared, the Gothic niche included a pseudo-stone windowseat on which she could be wooed in endlessly contorted positions. At least a pair of black velvet pillows would make the condemned woman's fate a tad more cushy while she was slowly crushed to death.

"Look at that neat wood post," an awed voice breathed beside her. "I can work with that."

Temple turned to face a stagestruck Quincey. "You actually look forward to this farce? Why are you doing it? And how did you get chosen, anyway?"

"Step-weasel." Quincey answered the last question first, while teasing the wispy tendrils at her ears into spit-curls.

"Are you referring to Crawford Buchanan?"

"Please! No names. Just thinking about the creep is awful enough. Though I must say that Step-Daddy Dearest did come through and get me this great gig."

"Now I know how, but why?"

"Why are *you* doin' this?" Quincey flicked sullen lashes over Temple's costume.

"Because—" The truth would never do. Maybe a half-truth geared to the audience would serve. "I'm mad at my boyfriend."

"Cool." Quincey snapped her everpresent gum.

"Actually"—Temple modified her previous statement with twenty-five percent more frankness—"boyfriends."

"Cooler." Quincey eyed Temple with new respect, then hiked her knee-length skirt and vamoosed into the shadowed wings, leaving Temple no wiser about her sixteen-year-old motives. Temple suspected that it had much to do with being—what else?—cool.

Actually, Temple was pretty cool herself. Here she was, about to undergo a serial pose-down, and she was no nearer a solution to Cheyenne's murder in these very wings than three days before. If she were playing the child's game where onlookers shouted "Hot!" and "Cold!" to guide someone in finding a missing item, everyone would be yelling "Frigid!" at Temple.

She shuddered again, this time at the iciness of her mental image. If she began this pose-down charade in her current mood, everyone would be yelling "Frigid!" at her anyway.

But don't think of the ignominy to come, she told herself. Don't even think of England. Think about committing murder.

She strolled alongside the entry ramp at stage left, then mounted the four steep steps at the end. Troy Tucker was right. This height was enough to give a midget hubris. The burgundy curtain that protected this area from the audience view also put anybody standing against it into shadow. So this route would be murder to negotiate in the semi-dark of a rehearsal, given the usual stampede for places backstage. Yet the murderer must have used it. Temple imagined a horse beside her on the stage level, about to enter, its rider's back within easy striking distance.

Death was usually symbolized as the Dark Rider. *Horseman, pass on by.* This time death had lain in wait to strike, and the dark rider passing by had died.

The killer must have taken the fatal arrow from Cheyenne's quiver before this point, even before the victim-to-be slung its leather strap across his chest. It would be easy to pluck an arrow from a quiver at this height, but the action would have alerted Cheyenne. So the murder had been premeditated by at least a few minutes. Still, Temple sensed an indecent haste in the act. It had been risky, even desperate. Was someone trying to silence Cheyenne? Or was the scene of the crime, the pageant, simply a distraction? Was Charlie Moon killed—not his alter ego Cheyenne, the pageant contestant and model—but Charlie Moon, for some ancient, unrelated reason?

Crew members rushed by below Temple, never glancing up at her alongside the burgundy curtain. Anyone preoccupied with the thousand hectic details of a large-cast production, Temple knew from her Guthrie Theatre experience, was far too harried to notice anyone else's actions.

So the murderer had participated in such events before, or had witnessed backstage action and knew how to use the situation. Great! That still left the cast of *Ben Hur* as suspects.

Could a scurrying crew member harbor an unsuspected motive, like the volunteer costume ladies, who had dubbed themselves the "Wardrobe Witches"?

Another bustled by, a prototypical grandmother unkindly described as dumpling-bland and nondescript, wearing the comfortable, concealing sweat-suit uniform some older women adopt as protective coloring. This edition was an ivory knit ensemble with a rearing navy unicorn etched upon the chest.

Perfect look for a murderer.

"Oh, my God," the woman was muttering, looking everywhere but up at Temple, thus proving how easily one could lurk backstage. "What am I gonna do?"

Temple never could resist a problem-solving challenge. Still unnoticed, she ran along the ramp on her stealthy-soled slippers (what had the murderer worn for footwear?), and dashed down the end steps to intercept this female version of Alice's befuddled, ever-tardy White Rabbit.

"Is something wrong?" Temple asked.

"Huh?" The woman almost collided with Temple, then eyed her costume in confusion. "Wrong? Hell, yes. You're all dressed and ready to go. Oh, what am I gonna do? There's no time."

Temple resisted the temptation to hunt for a rabbit hole. "What's wrong?"

"One of the boys—the contestants—he—oh, my—split out his costume and we have to start the rehearsal in a couple minutes and he's on first!"

"Isn't there an emergency-fix basket in the dressing room?"

"Huh?" Brown eyes set in maroon bezels of fatigue blinked dolefully. "We're not using the regular dressing rooms."

"Where is the side-splitting hunk?"

The woman gestured wildly toward the opposite wings. Temple took off in that direction, long brocade skirts swishing. Behind her came the bunny-trail thump-thumps of the hapless Wardrobe Witch.

"We're all assigned certain contestants to dress," the woman behind Temple chattered in breathless relief now that she had found a partner in panic. "We're responsible. It's not as if this is the actual pageant, but Mr. Dove demands promptness, and poor Lance is competing for the first time and so nervous. If he misses his cue, or worse, looks laughable, it will simply shatter his confidence for the actual pageant. Poor fellow—"

"Listen. If I can find that basket, and I know there's one somewhere, everything will be fine."

The object of their concern came into view like a lachrymose landmark: a tall young man wearing a white, full-sleeved shirt open to the navel. He was standing in pale relief against the backdrop, watching for his wardrobe witch like some Romeo aching for a glimpse of Juliet. He hardly glanced at Temple, which, given her lusty wench's getup, was a testimony either to his anxiety-level, or his sexual preferences.

"Follow me," Temple said briskly, passing him without a pause to snatch her duffel bag from the floor and continue offstage. Now the clump-clump of boots trailed the sneaker-muted thump-thumps of the Wardrobe Witch.

What a parade they must make! The Wench, the Witch and the Wardrobe. And the luckless Wearer of the torn-asunder Wardrobe.

Temple pattered down the concrete stairs to the basement and dashed into the Four Queens' dressing room. Last night she had automatically noticed just what they needed.

In the corner where dressing tables and mirrors met sat an innocuous basket overflowing with odds and ends—extra false eyelashes and fingernails, glue, safety and bobby pins, spare feathers and . . . *viola*, as we say in freshman French! A tidy sewing kit with scissors, needles and a rainbow variety of threads.

"Here!" She grabbed the kit and held it out to . . . "What's your name?" she asked the Wardrobe Witch.

"Mary Lou. And this is Lance." The hunk waited diffidently at the dressing-room door, head hung.

Temple nodded, thrusting the show-saving kit at Mary Lou, whose hands, even now wringing before the prancing unicorn on her sweatshirt, abruptly vanished behind her back.

"Oh, no. No, I couldn't," she demurred, bit her lip and backed away as if Temple was proffering Cleopatra's asp. "I can't . . . sew."

Mary Lou almost looked embarrassed, as well she should—a woman her age afraid of a little needle and thread.

Exasperated, Temple turned to Lance, getting a better gander at the hapless hunk. He was the usual good-looks-gifted, weight-lifted he-man hero with thick, wavy, coffee-colored shoulder-length hair Cher would envy. And, at a raw twenty-one or -two, he was one of the youngest contestants.

Mary Lou was backing all the way out of the room now. "I'll wait. Outside." She eyed a big-dialed watch whose pink plastic strap cut into her chubby wrist. "Hurry! Lance is due onstage in only a couple of minutes."

"So am I!" Temple said.

And she did loathe late entrances, for rehearsals, and especially for dress rehearsals, even when she loathed the forthcoming on-stage follies even more.

No time to wonder why the Wardrobe Witch had deserted her post. The show must go on! Temple pulled her glasses from the case in her duffel bag.

"Where's the problem?" she asked Lance, selecting a needle with a large, easily penetrated eye and hunting for white thread.

His odd silence in a crisis made her look up.

Lance was looking down.

Temple looked down.

Oh.

She began looking for black thread, and lots of it.

A seam in Lance's black leatherlike pants had split open. Temple could see why, now that his nether regions were no longer lost against the black backdrop of a curtain. The skin-tight legs laced up open sides. Apparently an enthusiastic, or nervous, lacer—like Mary Lou—had overtightened the lacing. Something had to give, and had, in the most unfortunate location: a seven-inch seam along the front fly.

"I can take 'em off," Lance suggested lamely, eyeing Temple's glasses with visible doubt.

"No time." But he knew that already, else why would he be so pale and wan, prithee? "Stand here."

The overhead light was thinner than chicken consommé, and theatrical makeup lights didn't shine past the dressing table edge. So Temple backed him tight against the table, knotted her double thread-end four secure times and went to her beskirted knees. At least the yardage cushioned the hard floor.

Needle poised to strike, she analyzed the truly prodigious problem. The needle had to pierce the fabric at an angle in order to suture the seam shut. Given the nature of the costume and the site of the split, any too-vigorous thrust ran the risk of spearing the wearer rather than the wearing apparel, and in a place best left unstimulated in any way, pleasant or painful.

Temple sighed. Lance said nothing.

Like national disasters, theatrical crises bring out the best in people, a neighborly no-nonsense coping. Each participant braced to ignore the task's inescapably delicate nature.

Lance gazed around the dressing room, his eyes on everything but the site of the tragedy and Temple's needle.

Temple concentrated on the task at hand, rather than its social ramifications. She had to draw the straining fabric closer, then quickly slice the needle through one side and out the other before tension sprung it apart again.

If the material hadn't been a somewhat sleazy leather substitute, she couldn't have done it at all. Still, the fabric was tough enough to resist the needle point.

"Two minutes, folks!" boomed Danny Dove's brisk, martinet voice from the dressing-room speaker set high on the wall. He meant it.

They both jumped, then froze.

Temple drove the needle into the next stitch, trying not to grunt and grit her teeth as she forced the tip through the resistant fabric. Grunting might make the guy nervous.

She couldn't help speculating idly as she struggled to close the gap in the rended seam. Rock stars were known to bolster their crotches with socks, just as women had used handkerchiefs in their bras long before the lingerie industry had thoughtfully provided the proper inflationary devices.

Did Incredible Hunk candidates resort to such cheesy stratagems? If so, dumping any stuffing would make her task much easier, and swifter to accomplish. Surely Lance would have thought of that, and suggested any sacrificeable flotsam to throw overboard in an emergency like this. Then again, Temple would hardly toss her Wonderbra at a male tailor were the situation reversed, so she could only . . . er, wonder.

And if this was not a case of artificial amplification, the interesting question became just how well-endowed Incredible Hunks were. Certainly considering the conundrum in long, Latinate words kept the speculations on a disinterested, academic plane. Plane . . . or fancy.

Temple's needle plunged on. She also explored black thoughts about amateur dressers who are not professional enough to perform awkward but necessary theatrical tasks. Grandmothers who were far better equipped than she to deal dispassionately with strange young men—rather, young men who were strangers—and the more private parts of their anatomy. Grandmothers who had diapered and potty-trained and done heaven-knows-what-else and should be as asexual as amoebas by now.

Grandmothers who got eaten by big bad wolves, but grandmothers who might turn the tables on the wolves, too. For grandmothers also read—and sometimes wrote—romance novels, and had once starred in a few sensual scenes of their own (or they wouldn't be grandmothers and supposedly beyond the socio-sexual fray, would they?). Grandmothers who were still earthy enough to enjoy being around handsome men young enough to be their grandsons, and canny enough to duck the issue when it came to confronting the underlying roots of their admiration.

Temple nodded as she worked. A fan could have killed Cheyenne, or any of these men. Someone like a Wardrobe Witch. Someone with outlandish fantasies? Someone spurned? It happened the other way all the time: much older men and young women who traded on their looks sometimes do-si-doed into messy situations where murder might out.

"Places, people!" boomed the speaker. "*Now!*" Danny sounded like Patton in a snit.

Temple took some last frantic stitches, triple-knotted the threat at ground zero, then patted the dressing-table top for the scissors. They weren't within reach.

"Scissors?" she asked, curt as a surgeon.

Lance twisted to look, nearly breaking the precious thread below the knot and undoing all Temple had redone, while she drew in an audibly appalled breath.

"Uh, sorry." He had to toss a brunette tress over his shoulder when he turned back. "I can't find the scissors."

Temple considered using her teeth, then decided that was above and beyond the call of wenchdom.

"The dangling thread won't show against the black," she told him. "You'll have to have it repaired again on a machine anyway." She took off her glasses and threw them into the gaping duffel bag.

Then she was up and running for the stairs, her skirts hiked almost as high as Quincey's. Lance thudded up the risers behind her, asking for little but reassurance.

"Thanks. Um, do you think it will . . . you know, hold up for the show?"

She devoutly hoped that he was asking about her repair job.

"Time will tell," she huffed back to him. "At least you only have to do your act once. I have to do mine eleven times."

And she was supposed to be onstage before the first trio of hunks.

Temple flew into the wings, Lance and his once-flapping fly forgotten. Lacey and Quincey were nowhere around, which meant that they already had melted onto the dimly lit set as directed.

Temple raced until the moment she could be seen from the audience, then braked herself to a saunter. No audience awaited except Danny Dove and some hangers-on, but she had to pretend that there was a houseful of eager watchers.

In the murky light, the glitter of Lacey's seven veils entwined a pillar. Temple's skirts swished soft as surf against the fake-stone riser of her Gothic corner as she stubbed an unprotected toe on it, then stifled a wail. Beyond her nook, Quincey leaned Lili Marlene–like against the barn set's ersatz lamppost. Temple swirled into place and settled against her own wall, gazing soulfully out the arched windowslit, which offered an unwavering view of backstage curtain.

At stage left, three hunks thumped from the wings. If Lance was assigned to her, after all they'd gone through together, wouldn't it be a . . . stitch? At least she'd know to discourage any costume-straining positions.

A Roman gladiator, oiled torso gleaming in his harness, hairy legs bristling, leather and brass slapping and ringing as he walked, headed for Lacey beyond Temple. She didn't like to imagine getting whacked by the gladiator's lethal costume during the pose-down.

A second figure eased around the stone wall encompassing Temple, shadowy in a short cloak and tights. Beyond her, Lance, a curled bullwhip slung over one shoulder, headed for Quincey. How romantic.

Temple, appropriately panting from her hundred-yard-dash upstairs, waited for the spotlights to illuminate the awful truth. Thank heaven she hadn't worn her glasses, which would be out of period anyway, but she knew the drill: three lady models, thirty-three remaining Incredible Hunks, eleven each. Entering male trios would move to the set appropriate for their garb and grab the proper girl for a minute or more of ersatz passion. The trick was to change positions and poses constantly, like cover models being photographed. Temple knew that Quincey and Lacey had huddled with their designated hunks to plan their routines. She had been busy with other matters, such as murder, and would have to wing it with whoever showed up on her doorstep.

She could only hope that Danny had chosen wisely and well.

And she only had to be pliant and malleable (the usual requirements for any medieval virgin-bride, she figured). Theatrical illusion would do the rest.

Although Temple should be able to hear whoever was standing in for the announcer introduce the candidates, the microphone blurred his voice onstage. That meant that her partners would always be as much as a surprise as their improvised routine.

The lighting slowly brightened as Temple's first hunk went to one knee before her, took her tenderly in his arms, then bent her back until her false hair pooled on the stage floor. If her hairpins didn't hold, her false hair would remain a blood-bright puddle on the stage floor.

The lights came up full. Against the blurry blazing suns of the spotlights, Temple squinted to decode the visage above her . . . the fine Italian face of a Fontana brother in Romeo disguise!

Piece of pasta! The hunk you know is always a better risk than the hunk you don't know.

Rico or maybe Armando or even Eduardo bent over her until the feather in his velvet cap nearly put out her unshielded right eye.

"Don't worry, kid. I will treat you like a sister."

"Fontana brothers don't have any sisters," she hissed back.

He shrugged, then began performing a cover tango while murmuring *dolce far niente*, or so the lyrics of some forgotten Broadway musical described sweet Italian nothings.

Temple murmured sweetly back, "Rigatoni, Ziti Pitti, Uffizi. Oh, Linguini!"

No one could hear them over the canned music that beat out *Bolero*-type rhythms suitable for seduction. She was finally deposited again on the windowseat to simper pensively as her swain backed away, bowing.

The lights dimmed. Temple squinted to see if the departing Lance was still intact, as far as trousers went, but she couldn't tell. Nor could she decide which of her ebbing attributes to check first: her false hair, or her authentically plunging neckline. She decided to semi-recline on the windowseat for the next suitor.

Her knight in shining armor clanked as he came. She barely registered the arrival of her neighbors' gentlemen callers, she was so busy wondering how she would cuddle up to an ambulatory Swiss army knife.

With one hand he pushed back his metal visor, with the other he encompassed her waist. Then he picked her up and turned in a circle, nearly ramming Temple's foot into a mock-stone wall while her heavy false hair threatened to elope in the arms of centrifugal force.

The grinning Fontana brother in the plumed helmet reassured her. "Fear not, fair lady, I will not drop you."

She had nothing to fear but fear itself, so she caressed his chill silver-metal cheek and ran her hands up and down his chain-mail chest as he lowered her back to the floor, very slowly, because he really did not bend very well. How refreshing to have a male contestant compelled to "dip."

She was definitely getting the hang of a pose-down, especially since it mostly involved hanging off the hunk until he could move her into one or another contorted position. Then they did pretend kissy-kissy until it came precariously close to real kissy-kissy, but by then she was kissing him offstage.

She was also quickly getting exhausted from inventing something different that she was willing to do, and she did feel obligated to help her assigned hunks win. Besides, she knew that Quincey and Lacey were not holding back. To let two teenage Lolitas outdo a mature woman in her prime was unthinkable.

So she posed down, and up, and sideways, sometimes half-climbing the wall or the hunk, sometimes swooning in lilylike languor. All the hunks seemed alike after a while. Actually, they all seemed like Fontana brothers.

And that they were, for Danny Dove had devised a fiendishly simple method to keep Temple on familiar ground. It was all in the Crystal Phoenix family, you see. A Fontana brother who hoped to be welcome again on the premises would never drop, French-kiss, or otherwise commit vulgar acts with their brother Nicky's employee.

In fact, Temple felt so secure that she soon was lulled into a lazy rhythm, even losing track of how many Fontanas had passed by her window. The rhythmically dimming and brightening lights were hypnotic, she noted.

How many more could there be? Temple watched the latest Fontana swagger offstage in doublet and boots, as lights and ladies were lowered again to their quiescent positions.

Three more figures emerged from the wings, then separated as they moved to the sets. Temple wondered what the next Fontana would be wearing as he tripped up the single step to her lair. He actually did trip, in fact, in the dark, and fell across her hard enough to knock the breath out of her chest.

Ufffth. She tried to speak, to breathe, but no words came.

Temple pounded her fists on the man's broad, bare chest to alert him to her predicament. He took the gesture for mock resistance, for he remained pressed atop her breathless body. It was terrifying, being unable to scream or say a word while a big lummox lay across her like a sledge of lead, his stupid long hair tickling her neck and falling into her mouth, which needed air—

She felt, maybe even saw, the lights coming up, but she didn't care how the audience would view the scene. She could not breathe. She. Could. Not. Breathe. Not draw air in, or push it out. She needed to breathe, but how could she with two hundred pounds of clumsy hunk sprawled all over her, even if he was a Fontana brother?

But he wasn't a Fontana brother.

The curtain of hair tenting their conjoined faces was blond. Had Danny finally run out of Fontanas? Of course, nine brothers to a set (too bad Nicky wouldn't moonlight), and eleven hunks on Temple's menu. Danny had been forced to fill in her pose-down program with a couple of odd hunks. Very odd, she thought. Why was this guy just lying on top of her like a weight, no wonder she couldn't breathe!

"*La Rossa,*" the impinging hunk whispered in a strange voice. Oh, no! Why had Danny let Fabrizio, of all hunks, into her safe cage of Fontana brothers?

His features twisted with some extraordinary emotion. "I— sorry."

He *darn well should* be sorry, Temple thought in rising panic.

His hands rested on her shoulders, thumbs pressing against her neck. One dug into her carotid artery until she could feel her pulse bucking under the fleshy pad.

His mouth hung over hers, a smothering not-quite-kiss.

But she still couldn't breathe! And he didn't know it. He could crush her to death with clumsy theatrics!

Then his hands tightened around her neck, huge hands that had promised to pick her up and never drop her. Her back slid half-off the windowseat. Still she was trapped in an airless silence, her rib cage crushed by the hot, heavy weight of Fabrizio's three-thousand-dollar chest.

She felt her throat arching back in the long, flowing line so beloved of romance cover artists, the pose that always reminded Temple of a woman in extremis, not ecstasy.

Now that she was in that exact position herself, she could . . . not . . . breathe . . . ever again. And Fabrizio thought he was so sexy, his hammy hands on her throat, his hot breath panting into her mouth! He was killing her. He. Was. Killing. Her.

The hands tightened, with palpable purpose. Fabrizio's too-close blue eyes squinted shut in a face his perpetual tan had deserted.

Black spots danced before Temple's eyes. From staring up at the spotlights . . . no, she didn't see spotlights or any light at all, just black spots and a narrowing tunnel of vision, tunnel vision, with a bright light at the end, like so many near-death experiences. . . . No!

Temple twisted, fought to fall off the ledge that half-held her, to slither out from under the crushing weight, to escape the hands circling her throat. Fought to breathe! Fabrizio grunted in his own battle to seal off all breath forever, as if he were a Samson whose strength was ebbing. But she felt his long hair brush her shoulders. He was invincible. . . .

One gasping inhalation took ragged hold. Rushing air dried her oxygen-starved throat and lungs as it drew deep into her chest, then reversed itself and burst outward with a rapid *whoosh*.

The shuddered breath, violent as a dry heave, jolted Fabrizio's hands loose. Temple inhaled again, another wrenching spasm of her entire torso, like giving birth. Giving breath. As she exhaled a turbulent hiccough, she twisted her body with all the life-fighting might in her.

Fabrizio tumbled to the stage floor on his back. Temple pushed herself up on one arm. She hung gasping above him, the ends of her long false locks mixing with the corona of yellow hair around his surprised face. No matter the embarrassment, he deserved it.

A few false crimson strands pooled on Fabrizio's smooth, golden chest. Some even curled around the knife hilt pressed tight against his washboard stomach.

Now that Temple *could* scream, she didn't dare.

The lights dimmed on cue.

Luckily, someone had glimpsed something amiss. Someone with power.

"Lights full up, dammit!" Danny yelled like an oncoming berserker.

Feet clumped toward them from all directions, but Temple still couldn't talk yet, and Fabrizio—?

Fabrizio wouldn't ever hear again.

Chapter 31

Murderous Suspicions

"I suppose you'll claim self-defense," Lieutenant Molina suggested sweetly.

Actually, Temple just pretended that Lieutenant Molina had spoken sweetly. Any other interpretation was too scary.

"He tried to strangle me," she said hoarsely, in her turn.

"So you killed him in self-defense, with a dagger you just happened to have in your garter."

"I don't know where the garter—the dagger—came from, but I know it must have been in his chest when he got to me."

"Then someone killed him before he could kill you."

"I suppose that person or persons unknown could claim credit for saving my life."

"Why would this"—Molina glanced at her notebook and sighed—"Fab-rizz-io want to kill you?"

"Maybe because I mispronounced his name."

"How is it said?"

"Fabreezio, as in Breezy."

"Why would this Fabreeezio want to kill you?"

"I don't know, but I *do* know that he went out of his way to do it. He wasn't supposed to be in my area. Danny Dove would never have assigned him to me—" Temple broke off.

"Because," Molina continued implacably, "according to witnesses, Fabrizio has picked on you since the conference started."

"He picked me up; there's a difference."

"You hated his attentions, though."

"But not enough to skewer him like a prosciutto ham. Besides, when he first landed on me, he knocked my breath out. I was . . . paralyzed. I couldn't do anything."

"So you suspect that he was stabbed offstage, like Charlie Moon, then stumbled out in the dark, not fully aware of what had happened. Therefore, he could have arrived at your . . . stand . . . accidentally."

Temple raised her eyebrows expressively. "Or he could have *meant* to kill me and, like Cheyenne, was so revved up while he waited to enter that he couldn't feel the killing blow."

"Knife wounds can fool a victim," Molina admitted.

"Besides, planning to kill someone onstage, with witnesses, would wind Fabrizio up beyond belief. That's why I think he meant to come to my area. He almost carried out his plan despite the fatal wound."

"Maybe." Molina was not convinced. "I don't see a motive. Well, I see a motive, but I just don't believe anybody will kill someone for being annoying."

Temple ignored the gratuitous put-down in the face of an inspiration. "Wait a minute! Who had Danny really assigned me for that time? Why didn't he show up as scheduled?"

Molina examined her notes. "A Jake Gotshall."

"Oh, no! Mr. Comedy Central. What happened to him?"

"Someone had 'borrowed' the bottom half of his costume."

"Or stolen it, so he'd be late. Ah, what was the bottom half of his costume? I need to know what I . . . missed."

Molina's intimidating blue eyes stayed on her notebook pages. Temple had a feeling that she was trying very hard not to laugh. "Fur shorts."

"Fur shorts? What was he dressing up as?"

"Every woman's secret fantasy, he claims: Santa making a special Christmas Eve delivery to the lady of the house. He said he planned to wear nothing but white fur shorts and a white wig and beard. And some mistletoe in appropriate places."

"Ooohh," said Temple. "He would have tickled!"

"I've never heard of anyone being tickled to death. Yet," Molina added cautiously. "I'm sure you'll run across one of those some day. Anyway, Gotshall couldn't go on without the key part of his costume and was scrambling around the dressing rooms looking for a substitution. It was just a dress rehearsal, and he figured the fur shorts would show up."

"So Fabrizio stole them to make Jake late." Temple put a hand to her neck.

Talking hurt her throat, and Fabrizio's last manual contractions hadn't helped. It was hard to prove that he had meant to hurt her, instead of simply blundering over to her and lashing out in his death throes. He certainly knew who she was. Why else say he was sorry?

Temple glanced at a coterie of supporters sitting in the theater's front row: Danny Dove, immobile for once, Electra and Kit huddled like fairy godmothers bereft of their magic wands and even Midnight Louie, lured away from his platinum ladylove by a roommate in distress. Word had gotten around fast.

"Why would Fabreeezio attack you?" Molina asked again.

Temple put a hand to her throat. It didn't help. "Maybe . . . maybe he knew that I knew his costume included a glove."

"Glove?" The glitter in Molina's eyes showed her instant grasp of its significance.

"The only pageant competitor," Temple said, to make it plain, "who was wearing anything on any hand onstage during the cover costume segment."

"A glove wasn't on the body."

"Exactly. He never wore it onstage, not even in rehearsals, but it was part of his costume originally. His costume. There wasn't much to it—tight pants, wrestling championship–size belt, long hair and one black leather glove. He was planning to enter with a hawk on his wrist."

"A live hawk?"

"A dead one wouldn't sit up straight."

"Which hand?"

Temple shook her head. She didn't know; besides, weren't the police supposed to find those things out?

"You'll have to come down to headquarters," Molina said, standing.

Temple remained sitting on the black velvet cushion she had once considered a scene of the crimes of the heart, not of homicide.

"Why?" she asked.

"We'll need your fingerprints. At least. Got someone to drive you?"

Oh, Lordy, she was a wanted woman. Temple stared toward Electra, Danny and Kit. She almost jumped out of her skin, or, rather, her decolletage. Matt Devine had materialized next to Electra. Was he starting to develop traits like the Mystifying Max's? She glanced back at Lieutenant Molina, who was noting Matt's presence with interest.

"Drive me? You mean I might be . . . edgy. I suppose so—"

"I'd expect some prints on the hilt, after the way you were flailing around, according to witnesses. I want to make sure I know whose prints are whose. You didn't know what you were doing, did you?"

Temple couldn't claim that she did, so she said nothing. She had a right to keep silent. She had a right to an attorney. She had a right to run for her life, but she wouldn't.

She begin to understand how Max might have felt if he'd found the body in the Goliath ceiling first. What's to say about being found hand-in-glove with a corpse? Better to skedaddle first and answer questions later, or never.

"Am I under arrest?"

"You just get right down to fingerprinting and let me worry about technicalities. I'll tell 'em you're coming."

"Thanks," Temple said faintly, rising and walking across the stage as if it were covered in seashells.

Fabrizio's body still lay faceup, worthy of a bestselling cover. Temple remembered the line from *The Duchess of Malfi*: "Cover her face. Mine eyes dazzle. She died young."

She averted her eyes and went to the runway's end. Nicky Fontana and Van von Rhine had joined the charmed circle, so a septate of human friends waited to help her down the stairs.

"Anybody got a Black Mariah?" she joked in a shaky croak from the runway. "I need a ride to headquarters."

Matt insisted on driving Temple. After all, he had said, ending the friends' debate, he wasn't involved in whatever this convention was, and could spare the time. Danny had to stay at the theater to insure that the investigation did not disrupt more than it had to. With the pageant scheduled for the next evening, the situation was critical. Nicky Fontana grudgingly agreed to Matt's acting as Temple's chauffeur; Temple knew he was aching to hot-rod to police headquarters in his traffic-cop-spurning silver Corvette.

Temple insisted on her own imperatives. First she went to the dressing room. Quincey was there, smoking a cigarette she had borrowed from someone. She tamped it out hastily in a makeup tin cover.

"Gosh, are you all right?" she asked, jumping up, big-eyed.

"Sort of," Temple said hoarsely. "Can you help me out of this rig? I've got to go to police headquarters."

"Oh, God!" Quincey's fingers were ice-cube cold on Temple's back, shaking as she undid hooks and pulled open underlying corset lacings. "That creep Lacey was telling that scary woman lieutenant all sorts of stuff about you and Fabrizio, about how he tried to force you into posing with him until Danny Dove stopped him. Rotten snitch!"

"It's okay. The lieutenant knows me. She wouldn't believe I stabbed him."

"You didn't, then?"

Temple turned to regard her emergency undresser. "No! If I

were going to kill someone, it would be for more serious crimes than attempted sweeping off the feet."

"I don't know—" Quincey's hands grew still on the lacings. "Some men keep making slimy remarks and treat the women they're with like dirt while ogling every other woman around . . . or girl. You could kill them."

Temple turned, jerking the laces from Quincey's nerveless fingers. "No," she said very definitely. "Not just for being creeps, or sexists. I wouldn't do it, and you wouldn't."

"I-I guess not. But . . . oh, what a groady mess this Incredible Hunk thing is! I thought doing this would be cool, glamorous, *something*, but I just feel . . . yucky."

Temple grinned. "It's not easy to be a *femme fatale*—oops! I didn't mean that literally. Everything will be okay. Only one more day until the pageant, and then this show is over forever." Temple slapped her bra to her newly useful chest (for holding up gowns) while her ebbing costume sank around her feet to a lavender cloud on the floor.

She stepped out of it as if avoiding dog doo-doo. "I hope I never have to wear this dopey costume again."

Quincey's pale smile looked automatic. She was scrounging the dressing room for a match to relight her crushed cigarette butt by the time Temple was dressed and ready to leave.

Matt was waiting upstairs, alone, a gilt vision in yellow sports shirt and buff slacks.

"Everybody did as you said and went about their business," he told her.

"Even Louie?" she wondered with a smile.

"He dashed off the minute you left us. Maybe he had urgent business downstairs, too."

"Yvette," Temple diagnosed as they walked through the casino to the parking garage exit. "Not a person," she said quickly. "A cat. Female. Persian. Savannah Ashleigh's pampered purebred darling. Louie crashed a cat-food commercial shooting to pay court, and Ms. Ashleigh, a one-time film star by her own lights, stopped me in the hall this morning to rake me over the Kitty Litter for not controlling my beast."

"*She* sounds like the uncontrolled beast." Matt handed her something. "I got you some throat lozenges."

"Thanks." Temple picked a roll open and took one. "I'm not good at keeping my mouth shut."

When he opened a glass exit door (the Crystal Phoenix had rising phoenix-shaped Plexiglas handles), the outside warmth and daylight struck her like molten honey.

"Aaah." She stopped to soak it up.

"Are you sure you're all right? Lieutenant Molina has no right to order you downtown for fingerprinting right after such an awful attack."

"She has the right. And I don't mind. I don't remember touching a knife-hilt, so I'm sure my prints aren't on it. I doubt anybody's will be, except maybe Fabrizio's."

As they walked to the parking ramp, Temple dutifully sucked the lozenge.

"What kind of convention is this, anyway?" Matt asked.

"Too complicated to explain and still save my voice. Romance novels and everybody who's involved in reading, writing and producing them."

"And your aunt is one of them?"

"An author. We hadn't seen each other since I was a kid."

Matt nodded, opening the door to the ramp. While they waited before the elevator for the doors to open, Temple husbanded her saliva so she could talk without rasping.

"You probably don't understand why I was wearing that lurid dress, letting strange men make pretend-love to me onstage."

"Well—"

"I was undercover. Yes, I know it's ridiculous; normally one doesn't have to undress to go undercover, except maybe female cops on the vice squad. But Molina encouraged me to snoop, believe it or not. Besides, I felt obligated to help find out why the first pageant competitor was killed."

"So that's what Molina meant." Matt's incredulity echoed in the small, stainless steel–lined elevator as they soundlessly headed for the third floor.

She nodded. "A guy from that striptease contest I did PR for a few months ago. He wanted to talk to me the night before he was killed. Kit and Electra were teasing me about being asked out by a hunk, and I felt so stupid that I said no. Now I think he wanted to talk to me about whatever led to his death."

"Temple!" Matt's tan face had darkened as they walked to her Storm, eight cars down the shadowy row. "What about what you owe to your friends? You leave the Circle Ritz without any word, then turn up at the Crystal Phoenix, taking insane risks. Think about your friends, if not yourself."

"Electra's here. And my aunt," she added. "And I'm not a bad detective. Fabrizio only tried to kill me because I knew too much."

"Great. We can put that on your tombstone: SHE KNEW TOO MUCH."

"Most cemeteries don't allow tombstones anymore. Takes all the fun out of graveyards."

Temple rummaged in her duffel bag, then handed Matt the key ring. He took it, but wouldn't look up at her.

"How can I make you see what it was like," he said slowly, "watching security people storm through the casino? Then a Fontana brother races by in some . . . ridiculous Halloween costume telling Nicky and Van about a 'new murder' and mentioning your name over and over. I thought—"

Temple put her hands on his wrists. "Thanks."

Matt looked up and the moment teetered on the brink of something more that neither was ready for.

"Maybe—" Temple gazed up at the uninspiring ramp ceiling, a coffered pattern of gray concrete beams. "It was supposed to be a murder-suicide! If Fabrizio killed Cheyenne and knew that I suspected him, he may have stabbed himself and then come out to kill the only witness who suspected he had committed the first murder!"

Matt's eyes narrowed with disbelief. Temple had meant to reassure him; in a way, she had succeeded beyond her expectations. He finally laughed and unlocked the Storm passenger door.

"You do have a uniquely creative mind for crime," he said, letting himself into the driver's seat. "Lieutenant Molina should be examining your brain, not your fingertips."

"I'd have to be dead first, and, fortunately, I'm not."

She pulled down the lozenge wrapper and offered Matt one. He shook his head, so she took another, letting it click against her teeth as the honey-herbal flavor coated her throat.

After the dark of the ramp, the shock of daylight had her clawing for the prescription sunglasses in her duffel bag.

Matt donned the drugstore pair in his shirt pocket. "You'll have to tell me where the police station is."

"Simple. Down the Strip, right on East Stewart for a few blocks. Big pale building with a soaring, curved section in front that's accessorized with an ersatz neon pattern, along with a colorful array of lounging transients."

"You sound like a veteran visitor, all right."

She shrugged and leaned her head against the seat. She felt as if she'd wrestled alligators, and perhaps she had. But now that she'd apologized for leaving home and having not-too-excellent adventures, Temple was inclined to resume her favorite role: offhand inquisitor.

"By the way." Her head turned toward Matt without lifting from the headrest. "Why were you in the Crystal Phoenix casino?"

"Ah . . . " He pretended to occupy himself with driving, ostentatiously peering in the rearview mirror, looking over his shoulder, frowning at the instrument panel.

Before he could lie, Temple decided to let him off the hook by throwing out another, deeper one. "And why were you and Max there together the other evening?"

Fingerprinting was not the kiddie-direct process Temple had imagined: stick your fingers in some wet gunk like fingerpaints, then slap them down on a sheet of paper.

Like all rituals, this had its protocol. The most distasteful part, besides the ink's chemical reek, was that the technician took control of each of her fingers, rolling the tip from side to side on the card. The process felt like automatic writing, as if she were a ghost of herself. It also pinched, and made her feel like a puppet.

Molina had sent a message ahead of her: wait.

So Temple did. Kit and Electra had taken a cab downtown to

join them, despite protests, so Matt took himself off. He had never quite answered Temple's question about his association with Max.

"That policewoman can't think you did it," Kit said as they huddled over lukewarm coffee in paper cups in the small waiting area, which was furnished with a visibly used leather sofa and chairs.

"No, but she would love an excuse to," Temple said, glad that Molina's assumption that Fabrizio had killed Cheyenne freed Kit from any suspicion.

"Why?" Kit demanded.

"We don't get along."

"Temple, you're my niece. My relatives don't have feuds with homicide detectives."

"It's not a feud, just . . . a personality conflict. And I happen to have suspicious associates."

"Us?" Kit asked in horror.

Temple shook her head and glanced at Electra, who looked as troubled as Temple had ever seen her.

"Electra, why don't you go back to the Phoenix? Who knows how long the inquisition will take, and you've got your contest submission to finish."

"Not now." Electra smiled for the first time that day. "It's done."

"You finished it? That's great."

"I suppose so, kiddo, but it would be better if you weren't in Dutch with that lieutenant."

"Oh, she just does these things to scare me into 'fessing up about Max."

"What's to 'fess up?" Kit asked.

"Nothing. That's the problem."

"More coffee?" Electra had risen and was looking toward the machine down the hall.

"Why not?" Temple said.

Molina came within the hour, a brown paper bag in each hand; her partner held two more.

"Maybe they brought us a snack," Temple whispered to her co-conspirators.

Moments later Molina materialized behind the counter and nodded Temple in.

Her office was long and narrow, just wide enough for a desk and a path to edge by it. Molina sat behind the desk, her partner on a battered office chair near the wall.

Temple took one of the two chairs placed to face the desk.

"You think of anything more?" Molina asked.

Temple shook her head.

"No prints on the knife hilt."

"Then you didn't need mine—"

"No glove," Molina added sternly, as if that were Temple's fault.

"You didn't find a glove?"

Molina shook her head.

"What about the bird?"

"The hawk was backstage, on its perch, hooded. A woman named Cindy Blyer confirmed that Fabrizio had planned to use the bird in his act."

"But he didn't."

"Blyer claims that he decided at the last minute that it would be too awkward."

"The last minute?"

"About fifteen minutes before he was to go on for the dress rehearsal. She hadn't seen the glove, ever, but she had to be there to tend the bird. Nice job, personal PR specialist."

Molina suddenly leaned forward to regard Temple through eyes narrowed gunfighter-tight. "You're getting some beauties?"

"What?"

"Neck bruises," she explained, sitting back. "We'll want photos when they're fully developed. Tomorrow."

"I have to come downtown again? At least I can go now—?"

"Go!" Molina ordered, as if dismissing an evil spirit.

Temple stood up. "And there was no glove in his dressing room?"

"Nothing but pretty-boy paraphernalia." Molina gestured at the paper bags. "Makeup and mousse; leather britches and shirts with sleeves the size of sails; big, trashy biker belts and boots."

Temple turned, then spun back. "Boots?"

Molina nodded. "You don't think he put a boot on one hand to keep his prints off the arrow?"

"No, but . . . what kind of boots?"

"That is odd." Molina leaned forward to flip through her notebook. "We found one like these in Moon's dressing room, too. Need to check if they're identical. Could be a freebie for all the contestants, or part of some costume they all have to wear."

Temple waited. Molina obliged by pulling something from one of the brown bags.

It was a galoot boot, size fourteen or fifteen, brand-new, with a pinkish tan sole and a silver-leather overlay. The rhinestones on its toe and heel glittered like dew on diamonds.

Interview with the Executioner

Any first-rate crime follower nowadays knows what it takes to solve a murder that has no witnesses: hard evidence. (Actually, finding all evidence is hard.)

Since Miss Temple Barr has put herself into deeper danger with every step of her investigation into the late Cheyenne's death, I feel obligated to put my paw into the pudding. I am also well aware that my romantic complications have kept me from guarding Miss Temple with the regularity and concentration I am noted for when on the hunt.

So, since I have not been able to help her find the stunning shoes in my likeness as yet, I can at least find an article of apparel that has become famous in legal circles, the black leather hawking gauntlet that Fabrizio so conveniently mislaid before his death.

While shoes have a certain leather scent that I find compelling, I am hoping that the missing glove carries an aroma that I am particularly equipped to sniff out: the victim's blood. I admit that, because of my nature and the opportunity, I often had Miss Temple's television remote control tuned to the jurisprudence channel in 1995. I can always use more prudence. It is obvious that, in this case, some scientific confirmation of everybody's suspicions is needed.

So off I go, on the trail of The Bloody Glove.

First, I need a witness, or the closest thing to one. So I hie to the Peacock Theater's backstage, where I find—besides dozens of humans readying for tonight's big show—one much overlooked individual.

Nobody has thought to question my secret witness. Even if anyone had, this tough customer would never talk. But Midnight Louie has his ways of communicating with the incorrigibly mute.

I leap atop a flat stored on its side, balance impeccably and warily inspect the suspect's vicinity. This is an individual so dangerous that it is kept caged. Even the cage is kept underwraps, so my first job is to drag off the cover. I accomplish it with a powerful swipe of my mitt and the assistance of my trusty built-in switchblades.

The canvas lies crumpled on the floor and I view my intimidating quarry.

This is a bird. Not the black bird of song and story, but a brown bird. A brown bird with long, curled claws that put my switchblades to shame. Those wicked talons can exert two thousand pounds of pressure when gripped around the prey's neck. My dear mama never exerted that kind of control when I was a kit and required toting from place to place.

This bird also has an awesome beak that could tear the hide off a rhinoceros. Luckily, I cannot see this biting, ripping, eating machine, for a small but sinister leather hood covers the creature's head.

This will be like interviewing an executioner.

I clear my throat with a low-throttle purr.

The hooded head jerks in my direction and eight lethal claws bite wood. I note that the perch is pitted with such marks. Better it than I.

Normally, this dude's relatives are prey for my family. But the birds we hunt are small, spry types, and this specimen is larger, and a raptor to boot. The velociraptors in *Jurassic Park,* the motion picture, scared the skin off many humans who saw them in action.

My interview subject is a surviving descendent. A hunting hawk.

I do not speak bird well, but I can croak out a few words in pigeon. I begin cautiously. "You alone."

"Awwk," it agrees, cocking its unseen head toward me.

"You not ride master's wrist."

"Last master buy hunter, not true hunter."

"So you not like Fabrizio?"

The feathered body sways from leg to leg, its claws tightening and loosening on the perch. Guess not.

"You would be star in show, though."

"Would rather hunt."

"He is dead."

"I hear but not see."

"You know new master?"

"No. She feeds."

"You sit on leather perch."

"Human arm."

"Where is gauntlet?"

The bird edges down the perch toward me. I cannot tell if it has grown tired of my interrogation or is just hungry.

"What are you?" it croaks.

"Investigator."

A silence. Birds do not have the keen sense of smell my kind does, but their eyes are A-one. Luckily, with their heads hooded, raptors are deprived of their most vital sense and are easy to deal with.

"Smell blood," it says.

"From the stage."

"Do not know 'stage.' "

"From a stream's width from here?"

"Yes. Two times."

"From the . . . glove?"

"Do not know 'glove.' "

"Leather perch on human."

"Yes."

"When?"

"Since three hunting moons ago."

The hair rises on my back. Although our lingo is primitive and sketchy on tenses, my avian source seems to be saying that he has smelled blood ever since Cheyenne's murder, which means the gauntlet is still in the area.

"Where?" I ask.

The bird rocks from side to side again, a gesture I now realize is frustration.

"Near. Too near. Hungry."

Although he is welcome to eat the glove by my lights, I cannot allow this when it is evidence.

"How near?"

"On ground."

I examine the stage floor, which is as bare as a bodkin. I even leap down to make a methodical search. Nothing. Nil. Zero. Zilch. I hate it when a snitch steers me wrong, but I am not about to take my ire out on this big bird. Resuming my own perch, I begin again.

"Glove on ground?"

"Yes. Just below."

"I do not see it."

"I do not see also."

Of course the hawk would not see the glove when it is hooded! What an Einstein. Then I realize that the numbskull is me.

I force myself to an unpleasant task. I examine the cage that contains the bird. It is large and square, made of strong wire. Because birds are caged, their litter boxes must come built into the bottom.

I look down to see a newspaper liner on which lies a dozen impressive-sized droppings, some clearly used and others dabs of fallen . . . body parts. Because this is a large cage, the bottom tray has a deeper dish than a Chicago pizza, pardon the parallel under the circumstances.

The papers are probably changed daily by the person known as "she," but the tray would be rarely removed. I reach up, snag the rim and pull. The tray is stuck. I pull with all my might. The tray moves toward me, but so does the entire cage.

Mr. Hawk and I are about to have a nasty fall. I tell him to hang onto his tailfeathers and then we hit the stage floor in a flurry of clashes, feathers and flying organic waste. As soon as I land on my feet, I dash behind a black curtain, where I am perfectly invisible.

The clatter has brought a full cast of characters to the site, including the PR woman who tended the bird for Fabrizio . . . and Danny Dove.

They gawk at the mess, and the hawk flapping its clipped wings in the cage, then quickly right it. The tray remains half out, so the PR woman tries to wrench it shut. Then Danny Dove takes over and decides to pull it all the way out before reinstalling it.

Smart fellow. When the tray comes out with a screech that would irritate the nerves of a jackhammer operator, so does something else.

I watch with satisfaction as the stage crew stares down at something black and crumpled and reeking of mouse on the floor.

The Bloody Glove.

A sensation ensues, while Danny Dove insures that no one touches the glove.

Blessed are the peacemakers.

I stroll away, so satisfied with myself that I decide to investigate another little matter of wearing apparel that has been overlooked by everybody else.

No, it is not my signature shoe—not yet—but it is not far off.

Chapter 33

A Clue to Chew On

Three boots sat on Lieutenant Molina's desk. Fabrizio's pair and the one found among Cheyenne's confiscated possessions after his death.

"Why didn't you mention your boot?" she asked Temple.

"I didn't know whose it was, or that it was related to the case."

"You found it during a rehearsal."

"Dozens and dozens of people use the downstairs dressing rooms for the hotel revue. I had no reason to suspect the boot was related to the Incredible Hunk pageant."

"What about the large size?"

"Showgirls are all treetop tall, with shoe sizes to match."

"You thought this was a *woman's* boot?"

"Pretty likely, given the glitzy design. Unless they're country-Western stars, most men prefer something a tad more conservative. And, as I said before, tall women wear big shoes, and every Vegas hotel dressing room is crammed with tall women."

"Even darling Clementine only wore number nine," Molina pointed out, glaring like a prosecuting attorney.

Temple kept silent, struck by the eerie coincidence: Molina citing the same folk song that Temple had remembered when finding the boot. She wondered what size shoe Molina wore. Ten, she would bet. That "only" had given the great detective away.

"The boot you found is exactly like these three?" Molina said.

"Yes . . . "

"Why do you hesitate?"

"I want to be precisely accurate. The boot I found was different in one respect. Some rhinestones were missing from the heel. Maybe that was why it was tossed."

"Defective," Molina commented, biting her lip thoughtfully. "Who would have gotten rid of it?"

"Cheyenne, obviously. It was his pair of boots. He must have been rushing to get onstage and dumped it as he went past the costume rack."

"Thrown out for a few missing rhinestones?"

Temple shrugged.

"I'll get you back to the Phoenix. I want that boot. It belongs with the evidence."

Temple couldn't argue about that, which often made being with Lieutenant Molina no fun.

Kit and Electra, however, had fun riding in the back of Molina's Caprice, which was roomy enough for three. Kit and Electra discussed changing genres from historical romance to contemporary romantic suspense, just so they could use the "atmosphere" in their next books.

Temple thought the atmosphere left much to be desired.

Once at the Crystal Phoenix, Kit and Electra returned to convention events. Temple escorted Lieutenant Molina downstairs to her humble dressing room.

"The boot is with my theatrical stuff," she explained as Molina ducked to enter the curtained cubicle. "In the bag."

"Big enough, isn't it?" Molina eyed the duffel bag.

And then the bag stirred.

"Don't tell me they have cockroaches down here!" Temple said, peering at her property.

Molina didn't waste time looking, but crouched down to jerk the unzipped top wide open.

Midnight Louie sprawled blinking in the brighter light, his forepaws wrapped cunningly around Cheyenne's boot.

"I've never had evidence contaminated by cat drool before," Molina said sardonically. "Good kitty. Give me the boot."

Temple could have told her she was taking the wrong tack with Midnight Louie. "Good kitty" didn't cut it. As Molina reached to tug the boot away, Louie's paws tightened in possession. He curled his back feet around it, kicking, and began gnawing the rhinestone-covered heel again.

"Come on!" Molina got her fingers on the heel and tugged. "Ouch." Her blue eyes glared over her shoulder as she appealed to Temple. "Your cat almost bit me!"

"No, he didn't. Your hand got in the way while he was chewing on the heel."

"A pathetically weak defense for obvious assault and battery, and why would he chew the heel anyway?"

"It's leather, which smells good to cats."

"Probably reminds them of prey. Come on!" Molina fought Louie again for the boot, earning a low, fierce growl that made her jerk her hand away.

"You get it," she ordered Temple, standing up. "If he bites anyone and breaks the skin, he'll be quarantined for rabies."

Temple hastened to take Molina's place beside the bag, then grabbed the boot-top and tugged. Midnight Louie put all his twenty pounds into keeping it.

Temple tugged again, hard, so hard that she fell back on her rear when the boot suddenly came free.

She held the boot up to the light. "Here's the spot that's missing rhinestones."

Molina cocked her head. "So I see, but I still don't see why the victim threw it away. Hand it up; I'll take back to headquarters so it's with the other effects." She frowned as she accepted custody.

"Sure is garish, and poorly made if the rhinestones flaked off so readily; maybe the victim was right to toss it."

Temple stood slowly, still aching from her last tango with Fabrizio. "No, the Four Queens said it was expensive. Rhinestones aren't cheap anymore, Lieutenant."

"The Four Queens? Some colorful romance-writing team, no doubt, or a quartet of pose-down girls?"

"Neither. The lead showgirls here at the Phoenix. I asked them if the boot belonged to anyone in the revue, but they said no."

"Bad taste is not necessarily cheap. Look, the heel has even been put on crooked."

Temple looked, and then she looked down at Louie, who was raptly licking his own foot leather. "Let me see that boot!"

Molina wasn't used to taking orders from civilians, but she dubiously handed over the boot.

"This heel was perfectly placed when I last saw the boot." Temple turned the boot in her hand. The heel definitely did not sit squarely to the sole anymore. She had the glimmer of an idea. "Those crystals in Cheyenne's medicine pouch, what were they like?"

"White crystals, like all the New Agers wear." Molina frowned. "Only they were much smaller and not oblong."

"Pointed on the bottom, like unset rhinestones?"

Molina's face reflected a dawning suspicion that still lay well below the horizon line of logic.

Temple grabbed the boot-heel—the rhinestone studding felt porcupine-prickly—and twisted. Ick. Cool drool from Louie's boot-licking wet her palm.

But something clicked, both in Molina's mind and in the boot. The lieutenant was reaching for the boot when Temple's efforts paid off. The heel twisted 180 degrees askew, releasing a shower of small white stones that flashed out and rained to the floor.

"Holy shit! Shut that thing!" Molina knelt and cupped her hands under the dazzling drizzle, until her palms filled with tiny glittering drops.

Temple snapped the heel back into place, then dove for the dressing table.

"Here's a makeup tin cover."

Temple held it under Molina's hands, which separated. Glitzy hail drummed the metal until Molina's hands had emptied, except for a few sparkling stones that stuck to her moist skin.

She picked them off, one by one, like priceless burrs.

Temple was on hands and knees by then, crawling over the floor to corral the first few stones that had bounced away.

"I'll send technicians over for an official search," Molina said, rising with the literal booty. "Get off the floor and tell me what and why and how you knew."

"I'm not sure," Temple said, dusting off her hands. "It just came to me."

"Something must have triggered your instincts, so think."

Temple leaned against the dressing table, gazing down at the shallow lid afloat with Austrian-crystal brilliance. Cut and uncut diamonds by the carat.

"Jake Gotshall told me Cheyenne had run out just before his first, fatal rehearsal. He'd come back in a hurry and seemed upset about something."

"The boot." Molina set the object beside its precious contents. "I should have thought of the hollow heel. It's an old smugglers' trick. So the men of steel and boys in bronze body makeup are moonlighting in smuggling."

Temple nodded and stared at the boot. Maybe she should not have been thinking of England during her trying moments lately, but of another foreign country. One famed for footwear and leather goods. One that recently had hosted both Cheyenne and Fabrizio. One shaped like a boot.

"Italy!" she said aloud.

Molina waited.

"Cheyenne had just completed a modeling job there, and Fabrizio was a native."

Molina touched the heel with the missing rhinestones. Then she lifted the boot from the tabletop. "Got a nail file handy?" She glanced pointedly at Temple's long, red-enameled fingernails.

Temple bent down to ravage her duffel bag until she came up with a metal file imbued with, ironically, diamond dust. She slapped it in Molina's extended hand like a nurse giving a surgeon a requested scalpel.

Molina used the file like a surgeon. She dug the tip into the soft leather and pried until a large rhinestone finally popped out.

Molina held it up to the makeup lights. "The larger stones were embedded in the leather. Clever, mixing real with fake stones. Looks like the amateur smugglers, Cheyenne and Fabrizio, had a falling out."

"But if Fabrizio killed Cheyenne—"

"Obviously to get Cheyenne's share of the diamonds. I bet when we check the boot of Cheyenne's we already have, it'll be clean. Only one in each pair was a mule; that way the bearer could try to pull a switch if a customs official got too curious. Cheyenne, sensing that Fabrizio planned to keep the goods in both pairs, hastily hid the boot of his that was loaded before Fabrizio got it. Only he was killed too soon, and when Fabrizio sneaked into Cheyenne's dressing room after he was dead to nick the diamond-bearing boot, he found only the real one, and left it in disgust."

"Then who killed Fabrizio?"

"Another confederate, maybe even the mob who arranged the smuggling. Believe me, these guys weren't meant to keep what they carried through customs. While Cheyenne and Fabrizio were tussling for possession of the gems, the people who had stolen them probably got impatient and used the pattern of Cheyenne's murder to off Fabrizio."

"Foreign assassins? Diamond lords loose at the Crystal Phoenix? But Fabrizio wanted to kill *me*—"

"Because you'd figured out he'd worn a glove, and could have killed Cheyenne. I got a call while we were en route. The backstage crew found a black leather gauntlet concealed under the waste tray in the hawk's cage. We'll test it, but the location alone pretty much nails Fabrizio for Cheyenne's death."

A yowl from the floor directed their attention to Midnight Louie, who was weaving against Molina's navy slacks and rubbing his chin on something bulky around her ankle.

She quickly moved away.

"I wish we'd realized that the stones in Cheyenne's medicine pouch were more than rock crystal," she went on. "But everything about the scene of the crime was so theatrical and fake—"

Molina's self-defense trickled down to a smile she quirked at Temple. "Anyway, thanks for the boot. I've got all I need here. You can pick up your cat and leave."

"Doesn't he get a medal?"

"For ensliming the evidence and nipping at an officer of the law? I think not."

But Molina patted Midnight Louie's head after Temple had nearly dismantled herself bending down and picking up the hefty tomcat.

Temple knew that Midnight Louie hated condescension as much as she did, but he let it go this time. After all, he had solved the case.

Chapter 34

Last Act

Once out of the dressing area, Midnight Louie wanted down, so Temple complied before he reminded her of his hind claws.

She watched him trot off, probably on a romantic mission. She had a mission or two herself.

First she saw Danny, who was working madly in the Peacock Theater, reblocking the contestants to reflect Fabrizio's absence.

The chaos suspended while Danny consulted with Temple, pointed to the stage once or twice, and finally patted her on the back. She left, smiling, a swing in her step.

She checked her watch without putting on her glasses as she walked up the theater's gorgeously carpeted aisle. That required squinting a lot.

When she looked up, someone tall was waiting for her by the royal blue velvet curtains at the entrance. She assumed it was Molina, but when she drew closer, she realized that it wasn't Molina after all.

"Max!"

The Hawaiian shirt was gone, replaced by his trademark black, and so were the sunglasses. He didn't smile in greeting, just looked at her.

"I was crazy to think that I could protect you by going away," he finally said. "You've managed to find more danger than I could ever lead your way."

"I'm all right," Temple said, betrayed by the fog in her voice.

Max cocked his head to hear the damage, then finally smiled. "You will be after your throat recovers. Are you planning to continue your role of put-upon romance heroine tonight?"

She appreciated that he had refrained from telling her what she should do. "No. I chickened out. The reason for doing it is gone. Danny's not feeling let down; he'll substitute a girl who did it last year and is wild to do it again."

"A veteran of the romance wars," Max noted.

"Yeah. She's all of eighteen."

"I wondered, because I wanted you to go out with me after the pageant tonight."

"Out? Is it safe for you?"

"It will probably be safer where we're going than here."

"And that is?"

"The Goliath."

"Max, that's not safe for you! Why there?"

His smile became mysterious. "I have a yen to see the Love Moat again."

That gave Temple pause. She and Max had "done" the Love Moat when they'd first arrived in Las Vegas over a year ago. The gondola ride on a waterway winding through the Goliath's vast lobby was amusing enough, but the portion that ran through a romantically-lit artificial grotto provided the kind of privacy that lovers were known to take full advantage of. Temple wasn't ready for that situation again with Max.

"I don't know—"

"If you're worried, I'll invite your martial arts instructor to come along as a bodyguard."

That almost gave Temple a heart attack.

"What is going on? What are you up to with Matt, and—"

"Shhh." Max's green eyes twinkled mysteriously. "Trust me."

That was a lot to ask, and he knew it. Temple was tired. She had not only survived a murder attempt, but several hours at the police station and in the company of her arch-antagonist Molina. Still—Temple smiled—Molina owed her now, thanks to Midnight Louie's love for boot leather, and her own putting two and two together and arriving at the Italian connection.

"You seem to have had a good day, despite your ordeal." Max's voice broke into her reverie. "Meet me at eleven by the Lalique phoenix, and I promise you'll have an even better night."

His confidential baritone made chills run up and down Temple's spine like it was an escalator made to play on. Now this was a genuine proposition with possibilities to die for! But Matt, coming along? What was Max up to? Something surprising; she saw it in his eyes. She also saw the silent intensity behind his words. *Do it!* his considerable magician's will was urging her. Svengali Central.

What did she have to lose? If she could fight off Fabrizio, she could certainly wrestle her own divided heart.

Temple nodded; Max disappeared behind the blue velvet curtain. Temple sighed. What would she wear to the pageant now that she was free of the Renaissance gown? Maybe something that could get wet. A frogman's suit. Max could be one wild and crazy guy.

A strange man stopped Temple as she was nearing the elevator.

"Excuse me. Are you Temple Barr, by any chance?"

"Yes." But she raised her eyebrows.

He pointed. "They said you had red hair. I'm Hal Richards, the Á La Cat commercial director."

He stuck out a hand, so Temple shook it, puzzled. Had Savannah Ashleigh sicced this guy on her to complain about Louie's little escapade?

"Ah, I guess there's more than one black cat around the hotel," he went on. "Miss von Rhine says the little one is a house cat, but that the big black guy is yours."

Temple nodded. What had Louie done now?

Hal Richards, a lean, Hollywood-tan man with close-clipped brown-gray hair, looked a bit tentative. "It's awkward to talk like this, like islands in the stream." He gestured to the crowds walking by. "But I wanted to suggest something to you."

Oh, no! Louie had done something new and unthinkable . . . instead of old and unthinkable.

"We ran the film from our interrupted shoot the other day—"

"I'm so sorry about Midnight Louie busting in on your filming. He has quite a thing for Yvette and—"

"That's just it. The footage is fabulous! Our lights weren't set up for a black cat, and the contrast with Yvette's silver-white coat is unfortunately extreme, but we all concluded the same thing. They're dynamite together. We'd like to hire Midnight Louie—that is, you and your cat—to do the commercial. In fact, the ad agency exec is talking an entire series of commercials. Do you think you and the animal could travel to L.A. in the future?"

"Sure, but . . . how much does this pay?"

Richards shrugged. "If Midnight Louie were an elephant, I'd say peanuts. A hundred and fifty a shooting day."

Temple blinked. "And I thought *human* actors were underpaid."

"There are residuals, of course, and other promotional tie-ins. We usually use animals provided by trainers, but the ad agency suggested a famous cat, which is how we got Yvette. And Miss Ashleigh," he added unhappily.

"Louie's famous," Temple said. "He's a crime-solving cat."

Hal Richards smiled weakly. Temple had a feeling he didn't put much faith in the reality quotient of cat people. "That's nice. Well, if you're agreeable, we could get contracts to you by tomorrow morning and shoot that afternoon. We're on a tight schedule. All right?"

Temple nodded, giving him her hotel room number as well as her home address and telephone, which he jotted down on a small notebook he carried in his shirt pocket. Hal Richards offered his hand again and it was a done deal. Midnight Louie was a media star in the making.

"I can't believe you," Electra said in their room that evening. "All you've been through, and you're still going to the Incredible Hunk pageant."

"At least I'll be there in an offstage capacity. What do you think?" She turned to show off her dress, the same short, silver-beaded number she had worn to the Gridiron with Matt.

"Great." Electra fluffed the long angel sleeves on her blue taffeta muumuu. "Too bad you aren't going to be onstage in that, though."

"I've had enough limelight," Temple said. "I want to sit quietly—unmolested—in the audience, like everyone else, and pick and choose winning hunks." She hesitated, then tied a black velvet ribbon around her neck. "It'll hide the bruises. I hate to say that Molina was right, but they'll be doosies by morning."

"Molina was right about the crime, too," Electra noted.

"But Louie discovered the diamonds in the boot, and I got the Italian connection."

"So you did. Where is that scamp? I've hardly seen him around here."

"He'll be closeted with Yvette while her mistress is onstage tonight, no doubt. She's so overprotective. I hope Louie gets enough beauty sleep tonight," she added fretfully. "He doesn't know it, but he has a big day tomorrow. And I'll be in late myself," she added super-casually, "so don't worry about me."

"How late?"

"Midnight, or maybe one. Or so. I'll try to be quiet when I get in."

"Anybody I know?"

"Nobody you don't know."

Electra narrowed her pale eyes. "So it's none of my business, but I should know who you're out with. Look at what happened the last time someone asked you out."

"I didn't go then. Maybe Cheyenne would still be alive if I had."

"Don't eat your heart out about his death. He was a jewel smuggler, dear."

"I still think he wanted help."

"Yeah, he probably wanted to talk you into some illegal scam. Forget it. This pageant should be a hoot tonight!"

Electra completed her outfit by spraying her hair an orchid color and donning emerald-green rhinestone earrings that hung to her shoulders.

The emerald rhinestones winked like the single Austrian crystals that represented the cat's eye on the Stuart Weitzman shoes. Temple still had time after the convention was over to search for the shoes, but she doubted she would find them. She'd already tried everywhere logical.

Temple picked up a tiny silver bag and waited by the door for Electra to finish gathering her evening things. By the time they got downstairs, the Peacock Theater lobby was crammed with women in sequined and beaded gowns, in rhinestones and pearls, in high heels and high hair.

Only a few men mingled with the crowd, refreshingly middle-aged men with looks that would never grace a book cover, but were somehow more inviting.

"Get you ladies a drink?"

Harvey Herbert (or Herbert Harvey), Sharon Rose's husband, stood before them. Temple squinted desperately at his nametag (tonight was not a spectacles night), but couldn't distinguish between the two similar names.

"Ah . . . thanks. This is my friend Electra, who's entered the Love's Leading Amateur writing contest. His wife is the bestselling author, Sharon Rose."

"Herbert Harvey," he said, shaking hands with Electra. "Sharon is an author-escort for a contestant, so I'm at loose ends. I'd love to buy you glamorous ladies a drink."

"Gibson," Electra said without hesitation, apparently infected by Kit.

"A Bloody Mary."

Herbert Harvey nodded and melted back into the crowd.

"What a nice man." Electra beamed.

"Don't get too impressed," Temple told her softly. "His wife is hell on mid-height heels and very possessive. Always calls him 'my Herb.' I wonder what glamorous outfit she'll wear to escort her hunk. Her fashion sense was purchased at the five-and-dime in nineteen-fifty-eight."

"That doesn't sound like you, Temple."

"She nearly ran me over for merely speaking to her husband. Poor man. I can see how he'd like to socialize for a few minutes without her."

Harvey soon made the traditional male return trip from the bar, three glasses crowded against his evening jacket.

Temple and Electra took their glasses and chimed their thanks.

"Happy to do it." He looked around with interest. "My, doesn't everybody look grand."

Temple sighed to herself. Why be jealous of a man who said innocuous things like that about a roomful of women in their most dazzling evening wear?

"What's Sharon wearing?" Temple asked.

"Ah . . . something pink, I think."

Temple nodded. What else would the Romance Queen of Mean wear? The woman's personality and public persona were at war, but for wardrobe, sweet conquered sour.

Herbert Harvey drifted away after a decent interval.

"Ahhh," Temple confided in Electra. "This drink is great."

"Your nerves were shattered. I'd be at the bar tossing back boilermakers if I'd been through what you had."

"Electra!"

"Hi, gang." Kit slipped beside them. She was resplendent in a black silk dinner suit with a floor-length skirt slit up to high heaven.

When Temple complimented her apparel, she stuck out a shapely leg in lace pantyhose. "The older author's compensation for a sagging middle. You look cute as a cricket, Temple. And Electra, you are truly electric."

"Cute," Temple complained.

"Relax and enjoy it," her aunt's most jaded alto advised. "The next stage is 'shaky and sinking fast.' " She finished her cocktail. "We better get some good seats. I want to see a show. You don't mind if I sit with my editor, do you? Her suggestion."

Temple and Electra shook their heads, so Kit glided off alone. While they were still looking at each other, a thin woman in a sequined floral suit joined them.

"Electra! Tomorrow's prize day, can you believe it? I've saved you a seat in the writing class section. Come on."

Electra turned spaniel eyes on Temple.

"Go ahead. I'll find a place."

The other woman pulled Electra away before she could protest.

Temple drank the dregs of her fiery Bloody Mary—the Crystal Phoenix had a first-rate bar, too—and left the glass on a tray.

She didn't feel left out. She wanted to see the show from the audience without having to discuss it with anyone. She wanted to judge how well Cheyenne would have done, had he been here to compete. Maybe she was rooting for a ghost.

The seats were filling up, so she grabbed one halfway down the aisle. If the pageant ran too long, she could leave early. Butterflies were fanning the Bloody Mary flames in her stomach, but she wasn't going to think about past or future. She was going to see the show, period.

"Mind if I sit here?"

The woman who asked was tall and angular, with silky, blunt-cut blond hair to her jawline, dressed in severe black. She seemed nervous, but that was probably her grayhound metabolism.

"Not at all," Temple said graciously. "This is my first pageant."

"Not mine." The woman pushed down the fold-up velvet seat. "Duty, not beauty," she added, assessing the runway. "Beautiful boys are not my poison of choice. What a racket!"

"You must have attended several of these."

"Have to. I'm an editor at Bard Books. Emma Ransom."

"I work PR for the hotel. Temple Barr."

"Well, get ready for the illusion of publishing hype. If you want a running commentary on the true lies, just ask me."

Temple did not want a running commentary; she wanted peace. She hoped the woman beside her would get the idea. Then the

woman bent down and lifted something from the floor. A plastic
low-ball glass filled with ice and a clear liquid. Oh-oh. One didn't
have to be an ace detective to deduce that the contents were not
water.

Temple squinched down in her seat, glad she didn't need her
glasses for distance. She would see the show with a fresh, unin-
volved eye, and put the dead to rest.

The house lights dimmed, the pre-recorded music swelled and
Emma Ransom's ice clinked. Temple slipped on her glasses.

The spotlights targeted stage right, where something like the
Blue Fairy from *Pinocchio* gleamed: Savannah Ashleigh in Jean
Harlow white satin and fox-fur stole, hopefully fake. Savannah
would have no reason to get real about anything at this late date.

"Good evening, ladies, ladies and a few good gentlemen," Savannah quipped in her breathy, artificial voice. "Welcome to the
West, where wanted men are what women are after."

Her co-host, a tuxedo-jacket-wearing biker-short kind of guy
with long, surfer-streaked blond hair and a smooth disc-jockey pat-
ter, took up the pre-written dialogue. "What about wanted
women, Savannah?"

"They're in fashion too, Vic. We're about to see a dress parade
of our guys and dolls: handsome cover heroes and the women who
dream them up."

"Then let the revels begin, Savannah," Vic suggested unorigi-
nally. These emcee types always overused each other's names, as
if to remind themselves who they were.

The lights dimmed on the dim-bulb couple beside the proscenium arch, flaring up on stage center. One by one, the Incredible
Hunk candidates strolled out, a woman in her glitzy best on his
arm, bearing a scarlet rose.

Many women were decades older than their escorts, Temple
noticed. How refreshing. Role reversal with a vengeance! The
competitors looked polished and handsome in their sometimes eccentric formal wear.

Troy Tucker topped his stovepipe-tight black jeans, cowboy
boots, tuxedo jacket and rhinestoned bolo tie with a white Stetson. An excited hoot drew Temple's eyes to Troy's wife Nan,

bouncing up and down in her seat, her hands clapping high above her head.

A clink to her left prepared Temple for a comment.

"A leading contender for the popular vote."

Temple nodded. She could see why. But the long glitzy line of judges in the front row would decide the winners.

Each couple parted at runway's end with some romantic gesture. Troy doffed his Stetson to display long, Wild Bill Hickock hair down his back and bow his escort offstage, to thunderous applause and whistles.

The next hunk may have been Fabio reincarnated, but he was unlucky enough to escort Ravenna Rivers. Her gown put Scarlett O'Hara's burgundy velvet Shameless dress to shame. It was red, clinging, bare and backless. She bid her man adieu with an R-rated, torso-to-torso shimmy routine that had the youthful hunk blushing to match her gown.

"All her talent is in her hormones," whispered Emma's vodka rasp.

Temple had to admit that her running commentary was astute, if unwelcome.

Next came Jake Gotshall, looking quite presentable despite the gigantic clown shoes he had donned. His entrance brought a laugh, and his author escort, Mary Ann Trenarry, was a dignified grande dame in contrast, wearing aqua crepe and pearls.

When they reached the end of the runway, Jake grinned and fingered the red carnation in his buttonhole. It squirted water into the audience, who squealed en masse. Then he pulled out the boutonniere and elaborately presented it to Mary Ann.

Laughter was still ringing when one of the most muscular hunks stalked out, arms swinging like stiff sausages because of his bulk. Yet his long hair flowed softly and a diamond stud sparked in his left earlobe. Temple tried to remember the sexual preference rules for earrings on men and couldn't. She was certain to mix it up, if it ever mattered.

She didn't know the author, a lovely, frail woman in her sixties dressed in a designer suit of citron beadwork. *Don't dip her,* Temple ordered the hunk with some of Max's unspoken willpower. She imagined Danny Dove in the wings, mentally urging the same thing. The poor woman placed one high-heeled foot in front of the other like a persnickety cat as she walked the runway. At the end, the hunk twirled her out the length of his arm.

NO DIPPING, YOU DIP! Then he reeled her back in, kissed her hand and watched her pussyfoot down the stairs.

Temple released a breath as the hunk received a rip-roaring round of applause for his chivalry. Standing center-stage, bursting out of his rental tuxedo, holding his hands up like Sylvester Stallone's Rocky.

"Anna Amber Leigh. Her career is dead," Emma confided as the applause died. "Too old-fashioned. No sizzle."

Temple nodded, resigned to her role of captive confidee. That's how the seating chart crumbles.

Another Conan the Barbarian clone came out, long dark hair flowing, moving like a robotic terminator. His author escort was much younger than the others, a buxom blonde in a strapless taffeta dress with a bouffant long skirt more at home at a high-school prom than a pageant.

"Love's Leading *Naif*," Emma commentated. "Where did she get that tacky dress? From *Carrie*?"

Temple knew true stage fright when she saw it; the poor girl was terrified. She seemed most terrified of her hunk, who grinned with awesome confidence as he lumbered down the runway. At the end, he turned to her. She blinked. Her hands curled into pale fists.

Then he grabbed her, twisted her, dipped her until her shoulder-length hair touched the stage floor. All the while she looked like a virgin sacrifice to the volcano gods. Temple glanced away. She had overheard some of the author escorts begging not to be dipped, but this guy was gonna dip her or die. It was a kind of social rape, like going to the prom with someone who got ugly or drunk.

The mostly female audience hooted and howled and applauded. They did love their dips, as long as someone else was being dipped. The blond woman tottered down the runway steps, looking as if she wished she were dead.

"Some of these guys are pigs!" Emma Ransom spat, none too softly.

Temple nodded. She had seen the Good, the Bad, and now the Ugly. The pageant was like life, and death, full of endless variety and wonder, sometimes surprisingly nice and sometimes gratuitously self-serving.

Another couple waited in the wings. Temple braced herself after that last unpleasant *pas de deux*.

They made an odd couple: he, young for a hunk, tentative. She, mature and almost aggressively poised. Her hair was a shellacked helmet. Her gown was structured pink polyester from the sixties. Her smile was stiffly broad. *Like* me, or else!

" ' . . . smile and smile and smile, and still be a villain,' " Emma quoted. "Makes Richard the Third look like a saint!"

Temple tried to ignore the comment.

"What a bitch."

That was harder to ignore.

No more ice was left to chatter in the drink next door, and damn little liquid. Emma Ransom held the plastic glass to her lips like a compress and mumbled into its rim.

"Got me fired from Chapter/Reynolds/Deuce. Needs all the credit. Needs to trample egos the way elephants trample flowers."

Temple tensed. She didn't need this after her really, really bad hair day. And she had been wearing a wig!

"Selfish bitch!"

Temple didn't need this.

"Poor bastard!"

Temple's ears perked up. Was the hunk an object of sympathy?

He did indeed look cowed as he went down on one gallant knee to a poised, triumphant Sharon Rose.

"Sells like pancakes."

Hotcakes, Temple the sometimes-editor herself corrected. Drink was a terrible weakness. It distorted even the weariest of cliches. And Emma an editor!

"Sells all over the world. Tours the East, the Riviera. Busts balls wherever she goes. She'd look good in the East River, don't you think?" A raucous, unhappy laugh.

Onstage, Sharon Rose drew her long-stemmed rose against the would-be hunk's cheek, from long thorny stem to the satin-soft petals at the blooming end. Oxymoron, the heart of romance: kind and cruel, soft and hard, illusion and reality.

"Busts butts. Busts babes. Bitch."

Hatred was addictive. Temple held herself apart from the tidal wave of venom looming over her. She was here to see the show. That's all.

"All over Europe. Sub-rights. Money rolling in. Millions! No justice. Even the Orient. Rich bitch. Villa in Via Reg, pied-a-terre in Paris, and the bitch can't even spell it! We rewrite her, stupid fool. Husband trotting after her every command. Hypocritical. Queen of sweet romance. Family values. Money, money, money."

"Excuse me." Temple stood up. She needed air.

Sharon Rose still smiled at her kneeling hunk. Temple's long-distance vision had seen the single drop of blood on his cheek. The name of the rose is coercion. The name of the game is greed. She saw it—oh, yes—but she didn't need to hear it, not tonight, although she had not listened when a murderer had breathed his murderer's name into her ear like an endearment. Not after the death threat and the diamonds, and the imminent date with Max. And Matt.

Oh, God, she had to get out of here!

Temple stumbled over the woman sitting in the traditional critic's seat on the aisle, the woman sinking on the aisle. Heads turned, then turned back to the stage.

Another hunk and escort came out, came on. She glittered, he shone. Savannah Ashleigh's vacant voice carried to the very last row. Vic showed his dimples for the cameras. Everyone was here, *Hard Copy, A Current Affair, Hot Heads.*

Temple was out of there, in the lobby, frantic for a phone. She never thought she'd be this desperate to talk to this person.

The telephone directory was set in eight-point type and even her glasses didn't help. She pushed one eye right to the page and dialed, impatient with the long recorded list of voice-mail options before she got a real person.

"Is there some way, any way, I can reach Lieutenant Molina tonight?"

Clicks and voices and finally a series of rings.

"Molina." Briskly, with a hint of very human annoyance.

"It's . . . Temple Barr."

"Yes?"

Questions for the policewoman. Answers for the PR woman.

"Inquiries are already underway," Molina said. "It'll take a few hours. International time zones," Molina said. "Interpol."

Temple winced. Then she spoke again, rushing her words.

"We'll look into it." Molina subscribed to the royal we of bureaucracy everywhere.

"Via Reggio," Temple suggested.

"Boots by design." Molina.

"Traveling." Temple.

"We'll look into it," Molina finished. "Don't worry. *Don't worry.* We're on it."

"Canada! Have you considered Canada?" Temple again.

"We will now." Molina.

Temple hung up the pay telephone near the Crystal Phoenix front desk. She wouldn't return to the pageant. Her watch, a delicate evening watch with a Barbie doll–size face she had to put her eye almost against, read ten o'clock.

She might as well walk to the Goliath. Fresh air would be welcome.

Chapter 35

Love in Vein

Max melted from among the crowds in the Goliath lobby, the man in black against a black curtain again. Temple couldn't even see his ponytail. "You're early," he said almost hopefully.

"You, too."

"Our chaperon isn't here yet."

"He'll come on time."

"I didn't know he worked nights."

"He'll come on time."

"Meanwhile, would you like a drink?"

"I'm considering teetotalism, but yes."

The Goliath lobby bar featured gilt camel-saddle tables and knee-high silk cushions for chairs.

Temple sank into one gratefully.

"You look frazzled," Max said. "The pageant?"

"Leaving the pageant."

"You don't know who won?"

"I did."

"You've really changed," he said, cocking his head.

"Have you?"

"Maybe not enough."

The waitress came, clad in harem veils. Max sent Temple an inquiring look.

"Bloody Mary," she said with feeling.

Max laughed. "That kind of night?"

"Yes."

"Isn't the case closed?"

"No." She paused, wondering if he'd understand how much she'd hated doing it. "I had to call Molina."

"Lieutenant C. R. Molina." His green eyes laughed at a private amusement, then sobered. "Are you all right?"

So the Four Queens had wondered a day or two ago. Did it show?

"Great. Louie's going to be a star. I'm out from under the hunk pageant, quite literally. I just gave Molina some vital information. It may resolve her case."

"So." Matt lifted his tall glass of exotic liqueur. "What do you want now?"

"Nothing." Temple was surprised to find that was the truth. "What killed Cheyenne—and Fabrizio—and almost killed me, was uglier than ambition, sillier than sex."

"Knowing too much is worse than knowing nothing at all," he warned.

"So you tell me, from self-interest."

"Granted." Max sipped his drink, green as absinthe, yet it couldn't be. Absinthe was illegal now.

"I meant to surprise you," he said. "Instead, you surprise me."

"Good." She was beginning to mellow, in her element.

"I hope I . . . don't disappoint you. Tonight."

"Modest Max."

"No, just hedging his bets. Ah. He was early, after all."

He stood, and Matt joined them.

How truly bizarre, Temple thought. Yet not as bizarre as what had happened at the Incredible Hunk pageant.

"Temple has contacted Lieutenant Molina," Max told him.

Matt sat, and refused the waitress an order. His wary eyes stayed on Temple. Her guardian angel against that ole devil previous involvement.

Dark. Light. Wrong. Right. Past. Present. Crime. Punishment. All these concepts were slouching toward their appointed end tonight.

"Do you want to cruise?" Max asked them.

"Why not?" Temple said.

They walked to the ticket booth, a mole-hole shrouded by trees decked in fairy lights. The Goliath gondolas were gilt and red-velvet, with two facing seats meant for four, or two, not three.

Three got in: Temple on one seat, the men opposite, their long legs filling the space between. The gondola rocked, like a cradle. This was sillier than sex, Temple thought, viewing the busy lobby from an alien angle.

Yet water was soothing, and this water reflected star-flowers from the trees. An automated timer pushed the narrow craft forward, away from the lobby's noise and bustle.

"You're probably wondering why I called all of you together tonight," Max intoned in his master-of-ceremonies voice.

They cruised beneath light-spangled trees, past people sitting down to dinner or dice.

A dark arch awaited them, the mouth of the monster, open and hungry. The gondola slipped inside, and Temple's hands clenched on its gilt sides.

New light reflected the eerie shimmer of neon green constellations on the cloud-shifting ceiling, of scintillating veins of green gold on the walls: laser hologram images cast on air.

"They updated it!" Temple exclaimed.

"I never saw it before." Matt's voice.

"They added illusion," Max said. "*Your* illusion, Temple."

She viewed the passing walls' panorama of gossamer three-dimensional images. Mere fiberglass and fantasy she knew, yet so very reminiscent of rock and substance. Reality according to Disney: great entertainment.

Lasers cast rainbows on the pseudo-rock. Sometimes they were shadows. Sometimes ghostly faces. She saw veins of exotic ores, lost Aztec treasures, Egyptian artifacts, all glittering in laser-green, all fairy dust and delusion.

Suddenly, Max's long arm shot out as the gondola glided near a wall. A portion of rock flipped open at some subtle touch. Max pressed a red emergency "Stop" button one usually finds in elevators.

"Go get it, swimmer," he said. "We've only got a couple of minutes before someone comes."

Matt started, then his eyes followed Max's other, pointing arm to a luminous display in the opposite wall, just visible in the eerie light.

Beyond the airy dancing of laser-light twinkled a recognizable form. A Cinderella shoe from the twenty-first century.

Matt stared from Temple to Max, then pulled off his shoes, his shirt, his trousers. He dropped into the dark, laser-dappled water, stroking for the niche of light.

"This is crazy," Temple warned Max. "I don't need the actual shoe, I just need to say where it is. How did you know I was looking for it, anyway?"

"A little bird told me."

Named Electra?

"And I know the hotel," he added modestly.

Did he ever . . . too well.

"Besides"—Max's grin was visible even in the artificial twilight—"Eightball O'Rourke is checking out the Goliath. Better that there be no question who found the shoe."

Matt was paddling back, something dazzling riding above the water in one hand. He pulled himself aboard, the gondola rocking until it almost capsized.

"Whoa!" Matt was laughing as he handed Temple a glittering something. "I guess this must be yours, Madame."

This reality was more incredible than the illusion. The low light emphasized the stones' Austrian-crystal flash as fire-opal sparks of red, green and blue. The shoe spanned the palms of her hands, white-diamond brilliant except for Midnight Louie's jet-black profile, which winked an emerald-green eye.

No one wondered if a cat's eye color was genuine. No one asked a cat where he had been, except possibly to see the Four Queens and sit on top of their dressing table. Midnight Louie *would* have more than one monarch to visit.

Temple laughed with delight. "If I turn up with this," she explained to Matt, who was stunned by the shoe, "I get a free pair in my size."

He had stopped gawking and was struggling to pull his clothes on over his damp skin. "That water was icier than Lake Michigan."

Temple remembered the lessons of her pose-down stint and emergency sewing job: she thought of England and not of underwear.

"Try it on," Matt suggested. So Temple slipped off her right pump with the steel heel and pushed her foot into all that flash and fire.

"Too big," she said, somehow disappointed. Glass slippers should fit the first time. "A six, probably."

"It looks . . . incredible. What size will yours be?"

"A five. It'll take a few weeks for my pair to be made. I can't believe the prize is mine, and two weeks before Halloween. Max, tell me how you knew?"

She looked to the opposite seat, and saw only the dark.

Max was gone.

The water was dark and still.

She turned to Matt. They'd been too busy dressing to notice.

He stopped pulling on his own shoes to shrug. "I think the Mystifying Max says 'Happy Halloween.' "

"What do you think of Max?"

"Don't know yet. I got wet, but he gets to play Prince Charming."

"Why did we come here at his invitation, then?"

"We're congenitally curious."

"Is that so bad?"

"Sometimes. Hey, this barge is moving again."

Temple cradled the shoe against her face, as if she petted Midnight Louie in person. "I won, but it doesn't feel like it yet."

"Winning never lives up to the advance PR."

"Why do you suppose he left?"

"I have no idea." Matt eyed her cautiously in the dimness. "Was it something you said?"

"Or you? You've been spending more time with him lately than I."

He was silent for a moment. "Divide and conquer."

"He'd hardly leave us alone . . . together . . . in the dark if that was his strategy."

"Maybe he would. Maybe he wants us to think just what we are thinking."

"Which is?"

"Look, Temple, we've got to settle this thing."

"Thing?"

"What's happening between you and Max?"

"Not much at the moment. We—I—can't just pick up where we left off. Too many rude questions come between us now."

"We can't pick up where we left off either." Matt didn't quite put a question mark on his final inflection, but it threatened.

"I suppose not." Temple trailed her fingers in the cool water that felt like liquid velvet.

"Maybe a moratorium is best for us all," he said.

"Maybe."

A silence.

"Maybe," Matt said suddenly, as the lobby lighting swelled beyond him, "we're doing exactly what the Mystifying Max wants."

Temple grimaced. "That's been known to happen before."

They floated into the fairy lights again, visible to passersby, on an enchanted raft Max had commandeered for a few even-more-enchanted seconds.

"He must be a hell of a magician," Matt admitted, squinting against the glare of Las Vegas's artificially lit night.

"Oh, yes." Temple smiled, serene again, holding the Cinderella slipper on her lap. "We all deserve each other."

Chapter 36

Swept Away

"Aren't you wearing your adorable Renaissance costume to the Awards Banquet and Ball this evening, dear?" Electra asked.

"I've had enough of long gowns and long hair—on either sex—to last me until 2001."

"Oh, testy." Electra glanced at Temple in the wide mirror above the makeup shelf. "Your late night out must have been a lulu. But don't stint on the glitz, girl! If you win an award and have to collect it at the podium, you'll regret not dressing up."

"Win an award? For what? Most Nearly Crushed to Death? Best Incredible Hunk Trampoline?" Temple stopped fluffing her curls to gaze at Electra.

Electra shrugged. "Maybe best unpublished writer. I noticed some new files appearing in the laptop. You're writing a romance, admit it!"

"Don't be ridiculous."

"That's kind of hard not to do in this airy-fairy getup." Electra continued, patting iridescent glitter gel on her face and hair.

The costume was more of a cloud, an amorphous gathering of shimmering fabric.

"Now if *you* win the writing contest," Temple went on indulgently, "you'll be dressed for the occasion. But, trust me; there's nothing in that computer but notes to myself about the Crystal Phoenix renovation. I tend to get ideas at odd hours."

"Hmmm." Electra didn't sound convinced, but that was her problem. "You're not even saying who killed Cheyenne and Fabrizio, and why."

"There's nothing to say. The jury is still out."

"I'm not used to waiting until the jury decides these matters, dear. I'm used to you spelling it all out for me, the moment the perpetrator has been apprehended."

"Maybe the perpetrator hasn't been apprehended yet."

"You *do* know something!"

Temple slammed her brush down on the travertine. "I don't even know who's going to win the writing contest. Why don't you concentrate on the big unanswered question in your life, and leave the murderer to Molina?"

"You don't."

"And what big, unanswered question do I have in my life?"

"Both of them start with M, as in Men."

Temple was silent, then she grinned. "Molina and I are cooperating lately. And Midnight Louie has just vaulted into a big TV contract."

"Playing innocent does not become you," Electra said tartly. "Good thing you reneged on the pose-down model role."

"I did not renege! I was nearly killed. Besides, a Lolita-in-waiting was rabid to take my place."

Electra shrugged. "Still, you don't have an escort for tonight."

"I don't need one. Besides, Matt's working and Max is working at being invisible again."

Electra stopped primping long enough to examine Temple's silver-beaded dress and steel-heel shoes. "I'm worried about you, Temple. You wore that outfit last night. It's not like you to forget to dress for every occasion."

"No one saw me last night, and I don't feel like traipsing around in costume again. I've wenched my last wench. I'm only going to this folderal tonight in case you win."

Electra beamed. "That's sweet. I suppose I shouldn't hope, but I think I have a real strong entry. He's a highwayman and she's a gently reared aristocrat."

Temple looked startled, then a bit uneasy. "Isn't that . . . a rather common romance scenario?"

"Perhaps, but it's how you execute the primal fairy tale that matters. Some situations reside so deeply in our psyches that we retell them again and again. Like *Beauty and the Beast*."

"Like *Cinderella*," Temple added, smiling at herself in the mirror as she clipped on long, dangling earrings. Too bad she had only one shoe, and two Prince Charmings, however dubious.

"Exactly." Electra regarded Temple with renewed suspicion, but gave up. "I expect you to tell me all about Louie at dinner. Time to go down and find out what happens."

"Amen." Temple picked up her tiny silver evening bag.

The ballroom that had hosted luncheons and dinners all week was decked in even more gossamer than before. All the tiny chandelier lights glittered through rainbow veils.

Beneath this celestial whimsy, an earthier artifice prevailed in a carnival's worth of costumes and masks, of brilliant jewelry and clothing.

"They're really puttin' on the glitz tonight," Temple noted.

"I suppose it seems like an anti-climax to you," Electra said. "You have no surprises in store this evening."

"I've had my surprise." Temple knew her mysterious smile would torment Electra, but that was as much as she was going to say about the shoe, and how she had gotten it.

"Let's find Kit and a table before everybody rushes for seats. I want to sit near the center front, in case—"

"In case you have to run up for an award," Temple finished. "I hope you do, Electra. I really hope you do."

"Kit's up for an award, you know."

"I didn't know that!"

"Neither did I, until an award candidates' list fell out of one of your author press kits."

"Well, that *sly boots*! Oops, unfortunate expression. I'll chide Kit severely for not telling us."

Just as they chose a table, Kit found them and pulled out an adjoining chair.

"You're too modest for an acting Carlson," Temple told her before she had sat down. "Why didn't you mention that you were up for a, a—"

"A Romie? So are about twelve thousand other authors. Don't put your white gloves on to cushion your hands while applauding for me. Although I hope our friend Electra will cause us to callous our palms."

"What does 'Romie' stand for?"

Kit frowned. "How the hell would I know?"

Electra leaned in to recite, in a true believer's voice, "RO-Mance Is Everything, Capital ROMIE."

"No kidding." Kit looked impressed. "Where'd you find that out?"

"In class."

"What's the award for?" Temple asked.

Kit dropped her beaded evening bag and dove under the table-cloth to search the floor.

Electra leaned over her bent back to whisper, "Best S-E-X."

"No!"

Electra nodded solemnly. "Only we call it sensuality. Looks better to the press."

"I would think so! Find anything, Auntie?"

"Two breath mints and a purse." Kit resurfaced, flushed and ready to change the subject. "What's the scoop on the Fabrizio offing? Surely the killer will not go unpunished? I'd sentence him to life—a lifetime of watching Fabrizio videos, and hearing Fabrizio motivation and romance tapes, Fabrizio playing the kazoo, Fabrizio gargling—"

"*She* might just like that."

"A woman did it?"

"Maybe."

"You're no fun." Kit pouted and kicked the long tablecloth skirt like a restless child. "I wish they'd get this show on the road; there are eighty-nine award categories, each with several candidates, which means that two thousand and eight possible wrist-slitters occupy this room."

"I can understand why they decided to do the awards before dinner," Electra said. "But did they consider that, since losers will outnumber winners, a lot of appetites will be lost before the waiters even serve the salad?"

Temple skimmed the award brochure lying across her dinner plate. Kit had exaggerated only a little. Award categories recognized every wrinkle on the much-traveled face of romance fiction: time travel and futuristics, historical and contemporary, suspense and intrigue, stand-alone and line titles. That only emphasized how many romances were published each month, and how they had become virtually half of the paperback market.

Yet at this convention Temple had heard tales of exploited and underpaid authors, of a midlist purge, of authors cut from publishers' lists by the tens and twenties. If there was big money to be made, only a few lucky authors hopped aboard the gravy train.

Those authors' names peppered the award brochure pages. Temple now knew and liked—or loathed—some of them. Sulah Savage, of course. Shannon Little and Misty Meadows. Mary Ann Trenarry and Sharon Rose, who must use her first and middle names as a writing pseudonym, although "Sharon Harvey" didn't sound too bad. Ah, yes: and Ravenna Rivers, the Homestud Man's Vamp of the West.

"Hello," a timbreless voice echoed through a microphone. "I'm Savannah Ashleigh, your surprise awards moderator tonight. And I'd like to extend all you G.R.O.W.L.ers a great big grrrrrrr."

Temple regarded the podium. A blitz of blond scintillated behind the speaker's box. Blond hair, blond body, blond gown. Spell it b-l-a-n-d and you'd be closer to the truth.

"First," Savannah's breathless monotone resumed, "the All-Time Readers' Favorites Awards. For Best Mistress . . . ah, for

Mistress Widow of Best Single Tittie . . . er, Title. Release. Oh."

Savannah gazed upon her attentive audience, decided their dropped jaws indicated adoration, and held out her hands to urge the silent mob to quiet. "It's Misty Meadows, Best Single Title Release!"

Kit slid onto her tailbone in embarrassment, hiding her face behind her open award brochure. "That woman is unbelievable! She's too vain to wear reading glasses. With that level of delivery, this awards list will take *hours* to get through. I hope to heaven I *don't* win. I can't imagine how she'd mangle my name."

"You overestimate her," Temple muttered. "Glasses wouldn't help her reading and speaking skills. She's a *film* actress, after all."

And so the evening stumbled on, with every ear and eye fixed on Savannah Ashleigh in the spotlight, struggling vainly to interpret award titles and winners' names.

"And for Best Sex!" Savannah looked up, proud, then down again. "Uh, Best Sexuality . . . no, Sense. Best Sense of . . . Reality? Sue LaSavage!" She used the French pronunciation, of course, or her best approximation of French. "Soo La Sa-*vahge*."

"I sound like a nymphomaniac railroad line!" Kit stood, threw her napkin to the table and stalked up to accept the award by graciously thanking every insensitive idiot who had ever stood in her way, therefore ensuring her sterling success.

Temple was still laughing when Kit returned to the table, slammed an object that resembled gold-plated mating dolphins down on the thick tablecloth, sat, picked up her discarded napkin, unfolded it and covered her head.

Temple was still laughing when Mary Ann Trenarry waltzed up to collect the "Most Innoculated Heroine" award.

"*Innovative!*" Kit, still under her peach-linen tent, translated with disgust.

Ravenna Rivers undulated up to retrieve a "Sexy West Hero Award."

"*Sexiest Western Hero,*" Kit droned ominously.

Seeing both women onstage was a study in super-feminine stereotypes, blonde on blonde.

Before Savannah Ashleigh could butcher another category, someone tapped Temple on the bare shoulder.

She turned to recognize Molina's moustached partner. He bent to whisper sweet somethings in her ear: "The Lieutenant would like you to meet with her now."

Molina, here? Had to be, if her partner was. What was up?

Temple excused herself, to little notice. Electra was so nervous she sat rapt at Savannah's maunderings, wringing the fabric of her diaphonous muumuu. And Kit, the Wise One from the East Who Speaks Only from Under a Veil, Soo La-Saa-*Vahge*, continued to commune with Thespis.

Molina stood against the wall like an idle waiter. With her neutral bearing and navy pantsuit, she could pass for one. She stood even with Savannah and the podium, watching both as if she expected them to creep, like Birnam Wood, utterly away.

Temple eased into place against the wall beside her, feeling like shrimpy Shirley Temple paired for a tap-dance with looming, lanky Buddy Ebsen.

Molina held out an awards brochure, and indicated a certain name. "You know her by sight?"

Temple nodded.

Molina leaned down to whisper.

"Don't *do* anything, for God's sake." Molina drew back against the wall. "Just point a finger."

"No kisses required?" Temple couldn't help asking. "This *is* a romance convention."

Molina glowered but didn't answer. Temple knew why. She was armed and dangerous. She was about to arrest a murderer.

Savannah Ashleigh, meanwhile, sounded quite giddy. She assumed that she was getting the hang of this awards thing, quite erroneously. She giggled between categories, and grew coy before she announced the winning name, which she invariably mangled.

"For . . . for Ass . . . Asset to the Feel Award—" Giggle. "That's *field*, everyone. For Field Asset Award, Sharon Rose!" Savannah drew the list to her face. "Is that it? Sharon Rose. I can do that!"

Sharon Rose moved toward the podium. Her gown was yellow

polyester chiffon, long and full. She had a matching yellow organdy bow pinned dead center of her brown hair, just above the curled fringe dusting her forehead. Her hands and unvarnished nails clasped the dolphins around what would be their waists, as if they never meant to let go.

"I can't tell you how much this means to me," her quivering voice trilled over the microphone to every nook and cranny of the ballroom. "I have labored so long and hard to make this field reach its full potential, to prove that good writing is the road to success, that our covers don't have to rely on the tawdry and tacky. Quality. That is the word I live by, and write by. Thank you so much for recognizing mine."

She rustled down to the dinner table level, afloat on sunshine chiffon and the audience of admiring fans.

Molina stepped forward and drew her toward the wall where a woman photographer waited. All the winners (except Kit) had paused to record this moment for posterity.

Molina whispered something to Sharon Rose while Savannah giggled and garbled at the microphone. Sharon Rose nodded. Molina turned to Temple, and passed on the message.

Temple, stunned, wove discreetly into the tables until she reached one. She spoke to someone there, who immediately rose and followed her, followed her back to Molina and the wall, and the silent partner by the waiter's portable tray table. Back to a triumphant Sharon Rose, beaming like a polyester daffodil.

The police closed in, including two uniformed officers, one male, one female, who materialized from the swinging doors to the kitchen.

Another author was weaving through tables to the podium in gratified suprise. Not Sharon Rose. Some other author was thanking whatever gods may be, not Sharon Rose. Some other author was hearing the applause of her peers and fans, the sweetest sound in the world. Not Sharon Rose.

Sharon Rose was hearing her Miranda warnings, delivered in a crisp, official drone that made Savannah Ashleigh sound animated.

Sharon Rose was extending her hands to surrender her trophy

. . . and extending them behind her for the handcuffs.

So was her husband, Herbert Harvey. Or was it Harvey Herbert?

Poor man, Temple thought, watching the stunned couple cowed, corraled and led discreetly through the kitchen doors. She glimpsed an anxious Nicky Fontana and Van von Rhine waiting against the institutional stainless steel.

Poor Herbert Harvey. Now that was an epitaph for a runner-up. A henchman. The lesser half in a merger of murder and greed. And, ultimately, a hit man with Fabrizio to his credit.

Molina handed Sharon Rose's award to Temple.

"You may wish to return this to the committee," she said. "And they may wish to forward it to her relatives. She did earn it."

"Why arrest them here and now?" Temple asked.

"To get them before everyone left town, and we had to wait for confirming information from Italy and the Orient, both on very different time zones, with very different languages. Especially the Italians, when it comes to efficiency. You have heard about Italian trains?"

"No doubt rank stereotype, Lieutenant. The Fontana Brothers are Italian."

"I rest my case."

"Was I right?"

"I'm afraid so. I checked. Sharon Rose and her husband were in Italy—Milan, in fact, meeting with her Italian publishing house—at the same time Cheyenne and Fabrizio were modeling for Armani there. The Harveys had commissioned the boots in Florence, noted for its leather goods. Both murdered models were 'given' the boots to commemorate their meeting with Sharon Rose and her husband in Milan a week ago. Both men considered such perks their due as rising romance-cover models. They never knew they were acting as mules for smuggled diamonds."

"Cheyenne was killed because he was going to reveal the scheme, wasn't he? That's what he wanted to ask me about the night before he died."

"Hey!" Molina smiled. "He may have just wanted to ask you out. You'll never know. But you're right. Cheyenne was not stupid. He went direct from Milan to Las Vegas, as did Fabrizio. Different flights, but not by much. We checked. Cheyenne also went straight to what passes for an honest pawnbroker in Las Vegas when he saw some stones from one boot heel had fallen off into his duffel bag during the transatlantic flight, and examined them. The pawnbroker gave us a statement: he identified the stones as gem-quality diamonds. I'd guess that Cheyenne told Fabrizio in his dressing room, then realized that Fabrizio wasn't about to give up the gold in any field. Finders, keepers. Cheyenne had to get on-stage in a hurry, thanks to dealing with the horse, so he ditched the evidence boot under the costume rack, planning to retrieve it later."

"There was no later." Temple picked up the scenario, though no one would ever know it for sure. "Minutes later, Fabrizio used his hawking gauntlet to stab Cheyenne with his own arrow."

"He ditched the glove under the waste tray in the hawk cage."

"A bloody glove?"

"I'm afraid so."

"How did you find it, Lieutenant? How do we know it isn't a plant?"

"Please. Backstage witnesses say a cat trying to get at the hawk tipped over the cage. The tray pulled out and the glove tumbled to the floor."

"A cat? What kind of cat would go after a hunting hawk?"

Molina blinked. "Witnesses say it was a black cat."

Temple refused to comment. "I never suspected Fabrizio until much later, when I learned that a single gauntlet had disappeared from his costume." She smiled wearily. "It's ironic. The only reason I suspected Herbert Harvey was learning that he was going hunting in Canada after the convention. Then I thought of bow-hunting. But he didn't kill Cheyenne with an arrow, though he finished off Fabrizio with a dagger."

"A dagger borrowed from general supplies in the joint costume cage, by the way," Molina said. "We got a warrant to search the Harveys's room on probable cause and found the *receipt* for the coverboys' damn boots concealed in their luggage. In a custom Italian western boot. Hers."

"They put a lot of faith in boots, didn't they?"

"Fabrizio figured he was safe. That Sharon Rose and her husband wouldn't dare tell the police if he kept the diamonds, because they'd have to admit their money-laundering scheme. And the diamonds were a perfect investment; anyone could sell them. Harvey had been backstage with his wife; it was easy to stab Fabrizio in the dark confusion of the lighting rehearsal. They planned to collect his and Cheyenne's boots later, although we had Fabrizio's and one of Cheyenne's boots and you had the other."

"Why was Sharon Rose laundering money? She has plenty."

"All is not enough for some people. You were right about her foreign sales having something to do with this. She's privately sold *all* her backlist books to the burgeoning Far East market. The money they paid her was converted to diamonds in Hong Kong. If anyone saw her books in Chinese, she could say they had reprinted them illegally; it happens a lot. Then Sharon Rose generously gifted her cover models with the commemorative boots. *Voila:* models and boots make it unchallenged into the U.S. Sharon Rose wanted to avoid taxes, but now she faces murder/conspiracy, tax dodge/money-laundering convictions."

"So the Arrow Man actually did one of the dirty deeds?" Temple mused.

Molina looked puzzled. "Arrow Man? You mean Harvey. Had Fabrizio's greed not encouraged him to keep the jewels, Herbert Harvey wouldn't have had to commit a murder. Unfortunately, you intervened before either of this murderous, larcenous couple could recover the gems from the boots. And Fabrizio, not knowing he was a marked man, was worried enough about your knowing about his missing glove to try to kill you, even as he was being stalked."

"Poor Herbert Harvey. Such a nice man," Temple murmured.

"Apparently."

"Apparently a pawn of his wife's. She was the brain driven by a bright, hot heart of pure greed. Just now she was claiming that the publishers are responsible for her scheme, for forcing authors to lead such scrimping, uncertain lives."

"At her rate of sales, please! She had it made. Why did she have to mess it up? I still can't picture her low-key husband as a killer."

"Any man who bow-hunts deer wouldn't be deterred by sudden death."

"How could he? Bambi-killer!"

"Some hunters eat the deer they kill."

"Cannibals!"

"They can't be that, unless they eat their own."

"Don't we all, Lieutenant, every day?"

A pause.

Applause.

Behind Temple, a thousand hands clapped as another author reached for the intangible award of professional recognition. Some things money can't buy. Freedom is another.

No one in the ballroom knew Sharon Rose's true award this night: Best Dressed Accessory to Murder. Tomorrow, the newspapers.

Tonight, the simple things.

Temple slipped back to the table and into her chair without undue notice. Her absence looked like a ladies' room run.

Kit had returned her napkin to her lap, and was bright-eyed again. "At last. The interminable published author awards are over. All the dolphins have mated and the ozone layer is saved for posterity. Would that our ears were redeemed. Savannah Ashleigh is about to announce the Love's Leading Amateur Awards."

"Third place is Valerie Menendez . . . I mean, Mendez, for *Heartbreak*."

Applause. Ecstatic would-be author at the mike.

"Second place is for . . . for *A Man for All Reasons*. Carolyn R. Podesta!"

More applause. More breathless gushing between awardee and awarder.

"And in first place, Elizabeth Lard for—" She squinted at the list to decode the title.

Applause.

No scurrying author.

Silence. Whispers.

Savannah Ashleigh strained to read the list. "Not Elizabeth, but . . . Electricity Loss. No, El . . . Cee Trisha—"

Kit stood up. Kit projected her voice to the ceiling light fixtures. "Electra Lark, you ninny!" Kit roared like a lion in winter.

The audience roared back.

Temple stood up beside Kit and applauded.

"*San Andreas Sunflower*," Savannah shouted out the winning title.

Electra found her way to the podium and captured a plaque with her name, spelled correctly, on it. The applause never died until she left the stage, so she never said thank you. But her face said it.

She settled back in her chair, breathless, putting the award where the centerpiece should be, for all to see and admire. "San *Antonio* Sunflower," she muttered when the room was quiet.

"And," a chastened Savannah Ashleigh was saying very slowly and very softly, "a last, special Honorable Mention. For an . . . unit . . . unique entry. A most clever parity—"

Kit stood up again and bellowed, "Parody!"

Savannah Ashleigh looked like she faced a firing squad. "Parroty," she repeated meekly. "Parroty of the Clichy . . . water?" She looked around helplessly, a broken woman.

A woman rushed up to the mike, covered it and whispered forcefully to Savannah.

"Cliched stereotype"—Savannah announced by rote, looking to either side and shrugging her shoulders—"of a romance novel. To Tempest Tower . . . " She grinned in relief at simple two-syllable words. "Author of *Sa-vahge Surrender!* Come and get it, Tempest!"

Electra was looking expectantly at Temple.

"I didn't do it!" she swore.

No one came and got it. The audience stirred, bereft.

A camera operator from *Hot Heads* zeroed in on the podium. Nada. Savannah stood alone, like all cheesy things.

Then someone was walking forward. The audience stirred. Uncertain applause began as a slight figure in a pale suit joined Savannah at the podium. ,

"I'd like to thank the G.R.O.W.L. committee, and the esteemed judges, and all who recognize literary merit," Crawford Buchanan's deep baritone boomed over the mike. "I never could have done it without all of you published writers as an example. And to my mother . . . keep the tuna casseroles coming, Mom! They're brain food."

He flourished his trophy and strutted back to a distant table, the *Hot Heads* camera dogging his every step.

"Gross," said someone near Temple.

She turned. Quincey, with a Fontana brother, was sitting only a table away.

Electra was looking disappointed, and looking at Temple. "I thought for sure that you—"

"Not guilty," Temple pled with perfect confidence.

She would never write a romance novel until she had plotted out her own lovelife, and that might take a while.

"By the way, who won the Incredible Hunk title last night?" she asked as people began rising and filing out of the ballroom.

"Troy Tucker got the popular vote of the convention at large."

"No surprise there," commented Kit, collecting her entwined dolphins.

"A nice guy," Temple approved.

"And Kyle Warren got the big award," Electra said, picking up her plaque.

"Kyle Warren? Which one was he?"

"Tall. Long dark hair. Muscles. One earring, two wrist cuffs."

Temple shook her head. "I couldn't tell him from Adam. Would Cheyenne have won, do you think?"

"Maybe, hon." Electra's face fell. "Say, you're the only one of us three who didn't get an award."

Temple smiled. "Don't be too sure about that."

Chapter 37

Confess

The brass vigil light hung from the high ceiling, glowing faintly in the daylight, striking the face of the madonna with a fever blister of bright red.

God bless Our Lady of Guadalupe, Matt thought, with its old-fashioned atmosphere of eternal Catholic verities: the vigil light and the Virgin.

He sat on the polished wooden pew, absorbing the peace and the piety. Statues of Mary and Joseph still kept guard on either side of the aisle. Stained-glass windows cast kaleidoscopic patterns on the stone floor varied enough to soothe the restless attention of the most fidgety child, at least for a few precious moments.

The pews were made from golden oak and waxed to piano-polish, hard but supportive, as all sturdy things are. The kneelers were padded in brown vinyl, a thirty-year-old concession to weak-kneed modern worshipers and unnecessary now that the modernized mass avoided long, trying stretches of kneeling. Matt remembered the bony knees of boyhood protesting hours on vinyl-tiled floors when special-occasion masses had been celebrated in the high school auditorium.

Now he sat. Now he thought rather than prayed. Now he worried about other issues, which were the same old issues in fresh form.

A door cracked somewhere in the church. Not the big thunderously echoing double doors at the front, but a smaller, discreet door beyond the altar. Perhaps the door to the sacristy, or a side door to the nearby school or rectory.

Was a janitor coming or going? The Ladies' Altar Society coming to dust? A church stood empty most of the time, a monument to scheduled sanctity. He liked this time of waiting best, the church itself as entity, the holy place in wait for a glimmer of random, unexpected spirituality, for a lost soul blundering in, snared by its ancient trap of shelter and sanctuary.

A man wearing a short-sleeved black shirt came around the communion rail, now also an outmoded symbol of a far more formal ritual. Communion was not taken kneeling on hard stone steps along an ornate guardrail anymore, with vulnerable closed lids and open mouth, but standing at center aisle with cupped hand and wide-open eyes. It was self-administered these days, like the sacrament of Penance, now called Reconciliation.

For all the softening of ancient habit, when it came to dogma, the church remained a hard mistress.

Father Rafael Hernandez recognized Matt, smiled and came forward.

"May I join you?"

"Certainly, Father."

The older man sat in the same pew and faced the same way, studying the elaborate carved plaster altarpiece, a rococo tribute as ornate as a Bach fugue.

"Even in the early sixties," he noted, "the parishioners wanted their florid folk art. I like it."

"Me too," Matt said with the ungrammatical ease of a schoolboy. "We Poles have our Black Madonna and our gilded Infant Jesus. Gilt doilies for the Lord, valentines for holy days."

"It is good to think of those Eastern European churches free of the shadow of the Kremlin these days, of people free to practice their faith with all the old traditions."

Father Hernandez's autocratic profile was tilted up toward the church's blue-painted nave, in the ancient pose of prophets and saints. Matt was surprised to see rays of good humor radiating from the corners of his eyes and mouth.

The priest sighed, his hands clasped simply on his lap. "My recent . . . difficulties have been the proverbial blessing in disguise. I had taken my priesthood for granted; I had too much pride of position and too little faith. It's a temptation. You've done parish work," he went on, assuming rightly. "Each parish is a little kingdom, and the priests are its princes. And the pastor, he is king. I took myself too seriously. I allowed myself to alienate an old woman from the church only days before her sudden death, and all over a matter of animals in heaven! No, that wasn't the issue. It was my authority. It was my being right, even about minutiae. And the blackmail, the notion of my being thought badly of, that was what unhinged me. Our Lord was falsely accused and made it into a means of redemption for all mankind, but I, Rafael Hernandez, could not survive a pointing finger. I had my pride. That is the root of all evil, not money. Pride."

"Money motivated Peter Burns to kill his great-aunt," Matt pointed out. "But pride did, too. He felt . . . shamed from birth and was never given leave to feel anything else, for a sin that was not his. He compared himself to Jesus, do you know? Asked who had given him room in the inn when he was an infant in need of shelter."

"You've talked to him recently?"

Matt nodded. "In jail a couple of weeks ago."

"Why? The man is poison, and he cannot blame the world for all the wrongs he did."

"I wanted to understand his hatred."

"You are not a priest anymore. You don't have to listen to confessions."

"No." Matt found himself glancing at the set of confessional booths on the nearest side aisle. "They look like something from Alice in Wonderland, strange, decorative doors to exitless closets, where you feel shrunken or inflated, depending on your sins that day, or your penance."

"I still use them." Father Hernandez shrugged at Matt's surprised glance, for confessions nowadays were face to face in faceless rectories or churches or schoolrooms. "The old timers can't countenance—excuse the expression—a cosy daylit conference with the parish priest. They must have their kneelers and their darkness, their pleated white linen curtain and the whispers in the dark, the slow slide of the priest's little door from side to side. I admit I enjoy the suspense, the anonymity, the drama, the guessing in the dark. So much about the church has changed. I wonder that anyone wishes to become priests anymore."

Matt smiled. "A lot of women do."

"Women! Don't start me on that, Matt. Next Miss Tyler's cats will find heaven not enough, and demand ordination. I'm too old for so much change."

"And yet church doctrine remains unswerving."

"For the most part."

"Do you never doubt?" Matt asked suddenly.

Father Hernandez's Spanish-olive eyes turned to him, all brine and bewilderment. "Doubt? Only myself, as you saw all too well. What should I doubt?"

"The boundaries of sin, I suppose. They seem . . . fuzzier outside the priesthood."

"Ah, well, my sins are of the self, an exclusive circle, you will admit. A social man must confront sin in plural situations. A priest is set aside from society, and therefore from some sins."

"Some priests have managed to sin grievously against society."

"And more grievously than ever for being priests," Father Hernandez added tartly. "Why do you meditate on sin, Matthias? It is nothing new."

"Some of it is, to me. Think about Peter Burns. If the church had not encouraged thinking of an unwed mother as an outcast, her son would not have been isolated and alienated."

"The church no longer shames unwed mothers."

"Not as much, and not if we want to oppose abortion; then we can't approve of situations that drive women to that extreme. But our new moderation seems self-serving, almost politically correct. Deep in our hearts, do we really accept the sinner? Or do we prefer that she not commit a graver sin that offends us more?"

"You are speaking of sexual sin and whether it is grave, or merely sensational."

Matt nodded, enjoying this theological debate. He missed these "wrestling with angels" sessions, in which nothing was answered but much was asked.

"We consider the slaying of the body the gravest sin," he began.

"Murder," Father Hernandez agreed. "Cain versus Abel."

"Slaying of the soul is harder to single out." Matt found himself speaking before he thought. "Father, I think I . . . need . . . would like to celebrate an old-fashioned sacrament called Confession."

"In there?" Father Hernandez eyed the facade of doors with their tightly decorative grills that let in air, if little light.

"Why not?"

"Why not indeed. I'll get my stole."

Matt watched him walk away, each footstep sharply echoing on the unforgiving stone floor. It was impossible to be furtive in a church.

Matt didn't wait for his return, but slipped into the confessional on the right. As a child, how many anxious moments had he stood in line, dreading and requiring this moment? When he could sink in the dark onto the kneeler and rest his folded hands on the small wooden shelf.

His world had shrunk to the thin line of light under the closed door—which always swung shut behind him without a sound, as if sealed by the Holy Ghost. Before him was the pale window of white linen, barely luminescent in what little light squeezed through the grill in the door.

How many anguished minutes had he shifted his weight from one hard-pressed knee to the other, as some old Polish babushka recited her endlessly trivial list of sins. They always took so long, the old. Were they confessing the sins of an entire lifetime while he waited, needing to go to the bathroom?

Ah, another fault to confess. Impatience, Father, with the elderly. Add it to the venial shopping list carried in the head from week to week. Like disrespect, or the vaguely thrilling "bad thoughts," or, even better, the delightfully mysterious "concupiscence." Six "Hail Marys" and ten "Our Fathers" and he would be off lightly.

He heard the approaching footsteps, pictured the purple stole of Penance around Father Hernandez's neck, wondered why he was doing this. Then his heart began to quicken and his bladder began to burn, like Pavlov's priest as a boy. Was he omitting any fault? Hiding anything? From Father or himself?

Hell, yes! the adult Matt admitted with an appropriately apt exclamation. He had hidden everything under a camouflaging cloak of petty misdemeanors, as he had hidden behind a collar for so long.

Bless me, Father, for I have sinned. It has been forever since my last, true confession. I have been disrespectful to my mother six times and to Sister Esperanza two times. I have been thoughtless of others four times, and I have wanted to kill my stepfather twelve times.

Matt shut his eyes as he heard the wooden window slide open. No more light entered the booth. Oops, wrong side, Father Hernandez. Perhaps priests weren't as prescient as the young Matt thought. The sliding sound came closer, like a nightmare monster's sucking footsteps. A glow illuminated the linen curtain, but let no shadow of a man fall on the neat, pleated folds.

"Bless me, Father, for I have sinned. It has been"—already he wanted to evade the truth—"eight months since my last confession." Eight months since he had visited a church, except for Our Lady of Guadalupe. He sounded like a fallen away priest; perhaps he was.

Father Hernandez made no comment. Confession was far more voluntary, and thus far less frequent these days. It was not like the weekly doom visited on impressionable children many decades before. He was here of his own free will. How many times had they debated free will in seminary?

Free will wasn't theoretical outside the seminary or the collar's discipline, he had discovered. Every act, every minute could require an ethical decision. His entanglement with Temple had raised dubious desires, ghosts and guilt. And now he had tapped a new source of anger against another powerful male figure, Max Kinsella, supermagician. Concupiscence was no longer Greek to him, nor was envy and rivalry. . . .

He spoke in generalities to a whispering voice beyond the milky veil, to the spiritual tradition and power beyond the unseen priest. He questioned himself, the past, the church. He didn't get answers, but he got more specific questions. And he found understanding, as a seasoned priest reduced Matt's feared mortal sins to venial offenses.

Then Father Hernandez cleared his throat before beginning the absolution. For a panicky, self-defeating moment Matt wondered if he would be told that he was beyond forgiveness, anyway.

The priest's hoarse whisper finally came again. "Bless you, my son, for your trust and courage. By revealing yourself to me, you have healed me of my shame and wounded pride for my failings that you witnessed through no fault of your own. By this sacrament, we are both absolved."

And he began the ritual words of absolution, in Latin. Matt finally felt a sense of closure with one father, at least.

Chapter 38

Checkmate

I wish that I could say that my lovelife works as well as a romance novel. You know the routine: boy meets girl, boy gets girl in the sack (and for my species, sacks are a real attraction), boy goes hunting and girl . . . does whatever girls do when they are with kits.

However, these are modern times, as I am soon reminded. While romance convention attendees are congratulating each other in the upstairs ballroom, I have padded (and I am one of the few dudes who can authentically "pad," since I have pads and not toes on my feet) downstairs to peruse the vicinity of the Divine Yvette.

A good thing, too.

Who do you suppose I find slinking around the Divine Yvette's door? You will assume the upstart Maurice.

No. It is an upstart of my own relationship, Midnight Louise.

"Well, Daddio," she hisses when I approach the Divine One's door, since I well know that Miss Savannah Ashleigh is detained above as long as her mispronunciation holds. "I suppose you are here to take advantage of a poor, ignorant, unsuspecting female."

That is not how I would describe it, and I am not about to describe things of an intimate nature between consenting kitties to my wayward daughter, who has renounced all such activity.

"I had no such plans toward you," I reply.

She hisses again. "I know you are besotted with that platinum airhead in the dressing room. And I know that your precious Yvette is now in no condition to reject your designs. Sssshe is in ssssteam heat."

Ah. So the stars have cooperated at last! My beloved is primed and I am on the scene. What more could a cat-about-town wish? How about a long-lost daughter who stays that way?

"If you truly care for Yvette, blond bimbo that she is," Midnight Louise goes on, "I beg you to consider her future. In her position, half-breed kits are the mark of shame. She will be drummed out of the Cat Fanciers Federation. She will shame her mistress, and her kits will be tossed out on the streets to eat insects. She will be a queen without a country, a marked feline. For once in your life, think before you act."

She has a point, being my daughter and no fool. I see two facts: the Divine Yvette is in that blessed condition called "heat," and any red-blooded male cat worth his hormones will be clawing down the doors to get to her . . . ergo—

I dash past Midnight Louise, throwing my entire weight against the dressing-room door. It gives with a creak and a crack.

Nosing my way in, I confront my worst suspicions: Maurice is inside, and the Divine Yvette's carrier has been knocked to the floor. Maurice is fussing over the zipper like a monkey trying to type Shakespeare to order on the first try.

I am on him like a banshee, all sound and fury. My claws are sawblades and he is yellow pine . . . yellow supine. I have him nailed on his back, while the females yowl in counterpoint.

A few biffs to the whiskers, and he finally gets the message. This is Midnight Louie's turf. He backs out into the corridor, back curled, tail kinked, hissing all the way.

I am not impressed, but Midnight Louise is.

"Good brawl, Daddio. Now do the right thing."

What can I say? I amble over to my Divine One's toppled carrier.

She is panting within, her eyes wide and wicked. The fall has done nothing to cool her ardor. We are talking platinum passion here. I can smell my future on a pheromone. Every fiber of my body screams for satisfaction, and the Divine Yvette is willing to indulge my every instinct.

Of course, I have a witness. My own kith and kin, suitably and surgically altered. She would never understand.

I sigh.

"Louie, Louie," the Divine Yvette mows, hot to trot.

One of us must do the right thing.

I push and pull her carrier into its proper upright position, then hook an incisor in the zipper tab and draw the bag slightly open. The Divine Yvette's long, spidery whiskers poke through the gap.

"Louie, *mon amour!*"

That French does it every time.

"*Ma cherie.* We must wait and be wise. We will always have another Á La Cat commercial."

"Louie!" she wails.

(And the Divine Yvette, for all her sublime delicacy, does indeed know how to wail, especially when she is in a wanton condition.)

"Until we meet again," I promise, withdrawing before I forget myself, knock Midnight Louise into a wall and have some long-deserved fun.

It is hard being a responsible male in these modern days. In fact, it is Hell.

The next evening I return to the Circle Ritz and Miss Temple Barr, a female I will never be tempted to ravage, given our separate species.

She seems glad to be home again, and is preparing for bed.

I notice a new object on her nightstand: a lone shoe that glitters like a Broadway opening. It bears a handsome representation of a black cat with a single green eye upon the heel. I prefer two eyes, but I have not seen the mate to this one yet.

"Louie!" Miss Temple greets me with an enthusiasm that is not steamy, but is most welcome, and even soothing after my many travails at the Crystal Phoenix. "Are you as tired of the romance ride as I am? Come on, your spot is waiting."

She pats the coverlet near her knees. Miss Temple has the most endearing habit of flexing her knees when she sleeps, at an angle custom-tailored for a dude of my size and temperament to curl into. And she will not carp about my reproductive habits, or, rather, my former thoughtless acts that resulted in unplanned pregnancies. I do understand that Midnight Louise's attitude is politically correct, but nobody ever had much fun being politically correct.

Miss Temple knows that well.

She pats my head and shoulders, and does delirious things to my ears that almost make me forget myself.

"Louie," she says, "love is murder, and love of money is the most murderous thing of all."

I would not know. Money is not one of my weaknesses, which is why I am such an ace crime-solver.

"And thanks for turning up the bloody glove." She goes on to confide all that happened on both the romance and crime-solving fronts, including the good news about "my" shoe.

It is nice to be the hero of the hour. I settle into my perfect spot and listen sagely, reflecting on the symmetry of life.

We are all in our proper places, and most is right with our world.

The murderers have met their just rewards: Fabrizio became a victim himself and Sharon Rose will be writing her bestsellers from prison in the future. No doubt her mild-mannered husband will miss the opportunity to bow-hunt, but the deer will be pleased. I applaud with silent cat feet. I never approve of wanton predation, unless it is mine.

And even I am reforming.

After our on-camera tryst tomorrow, the Divine Yvette will depart for Malibu with her human, Miss Savannah Ashleigh, ecstatic that I will play opposite her again in these little exercises of television advertising.

Miss Savannah Ashleigh is ecstatic that she will appear in a videotape of the infamous Incredible Hunk pageant featuring two murders, which will air interminably and simultaneously on *Hot Heads*, *A Current Affair* and *Hard Copy*. The Divine Yvette told me this morning that her mistress was disappointed to learn that she has lost a pair of prize shoes to some anonymous shoe-hunter, but that she has enough money from Yvette's commercials to order a custom pair of Pavé Collection shoes with Incredible Hunks on the heels.

Maurice will return to the trained-animal farm from whence he came.

Miss Temple has brought me home in both my forms: self and shoe. She has already presented this incontrovertible evidence that she found the location of the prize shoe to the Stuart Weitzman store. I expect to have a body double, times two, on the premises by Thanksgiving.

Speaking of which . . . Thanksgiving, that is, not premises, I learn that:

Mr. Matt Devine feels that his aquatic skills have justified themselves.

The Mystifying Max, wherever he is, has once again manipulated circumstances to his liking, and in a most generous manner, too.

Miss Temple Barr has come to terms with the fact that she must rely on the professional connections of Lieutenant C. R. Molina for some investigative work, such as international inquiries.

What more could one want? Midnight Louise would not understand. I muse upon my favorite lines in all literature:

It is a far better thing that I do, than I have ever done.

It is a far better place to which I go, than I have ever gone. . . .

Of course, Sidney Carton did not have much self-esteem, and was co-dependent on top of that. He also did not get the girl. My world, and welcome to it, Sidney. Have I got a spokescat job for you. . . .

Midnight Louie Celebrates

Well, this is more like it! All things come to he who waits, and I have been waiting for my just desserts for some time. I had just expected them to be edible instead of esthetic. But that is okay. I can roll with the rewards.

I have been the object of a kick more than once before, during my street days, but I have never been *on* a shoe before.

"The Midnight Louie Shoe." That phrase has a ring to it. "The Midnight Louie Pussyfoot Pump." Toney. "The Midnight Louie Sophisticat Spikes." Better! More guts. These shoes were made for stompin'—not at the Savoy, but at the Crystal Phoenix.

You may distrust my exuberance. You may suspect that I have been dipping into the nip too much lately. I may even sound a trifle giddy. But I am one to whom recognition has come late . . . er, later . . . in life. Observing the shenanigans of these romance cover-model hunks, what reader may have considered that Midnight Louie once nearly was one? True, I am a cover model *now,* but only after much time and travail, and only after a golden opportunity for fame was cruelly snatched away in my youth, when

I was svelte and swell-headed enough to really enjoy it.

You may recall my abortive venture into a romance-novel quartet a decade ago, wherein I was soundly scolded for conduct unbecoming a romance character and relieved of forty percent of my literary weight (i.e., almost half of my lines ended up on the cutting room floor), thanks to the ministrations of a nervous editor who judged Midnight Louie too powerful for the romance reader of a decade ago.

Savvy early thought of using me as a cover image, albeit minor, was soon quashed by a flurry of actions to conceal all things furry and feline about the romances in question. I did make it onto a promotional page at the books' rear, but the volumes quickly plunged into the river of pulp from whence all paperbacks flow and eventually return. Now, of course, romance series with continuing cat characters are the "in" thing; some even pretend to talk, like me. (I refuse to talk to inferior species, which is why I write my opinions.) Today romance short-fiction anthologies are built around those of my ilk, on the cover and inside it. I was obviously (I say with almost no hubris) ahead of my time.

But the future was unseen during that bleak period of rejection and exile. Oh, I soldiered on with my customary bravado, but the entire episode stuck in my claw. So how I relish my long-overdue vindication as a rightfully celebrated covercat not only on my own mystery series . . . but on a custom pair of designer high heels as well. I can hardly wait to see what heights of fame my forthcoming cat food gig will bring!

Very best fishes,

Midnight Louie, Esq.

P.S. You can reach Midnight Louie on the Internet at:
http://www.catwriter.com/cdouglas

—CND

Carole Nelson Douglas Talks Shoes and Show Biz

Midnight Louie and I agree for once: his new prominence in the fashion-footwear world is the cat's meow.

Writers sometimes burden characters with their own quirks; Temple's high-heel addiction is such an inherited trait. So do the details of a writer's life and fiction blend.

Here's another relevant example of this eternal intertwining: At the 1995 *Romantic Times* magazine Booklovers Convention in Fort Worth, a grandmotherly costume volunteer delivered a drop-dead hilarious monologue about her adventures with the daring young men in the cover model pageant. These included emergency repairs of a delicate nature, given the men's costuming, or lack of same.

Romance convention attendees might assume that this true-to-life incident inspired a scene in this book in which Temple faces a similar crisis. Not so. Time passes, but classic human dilemmas do not.

During college theatrical days I myself confronted a panicked

Mountie from *Little Mary Sunshine* who had altogether too much sun shining on a place where it shouldn't, and was due onstage for an athletic dance number in minutes . . . heck, seconds! He, too, had no time to remove his pants. He also had a lot more panicking to do before the situation was all sewed up, but he didn't miss his cue . . . or suffer any pain, although I can't speak for humiliation on either of our parts.

This is one story that leaves everyone in stitches.